Revenants

Revenants

by
Paul Féval

translated, annotated and introduced by
Brian Stableford

A Black Coat Press Book

Acknowledgements: We are indebted to David McDonnell for proofreading the typescript.

English adaptation, introduction and afterword Copyright © 2006 by Brian Stableford.
Cover illustration Copyright © 2006 by Arnaud Demaegd.

Visit our website at www.blackcoatpress.com

Introduction

The original version of this book was a serial that ran in the daily newspaper *Le Pays* from May 25 to July 10, 1852 under the title *Le livre des mystères* [*The Book of Mysteries*]. That title did not suit it very well, but Paul Féval evidently found it difficult to find one that seemed to him to suit it better. The first edition in book form, published in three volumes by Cadot in 1852, bore the title *La soeur des fantômes* [*The Sister of Ghosts*], but when Dentu reissued it in 1867 it was retitled *Les revenants*—a word that has no economical English equivalent and is therefore sometimes granted English usage, although it is also rendered into English as "they who return."

Following his sudden destitution in 1875 and his much-trumpeted "conversion" to religious piety the following year, *Les revenants* was one of the novels that Féval revised for publication in a new edition of "corrected" texts; that version was initially issued in two volumes by Palmé as *Une histoire de revenants* [*A Tale of Revenants*] in 1881. The revised text was frequently reprinted thereafter, the second volume often being given the separate title of *L'homme sans bras* [*The Man With No Arms*]. One modern reprint was retitled *Nuits de terreur* [*Nights of Terror*]. As the plot of the novel revolves around a double meaning of the term *revenant*, I thought it best to call this English version *Revenants*, even though I was acutely aware of the prior existence of Geoffrey Farrington's novel *The Revenants* (Dedalus, 1983).

1852 was a notable year in Féval's career because he was able to resume the prolific publication of serial *romans feuilletons* after a difficult three-year period occasioned by the economic and political upheavals of the aftermath of the Revolution of 1848. Although Féval had completed three such serials in 1850, and one in 1851, much of his production in 1849-51 had gone straight into book form, and it was not until Louis-Napoléon's *coup d'état* of December 1851 that order was more fully restored. In the early months of 1852, Féval

5

launched three serials; *La forêt noire* [*The Black Forest*] began in *L'Assemblée Nationale* in February and the relatively short *Le Comte Barbe-Bleue* [*Count Bluebeard*] ran in *La Patrie* from March to April before *Le livre des mystères* began in *Le Pays*.

Le Comte Barbe-Bleue was the latest addition to a series of novels that Féval had set in his native Brittany in various periods of history, most of which drew on the folklore of the region and lamented the deep decline into which the local aristocracy had fallen since what Féval liked to think of as the glorious Golden Age of Chivalry: the late Medieval era in which the actual history of feudal baronies had been lavishly confused by the composers of *romanz* with legends of unparalleled heroism, like those built around the legends of King Arthur's Round Table by Chrétien de Troyes. Its immediate predecessor in this sequence, *La fée des grèves*—serialized in *La Gazette de France* in 1850—became one of Féval's most popular and frequently-reprinted books. Although both novels made use of motifs derived from folklore, both followed the policy customary in novels of the period by refusing to countenance explicit use of the supernatural.

This policy may seem a little odd, in that the supernatural was still tolerated, and lavishly deployed, in short fiction. Féval was one of many writers of the period—including English and German writers as well as French ones—who were perfectly happy to write supernatural short stories while preferring to address supernatural ideas from a naturalistic viewpoint in their novels. This reflects a noticeable difference in narrative method between short and long fiction, the former still being frequently modeled on traditional *contes populaires* [popular tales] that mimicked oral narratives in being conspicuously told, and relating back to a mythic past when the workability of magic and the existence of supernatural beings had been taken for granted. Longer fictions, by contrast, made far more use of a mimetic mode of narration in which the reader is "shown" what is happening, usually by means of a viewpoint tied to a single active character or by means of the recording of dialogue. Such fiction relates back to a historical past rather than a mythical one, and belief in magic and supernatural beings is assumed *a priori* to be mere superstition.

Le livre des mystères is a partial break with this pattern, which takes a much more ambivalent view of the reality of the supernatural, and trades on that ambivalence in shaping the mysteries that drive its plot. It was the first novel in which Féval had juxtaposed Breton and Parisian settings, explicitly comparing the two in terms of prevailing attitudes to the supernatural. Had he undertaken to do this in 1850, he might well have done so in terms of a straightforward contrast, in which Brittany was a reservoir of primitive superstitions while Paris was a milieu from which superstition had been conclusively balanced: the epitome of modern Enlightenment. *Le livre de mystères* did not do that; indeed, the story implies that the two environments are more similar than they might seem.

Within the novel, superstition is at home in Paris, as it is in Brittany, but its context is markedly different. The superstition of Brittany is old superstition, continuing traditions that have been in place for centuries, occasionally modifying its superficial aspect but always remaining, in essence, the same thing. Parisian superstition is new: a matter of fashion. Ghost stories are told at *soirées* and literary salons for the sake of sensation—but that does not mean that they are not taken seriously. Spiritualism had not yet arrived in Paris in 1852, but the city was fertile ground for some such fad, and Féval was aware of that.

This awareness permitted Féval to exercise greater and more ingenious license in the deployment of supernatural motifs than he had been prepared to do in the earlier novels in his Breton series. He is highly selective in deciding which aspects of superstition can be allowed a measure of hypothetical reality—although he appears to have remained uncertain in his own mind with regard to one particular apparition—but his primary interest is not so much in different kinds of supernatural phenomena as in different responses to confrontation with them, be they real or apparent. The work he did in this book helped lay the initial groundwork for the idiosyncratic supernatural fiction of his later years, including the novellas translated for Black Coat Press as *Knightshade* and *Vampire City*.

The proximal cause of this shift in emphasis is clearly indicated within the text, in the first Chapter of Part Two, when the action first shifts to Paris—specifically to the Bois de Boulogne, where the Parisian *beau monde* exhibits itself on weekends. A group of fashionable young men riding out one Saturday morning is asked: "Have you seen the play that's on at the new Théâtre de la Porte Saint-Martin, called *The Vampire*?" There is no need for them to reply; the narrative voice immediately observes: "Everyone had seen *The Vampire*. In 1820, *The Vampire* was a runaway success."

The play in question, *Le vampire*, was a loose French adaptation of the anonymously-published English novella *The Vampyre*, which was then widely rumored to be the work of Lord Byron (it was actually by John William Polidori, Byron's embittered former physician, who had modeled its protagonist on the poet). The script was cobbled together by Charles Nodier, the great pioneer of French Romanticism, with uncredited assistance from Achille de Jouffroy, the son of a famous steamboat pioneer, Carmouche and the director of the Porte Saint-Martin theatre himself, Jean Toussaint Merle.

In 1852, while *Le livre des mystères* was being serialized, *Le vampire* was enjoying a runaway success at the Porte Saint-Martin for a second time, in a new adaptation scripted by Alexandre Dumas which premièred in 1851. (Dumas records in his autobiography that one of the first things he had done on his initial arrival in Paris in 1820 had been to go to the opening night of *Le vampire*, where he had found himself sitting next to a grumpy old man, who muttered incessant complaints and expressions of disapproval throughout the performance—and who turned out to be Nodier.)

Frank J. Morlock's recent translations of both Nodier's and Dumas' plays, as well as Polidori's original novella, were published in 2004 by Black Coat Press as *Lord Ruthven the Vampire* and *The Return of Lord Ruthven*.

The success of Dumas' play probably prompted *Le Pays* to commission Féval to write *Le livre des mystères*, although he might have come up with the idea himself. It was not the only work he produced in direct response to that stimulus; his own *La vampire*—translated as *The Vampire Countess* in a Black Coat Press edition—was probably written and published in the same year, although Jean-Pierre Galvan's bibliography of Féval's work—which does not include a serial version of the novel—gives the date of the book version as 1862. (The catalogue of the Bibliothèque Nationale lists an edition of 1852 in advance of the 1862 edition, but Galvan appears to think that the earlier date is a misprint.) There is, in any case, a sense in which *Le livre des mystères* and *La vampire* are companion-pieces, and it is partly for that reason that I have followed up my version of *The Vampire Countess* with *Revenants*. As typically-uneasy novel-length examples of mid-19th-century supernatural fiction, they make an interesting pair.

Le livre des mystères is also interesting for another reason, connected with its attitude to speculation. The author would presumably have been very surprised had anyone told him in 1852 that he would, one day, lose a large fortune by unwise speculation, thus rendering himself and his family destitute—but he knew it only too well when he prepared the revised edition in 1881, having suffered exactly such a reverse in 1875. The novel's ambivalent attitude towards the scheme for enrichment that forms the core of its plot takes on an extra dimension of irony by virtue of this fact. Féval was forced to make every effort to make a comeback of his own, in one of the senses implied by the word *revenant* in the novel, and the new edition of *Une histoire de revenants* was a significant element of that effort.

The version of the text from which this translation is taken is the "revised and corrected" edition of 1881. I have not had the opportunity to compare the two versions of the novel in full, because the earlier one is very difficult to obtain, but

two of the earlier version's Chapters (III and IV) are repro-
duced at *www.bibliosem.net*, and the only significant difference between those chapters and their equivalents in the 1881
version is that the name of one of the characters has been
changed (the Etienne of the revised version was originally
Roland Montfort—a name of dubious propriety, given that the
character is a loyal servant of the Treguerns, who are said in
the text to have once fought in a Civil War against the
Montforts).

The majority of the "corrections" Féval introduced into
the new version, in line with his conversion, probably involved the addition of more references to God, and the revision of existing references to increase their reverent piety. It is
not impossible that some changes were made in the structure
of the story, but Féval does not appear to have made any attempt to tidy up the problems and inconsistencies discussed in
the afterword, so it seems more likely that the changes were
minor, and restricted to what could reasonably be done by
altering the publisher's proofs.

I have followed my usual policy of leaving proper names
in French, providing translations in the notes where appropriate, but have deviated from the rule in two instances. It would
have been awkward to refer continually to the Manoir de
Treguern because it would have committed me to using
manoir rather than manor every time the edifice is referred to
in shorthand fashion, so I have substituted "Treguern Manor."
I have also rendered the name of the "Three Rooks" into English, because it would have been similarly awkward to refer
continually to the *Trois Freux*.

I have corrected a few mistakes in Féval's text without
annotating them. It was probably unwise of the author to tempt
fate by naming three of his characters Mathurin, Mathelin and
Michelan, especially as the latter two are invariably on stage
together and that all three are present in a key scene in the
novel's gathering climax; I have corrected a couple of instances where Féval seems accidentally to have used the
wrong name from this set of three, and several in which

Jérôme Clément's Christian name is misrendered as Joseph. I have also made a couple of trivial deletions in order to repair slight "continuity errors" of no significance to the storyline.

The only significant change I have made to the organization of the text is that I have taken the liberty of moving Féval's preface to the end, where it appears as an appendix. I have done so because it gave away in advance a little too much of the solution to the mystery set out in Part One, and might have spoiled more than one reader's enjoyment slightly in its original situation. Féval, or the editor of *Le Pays*, appears to have had the opposite anxiety, given the amount of space given in the early chapters of Part Two to making explicit everything that an alert reader would surely have inferred while reading Part One. Serial novels routinely involved a certain amount of recapping and repeated explanation, for the benefit of readers who had not started at the beginning, but I have resisted the temptation to excise the repetitive material, which does no real harm to the progress of the plot.

Brian Stableford

Part One
Life Insurance

I. Guillaume Féru's Mill

The old church nestled in a little valley; the bell-tower displayed its copper weathercock, its slanting shaft warped by the weather, above a group of pruned oak-trees, reminiscent at a distance of deformed giants.

It was a crossroads in the open country between Redon and Malestroit, in Brittany. There was a stone table there, resting on three unequal supports. Thorny furze, broom and tall ferns grew around the monument like a Druidic hedge, which no inhabitant of the parish of Orlan would ever have dared to touch with a finger or a toe. It was known as the *Pierre-des-Païens*.[1]

It was rumored that, under that granite table, there was an oval-shaped hole, hidden by the brambles, and that the hole gave access to a tunnel connected to the cellars of Treguern Manor. It was rumored, but no one had gone into it to see, because the girdle of brambles, broom and furze was inviolate, presenting no apparent opening that could give passage to a rabbit.

A quarter of a league away, the upper half of the melancholy walls of Treguern Manor were visible in front of the forest. The ivy draped over the cracks in its walls spoke of sadness, abandonment and poverty—testimony repeated by the great windows, where the wind drove the rain through holes in the long-broken panes.

In the choir of Orlan's church, there was a tomb proudly hewn in black granite which bore the recumbent figure of a knight. It was called the Tomb of Tanneguy; there, it was said, rested the remains of the first lord of Treguern, Tanneguy-

---

[1] (See Notes p. 316.)

Filhol-Aimé Le Mâdre, created Comte de Treguern by King Louis XII in 1513. Beyond the tomb, at the border of the choir and the nave, there was another funereal monument, also in black granite, but more modest and bearing no statue. It was the last resting-place of the second lord of Treguern. Then, for the third, came a simple cube of masonry, covered by an unornamented stone. Then, for the fourth, nothing but a slab of slate set in the floor. It was necessary to leave the church to find the fifth, who had a marble cross at the highest point in the cemetery.

The cemetery, like the only pathway in Orlan that bordered it, was on a slope. The sixth Treguern followed the slope downwards; the cross on which his names and titles were inscribed was in Saint-Pern sandstone, less tall that that of his predecessor. The seventh was already reduced to a cross of grey slate. For the eighth, two shafts of iron had been bound together, which had rusted and no longer retained any trace of inscription. Then, there were wooden crosses that became smaller and poorer as they descended the slope, until the last was not even set upright, but laid down flat, upon a grave so recent that the grass had not had time to sprout. On this one, ill-written letters displayed the legend: Filhol-Aimé-Tanneguy Le Mâdre, Chevalier, Comte de Treguern, August 1800. The inscription also said that he had died at the age of 21, and invited Christians to pray for the peace of his soul.

There are families that rise, as if Providence were leading them by the hand; there are families that decline, as if the hand of God weighed upon them. Treguern had once owned all the land between the Vilaine and the Oust; no one had been able to point to a greater lord than Treguern between Redon and Vannes. But that slope recounted a history of decadence; it was a long way from the proud mausoleum of the Tomb of Tanneguy to the little heap of freshly-turned earth on which lay the humble cross bearing the name of Filhol, the last Comte de Treguern.

At the *Pierre-des-Païens*, six roads met, forming a large star; this space, an irregular circle, was situated some 300 paces from the hill that overlooked the parish of Orlan. One of the paths, passing between two compost-heaps, led directly to the top of the hill, where a windmill was perched. The road directly opposite, on the other side of the Druidic stone, went into the fields where the little river Oust wandered along its sinuous course. To the left, a third path steered towards the village, while the fourth, heading slightly uphill, led to a large and decrepit edifice whose thatched roofs were crowned by an old crenellated tower. This was a farm, built on the ruins of a manor house, which still bore the name of Château-le-Brec.

The two paths on the right were more widely angled. The first ran parallel to the hill, heading for Treguern Manor and the forest; the second plunged, rather than merely descending, to the bottom of a dark ravine that was called the *Trou-de-la-Dette*.[2]

It was the month of August in the first year of the century.[3] Night was falling; the warm and electrically-charged wind was sighing in the heather; the crescent Moon, it its first quarter, was already descending towards the horizon, outlining the black silhouette of Château-le-Brec, with its toothed tower, and Orlan's church, whose bell-tower topped the tallest trees. Dark clouds were coursing hurriedly across the sky.

Two women were walking slowly along the path that led to Treguern Manor. One had a forest of grey hair beneath the brown hood of a Morbihan countrywoman. The other seemed very young; she wore neither hat nor hood, but a veil attached to the tresses of her hair covered her face. As the wind lifted the folds of the veil, when the Moon shone between two clouds, her companion stopped to look her in the face.

"Be brave, Marianne," she murmured.

The young woman's eyes were full of tears.

"Where is he," she said, "at this hour, when I am suffering, and when I might perhaps die? Where is my husband?"

The old countrywoman took her in her arms, because she saw her stagger.

"Be brave, Marianne," she said, again. "I love no one on Earth but you and him. You shall be rich, Marianne—Marianne de Treguern—and you shall live for a long time!"

A sigh elevated the young woman's breast. "Dowager," [4] she pronounced, effortfully. "I'd rather be told that I'll be happy!"

The old countrywoman shook her head, and a bitter smile formed amid the wrinkles of her lips. "Yes, yes, Marianne," she replied, in the tone one adopts to calm the impatience of children, "you shall be very happy! Your husband is seeking your fortune." She was a tall woman, whose stern face seemed to be hewn in marble.

The heath was deserted and silent. The *Pierre-des-Païens* stood out whitely in the middle of its dark thicket, like a linen cloth laid out on the grass in order that the dew might give it a sparkling sheen.

"There it is," said Marianne de Treguern, shuddering and averting her eyes. "That's where he comes back—my dead brother, my poor brother!"

The old woman shrugged her shoulders and stopped, leaning on the long white staff, like a crozier, that she carried. "Who has seen him?" she murmured. "I've passed by here many times after nightfall—why doesn't your brother show himself to me as to others?"

"Because you love me too much, Dowager," Marianne replied in a low tone, "and because you do not love my father's other children enough."

Dowager Le Brec drew nearer to the young girl and kissed her. You might have felt a strange sensation in seeing that woman's caresses, which did not seem to be born of love. Her hard face refuted any notion of tenderness or femininity; there was a sort of tragic pride in the stark set of her features.

"Le Brec and Treguern were enemies for a long time," she said, drawing herself up to her full height, while the storm-wind lifted the grey wisps of her hair from behind. "A long time! The first man named Le Brec de Kervoz detested the first man who bore the name Le Mâdre de Treguern. There was, however, a daughter of the Le Brecs who married a son of Treguern. That was my sister; I loved her so tenderly that I gave her my inheritance, in order to satisfy the avarice of Treguern. I love you because you are her daughter. It is my blood that draws me to you; but my poor sister Jeanne died bringing you into the world, and another took her place in the house of Treguern. Why should I love the children that the enemy of our race had much later, by a stranger?"

There was a noise in the undergrowth that surrounded the Druidic table. Marianne threw herself backwards; terror made her teeth chatter. Dowager Le Brec extended her white staff towards the stone; she did not tremble.

"If that's the late Filhol de Treguern," she said in a loud voice, "don't hide yourself away! I'm Françoise Le Brec, and this is your sister Marianne. We'd like to know why you aren't resting peacefully in your grave."

Marianne hid her face in the old woman's bosom; fear had taken her breath away. If she was expecting to see the pale phantom of the last Treguern appear in response to the voice, the actuality alleviated her dread; nothing appeared in front of the table, and no voice was raised within the furze. The noise continued, though, and a slight movement could be discerned in the tips of the branches, despite the gloom.

The crescent Moon, having descended to the level of the bell-tower, was floating in a small pool of blue sky surrounded by huge clouds. After a few seconds, just as the Moon was sliding one of its horns beneath the cloud, a human form became visible, coming out of the undergrowth on the other side of the *Pierre-des-Païens*. If it was a specter, it was the specter of a woman. The apparition came around the circular path at a slow and graceful pace. She passed within some 15 paces of Dowager Le Brec and her companion. For an instant, they could make out a face of angelic beauty, around which tousled curls of blonde hair tumbled profusely.

Dowager Le Brec extended her wrinkled finger; a sardonic and mischievous smile elevated the corners of her mouth.

"Do you recognize her?" she asked.

"Geneviève," murmured Marianne.

"Yes, Geneviève," the Dowager repeated. "Geneviève, your brother's widow!"

"Where is she going?"

"To see her son, as you have come to see yours. Do they not have the same nurse?"

"That's true, mother," Marianne said. "You wanted it that way."

The old woman's smile became more incisive. "Our Breton prophecies never lie," she said. "The name of Treguern will be restored."

"I'm the wife of Gabriel Le Brec," Marianne said, indifferently. "What does that matter to me?"

Dowager Le Brec took her hand and looked her in the face. Her eyes shone with a strange enthusiasm.

"Sometimes," she said, "chance plays tricks. I can't hear him with my bodily ears, for my Gabriel is far away, but I sense that he's coming. Is he not handsome enough, and bold enough, to take the name of Treguern, which no longer belongs to anyone?"

"Commander Malo..." Marianne began.

"Commander Malo is a Knight of Malta;[5] a Knight of Malta is like a priest: there's no one but the little child..."

In speaking thus, the old woman's voice seemed to lose its natural firmness, taking on a blustering manner. One might have thought that she was afraid of the person whose name she had pronounced: *Commander Malo*. "Let's go," she said, with sudden harshness. "You sleep under the Treguern roof, but you're the wife of Gabriel Le Brec, my son. Go on, my daughter—you shall be rich!"

"Will I be happy?" Marianne asked.

Nothing more could be heard on the heath; the two women circled around the *Pierre-des-Païens* and took the narrow path that led to the windmill, between the two compost-heaps.

When they were halfway up the hill, they heard the door of the mill open and close again.

"Geneviève has got there first," said Marianne. "She's come for the baptism of her child. When will mine be baptized?"

"Whenever you wish," the old woman replied. "The priests are coming back to the churches now. The world went well without all that... Hey! Guillaume!" She rapped on the door of the mill with her staff and repeated: "Hey! Guillaume Féru—it's me, Dowager Le Brec, your lady!"

Guillaume's thick clogs sounded on the interior flagstones. The door turned on its rusty hinges for a second time.

"God bless you, Dowager," the miller said, not having noticed Marianne yet. "You could have waited till tomorrow, for the weather's getting bad and I'll not be putting my sails to the wind tonight."

"You're mistaken, Guillaume Féru," the Dowager replied. "What I want, you can provide. I want to see your wife."

Guillaume burst out laughing.

"Oh ho!" he said. "We're on treacherous ground. Fanchette isn't here just now. Someone came for her at dusk..."

"You're lying," Dowager Le Brec cut in, putting her withered hand on the man's arm. He tried to pull away, but the Dowager was stronger than he was. "You're lying," she repeated, looking him in the eye. "Go get Fanchette for me, right away. I want her!"

"Only the King says 'we want,' " Guillaume Féru grumbled, who did not appear to be in any hurry to obey—but the stare that he directed at the old woman testified to his dread. "You see, Dowager," he went on, "in all fairness, Fanchette cannot be here and in Bains."

Dowager Le Brec let go of the miller's arm. "Get up," she said, taking Marianne by the hand.

Marianne obeyed.

"Get out of the way," the old woman said, addressing herself to Guillaume—who hesitated, and did not move.

Dowager Le Brec took a step towards him. "Watch out!" she said, in a tone so imperious that the miller bowed his head involuntarily. "I know what goes on in your house better than you, and those that have stood in my way so far have been the worse for it!"

Guillaume was very pale.

"I don't speak thus," the Dowager continued, "because I'm your lady; I speak thus because you love Fanchette, your wife, and because you've long been in the habit of staying in together to look at your little child in its crib."

The miller was frowning harshly, but he was trembling. "I'll do as you wish, Dowager," he murmured, after a pause. "Don't put a spell on us."

"Good!" said the old woman. "Can Fanchette hear me?"

"Yes," replied a different voice, which seemed to come from the next room. "I hear you distinctly, Dowager; whatever you want shall be done."

"For your part, Fanchette," the old woman resumed, "I believe you'll obey me, for you know me and you're a good mother, but your husband Guillaume..."

"You can stay here and keep an eye on me," the miller put in, in a surly manner.

"That's not good enough," said the Dowager. "Go up to the flour-bolter, Guillaume Féru, and I'll lock the trapdoor behind you."

"A prisoner in my own house!" the man protested.

"That way," Dowager Le Brec went on, "you won't be tempted by curiosity."

"Go up, my man," said Fanchette's voice. "Go up for the sake of our child."

The miller set his foot on the ladder that led up to the upper floor. When he had disappeared through the trapdoor, he turned around, because the ladder was vibrating under a new weight. It was Dowager Le Brec, who was climbing up behind him in order to shoot the bolt.

"While you're up there," she said, "you can grind a por-
tion of grain or two so as not to waste the time."

"In this wind! On the eve of a holiday!"

"It has to be done," the Dowager said, in a peremptory
tone.

The open trap fell back; the thick bolt slid firmly into its
hole; Dowager Le Brec went down the ladder's steps and drew
Marianne towards the other room.

"Open the door, Fanchette," she said.

The other room was plunged in total darkness. The old
woman had obviously expected that, for she made no comment. "Fanchette," she said, simply, "if you do as you're told,
your son Josille will grow up and grow strong. Come closer—
I'm not alone."

Fanchette emerged from the shadows and recognized
Marianne. *The half-sister!* she thought. *The late Treguern's
half-sister!*

Marianne came in. The Dowager spoke to Fanchette in a
whisper for some time. As she went out, she said: "I know the
other one's here; take care!" Then, she went outside, where
the wind was blowing with increasing violence and large raindrops were beginning to fall.

Dowager Le Brec pushed back the hood of her cloak so
that the wind and the rainwater could cool her feverish head.
She took up a position on the other side of the path, at the foot
of a bank, and stood still, leaning on her great white staff. She
stared at the mill, whose windows were lit by a pale glow.

Guillaume obediently set the vanes to the stormy wind,
which seized them furiously.

The immobile Dowager thought: *They are two children
of the same age and the same blood. Which of them shall be
Comte? Gabriel, Gabriel! Where can he be at this hour, and
what is keeping him so late?* She pursed her lips, while murmuring: "If I could only pray!"

Almost immediately, though, her lowered forehead was
raised again and her eyes defied the darkness of the night sky.
The first ray of light breaching the clouds illuminated her

haughty face, which seemed to be challenging the almightiness of God. A distant thunderclap extended its dull and profound echoes over the heath.

When the thunder died away, a sonorous male voice could be heard on the far side of the hill, on the Redon road, singing a joyful Ille-et-Vilaine song at full blast, despite the thunder and the rain. Dowager Le Brec thought she was dreaming. The Redon road was in front of her, but it was as dark now as a cellar, and nothing could be seen beyond 15 paces. From the depths of that darkness came a double burst of spontaneous laughter, and another voice joined in with the first to repeat the chorus of the song uninhibitedly:

> *If you want a drink, I've Adam's ale,*
> *My bucket's full and so's my pail,*
> *Jean, my poor old duckie;*
> *Dum-de-dum and dum-de-doo!*
> *I've got no water, good cider for you*
> *My pail's full, and so's my bucket!* [6]

"It must be the Devil, to sing at a time like this!" Guillaume Féru muttered, shivering behind the bay of his window as his fearful eye followed the unsteady movement of his machinery.

It sounds like the voice of that boy Etienne who joined the Army, thought the old woman. *Why has he come back here, when he still has five years to serve?*

"Lady Le Brec!" shouted the miller. "This beam's going to break and the millstones will shatter like glass. In God's name, the sails must be brought round!"

"Let the beam break, Guillaume Féru," the old woman replied, "and the millstones shatter like glass."

Guillaume made the sign of the cross and sat down on a sack of flour. The people coming along the Redon road drew closer. Dowager Le Brec went along the path, which had changed into a torrent; the filthy water, covered with yellowish scum, came up to her knees. She crouched against a wall on the moist ground. The joyful companions, who were defying the tempest with their singing, were now so close that they could be seen advancing through the darkness.

"Ah, well!" one of them exclaimed, with imperturbable gaiety. "One can't say that we've brought good weather to the region, Mathurin!"

"As long as we haven't lost our way, Etienne!" the other replied. "Hang on! I can see a light!"

"Dum-dum-de-doo, good cider for you! Here's a light, just at the right time! Can you hear that noise, though?"

They stopped.

"I think it's a mill..." Mathurin began.

"Right!" Etienne replied. "I think I recognize it! We're on the road that goes down to the *Pierre-des-Païens*, and it's Guillaume Féru's mill."

"What sort of diabolical Sabbath is Père Guillaume holding in there tonight?"

"If you want to know, and to dry off a bit, we've only to knock on the door."

Mathurin hesitated for a moment. Dowager Le Brec held her breath.

"Although it's raining shells and bayonets," Mathurin said, finally, "the first house I'll enter tonight will be that of my dear old mother. We must go our separate ways here, Etienne my friend. You're going straight on and I'm turning left. Let's shake hands and say our goodbyes."

Etienne's voice was impregnated with sadness. "That's true," he said. "You have a mother."

A second flash of lightning was ignited at that moment; the inundated heath emerged from the darkness. A few paces away, on the ridge of the hill, Dowager Le Brec saw two young men in uniform shaking hands. They were two fine soldiers, but there was an empty sleeve hanging from the shoulder of one of them.

Dowager Le Brec's eyes opened very wide. "Oh!" she murmured, with a gasp. "Treguern's friend Etienne has lost his right arm: Gabriel will be happy!"

The lightning-flash was extinguished.

"Good luck!" said Mathurin.

"Good luck!" Etienne replied.

Mathurin took the path that led to the forest. Etienne set the stick supporting his petty belongings upon his shoulder, and headed straight for the door of the mill.

II. Two Sergeants

A few hours earlier, beneath the porch of the last house in the suburb of Redon that extended towards the road to Vannes, our two soldiers had been sitting at a table, with their backs to the wall, chatting like old friends. It had been stiflingly hot all day and their dust-covered uniforms bore testimony to the stress of a long journey; they gave every appearance of savoring the moment's rest to the full. The pitcher of froth-crowned cider that stood between them had been filled and emptied several times.

It was a fairly well-appointed inn. Through the carriage entrance a capacious yard could be seen, with very airy stables, where three or four of the region's small horses were taking their evening meal. Our soldiers were non-commissioned officers; both of them wore sergeants' stripes. The older might have been nearly 30; the other, who had one arm fewer, did not appear to be more than 22 or 23. The latter was a handsome lad, with frank and cheerful features, whose forehead was crowned with black curls.

"There it is, Mathurin, old chap," he said, letting loose a deep sigh. "When one has a broken paw, one must choose between the Invalides and the village. I thought it better to return here, to see if my left hand is still good for planting cabbages." He did his best to smile, but behind that forced gaiety there was a good deal of sadness.

"It's a shame," said Mathurin. "At the rate you were going, you were certain to make captain. How long had you been in the Army?"

"Fifteen months, when I stopped that accursed bullet. And I'd already been a sergeant for some time."

"Not captain, then," Mathurin exclaimed. "You'd have been a colonel before your moustache turned grey!"

Etienne moistened his lips in his cider-bowl. One might have thought that he was drinking bile.

"Now, old fellow," he said, abruptly putting his bowl on the table, "let's not talk about that, for my eyes are pricking and it wouldn't do you any good to make me cry like an infant."

Mathurin silently held up his hand.

"By the way," Etienne went on, "has your mother said anything in her letters about that famous *cloarec*, Gabriel?" The word *cloarec* is used in colloquial Breton to describe the pupils of a seminary.

"Not much. The good woman said that there was some sort of fop at the Orlan presbytery—who knew better than the books, and was the nephew or godson of Dowager Le Brec—who was bound to replace the old rector some day."

Etienne frowned. "An evil family!" he said. "That one's no priest, despite his seminarist's habit. If he becomes one, there'll be the Devil in his blessing!"

The Sun was sinking towards the horizon and was already hidden behind the square foundation of a tower in the form of an obelisk, where the Chouans had withstood the assault of the Republican Army some years previously. A horseman dressed in black, mounted on a horse that seemed exhausted, appeared at the corner of the street. He came straight towards the inn.

"How far is it from here to the parish of Orlan?" he asked the innkeeper, who had gone to meet him.

The two sergeants pricked up their ears.

"He's going to our home ground," Etienne said.

"And he's an Englishman," Mathurin added. "I've learned to recognize the accent."

"Four leagues across country," the innkeeper relied to the foreigner's question.

The foreigner hesitated for a moment, then threw his bridle to the innkeeper. He dismounted and undid the straps of his valise, which he put on his shoulder, refusing the assistance pressed upon him by the stable-boy.

"A room," he said. "A good meal, if that's possible, and a fresh horse in an hour's time."

"It appears that he has something valuable in the valise," said Etienne.

"These *goddams*," Mathurin replied, "are nothing like other people." When the foreigner had gone into the inn, he added: "What the Devil have you got against that poor old woman Le Brec?"

"The damned witch!" Etienne muttered. "She's tried many a time to put a spell on Treguern."

Mathurin burst out laughing. Etienne looked at him disapprovingly and went on: "You've been away too long. You no longer believe in anything."

"As to that," Mathurin put in, "I believe in the good God. You like him as much as that, then, your Treguern?"

"Yes," Etienne replied, simply. "I like him a great deal. I could not love him more if he were my own brother."

Mathurin bit his lip as if to hold back a word that was trying to escape. Etienne continued in a dreamy voice: "It was always that way between Treguern and us. Treguern was a good lord; we have been loyal vassals."

Mathurin shrugged his shoulders. "Lord! Vassal!" he repeated. "There's ancient history for you!"

"My grandfather had five sons," Etienne went on, as if he had not heard a word. "Five handsome young fellows, as strong and brave as lions. They followed the last-but-one Comte de Treguern to America when he went there to fight the English. My grandfather died putting his breast in front of Treguern's. He said to his sons: do as I do; and his sons obeyed. When Treguern returned to Brittany, he only had one of my grandfather's five sons with him; the other four had died saving his life. I've seen a saber cut on the forehead of the one who remained—who was my father—which an English dragoon aimed at Treguern's forehead. As he died, my father said to me: do as we do. I would not regret the loss of my right arm so much if I had given it for Treguern."

"Each to his own..." Mathurin began. "I've been told, though, that you've given him more than that."

The young soldier's handsome face became sad and serious. "That's true," he replied. "I gave him my happiness."

Mathurin leaned forward and filled the two bowls.

"When you left to join the Army, Mathurin," Etienne went on, "Geneviève Le Hir was still a child, wasn't she?"

"Eight or ten years old, at the most."

"You don't remember her at all?"

"Of course! The prettiest little girl I've met in my entire life. She must have been very beautiful when she got to 16."

"Very beautiful," confirmed Etienne, whose voice had changed. "Yes, as beautiful as the angels!"

"Oh, ho!" said Mathurin. "So there's a story?"

"Has your mother never mentioned in her letters the name of the wife of Filhol de Treguern?"

"I don't remember it," Mathurin replied.

Etienne passed the fingers of his left hand over his forehead. "We were the same ages, Filhol and I," he went on. "The house of Treguern had become so poor that we were brought up together, as fast friends. I was like Filhol's brother. Until the age of 20, I never thought of spending a single day without sharing his pains or his pleasures. One evening, when we had reached our 18th year, there was a party at the manor despite the evil times. What remained of the gentry of the region came together in the great hall. The rumor had gone around that Commander Malo had been killed by the Blues,[7] in that tower that you see over there above the houses in the street. It was several months since anyone had seen him, but he appeared all of a sudden, that evening, without having himself announced, and came to stand in the middle of the circle surrounding the chimney..."

"Ah yes!" Mathurin interrupted him. "I'm quite content to talk about your Commander Malo. Is he a sorcerer or a madman, that one?"

"Commander Malo is a younger brother of Treguern," Etienne replied, sternly. "That name must be pronounced with respect. Have you heard of the Veil?"

"What veil?"

28

"The Veil that presages death."

"Ah!" said Mathurin, whose hearty laughter became a trifle forced. "The Veil of Treguern! Yes, I've heard talk of that. Truly, I believe we change as soon as we find ourselves back in our homeland. I haven't thought about all these devilries for ten years, and God knows that I would have laughed like a hunchback if anyone had told me a ghost story in the Army of Sambre-et-Meuse. Look how close I am to coming out in goose-pimples now!"

"If you've heard talk of the Veil of Treguern," Etienne went on, his tone calm and melancholy, "you know that since the great knight Tanneguy, whose tomb is in Orlan's church, all the males of the Treguern blood have the gift of foreseeing the deaths of their friends and their enemies."

"Well enough," Mathurin muttered, "that, when that Malo used to look me in the eyes, although I was neither his friend nor his enemy, I hurried away as if I had seen the Devil!"

Etienne continued without pause: "So, that evening, the good Comtesse, Filhol's mother, was sitting under the chimney mantelpiece. She was wearing her widow's weeds, because the Comte had died the preceding year. Commander Malo looked at her and suddenly turned very pale.

" 'Madame my cousin,' he said, 'you must turn your thoughts to God.'

"The Comtesse was a devout woman; she got up and went straight to the Commander.

" 'Monsieur my cousin,' she said to him, 'since my husband the Comte is no longer in this world, I think of nothing but God.'

"The merriment on every face had frozen, and at the far end of the room, where Filhol and I were dancing with the young women, we heard the word repeated everywhere, echoing in the silence: 'The Veil! The Veil!'

"The Comtesse called Filhol over and told him to fetch a priest.

"I remember clearly that Geneviève, poor child, was dancing with me. She murmured, without being aware that she was speaking aloud: 'It would be a brave woman who would dare marry into the Treguern family!'

"The Comtesse died a Christian death without seeing the Sun again. Commander Malo stayed at the manor until the funeral, then departed without saying where he was going, as was his custom.

"Filhol no longer had a father or mother; he was his own master. A great sadness took hold of him—and I felt that sadness myself, for it seemed that our two hearts had become twinned. The circumstance that had preceded the death of the Comtesse had struck us vividly, and we no longer occupied ourselves with any but supernatural matters. It was at that time that we exchanged a promise, which may have been a sin..."

"What promise?" Mathurin asked. He was no longer the joyful person of a little while ago. The Sun had disappeared behind the gables of the suburb; dusk was falling rapidly. The sky, whose horizon was charged with clouds, seemed on the point of dissolving its somber circular outline into the darker line of the mountains of Saint-Pern. The road, beyond the neighborhood, curved up a slope and vanished between two walls of slate. Beyond that point, all was darkness: the immense and deserted heathland, which they would be obliged to cross in the dark.

"The promise that Filhol and I exchanged," Etienne went on, "could not be fulfilled until one of us died—and, thank God, he and I are both still in the world. I shall explain more clearly in a little while; first we must speak of Geneviève. I could never look at her, so gentle and so pious, without wanting her for my wife when I came of age. I thought that I was alone in courting her. I was hopeful; it seemed to me that her smiles were for me. Sometimes, however, I became anxious. Filhol was so handsome and so good! But Filhol had never said anything to me, and I could not help remembering Geneviève's words: 'It would be a brave woman who would dare marry into the Treguern family!'

"Two years later, in May 1798, Filhol and I had both attained our 20th year. We were entered together into the ballot for conscription. I drew a good number, but Filhol was selected by the draw. I didn't think about Geneviève right away, thinking only of myself. As I returned to the manor, full of joy, I heard someone weeping behind the orchard hedge; my heart was gripped, for I said to myself: 'That's Marianne de Treguern, Filhol's half-sister, and his little sister Laurence, weeping over poor Filhol's departure.'

"They all lived together at the manor: Marianne, the daughter of the first wife, Filhol, and Laurence, a young child. It was thought that Laurence would not live long; she was reminiscent of those souls that are ready for Heaven.

"The foliage wasn't very thick as yet; I put my eye to the hedge, and I saw Geneviève with her lush blonde hair in disarray, sobbing." Etienne interrupted himself at this point to say: "Mathurin, my friend, I did not feel such a pain when they cut off my right arm." He continued: "I went on my way toward the manor, where I had been given a place in the old servants' quarters—for I was already fatherless and motherless, like Filhol. I made a little bundle of my personal effects, and I said to my sister Marion: 'I've been selected by the ballot. I must go. Goodbye! Be happy.'

"We were still at war; the conscripts had to leave that evening for Redon. I put my package over my shoulder on the end of a stick, and I ran to the manor, where Filhol and Geneviève were together.

"They saw me coming, and perhaps they expected me, for Geneviève threw herself on her knees on the grass and thanked God, while Filhol drew me to his bosom. Filhol and I went into town, and formally exchanged our numbers in the presence of the Mayor. I left the same evening. Filhol came with me as far as Redon. What I had done for Filhol, Filhol would have done for me."

"Perhaps..." Mathurin murmured.

"Besides which, I was obeying my father's final command. Since then, I've received two letters from home: one in which Filhol told me of his marriage to Geneviève, the other informing me of the birth of their first child, little Olympe de Treguern."

Etienne fell silent, his bowed head slumped over his breast.

"How long has it been since you received the second letter?" Mathurin asked.

"A year."

"And the worthy Marion has not sent you any news?"

"My sister Marion cannot write."

"And now that you've come back home, Etienne," Mathurin said, full of emotion, as if he could not hold back the words, "what if you find Geneviève widowed... free?"

Etienne drew himself upright and became so pale that one might have thought him a dead man. He fixed his wide-open eyes on his companion, as if he did not dare to interrogate him by any other means than his gaze.

At the corner of the street, where the black-clad horseman whom Mathurin had identified as an Englishman had made his appearance, the sound of another galloping horse was audible. Dusk had fallen some time ago; a few lights were already shining in the narrow casement windows. A dark silhouette was vaguely discernible in the gloom. It was another rider dressed in black. He covered the distance separating him from the hostelry in a matter of seconds; his horse, whose flanks were flecked with foam, came to an abrupt halt in front of the table where the two sergeants were sitting.

There was a street-lamp attached on one side to the wall of the inn, and on the other to a pole planted on the other side of the pavement. The newcomer cracked the little whip he was holding in his hand to summon the inn's servants. He stayed on his horse, though, as if he were afraid to dismount unaided. He was a very young man, who seemed to be at least a year or two younger than Etienne. The curls of his abundant fine blond hair were sagging beneath his broad-brimmed hat, moist with sweat. He wore a short cape, trousers secured at the knee with silk ribbons, and calf-length boots with spurs. Despite his riding costume, however, there was something gauche and timorous in his manner that revealed him as a man used to a sedentary and retiring life. It did not require a keen observer to see that; it was obvious to Etienne.

It needed something very serious to distract Etienne's attention following his comrade's last words; his attention was, however, distracted. As soon as he had fixed his eyes on the new arrival, his gaze could not be detached from him.

"Do you recognize him?" Mathurin asked, in a low voice.

"I've never seen him before," Etienne replied, "but I believe that I know him."

"Hey!" shouted the horseman, in a voice that was youthful, but seemed nevertheless to adopt a naturally imperious tone. "Is there no one here to welcome me?"

It was the wind, which was beginning to rise, that prevented him from being heard inside the inn. In the distance, the clouds were accumulating over the heath, and the dust on the road was beginning to swirl. The young man, his patience exhausted, put his whip down and released his bridle, in order to get down with the aid of the horse's mane. He was definitely a poor horseman. The horse, which could do no more, did not budge, and the young man got down without difficulty—but while both his hands were occupied, a gust of wind got hold of the broad brim of his hat, and carried it 20 paces away.

The light of the street-lamp fell on a face of almost feminine beauty, which seemed too small for the prodigal richness of the blond hair that framed it. On closer inspection, though, the face, whose complexion was too pale and whose features were too fine and delicate, revealed a hint of bold intelligence and obstinate will. The forehead was high; it was evident that it extended into the roots of his hair; the contours of the thin-lipped mouth were firmly shaped; the nose presented an indecisive curve that was not quite aquiline; the flared and almost transparent nostrils were already emphasizing the flatness of the frontal bone, which is normally squared off by age alone.

His arched eyebrows, as beautiful and neat as if they had been skillfully sculpted in marble, were mounted over dark blue eyes. At first glance, it was a charming head. The second glance searched the harmonious ensemble in vain for the slightly reckless frankness and cheerful temerity of youth.

"Fetch my hat," said the newcomer to the waiter, who had finally presented himself, "and next time, make sure you come more quickly when I call!"

Etienne squeezed his companion's hand.

"It's him!" he murmured. "I'd bet my life that it's him!"

"Who do you mean?" Mathurin asked.

"The *cloarec* Gabriel!"

"In spurred boots...?" Mathurin began, laughing.

But he did not finish, for the newcomer had turned to take his hat from the hands of the waiter, who said to him: "Oh, Monsieur Gabriel, you've arrived just in time. It will be better to be here with us than on the heath tonight!"

The young traveler went towards the door without replying.

"You guessed right, though," Mathurin whispered in Etienne's ear. "It's your *cloarec* from Orlan!"

Etienne silenced him with a gesture and cocked his head to hear better. Gabriel was speaking.

"A room," he said, "broth, bread and wine—and a horse ready at the door in a quarter of an hour."

"What!" cried the waiter. "You're going to take to the road again in weather like this, Monsieur Gabriel?"

Etienne immediately leaned forwards to catch the reply, but the young traveler had already passed over the threshold.

"What about us?" Mathurin said, looking up at the threatening sky. "Should we bed down here? It'll be light tomorrow." When the younger sergeant remained silent, he added: "What do you think?"

"I think," said Etienne slowly, in a different voice, "that that man arrived at the Orlan presbytery a week after my departure for the Army. It's like destiny: Filhol was alone and Filhol is weak. I think that Filhol has only written to me twice, a dozen lines in each letter, since the day when I said good-bye to him on this very spot. I think that it's a singular occurrence, and an evil omen, that as soon as my path has brought me home, I should immediately encounter the face of the man who has stolen the heart of my brother Filhol from me."

Mathurin wanted to say "Bah!"

Etienne raised his head again and studied the sky in his turn; the clouds, growing ever darker, seemed to be getting closer to the ground, touching the gables of the houses. "He must be in a great hurry, that Gabriel!" he murmured, as if talking to himself.

"What does that matter to us?" Mathurin said.

"And what of the other one?" Etienne went on. "The one with the heavy valise on his shoulder. Why are they both here, on the same day, at the same hour?"

"Why did you and I meet up on the highway?" Mathurin asked him, laughing.

"Yes... why?" Etienne repeated. "I've seen whole seasons pass without a single traveler arriving in the parish of Orlan."

Mathurin shrugged his shoulders. "Look!" he cried. "The pitcher's empty and there's nothing in the bowls. Shall we stay? Shall we go? Me, I vote that we stay."

Etienne got up and rapped on the table with the end of his stick. "Stay if you want, Mathurin my friend," he said. "Myself, I think that something is happening tonight in Orlan. Why I think so, I don't know; but there's a kind of voice sounding in my ears, which is crying out to me: Be on your way! I have but one arm now, but that's all right—thank God, I'm going. It's not natural that a Le Brec should befriend a Treguern."

He put a few coins in the waiter's hand to settle the bill.

"Give me time to fill my waterskin," Mathurin cried. "You shan't be alone, by thunder! And that's the right word, for the clouds are already striking the flint behind the mount of Saint-Pern. We've seen plenty like that in the Army of Sambre-et-Meuse! Waiter, put brandy in that up to the neck, and we'll be off!"

III. Nocturnal Terrors

It was eight o'clock in the evening, or thereabouts, when the one-armed Etienne and his comrade left the inn on the outskirts of Redon. The first steps they took brought them into open country, for there were no more houses beyond the little enclosure of the inn. Mathurin's waterskin had been filled to the brim, according to his instructions, and it was a capacious vessel; what was in it would give them heart.

The two sergeants climbed the slope in silence, heads bowed to avoid the dust-charged wind, marching with great strides. As they advanced, the turning path, curtailed by the slate, was hemmed in by precipitous walls. Mathurin looked back frequently; while he could still see the scattered lights that indicated the location of the town all was well, but when the walls of slate closed in, extinguishing the last glimmer, he drew a sigh from the depths of his bosom.

Etienne and he were in a sort of tunnel, whose ceiling was formed by the low black sky. The storm-wind flooded it with furious violence. Then, when the wind chanced to die down, there was a dreary silence, in the midst of which the footsteps of the two travelers echoed eerily.

"It's ten years since I last passed this way," Mathurin said, in a hesitant voice. "How long have we to stay in these rocks?"

"Less than a quarter of an hour," Etienne replied.

"My God!" Mathurin muttered, envious of his companion's calm. "I've crossed defiles full of snow in my time, where comrades fell frozen all along the route; I don't know why I wasn't chilled, as I am here, to the marrow of my bones."

It was getting warmer, though, and poor Sergeant Mathurin had sweat on his brow. At the top of one of the neighboring slopes a sad voice raised a song that the local laborers sang in the fields. Another voice replied from the

37

opposite slope, and for a few minutes there was a plaintive and prolonged exchange. Then there was the sound of the little bells worn by goats, and the wind carried the bellowing of cattle being led to the byre.

Mathurin pulled himself together bravely; these melancholy and familiar sounds were, at least, evidence of the world of living men. The barefoot herdsman and the shepherd-boy speaking from one crag to the other, the bellowing herd and the tinkling bells, all in unison, was the true voice of the region, and Mathurin loved his little realm of Brittany very dearly. If he had been at the fireside of some friendly farmhouse just then, surrounded by boys and girls, smallholders and their wives, in the parish of Orlan, there would not have been a happier man than Sergeant Mathurin in the entire universe. But Breton leagues are so long! And the *Grand'Lande* [8] hides so many specters among its white-tipped and heather-clad crags!

Etiennne had been correct in what he said; in the Army, Mathurin had forgotten the traditional superstitions of his native region. The bivouac fire is a sovereign remedy for such vague terrors. Not even once, perhaps, since he had put on his uniform, had Mathurin thought about those fantastic dances that the *kourils* [9] lead around granite crosses, accompanied by the lugubrious mewing of the *chats courtauds* [10] holding their councils on the capstones. Nor had he thought about the giant beasts harnessed to Satan's carriage, which have hundred-year-old oaks for horns and which graze the forests like ewes cropping meadow-grass. Nor had he thought about the *corniquets*, [11] the crafty goblins that jump on the necks of travelers to strangle them and abandon them in the bogs, nor the *laveuses de nuit*, [12] those huge pale young women with expressionless eyes who force passers-by to wind the moist linen of shrouds in the wrong direction.

Memories of this sort, however, lie dormant without dying; the Breton native can go around the world, but recover his childhood impressions the moment he sets foot again on the soil of Brittany. There is something indefinable in the air: the

nocturnal solitude is populous; the silence speaks; the empti-
ness acquires a body; every rock seems to be a crouching
form; every tree extends long, emaciated and menacing arms;
plaints are heard in the mist, where veils can be seen floating
in the wind behind the *belles-de-nuit*: virgins who died before
the hour of their betrothal.[13]

Amid the clouds you see the mountains with bare slopes,
immense forests bordering the somber profundity of great
lakes, cathedral towers, and a colossal recumbent figure that is
always looking down at the Earth. Then, in the distance, on
the traveled road, you hear the screech of the Black Cart's
axle. No one has ever seen that cart, but everyone has heard
that funereal grinding a hundred times over in the course of a
lifetime. The *carriguel an ancou*, the ancient gallic language
calls it: Death's wheelbarrow!

Then the undergrowth stirs; the sound of a horn sounds
in the covert; a roe deer bounds across the path, its eyes two
glowing coals and its bones piercing its hide. Behind the deer
a horse's skeleton passes, as rapid as a lightning-flash; on that
bizarre mount there is a tall knight, fully-clad in steel armor—
save only for the helmet, which is missing. What good would
a helmet be? On the knight's shoulders there is no head. It is
the ghostly hunter who races through the forest from nightfall
till dawn. And down there, those little pale flames that leap up,
cresting the water-filled ditches: souls in torment in search of
lost prayers, like beggars awaiting the crumbs from an opulent
table. And, further distant, at the bend of the river, that sway-
ing form, as white as an alabaster statue, which is magnified as
you move away, until its forehead touches the stars...

Some time had passed since they had heard the herdsman
and the shepherd-boy, the goats' bells and the bellowing of the
cattle.

"Mathurin," said Etienne in a low voice, "why did you
speak to me of Geneviève, widowed and free?"

"Why?" Mathurin repeated. "Too late... not here! I'm
choking between these dark walls." In order to recover some
of his composure, he took the stopper from his waterskin for

the first time, and drank a mouthful. Etienne continued walking.

"Do you want some?" Mathurin asked from in rear.

Etienne made no reply. His head was bowed and he was lost in thought. *Widowed and free!* he said to himself. *That's not possible. How could Filhol be dead, since I have never seen, whether waking or dreaming, that which he promised me?*

Mathurin made haste to catch up with him; the darkness of the hollow lightened little by little as the heights declined, while the sky became less gloomy. The path turned abruptly, and there was a sort of *coup de théâtre*. The horizon opened up before the travelers as far as the eye could see; the wall continued to the right, while to the left there was a void—for the road, which had hitherto been making its way through the mountain, now clung to its flank.

The wind had got the better of the clouds for the moment, thick and heavy as they were; great gaps appeared here and there that allowed the starry sky to show through. The crescent Moon appeared periodically, swallowed up again by the avid vapor only to reappear again, radiant and victorious, between the clouds.

In broad daylight, it is a large and fertile countryside that presents itself to the eyes of travelers arriving at the far side of the mount of Saint-Pern. Beneath their feet, the slate expanse descends to an immense depth, bearing vegetation according to the whims of its strata, maintaining little hummocks carpeted with grass and flowers close at hand, while dipping down more distantly into abysses that the eye cannot penetrate.

A hundred paces from the foot of the mountain, the river Ise, a tributary of the Vilaine, meanders gracefully along its course, eventually bathing the feet of the chapel that serves the quarrymen's encampment as a parish church. On the far side of the Ise, meadows populated by livestock climb a gentle slope that extends to the town of Bains, towards which the roadway rises through plantations of pines to the arid heights of the *Grand'Lande*. The entire scene is full of movement and life, as the laborers swarm like ants.

At night, it is different. People go to bed early on the slopes of Saint-Pern, in order to rise early. Silence replaces the thousand noises of travail; the fires are extinguished; the huts vanish into the shadows and the entire agricultural endeavor resembles a black and bottomless pit.

Etienne stopped; Mathurin was seized by vertigo as he saw the void bordering their route.

"I've never felt anything like it," Etienne thought, aloud. "I knew, though, that I'd be very glad to take the first breath of this country's air. Here's the Ise, in which I bathed many a time; I've led the manor's herds as far as these meadows. Look, Mathurin, while the moonlight lasts: there's the forest of Grandpré, there's the Moulin-Neuf, in front of the town of Bains—and it seems to me that I can make out both wings of the beautiful Château de Moeil."

"You see all that," said Mathurin, retreating to the shelter of the slope, "and you're very happy. Me, I can't see anything but that devilish precipice into which you'll fall head-first if you stand on the edge like that. I see the shadow of the clouds racing across the landscape, and way down there, the far side of the *Grand'Lande* seems to be illuminated by I don't know what diabolical light."

He was right. The crescent Moon was about to be hidden from the travelers' view, but it lit the horizon vividly; behind the darkened regions of the nearer landscape, the more distant regions of the *Grand'Lande* stood out against the black horizon.

"That's not natural," Etienne went on, speaking of his own impressions.

"No!" cried Mathurin, "It's not natural! It's necessary to be somewhere other than the *Grand'Lande* if one desires to see natural things, at the hour of night when we, for our sins, are abroad. There's still time to return to Redon. What do you say?"

Etienne replaced his stick on his shoulder and resumed his march. They descended the path in silence.

"Have the marriage laws also been changed in Brittany?" Etienne asked, suddenly.

"Why do you ask that?" Mathurin said.

"I believe they call it divorce," Etienne went on. "Divorce must have been established here, since you speak to me of Geneviève, widowed and free?"

"As regards that," Mathurin said, in a level voice, "I haven't heard anything. But let's hurry, if you will. The storm that flags becomes a tempest and the best thing for us would be to get on swiftly."

The young sergeant made no move. He had been obsessed with the same notion since they had first set foot in the region. "In that case," he said, trying to make out his companion's expression, "you have heard a rumor that Filhol de Treguern is dead?"

"Sooner or later," Mathurin replied, warily, "everyone finishes up that way. We all die."

Despite the darkness, an extraordinary agitation was discernible in Etienne's features. "Whoever told you that was lying," he added, resuming his march. "When Filhol de Treguern dies, I'll be the first to know."

Mathurin was disinclined to discuss the matter; he had embraced his waterskin three or four times, but it had not put the heart back into him. For the moment, this one-armed Etienne was a miserable companion. It was impossible to get a rational word out of him! Mathurin heard him murmur between clenched teeth: "But what if God did not wish it? What if the dead cannot fulfil promises made in life?"

The road began to slope upwards. On the left hand side, the tall chimneys of the Château de Moeil became perceptible when there was a glimmer of light. In front of them, a great dark mass cut across the path: the forest of Grandpré. A few steps further, and the old oaks surrounded them with the vault of their enormous crowns.

Once they were in the forest, the two soldiers were literally unable to see either the sky or the ground. Mathurin's breath caught in his throat; he found it difficult to match the steady and tranquil pace of his companion. The wind no longer blew in his face, as it had before, now that they were engulfed by the forest—although brief gusts sometimes blew from the left or the right, and the tempest bore down upon the roof of the forest, whose thick trunks swayed and shivered. Mathurin felt more dead than alive.

"There's one!" Etienne said, suddenly, stopping abruptly and seemingly cocking his ear.

"One what?" stammered Mathurin, oppressed by fear.

"Listen!"

The noise of a horse galloping through the forest was distinctly audible, although it was impossible to determine the direction from which it came.

"The Ghostly Hunter..." Mathurin began.

"There were two at the inn," Etienne put in. "This one's the first to arrive." Then he lifted his ear to another breath of wind and said: "Not by much. I can hear a second horse."

"And here's a third halted in the middle of the road!" cried Mathurin, putting out his arms as if to repel a vision. "Lord, what a night!"

There was indeed a horseman motionless at a crossroads in the center of a clearing some 40 or 50 paces away. There was nothing there to block out the rays of moonlight, filtered through lighter clouds. The rider seemed to be surrounded by an aureole of light. He was bare-headed; it was already possible to make out his pale, thin face beneath the floating strands of his greying hair. He was tall, and the folds of a cloak of uncommon length descended from his shoulders as far as the legs of his horse.

They saw him gesture with his hand, and his voice was raised while the wind fell silent.

"Hey there!" he cried. "If you're Christians, answer me. Have you seen two horsemen coming through the forest, heading for the parish of Orlan?"

"Commander Malo!" Etienne murmured. "When he comes here, it's because misfortune is about to knock on Treguern's door!" In a louder voice, he said: "We've heard two horses galloping, but we've seen nothing."

The rider turned his mount's head towards the *Grand'Lande.*

"Listen!" cried Etienne. "They're very close now, and they're coming towards you; if you need help, say so, Malo de Treguern."

The rider's spurs touched the flank of his mount, which leapt forward and disappeared into the trees. Nevertheless, his response was audible. He said: "I go where the Lord leads me, and I don't need anyone!"

Before Etienne and Mathurin could traverse the short distance that separated them from the clearing, the dust of the road erupted in whirlwinds beneath the hooves of the two horses, which flashed through it like arrows, to be lost almost immediately in the shadows. For a few seconds more, the double gallop was audible beneath the vaults of the forest, then everything fell silent—except for the storm, whose menacing voice was on the increase.

IV. The Croix-qui-Marche

From that moment on, poor Sergeant Mathurin was no longer living in the real world. He had a fever, and the contents of his waterskin could only exacerbate his fears. The rider in the long black cloak, positioned in the center of the clearing, had seemed to him to be more than human; his dazzled eyes had seen trails of fire behind the two other horsemen, whose reckless course had lifted whirlwinds of dust from the road.

Etienne's presence no longer reassured him; on the contrary, it was not without a certain terror that he matched the assured and steady march of his companion; since he remained so calm, he must feel that he was in his element here! And now that poor Mathurin thought about it, he clearly recalled that he had thought that there was something strange about the fellow when he encountered him the previous evening, on the Paris road.

Perhaps Etienne himself was one of those dead men who returned, and who drew the living down into the graveyard. Such things were known to happen, Mathurin told himself, shivering, and the belated suspicion was not without wisdom. Even so, he followed Etienne—followed him like a dog, one might have said—making all the same turns and not daring to let him out of sight for an instant. It is always thus. In all the legends, a chain stronger than steel attaches the living to the dead. To be sure, an hour or two earlier, under the porch of the inn, on the outskirts of Redon, Etienne had had an honest face—Mathurin could not deny it—but that did not reassure him in the least, because he thought: Why does he no longer show his face?

In fact, Etienne had not turned once since the Saint-Pern bridge. He had gone straight ahead, without ever hesitating, as if the Sun were illuminating the road's obstacles. Enough time had passed for the noise of galloping horses to be lost in the

45

distance. Etienne was leaning on his stick in the center of the crossroads.

"I certainly recognized the *cloarec*," he murmured, talking to himself. "He's followed the same path as Commander Malo. The other has taken the road that leads to the manor of Treguern. Mathurin!"

"What now?" the latter said. He was standing a few paces away, similarly leaning on his staff.

"Did your mother ever mention Marianne, the half-sister, in her letters?"

"Shall I see her again in this world, my poor old mother?" Mathurin muttered. He added: "She spoke to me of this and that, Monsieur Etienne, but I've no clear memory of it just now."

"Why do you call me monsieur?" the young sergeant asked, turning in astonishment.

Mathurin saw the movement and closed his eyes, as if he dreaded seeing that the face had two empty holes instead of eyes. "It's not out of malice," he replied, trying to smile. "As regards Marianne de Treguern, Filhol's half-sister, there was some story or other, in which the name of the *cloarec* Gabriel was also mentioned. What does it matter to us? I'd willingly give everything I have in my sack to be at the far side of the *Grand'Lande*, in front of Guillaume Féru's windmill."

"We'll get there," the young sergeant said, setting off again, "and you'll keep everything in your sack, Mathurin my friend... but between here to there, I must find out the news."

"The news? Who are we going to ask? Between here and Guillaume Féru's mill is the *Grand'Lande*—and I don't know of a single human dwelling on it."

"Perhaps the one who will tell me the news," the young soldier said, lowering his voice reflexively, "is no longer in a human dwelling."

Sergeant Methurin had not thought that his anxiety could be further magnified. He was mistaken. His heart suddenly skipped a beat. "In the name of the Lord, Monsieur Etienne!" he stammered. "Don't tempt the secrets of the tomb!"

"You've told me that Geneviève is widowed and free," Etienne replied, firmly. "I want to know if that's true. I want to know it from the man who is sworn to tell me, by his solemn oath."

"Listen, my friend—my brother," Mathurin said, whose very distress gave him the courage to reproach himself. "I see where you intend to go: the road to the *Pierres-Plantées*, the road to the *Croix-qui-Marche*![14] Misfortune always comes to those who pass that way!"

"It's by that route, nevertheless, that I must go," Etienne replied.

Mathurin tried to come to a halt and adopted a fervent tone of supplication. "This isn't the road to the village!" he said, with tears in his eyes, more helpless for the moment than a babe in arms. "If you're dead, Etienne, tell me—don't draw me to my doom!"

There was a smile on the young sergeant's pale face.

"It's necessary that I sit down on the steps of the *Croix-qui-Marche* tonight," he said.

Mathurin fell to his knees, put his hands together, and cried: "My true comrade, if it's to have certain knowledge of the death of the last Treguern, don't go as far as that, for I can give you the bad news. Filhol de Treguern died in his manor almost a year ago."

"I don't believe you!" Etienne said. A few hours earlier, he would not have been so impolite as to say *I don't believe you!* to Sergeant Mathurin's face—but the Lord knew that he was under duress. "I don't believe you," Etienne repeated, "and if the entire parish of Orlan comes to tell me what you have told me, I would still say: It's impossible! Treguern and I made a pact, and Treguern is the son of knights: why would he have forgotten his promise?" The young soldier's stride increased reflexively; he was speaking with a certain agitation now.

"So," Mathurin said, his voice catching in his throat, "you believe that the dead man is waiting for you among the *Pierres-Plantées*?"

"I pray to God that there is no dead man," Etienne replied. Then, seeing that Mathurin's pace had slowed, he added: "This is my road. The other path leads straight to the parish of Orlan. I don't need you to go with me to the *Croix-qui-Marche*. Let's separate here."

They had reached the edge of the forest. The open country in front of them was illuminated by the fantastic and changeable light that the clouds let through as they moved. It was like an immense black short-piled carpet, sliced here and there by rocks of a startling whiteness. As far as the eye could see, that was the way of things: white points against a black background. There they were, drawn up and aligned in bizarre order. It was said that every year, on Good Friday, a new one emerged. Who had set them up in this fashion, these stone colossi that no human force could have lifted?

The two paths that Etienne had indicated formed an acute angle. One of them climbed up towards the end of the heath, to the stoutest of the *Pierres-Plantées*; the other remained on the level, leading to the cultivated fields. Mathurin hesitated, awkwardly. The mere idea of following one of the heathland paths all alone gave him a foretaste of anxiety.

"Go on, then!" he murmured, brokenly. "I'm with you. But my death will be on your conscience if I die unshriven."

For a quarter of an hour, they walked without exchanging a single word. Periodically, raindrops as large as coins fell noisily on every side, but they were insufficient to beat down the dust of the road. After a few minutes, the sky closed again and the crescent Moon that was descending towards the horizon caused the moist tips of the heather-tufts to sparkle like diamonds.

There are upright stones almost everywhere on the *Grand'Lande*. The ones that are singled out as the *Pierres-Plantées* from a sort of irregular ovoid circle, comprising several concentric arrays of rocks, in the middle of which there is a granite table like the one we have described under the name of the *Pierre-des-Païens*. All around the circle, the rocks are more distantly placed along each radius; if one were to look at

48

the gigantic monument as a whole, from above—from a balloon, for example—one would see the figure of a star with six unequal branches.

The *Croix-qui-Marche* is situated a hundred paces from the circle, at a place where the heath, being less arid, allows brambles to flourish. It is much taller than an ordinary signpost, and hewn from a single block of granite. The nature of the half-effaced sculptures with which it is covered suggest a very ancient date of origin. On the shaft, there are horned monsters and demonic heads. It is raised above three sandstone steps, and surrounded by huge slates driven into the ground.

Once, a long time ago, the noble knight Tanneguy de Treguern, pursued by a dozen Englishmen and bleeding copiously, had happened to fall on the steps of the cross. The cross was then a little further away, and one could still see the square shape of its base at short range.

When the Englishmen appeared, coming out of the stones, Treguern drew his sword and tried to get up, but he could not, for all his blood was bathing the steps of the cross. He said: "Holy cross, either give me back my blood so that I might die standing up, like a knight, or come to my aid!"

The cross immediately started marching, throwing the good Tanneguy de Treguern rather rudely aside. When the English heretics saw the miracle, they huddled together in fright; even though they were a dozen strong, they occupied no more space than the bottommost step of the cross. The cross reached them, detached itself from the ground, and made its large base into a tomb, after having crushed them. That was one account of the origin of the name *Croix-qui-Marche*, although there were other versions; there are at least 50 legends on the same theme.

Etienne went through the circle of the *Pierres-Plantées*, not pausing until he reached the foot of the cross. "It was here," he said, baring his head, "that we once came, Filhol Treguern and I, at midnight. It was here that each of us said, on oath: *If I die first, I shall return to tell you what there is beyond the tomb.*"

Mathurin's legs turned to jelly, and it seemed to him that the ground was opening up beneath his feet.

"We were sitting on the steps of the cross." Etienne said. "I'm going to sit on the steps of the cross."

As he said it, he did it. Mathurin's blood ran cold in his veins.

"Filhol!" Etienne intoned, in a voice that was trembling with emotion rather than dread. "If you are dead, remember your promise!"

A distinct voice was raised in the silence of the night to reply: "I am dead, and I remember."

Mathurin let out a cry of anguish and fell face down on the Earth. He did not move again.

Etienne got up straight away, breathing forcefully, and scanned the thicket surrounding the cross with an avid eye. His forehead was feverishly red, and there was a hectic boldness in his heart.

He saw nothing; the wind left the brambles motionless, and no living object showed itself in the black depths of the thicket.

"Where are you?" he demanded.

"In the air that you breathe," the voice replied.

"Can you not show yourself to me?"

There was silence, and the first lightning-flash split the sky to the west. When the voice replied again, it seemed to be more distant, and because the wind was howling furiously, Etienne could scarcely grasp the meaning of the words.

The voice said: "When you are alone and the Moon descends upon the bell-tower at Orlan, I shall meet you at the *Pierre-des-Païens*. Don't believe anything anyone says to you about my wife Geneviève."

V. The Apparition

Etienne continued listening, although his ear could not detect any further sound—but he thought that he saw a vague shape in the distance, gliding over the heather as if borne by the storm-wind. Then he wiped the sweat from his forehead and put his hand to his heart, which was beating in his breast as if it might burst. Nature got the better of him; tears streamed from his eyes, and the frenetic exaltation that had sustained him a little while ago was replaced by a profound misery.

Filhol de Treguern was dead—Filhol, whom he loved as others loved their brothers and sisters, their father and their mother! Etienne had no family, save for his sister Marion, who had married long ago and had soon been widowed; his real family was Filhol, his master and his friend.

Once, the sentiment that is in the heart of every young man had drawn Etienne to think of marriage, and because he had a faithful heart his tender feelings had been sincere and profound. She was so beautiful, the blonde Geneviève, whom he had seen smiling at God among the flowers that surrounded the image of the Virgin Mary in Orlan's church! She was so pure, so good, so pious, and the man destined to be her spouse would have the sweetest heaven on Earth! Ah well! To the blonde Geneviève, who had had the best of his heart and was the hope of his life, Etienne had bid adieu, without complaint, because his rival was Filhol de Treguern. He had not hesitated for an instant; the thought had not even crossed his mind that he might do anything other than give Filhol seven years of liberty, while he sacrificed the happiness of his entire life!

And now, Filhol de Treguern was dead—dead at 21, leaving Geneviève a widow in charge of a meager crib.

Etienne protested as hard as he could, but he had, in the end, to accept it. Sobs tore at his bosom, and who can tell what glimmer of light shone amid his tears when a temptress voice whispered in his ear: *Widowed and free!* It was the image of Geneviève that passed before his eyes. He was horrified at himself.

"Hey, Mathurin!" he cried, shaking his rain-soaked hair—for the storm had finally burst, and the clouds were pouring their torrents upon the heath.

Mathurin was still there, stretched out like a lumpen mass, half-drowned in the mud. Etienne drew him to his feet, and the poor devil finally opened his eyes. He had no memory of what had happened, but when he saw, by a flicker of lightning, the pale and ravaged face of his companion, instinct set him trembling.

"Where are we?" he murmured, dazedly.

"On the road home," Etienne replied, with a bitter laugh. "And there's no more joyous hour than the one in which one returns to one's homeland."

"Yes," Mathurin stammered, patting himself as he began to feel the chill in his damp clothes. "That's a joyous hour! But why are we in this place?"

"Pass me the waterskin," Etienne said.

Mathurin obeyed. Etienne tested the weight of the vessel to gauge its contents, then gave it back to Mathurin, saying: "You can drink."

The waterskin was large, and it was still three-quarters full. Mathurin drank. Every time he stopped, Etienne said "Again! Again!"—to such effect that the gourd was soon only half-full. Etienne took a single draught then—but when he returned it to Mathurin, it was empty.

"Oh!" said Mathurin—whose last libation, coming directly after a fainting fit, had rendered him drunk—"you've had a good mouthful!"

Etienne brandished his stick above his head; his brain was on fire. "Can you feel the coolness of the good Lord's deluge on your forehead?" he cried. "Let's go! Those who love us await us!"

"Let's go!" Mathurin repeated.

"A song!" Etienne continued. "So that people can hear us coming from a long way off, and no one can say that soldiers like us are afraid of thunder!"

Mathurin, being in no condition to detect the cruel misery in his comrade's gaiety, immediately launched into the chorus of a sing, rendering it at the top of his voice:

If you want a drink, I've Adam's ale,
My bucket's full and so's my pail,
Jean, my poor old duckie;
Dum-de-dum and dum-de-doo!
I've got no water, good cider for you
My pail's full, and so's my bucket! [6]

"Come on, Etienne," he added. "Let it rip, man, let it rip!"

They marched off through the battering rain, along a path that had become a torrent, and they sang.

As Etienne had said, someone heard them coming. As they reached the chorus again, after one last verse, they saw the great sails of Guillaume Féru's windmill, turning with mad swiftness in the wind. The heath had been crossed, and Mathurin felt so brave now that he took the path that led to his mother's house of his own accord. Etienne went on by himself towards the mill.

As he knocked on the door, the tall and lean figure of Dowager Le Brec appeared in silhouette in front of the lighted widow.

"Greetings, soldier," she said. "You arrive singing, and that's all right. You weren't at the funeral, but you'll be at the baptism."

Etienne made no reply. He asked himself why the old woman was there, in a great storm, at this hour of the night. He thought—because, despite his intrepid courage, there was a corner of his heart open to superstition—that this encounter was a bad omen.

The first person he had seen on arriving in the district was the *cloarec* Gabriel, his mysterious enemy. The second was Dowager Le Brec, whose violent and implacable hatred was a mystery to no one. What was this talk of funerals and baptisms?

"You'll lose time, Sergeant Etienne," Dowager Le Brec went on, "if you intend to go in to that house. Continue on your way, and go to the one who's waiting for you."

"The one who's waiting for me?" the young sergeant repeated.

The old woman let loose a dry and mocking laugh. "The brambles of the *Croix-qui-Marche* have ears," she murmured. "If the dead can waste time, Filhol de Treguern must have wasted some of yours since the hour of his demise."

At that moment, in the midst of the racket that the wind-mill was making, voices became audible. Etienne, who was already drawing away, came to a halt. "I want to know what's going on in there," he said.

When Dowager Le Brec had told him that he ought not to go into the mill, she had positioned herself in front of the door, her white staff in her hand, as if she intended to prevent his passing by force—but she seemed to think better of it.

"You're not just anyone," she said, sarcastically. "You're family. Go in if you want to."

Etienne did not go in. A hand of iron gripped his heart within his breast. He thought that he had recognized one of the voices that had spoken a moment earlier, and the name of Geneviève sprang to his lips.

"Well?" said Dowager Le Brec, standing aside to let him pass.

Etienne went away, his head bowed, without making any reply. As he went down the path that led to the *Pierre-des Païens*, he was able to hear the old woman repeat, along with her strident laugh: "You weren't at the funeral, but you'll be at the baptism!"

Geneviève! Geneviève! thought Etienne, whose heart was breaking.

While he was going slowly down the path, the wind had swept away the last clouds. The rain was still streaming from the foliage to either side of the path, but the dark blue of the sky was sparkling with a thousand fires. The stars had the diamantine sharpness that they take on after a storm. When Etienne arrived at the *Pierre-des-Païens*, the purified sky displayed the prodigious marvels of the landscape's magnificence. The dewy heath released its stringent perfumes into the night, and the little torrents left on the weary slopes by the tempest were the only audible sound.

Etienne was not the first to reach the rendezvous. He recognized Filhol de Treguern from a distance, standing in the midst of the furze-bushes, resting his elbow on the stone table.

Treguern did not have the appearance that might be expected of one returned from the other world. True, the darkness was too profound to allow Etienne to make out his facial features, but the attitude of his body retained the youthful grace that had distinguished him previously. His fine blond hair hung down to his shoulders, his head cupped in his hand.

The young sergeant was overflowing with emotion. Perhaps he would have been more able to bear the sight of one of those funereal apparitions that strike the imagination more than the heart: a long pale form, dressed in the shroud that the dead carry with them. On the contrary, though; he saw Filhol just as he had left him before his departure.

That which the night hid might be horrible; that which the night allowed to be seen was entirely graceful and youthful.

The idea of death vanished from Etienne's mind; consciousness of elapsed time also disappeared. He wondered whether he might have had a cruel dream, and whether this might be the eve on which he had last embraced his brother Filhol. He experienced the joy of people who awake and dismiss a vanquished nightmare.

He threw himself forward, transported by his impulse, and plunged into the thicket, eager to clasp Treguern to his bosom.

"Stay there!" said the apparition, simultaneously gesturing with his hand.

Etienne came to an abrupt halt. Treguern had struck a commanding attitude; Etienne felt a chill extending to the marrow of his bones, because his eyes, accustomed to the gloom, made out something vague and dark beneath his brother's blond hair that was no longer a face. Poignant reality took hold of him again.

"Are you suffering, Filhol, my brother?" he asked, with tears in his eyes.

"Yes," Treguern replied, "and I deserve it."

"I've come back as poor as I left," cried the young sergeant, "and I have but one arm—but if this arm can still work, you shall have the measure of your prayers. Filhol, my poor Filhol!"

The apparition put his head in his hand again and Etienne received no reply. "Have you something to demand of me?" he said, after a pause. "Dead or alive, Treguern is my master, and I shall obey him."

The apparition shook its head, equivocally, and the young sergeant thought he heard him murmur: "Perhaps."

There was a second pause; then the specter continued, in a slow voice laden with sadness: "Do you remember, Etienne, the eve of your departure? We went together to Orlan's church. We knelt down before the great tomb of Tanneguy, which speaks so loudly of the power of my ancestors, and we prayed. And thus we went from tomb to tomb, wherever the name of Treguern was inscribed, kneeling and praying."

"I remember," Etienne said.

"I said to you," Filhol went on, "because my heart was distressed by my family's decline, while following the course of the ever-diminishing sepulchres: It's like a staircase whose topmost step, wrought in marble, supports the colonnades of a portico, while the last, broken by the feet of passers-by, has vanished in the mire. I said that, while looking at my father's grave, on which we could only set a humble wooden cross. Do you remember, Etienne?"

"I remember."

"Good! Beneath that last step, miry and mutilated, there is one more. After my father's grave, there is one more, even poorer—and that is mine."

"On my salvation, Filhol," cried Etienne, sobbing, "If I have to beg in the streets, you shall have a marble tablet appropriate to your birth: a tablet with your name, your titles and your coat-of-arms!"

Filhol shook his head. Etienne thought he could make out something like a smile beneath the curls of blond hair that inundated his face. When Filhol spoke again, his voice had changed.

"What is required," he said, in a curt and imperious tone, "is not a tomb for a dead Treguern but a palace for a living Treguern!"

"A living Treguern!" Etienne repeated, prompted to hope.

The specter interrupted him. "Time is passing, and the minutes are strictly rationed. I must question you. Tell me: what have you seen tonight on the Redon road?"

"Three men on horseback," Etienne replied.

"Who were?"

"Your new friend, Filhol: Gabriel..."

"Next!" said the apparition. "That one could not help but come."

"Your uncle, Commander Malo..."

"Next! He is, it's said, the kind of bird that only quits its nest in a storm. The third?"

"A foreigner."

"An Englishman?"

"So I was told."

A long sigh escaped Treguern's breast. Was it misery or joy?

The specter went on: "You passed close by Guillaume's mill. Did you see or hear anything?"

"I heard voices. I saw a lighted window, with Dowager Le Brec in front of it."

The apparition shivered at that name. "The day is coming," he said, "when all will be recompensed, according to their works. A woman with the name of Treguern has been deceived by those who should have given her aid and assistance. May her seducer be accursed!"

"Say the word," Etienne cried, "and whoever has done wrong to Geneviève..."

"I'm not talking about Geneviève," the specter put in, emotionlessly. "I'm talking about my half-sister Marianne. I told you not to believe anything against Geneviève."

"Pardon me," said Etienne. "I was mistaken."

Filhol continued in a calm and serious tone. "The poor grave that comes after my father's—my own tomb—was dug, as you were told, a year ago. Even so, my wife Geneviève has given me a son. Don't interrupt me—time is pressing. The child is legitimate, and it's through him that the name of Treguern will be revived. You shall be his godfather, and you shall carry him to his baptism tomorrow, despite the protests of the parishioners. You will name him Tanneguy, as my father was named, as all our great ancestors were named, and as I am named myself. After the baptism, the child will have no further need of you. Someone will watch over him, and his mother too. Now, adieu, Etienne my brother."

The young sergeant seemed to be about to ask a question when a faint noise sounded behind him. He turned round swiftly. The tall figure of Dowager Le Brec appeared in the middle of the road.

"What did I tell you, soldier Etienne?" she muttered, with a derisive laugh. "You weren't at the funeral, but you'll be at the baptism!"

Etienne turned his gaze back to the *Pierre-des-Païens*, but Filhol's specter was no longer there—except that he heard, from very close by in the thicket, a faint murmur, which said once more; "Adieu, my brother. Pray for me!"

Then a few more words reached him, vaguely: "Don't go near Treguern Manor tonight—I forbid it!"

VI. Worthy Marion

"Don't think," said Père Michelan forcefully, "that a storm like that will make the buckwheat sprout. No, by damn—trust me on that."

"The more time goes by," replied Vincent Féru, the miller's brother, "the more difficult it becomes to get anything out of the ground. My father remembers a time when the wheat grew a fathom and a half high above the furrow all by itself, without manure."

"And my grandfather," added young Mathelin, who was a farmhand, "saw apples from Le Brec's enclosure as fat as skittle-balls and redder than Toinette Maréchal's cheeks!"

This compliment did nothing to make Toinette's cheeks any paler. They must have been fine apples to rival the poppy-bright glow of her complexion.

They were all sitting around a table, men and women together, celebrating the eve of the mid-August feast of the Assumption, in the home of worthy Marion Lécuyer, the tenant of Treguern Farm. Treguern Farm bore that name purely for old time's sake. Even though its lands extended to the manor's bounds, it had been a long time since it changed masters.

The farm's downstairs room was large; steps cut out of the soil and maintained by little palings separated it from the cowshed, where two fat milk cows were sleeping on the straw, not far from the dreaming pigs, whose long backbones formed a semicircle as they snored, with their groins beneath their bellies. On the table there was a pot of *gigoudaine*, or buckwheat soup—a local dish with which Paris, behind the times, has not yet caught up. Here and there were pitchers, whose crowns of foam set off the brown earthenware of their bellies. Worthy Marion Lécuyer had what it took, as they said in Orlan: she could put on a spread for the friends and neighbors gathered in her home to celebrate the eve of the feast-day.

Large, deep bowls were filled and emptied quite rapidly, for *gigoudaine* generates a thirst and it doesn't take much to fill up a healthy man. While they talked about the tempest that was pouring out its torrents of rain for a second time outside, old Michelan, Vincent Féru, Pelo the basket-maker, young Mathelin and the rest occasionally darted sly glances at the hearth. There was someone there, beneath the vast mantel of the chimney, who had not yet said a word. It was a soldier. His rain-soaked uniform was steaming; he had his back turned to the assembled company, and was supporting his head on his hand.

The room's only illumination was provided by a resin lamp held by a little stave split into two, which was hanging from a beam. The fire was going out, and no longer gave out more than a glimmer. Nothing could be seen of the stranger's face, and the good people who were spending the evening at Marion Lécuyer's house were losing patience in their desire to see his features. He had come in a quarter of an hour earlier and had sat down without saying a word on an empty stool in the corner of the fireplace.

Although Breton hospitality, strictly interpreted, permits this fashion of introducing oneself, it is the custom nevertheless to offer greetings to everyone, or good evening to the household, or some other politeness, as one enters. The soldier—the *blue*, as the worthy Lécuyer's guests were already calling him—had dispensed with that simple formula. Since crossing the threshold, he had kept his head in his left hand, absorbed in his thoughts, periodically releasing deep sighs.

At the time of his arrival, there had been a lively discussion going on around the pot of *gigoudaine*. There was a subject of conversation on the agenda that was of the very highest interest, and full of mystery. It concerned the two orphans of the young widow who lived in Treguern Manor—living God knew how and bound for God knew where. It concerned the strange decline of the great Treguern family, for whom the entire region still retained an involuntary respect. It concerned the thousand rumors that were running around concerning the premature death of Filhol, his half-sister Marianne—who was under the spell of the accursed Dowager Le Brec—and Geneviève, living alone at the manor with the little sister, Laurence.

The *blue*'s entrance had shut every mouth. Brittany was at peace, but the memory of the Chouan Wars remained very vivid, and there was a residue of mistrust in every heart, against every unknown wearing the uniform. It was because of the soldier that they had begun talking about rain and good weather.

"For that matter," old Michelan went on, taking out the hollowed-out ox-horn that served as his snuffbox, "I've seen vatfuls of grapes in my press—and the largest apples don't always make the best cider, I tell you no lie."

"They need to be of medium size," added Vincent Féru, pedantically. "Not too big and not too small; but whatever goes into neighbor Marion's cider is bang on target for strength and fruitiness. Yes, by damn!"

"Yes, by damn, that's true!" supplied the chorus, while every thirsty lip was moistened at the lip of a bowl.

Of all the glances that were darted at the black and frizzy hair of the soldier, Marion Lécuyer's were the most obstinately curious. She had already asked once, in order to fulfill her duty, whether the soldier wanted a bowl of warm *gigoudaine*. The soldier had said no without turning round. On hearing the sound of that voice, worthy Marion would have given a 50-*sou* piece to study the stranger's face at her leisure.

"Man!" she said, addressing him for a second time, "if you crossed the heath during the first flood, my opinion is that you're in dire need of warming your insides. Get up and take a seat at the table."

The soldier made no move. The company assembled for the feast exchanged significant glances.

"He's asleep!" said Toinette Maréchal.

Marion Lécuyer was a woman of 30 or thereabouts. Her face, honest and soft, possessed the dignified benevolence that is the beauty of the Breton housewife. Out there, though, women work hard, as Père Michelan had said, and hard work ages one. Marion Lécuyer, a widow for some time, was no longer a young woman; she had the rank of *worthy*, which is something akin to a badge of virility granted to the mistresses of big farms who remain alone, without a man's assistance, to supervise the ploughmen, the storehouse laborers and hands in the cider-press. Respectfully ranked as she was, the timid glances worthy Marion directed at the unknown man were becoming pensive.

Into the little recess where the two muscles of his thumb were attached to his wrist, Michelan had tipped out a little heap of the impalpable powder that Breton peasants take by way of defrauding the state.[15] He shook his head slowly and breathed in the yellowish dust, which brought tears to his eyes. "In the days when I went poaching in the forest," he murmured, "I saw more than one hare that became motionless when the shot was fired, but escaped between my legs as soon as I had put my rifle back on my shoulder."

"You think that he's faking it?" asked several timorous voices.

Michelan put his horn back into his pocket and took up the pitcher, saying in a loud and clear voice: "As to that, my lads, even storms don't make the buckwheat sprout, by damn! Not that sort."

While everyone was admiring the old man's diplomacy, Marion Lécuyer, the smallholder, took hold of the lamp and got up. She went to the hearth and set about examining her most recent guest. It was not an easy thing to do, because the soldier's hand was spread like a mask from his forehead to his mouth. Marion came back and said with a sigh of regret: "It's not who I thought it was; he's only got one arm."

"He's only got one arm?" repeated the astonished company. "So he's a cripple!"

"And you can say whatever you like," the worthy added, "for he's sleeping—snoring like a chimney-stack."

"Oh well," said Mathelin the farmhand, "I say that Dowager Le Brec—for whom I work, for my sins—took up her white staff at dusk to go for a stroll on the heath. It's the day of the Sabbath, for sure, and last night, I heard talking until morning at the base of the Tour-de-Kervoz."

"Perhaps it was Commander Malo singing his litanies?" said Vincent Féru.

"When Commander Malo's in the tower," young Mathelin replied, "you can see the light of his lamp through the loopholes on the first floor. I know what goes on at his place, because it's me who fills in the holes in his walls with moist earth. It's been a month since the Commander last came to the tower."

"He'll be there tonight," Pelo the basket-maker put in. "As I came through the chestnut-wood, I heard his wheezy horse coughing and whinnying in the bushes."

"He's come in search of the Broken Stone," Marion intoned, gravely.

"Do you believe in the Broken Stone, Marion?" asked Vincent Féru, who was sometimes inclined to skepticism.

"As I believe in the Treguern Prophecy!" the smallholder exclaimed, her tranquil features becoming animated. "And why should I not believe in it, since my father and grandfather believed in it before me? Every Christian who goes to High Mass on Sunday can see that there's a corner missing from the Tomb of Tanneguy. It's been like that for hundreds of years— and ever since it's been that way, Treguern has always been in decline. Always! The Prophecy foretold it. And for Treguern to regain all that it has lost, it's necessary to find the stone cornerpiece that's missing from the Tomb of Tanneguy!"

"Given the time they've been searching..." Vincent began—but the women were already making the sign of the cross.

"Treguern is not of this world, as others are," said Michelan. "There's yet another prophecy, which says: *Before the resurrection, Treguern will die three times.* Those of us who are young may yet have many things to see!"

"But not as much as we who are old have seen!" put in Marion Lécuyer, who had crossed her arms in front of her on the table. "One sees for a long time before dying, Vincent Féru, and yet death never leaves anyone out. Anyway, one can search for something for a long time before finding it. When my mother was a young girl, this house still belonged to Treguern, and you know how good a master he was! The Le Brecs de Kervoz were then beginning to make their fortune; to the extent that Le Brec prospered, Treguern declined.

"My mother said that Comte Tanneguy's three young brothers once met Le Brec's five sons in the Margerie pasturelands. There was a battle, for the two families have an instinctive hatred for one another, as brave guard-dogs have for wolves. Four of the five Le Brecs were laid out on the grass; one Treguern was always worth two men. Françoise Le Brec, whom they now call the Dowager, dipped the corner of her mourning-sash in the blood. When the Bishop of Vannes came to the region to reconcile Le Brec and Treguern, who embraced three times on the altar steps, and the eldest daughter of Le Brec married Comte Tanneguy, Françoise Le Brec would never set foot in the manor. It's said that ever since that time, she goes to the *Pierres-Plantées*, and that a false priest from Lorraine, a heretic, a Jansenist [16] and a juror,[17] who said Mass at the *Croix-qui-Marche*, taught her to cast evil spells. The three younger Treguern brothers, who had drawn swords on the Margerie pastureland, died in the year following the marriage—and Marianne, poor Filhol's half-sister, came into the world on the very day when the last of the three perished..."

Everyone around the table was listening; the bowls remained full now. The younger women and the younger men leaned forward, wide-eyed. The history of the Treguern family was more or less familiar to all those who had come to spend the evening at Marion Lécuyer's, but for these simple people, avid for marvels, the history of Treguern was the most marvelous of all legends. It was well-known, but one never knew everything. It was like an inexhaustible mine, from the bottom of which some new mystery was ever-ready to emerge,

"The three dead brothers came back at the *Pierre-des-Païens* for a year," said old Michelan, in a low voice, while all those in the assembly who still had hair felt it stand on end. "They were called the Three Rooks, because they screeched in the night like birds of ill-omen. Marion's mother was no liar. At the end of the year, Hélène le Brec, Comtesse de Treguern, Marianne's mother, slept so well one night that she never woke up again. All night long the Three Rooks had been heard calling her by name, in the manner of a curse."

"Then," Marion Lécuyer, went on, "Françoise Le Brec, the Dowager, went into the manor for the first time. She set about caring for little Marianne, her dead sister's child. Perhaps she would have forgotten her hatred if Comte Tanneguy—who was still young—hadn't married another woman..."

"The good Comtesse!" cried several voices within the company. "The mother of Filhol and little demoiselle Laurence."

"Françoise Le Brec quit the manor again, to return to her farmhouse; this time, she never forgot or forgave. She was already the widow of her cousin, Jean Le Brec, who had left her a large farm, Château le Brec, and Guillaume's mill. She had been living previously in the town of Feuillans in Saint-Brieuc, and she came back with a young boy; no one ever found out who his mother and father were."

Around the table several voices pronounced the name of the young *cloarec*, Gabriel, in a whisper. The smallholder continued as if she had not heard. "When Marianne de Treguern was of an age to walk," she went on, "you might have thought that her little legs carried her instinctively towards Château le Brec. That one has no Treguern in her heart! She resembles the Le Brecs de Kervoz in her features and her soul."

"She's not an unpleasant demoiselle," said Mathelin the farmhand, "but she's certainly different. I don't know what goes on at the manor but I can certainly talk about Château-le-Brec, since I live there. Well, whenever Marianne came to visit her aunt last autumn, you could be sure of seeing Gabriel the *cloarec* rushing down the road from town. It was scarcely a month after Filhol's death that they were having a high time in the big room at Château-le-Brec. The Dowager shut the doors, but when one laughs too heartily, closed doors don't prevent one from being heard. I often heard the Dowager say that there was no good Lord, that Gabriel would never take the skull-cap, and that he would marry Marianne at the *Croix-qui-Marche* with the blessing of the false priest. Worthy Marion, you who know everything, is it true that the subterranean passages of Château-le-Brec extend as far as Treguern Manor, passing beneath the *Pierre-des-Païens*?"

"My mother often said so," the smallholder replied.

"I ask because I didn't finish just now, when I mentioned the noises to be heard beneath the Tour-de-Kervoz. At least Commander Malo reads his grimoires in a low voice, and he doesn't make much of a racket while searching for the Broken Stone. But under the hole in which he chooses to live, there are the cellars of the tower. I've tried 20 times over, when broad daylight gives me the courage, to find the door that leads down there, and I assure you that none exists—but in the deepest undergrowth I can get into by crawling, I found a kind of crevice that a rabbit would have difficulty getting through. I put my hands to either side of my eyes and I looked into it."

"And what did you see, Mathelin?" everyone asked.

"What did I see?" the farmhand repeated. "I don't know that myself. It was as dark inside as the basement of Hell, and I felt a damp draught hitting me in the face. Even so, I vaguely made out something: it looked like a body laid out at full length, and I seemed to hear the breathing of a sleeping man."

"It's possible," said Père Michelan, reaching for his ox-horn.

The young women were holding their breath, frightened and entranced at the same time. The men exchanged astonished glances. Everyone's curiosity was violently excited. A human being asleep beneath the ruined mass they called the Tour-de-Kervoz!

66

"What happened next, lad?" asked worthy Marion, who was no less impatient to know than anyone else.

"Well," Mathelin went on. "Whatever he was, man or devil, he had companions when night fell, for in my little room, which is next to the wall of the tower, I heard confused voices talking beneath my bed."

"And you didn't say anything to Dowager Le Brec?" Marion Lécuyer asked.

"I certainly did—nearer ten times than once."

"What did she say?"

"That I was a poltroon, that I was dreaming while I was wide awake, and that she would send me packing if I heard anything else."

No one spared a thought any longer for the poor soldier who was asleep in the fireplace.

"So forcefully," Mathelin went on, "that I became determined to find out the truth for once in my life. I can't be any braver than I am, but all the same, I have my pride!"

There was a general movement on the benches surrounding the table. No one asked any more questions, but the wide eyes and gaping mouths spoke more loudly than all the questions in the world. Mathelin felt that he had become a celebrity.

"So then, thankfully," he continued, "I had an idea! To chat for such a long time, it's necessary to light a candle, and it occurred to me that the cellar might not be as dark by night as it was by day. Yesterday, at eleven o'clock, I heard the conversation start up under my bed. I got up very quietly, got my trousers and jacket and dressed myself from top to toe— except that I didn't put my clogs for fear of waking the Dowager. I was shivering hard. I'd put a drop of brandy in a broken cup to warm me up for the business in hand. I drank it; then I opened my window and went out."

At that moment, one could have heard a mouse running through the room.

"On my oath," Mathelin said, now sure of his success, "I've never seen the tower like that, standing out in front of

67

the Moon, which was already setting behind the trees in the cemetery. It was black, and all in ruins; the ivy hanging down from the cracks in the battlements was like a vast mourning-curtain. Owls have good ears and I'd woken them up; they hooted as turned on their nests.

"There was no light at all in Commander Malo's retreat on the first floor. But at the place where I'd seen the crevice, at ground level, beneath the undergrowth, there was a glimmer. I put my soul in the hands of the good Lord, for I sensed that I was risking my very life, and for the second time I slithered through the brambles on my belly, as far as the entrance of the air-hole..."

At this point Mathelin paused to drink a mouthful from his bowl. Everyone, in his or her imagination, attached a dénouement to the farmhand's interrupted story, seeing prodigious things by the pale light emerging from that air-hole. There are bedtime stories that commence in exactly this fashion, and Lord knows what one might find at the bottom of mysterious subterranean passages!

"It was like a sort of room," Mathelin continued, "rounded in accordance with the shape of the tower. A lamp was lit in the middle, on a cask set upright. A kind of bed with a mattress and curtains of thick serge was to the right of the crack; to the left, on the farmhouse side, masonry was arranged to serve as a hearth, and as I got my bearings, I realized that the smoke from the firebrands must go up Dowager Le Brec's own chimney. At the back, the lamplight petered out in a dark opening that seemed to be a corridor. Where does that tunnel lead? God knows! Around the cask on which the lamp stood there were three people."

"Three people!" the stupefied audience repeated. "The Three Rooks, perhaps?"

"Sleep peacefully, after that!" Mathelin added. "When you know that things like that are happening in your own parish!"

"Did you recognize the three people, scamp?" asked Marion Lécuyer.

"I was certain that I recognized two," the farmhand replied, "and if I say nothing about the third, it's because I didn't see his face."

"Who was it? Who was it?" cried the assembly, in an explosion of curiosity.

"Guess!" said the farmhand.

VII. The Man in Black

Mathelin the farmhand paused for a minute. When no one ventured a guess, he struck a solemn pose.

"No," he intoned, slowly "it was not the Three Rooks. There were two men and a woman. One of the two men, entirely dressed in black, was sitting in the middle—I couldn't identify him because he had his back to me. To the right, the *cloarec* Gabriel was reading papers by the light of the lamp. To the left, Madame Geneviève was weeping beneath her widow's veil."

A considerable murmur went up around the table; some repeated the name of Gabriel, some that of Geneviève, while others said: "Who was the third? Who was the third?"

Mathelin remained silent.

Worthy Marion Lécuyer shook her head gravely. "The third?" she said. "The younger brothers of Treguern were revenants for a whole year at the *Pierre-des-Païens*. My grandmother often said that the late Comte's father, Filhol's grandfather, showed himself for 12 months in the avenue of the manor. The Comte himself, remember..."

"So you think the third was the deceased Comte de Treguern?" several voices put in.

"Why shouldn't the late Comte Filhol not have the privilege of his family?" Marion murmured. "Everyone knows that it takes a year and a day for a Treguern to go to his final rest."

This explanation fitted in too well with the company's preconceived notions for anyone to deny it. Even young Mathelin's silence lent support to the smallholder. But Vincent Féru said: "Many others have encountered this man whose face the farmhand couldn't see over the last few months, in the fields and on the heath. I've caught him myself, prowling around the manor."

"Me too," murmured Pelo the basket-maker.

"Others also said: "Me too!""

"And that one," Vincent Féru continued, "isn't Filhol de Treguern. Listen to me: Treguern's father was a good landlord before he became a poor man; I've nothing against Treguern. But you're wasting your time, believe me, trying to explain what's going on hereabouts. There's only one who has the final word, and he's not talking."

"Do you mean Gabriel, Vincent?" Marion Lécuyer put in, frowning.

"I know what I mean, and so do you, you old gossip. That's enough. Gabriel has no need to go into the cellars of the Tour-de-Kervoz, since Gabriel is master at the manor. And if he chucks his cassock into the nettles—as he ought have done a long time ago, so it's said, if he had a farthing's-worth of religion or honor—it won't be for Geneviève but for Marianne."

"You've got that right, Vincent Féru!" cried the small-holder, breathing as if a weight had been lifted from her breast. "There's no stain on Geneviève's dress!"

All eyes were turned to Vincent Féru, who had made an abrupt gesture with his hand. "I was in Orlan's church," he said, "when Geneviève came to kneel at the altar with her bridegroom, Filhol. I don't believe there's a sweeter angel in Paradise! I wished them both happiness from the bottom of my heart." He stopped, and seemed to hesitate, then he re-sumed in a changed tone: "I'd prefer to say this somewhere other than in front of you, Marion Lécuyer, for you're a good woman and you're the daughter of old Etienne, who gave his all for the children of Treguern. You love the Treguerns as you did when they were your masters. But it's 11 months since Filhol died..."

"And you dare to say...?" Marion broke off, choked by anger.

"I say that the only servant who survived the misfortunes of the Treguerns is very often sent away as night falls. I say that the crib of Olympe, Filhol's poor orphan, who never knew her father, is very often left in the care of another child—the

71

little sister, Laurence—and that they remain all alone in that great manor, while Marianne and Geneviève go where the evil spirit leads them."

"You're a liar!" cried Marion Lécuyer, rising to her feet like a man.

"No, I'm not a liar... and why would I lie? I say that this unknown, the Man in Black, as the villagers call him..."

"Liar! Liar!" worthy Marion repeated twice over, her eyes full of tears. "And if my poor dear brother Etienne was here, you'd pay for your lies in blood, Vincent Féru."

A dull groan was heard from the side of the hearth, and all eyes turned towards the soldier, who had doubtless moaned in his sleep. In the silence that followed, the clamorous noise of the tempest that was raging without became audible.

"Ah, by damn!" said Père Michelan, gladly returning to the conversation's point of departure. "That's not the kind of weather that'll make the buckwheat sprout. Surely and certainly, that's the absolute truth!"

But Vincent Féru was not the kind of man to be reined in like that. "Worthy Marion," he said, "your young brother used to be a mate of mine. He could easily break my head, if I didn't break his bones—but that doesn't make any difference to the fact that as I speak, Treguern's widow and sister are both abroad. And if you like, Marion Lécuyer, we can all go round to the manor together—and we'll find it empty, I promise you, save for poor little sister Laurence, who replaces the absent mother beside Olympe's abandoned cradle."

The smallholder got up again to accept the challenge. She was beautiful in her anger, and her pious faith in the honor of Treguern; you would easily have recognized brave Etienne's sister. But, at that moment, the farmhouse door opened and a newcomer came in. It was a poor fellow dressed in a threadbare fustian jacket, soaked to the skin. His cheeks were very pale beneath the wisps of his grey hair.

"Claude!" the cry went up around the table. Claude was the servant at the manor.

It seemed that chance had brought him there for the express purpose of settling the dispute between Vincent Féru and the smallholder Marion Lécuyer. As he approached the table, they saw that he was shivering in his damp clothes and that his livid lips were trembling.

"A bowl of cider, for the love of God, worthy Marion," he said, in a quavering voice. "I've just seen the Devil!"

The two benches that flanked the table were overturned at the same time by the start that affected the entire company. Claude's trembling hands seized a pitcher; he drank directly from it, and his teeth could be heard chattering against the earthenware.

"Lord God! Lord God!" he stammered, letting himself fall upon a stool. "Who among us will be alive tomorrow morning?"

"Come on, Claude, old chap," said Vincent Féru. "What's happened to you?"

Claude mopped his sweat-bathed brow. Everyone looked at him, mouths agape.

"God help me!" replied the servant, whose did not seem quite right in the head. "I went around the *Pierre-des-Païens*, because I saw Dowager Le Brec standing in the rain in the middle of the road going up to the heath—and who would dare to cross her path at this hour of the night? All of a sudden, Filhol, my young master, was standing on the stone, talking to someone I couldn't see, but whom he called Etienne."

"We must pray for the salvation of soldier Etienne's soul," said old Michelan, while Marion Lécuyer covered her moist eyes with both hands. "When one hears a dead man pronounce the name of someone absent, the relatives can surely put on their mourning-dress."

"My poor brother!" sobbed Marion Lécuyer.

"I wouldn't have stayed there for all the world," Claude went on. "I picked up my legs ready to run across country to Guillaume's mill. He's a good fellow, and he opens his door willingly. When I arrived at the opening to the heath, I heard the hoofbeats of horses galloping all around me—but I thought

73

that it was my poor head that was deranged, for I had a high fever and a ringing in my ears. I could also hear Guillaume's mill, which was going in spite of the holiday—going as if Satan was shaking it to bits!

" 'Hey, Claude!' a voice said to me. And Malo de Treguern was right beside me, on his skinny horse. God help me! I let myself fall to my knees.

" 'Why aren't you attending to your duties?' Commander Malo asked me. 'Is this how you look after the house of Treguern?'

"I replied, all a-tremble as I was: 'I've been sent away from the house of Treguern tonight.'

" 'Quickly. Go quickly!' cried Commander Malo. 'Get back to the manor. The evil spirit is abroad, and wants to get in. Quickly—go quickly!' "

"Claude," the smallholder put in at this point, "it was Marianne de Treguern who put you out of the manor tonight, wasn't it?"

"No," the good servant replied. "It was Madame Geneviève."

Marion Lécuyer bowed her head to avoid the triumphant gaze of Vincent Féru.

"Commander Malo," Claude went on, "pricked the side of his mount, which cleared the palings with one leap and galloped off towards the Tour-de-Kervoz. It seemed to me that I could still hear his voice repeating in the distance: 'Quickly—go quickly!'

"As I tried to get to my feet, another horse, going full tilt, passed so close to me that I could see the steam from its nostrils. If Gabriel the *cloarec* had not left yesterday, I would have sworn that the second rider was Gabriel. He went down the road that led to the town. Then came the sound of yet another galloping horse, and another rider in the night!

" 'Which road to Treguern Manor?' this one said to me, in a voice like none I've ever heard in my life.

"I don't know what I said in reply. We were under the windmill; the wind had forced the four sails backwards and wrenched them free, to carry them 200 paces across the heath. My crazy ears heard something like screaming in the interior. The third rider had disappeared. Then someone who had the voice of Dowager le Brec spoke in the darkness, saying: 'You weren't at the funeral, but you'll be at the baptism!' I've been with the Treguerns for 40 years; I took the path to the manor as Commander Malo had ordered me to do. Not far from here, at the end of the avenue, I heard someone drawing the bolts of the main door.

" 'At any cost,' I said to myself, 'I shall serve the Treguerns to my final hour!' And I plucked up my courage to go through the open gate.

"Was it Satan riding through the storm on a horse as black as night? Had not Malo spoken to me of the Evil Spirit? Who had opened the door? I couldn't say, for there are only women in the manor and the bolts are heavy, even for a man's hand. A lightning-flash lit up the sky. I saw the rider that had questioned me on the heath, as large as a giant and utterly dark in the midst of that dazzling light..."

"The Man in Black!" murmured Vincent Féru.

A frisson ran around the table, while a chorus of fearful voices repeated: "The Man in Black!"

"He had passed over the threshold," the good servant went on, "and the door closed again just as I went to go through it myself. Before going out, I had let out the two mastiffs. Last year, those two dogs brought down a thief who had climbed over the courtyard wall—but they were not even barking!"

"The two dogs must know the Man in Black!" Vincent Féru deduced.

Poor Claude took up another pitcher. "Me," he murmured, between two copious swigs, "I say the demon is like the two Treguern mastiffs—someone has let him loose. There are omens of death all around us, and you'll see more than one empty bench at Mass tomorrow."

The dinner-party had been over for a long time, and the clock, whose machinery was groaning in its casing of carved oak, had sounded the half-hour after eleven o'clock. The wind could still be heard whistling in the trees on the common and crying in the cracks in the windows, but the rain had stopped. The friends and neighbors had taken advantage of the respite to return to their homes. Pelo the basket-maker, young Mathelin, Vincent Féru and he rest had gone out with Père Michelan, who had not neglected to say to them as they went: "Weather like this won't make the buckwheat sprout!"

Inside the farmhouse, the male and female servants were roosting in their respective nests. Poor Claude had been given a good spot on the straw in the cowshed. No one had given a second thought to the soldier sleeping on his stool, his feet in the cinders of the fire. That is the way of Breton hospitality; it refuses nothing, but it offers little; the guest gets exactly what he asks for. If you go to sleep in the corner of the fireplace in a Morbihan farm, you won't be woken up until the morning's work begins. Whatever one wants, one asks for; that's the rule. As the soldier had asked for nothing, no one had given him anything.

Elsewhere, or from another viewpoint, one might perhaps have been anxious at the prospect of a man sleeping alone, ten paces from a woman's bed after the departure of the neighbors and the servants—but thieves are rare in that poor country, and there is no mistrust.

When worthy Marion was alone, she knelt down in front of the decorated trunk that served as a mounting-block for her bed. She prayed for the house of Treguern and for her brother Etienne, to whom she had been almost a mother. They were all she loved in the world. Alas, the house of Treguern was following the fatal decline to which destiny had consigned it—and as for Etienne, who was at war, worthy Marion had too much Breton blood in her veins to disregard the dire omens. So many young men, as handsome and brave as Etienne, had departed thus, never to return!

While she prayed, Marion Lécuyer wept.

She finally got up, wiping her reddened eyes, somewhat consoled by her fervent orison. She took hold of the cord that opened the thick curtains of her bed. Before climbing into it, however, she turned instinctively to dart one last glance at the place where the *blue* was sleeping.

When she had begun her prayer, he had been sitting on the stool. Now she found him standing upright. Because the smallholder's eyes were troubled by tears, and because the glow of the resin-lamp was insufficient to illuminate the room, she could not make out his features.

"Man," she said, beginning to feel anxious, "has hunger overtaken you as you slept? Do you need to eat now?"

The unknown shook his head. At that moment, the resin-lamp perked up slightly and shot out a brighter ray of light. Marion's hands trembled; she experienced something akin to a vision.

"I've wept too much," she murmured. "My eyes are feverish!" As the flame of the resin-lamp died down and the man's face retreated into darkness, she continued: "Man, do you need a bed, or would you like someone to open the door so that you can continue your journey?"

"I don't need a bed," the soldier replied. "I shan't sleep a wink tonight; but I shan't continue my journey, because I've arrived."

The smallholder joined her cold hands together, and put them to her bosom. "Lord Jesus!" she murmured. "Have they driven me mad with their tales of misfortune?"

"May the Lord protect you, Marion, my sister!" the soldier said, unhooking the resin-lamp and holding it before his face. "You haven't forgotten your brother!"

The good woman's legs grew weak beneath the weight of her body. She put out her arms, and the young sergeant was obliged to leap forward to clutch her to his bosom.

"Etienne!" she said, looking at him through her tears. "The son of our beloved mother! Thanks be to the Holy Virgin for having answered my prayer, for I dreaded for an instant, my brother, my dear brother, that I would never see you again!"

Etienne pressed her to his heart; he called her his sister and his mother. Marion's eyes fell upon the empty sleeve that was pinned to the back of the uniform. She lowered her eyes and said nothing. Etienne understood her silence, and murmured: "My sister, may God's will be done! We have no time to think of ourselves."

"That's true!" exclaimed the smallholder, looking at him anxiously. "You said that you wouldn't be going to bed tonight. Why did not tell me that?"

"Because," Etienne replied, "I heard what was said tonight, about those who were our masters."

"Ah!" said Marion. "So you weren't asleep over there, under the mantel of the chimney?"

"I was wide awake, and I didn't miss a single word." The young sergeant's pale features had straightened. "My sister," he said, in a slow voice laden with sadness, "there was no one but you here to defend the name of Treguern!"

"But now we are two, aren't we?" cried the valiant woman, putting her hand on her hip, defiantly. "And the miserable wretches who waited for Filhol's death to insult his widow had better watch out!"

"Yes, my sister, we are two," the young sergeant replied. "So long as there is blood in my veins, that blood—to the very last drop—belongs to the children of Treguern. But they were telling the truth, the people at the party: Geneviève has given Treguern a son."

Marion Lécuyer took a step back.

"You too!" she cried. "It's you who say that, Etienne, my brother!"

"My sister," the young sergeant put in, "the dead don't emerge from their graves to tell lies!"

The smallholder lowered her eyes. "So it's really true that the dead Filhol has spoken to you?" she murmured.

"Filhol has spoken to me. I'm going to disobey him for the first time in my life. I shan't go to bed beneath your roof, my sister, because it's imperative that I go to the manor to-night, in spite of Treguern's prohibition."

Marion Lécuyer began shivering from top to toe. "Don't do that, my brother!" she cried. "You heard what they said: the Man in Black... the evil spirit has crossed the threshold of the manor!"

"I know too much already not to delve to the bottom of this mystery. There is a man in the house of Treguern. I want to know who that man is and what business he has with my brother's widow!"

"The door is closed," Marion Lécuyer objected, feebly. "No one will open it."

"Is the route we used to take to gain entry to Treguern blocked off?" asked Etienne.

The good woman folded her arms across her bosom. "If I beg you to stay with me tonight, Etienne, my dear child," she murmured, tenderly, "Will you refuse me?"

"I shall refuse you, my dear sister."

Marion Lécuyer took the resin-lamp.

"Go on then," she said. "And may God go with you!"

She went behind her bed. In the space between the bed and the wall there was a little door, which she opened. She gave the resin-lamp back to Etienne, who kissed her forehead and went into a narrow corridor.

Marion Lécuyer closed the door behind him, and re-mained on the threshold, praying.

VIII. Geneviève

What was now called Treguern Manor had once been an immense castle, surrounded by walls and fortified according to the fashions of the Middle Ages. The angular design could was still detectable on the lawns, and half a dozen regularly-spaced knolls permitted the antiquaries of Vannes and Redon to establish the precise location of the six supplementary towers. A circular depression in the terrain still marked the moat, and the ruins of an exotically-styled chapel that had been integrated into the primitive buildings could be found more than a hundred paces from the sad grey house.

These old Breton castles were townships. They were made large enough to give shelter to all the vassals who abandoned their tenancies when an enemy entered the region. After measuring the surface area enclosed within the six towers and the chapel, the antiquaries of Vannes and Redon had declared that in its heyday Treguern Castle could have provided a retreat for two hundred families, including the teams that pulled their carts and their livestock.

Local tradition had preserved the memory of that power, but what secured the renown of Treguern more than anything else was the extraordinary extent of its subterranean workings. The good people of Orlan were inclined to believe that these underground passages extended in zigzag fashion to the borders of the *Grand'Lande*. Some contended that their course concluded at the *Croix-qui-Marche*, but there were skeptics who would only grant these dark galleries the interval between Treguern Manor and Château-le-Brec, by way of the *Pierre-des-Païens*. According to the latter party, the manor's subterranean passages terminated in a vast vaulted hall, on top of which the Tour-de-Kervoz had been constructed.

Why was there an intimate connection between two houses that had been enemies for so many centuries? The good people of the district had no idea. That was the way it

80

was—or, at least, was believed to be. That was all. And there were some fine stories concerning these tunnels. More than once, it was said, in the Age of Chivalry, Treguern and Le Brec had met one another in those vaults on horseback, fully-armored and bearing lances.[18]

Immediately beneath the *Pierre-des-Païens*, the subterranean workings were enlarged so as to form a circular arena. In the era of the wars of succession between Charles de Blois and Jean de Montfort,[19] Treguern had fought for Blois with Bertrand Duguesclin, Le Brec for Montfort with Olivier de Clisson and many others. In the dark enclosed space of which we speak, there was a veritable pitched battle, and Tanneguy de Treguern, the victor, had been able to inscribe the names of 100 dead foes in the stone of the subterranean walls.

A bas-relief on the outer wall of the ruined chapel, situated to the east of the ancient castle, presented a grotesque parody of this memorable event. The artistic Renaissance was fanciful and teasing; although one cannot say that it always disdained drama, it certainly took greater pleasure in farce. In the chapel bas-relief, the knights were transformed into scullions—scullions with horns and tails, of course, as the gaiety of the time required. The lances were skewers, the maces saucepans—but the boldest transformation of all was undoubtedly that to which the artist's bizarre invention had submitted the noble warhorses. The artist had been further from the mark than Cervantes; these were not Rosinantes which served the combatants as mounts, nor even Sancho's humble Roussin. The paladins of the skewers and frying-pans were mounted on long and slender pigs, ironclad like chargers, stretching their slanting groins and twisting tails, thinner than the threads beneath the magnificent fringes of their cruppers.[20]

This bas-relief had the privilege of making the big and little children of Orlan roar with laughter. Perhaps they could not appreciate the satirical intentions of the artist as well as the antiquaries of Redon and Vannes, but the saucepans, the skewers and the pigs disguised as warhorses were sufficient to amuse them—and the chapel bas-relief was, for them, irrefutable proof of the existence of a subterranean passage linking the cellars of Treguern Manor with the foundations of the Tour-de-Kervoz.

What remained of the manor in the epoch of our story seemed to have retreated westwards. The buildings could not have been of any great antiquity, and yet their sad, almost desolate, ensemble presented a certain appearance of grandeur. This was not that solitary and robust melancholy painted in such broad strokes by Walter Scott in the tower of Ravenswood,[21] that eagle's nest perched on the point of a headland overlooking the open sea; this was a noble house growing old and decrepit next to a prosperous farm that was repaired annually. Alas, the prosperous farm, joyous and luxuriant, situated too close beside the poor manor, rendered the sight of the manor even more painful. In comparing one misery with another, we prefer that which perishes proudly in solitude—but one did not have the choice. Besides, there was no longer any but women behind those poor walls, and who could tell whether the fertile and prosperous farm might not occasionally have given alms, after the death of the last Treguern, to the suffering manor?

Worthy Marion's farm was situated outside the ancient wall, bordering the southwest corner of the manor, whose main entrance opened on to the lawn on the opposite side. The passage into which Etienne had gone with his resin-lamp after leaving the downstairs room of the farm did not form part of the famous subterranean passages of Treguern; it was at ground level, and the least maintenance would have made it into an ordinary corridor. Since Etienne's departure for the Army, however, no one had followed that route. His feet sank into the cold dirt; cobwebs hung from the ceiling like vast rags, and bare stones projected from the damp walls.

Etienne felt a constriction in his chest. The heavy and humid atmosphere weighed upon his lungs. He reached a door situated at the other end of the passage, equipped with a veritable prison-lock. Closed, that lock would have been an insurmountable obstacle, but Etienne knew well enough that it

82

had no key. It was the door to the room in the manor that he had occupied in his youth.

He pushed the door, which gave no other opposition to his pressure than its own weight and the inveterate rust on its hinges. An indefinable sentiment, compounded of pain and joy, took hold of him. The room was exactly as he had left it upon his departure. The straw bed was unmade, the hunting and fishing equipment were hanging on the walls, and on the bench that had once served as a nightstand the forgotten prayer-book that he had so often missed while in the Army, still lay open.

For some unknown reason, these objects reminded him of Filhol even more than himself. When he lay down there by night, on his poor bed, he always exchanged his goodnights with Filhol, whose room was next door. Sometimes, before going to sleep, they both lay there for a long time, chatting through the open door. Filhol always talked about fortune and the future. Filhol was ambitious; Filhol always saw, beyond the misery of the present, a radiant new day bursting forth for the eclipsed glory of Treguern.

He was young, he was handsome, he was brave; who could tell whether the Lord might not have realized his hopes?

Etienne needed to gather himself to enter the neighboring room, which had belonged to Filhol. There, everything was much changed. As soon as he crossed threshold, Etienne was overtaken by thoughts of death that wrung his heart. Poor as it may be, ingenious youth knows how to furnish its redoubt. There had been a bed with white curtains in Filhol's room; hunting trophies had been arranged all around it. His mother, the Comtesse, had hung a few pictures on the wainscot. Filhol loved flowers; there were two huge antique porcelain vases, rich debris that misery had forgotten in the midst of profound desolation. He had his little library, and butterflies he had collected were displayed, the shimmering velvet of their wings under glass.

All that was in Etienne's memory. During his absence, he had often summoned up the memory of his brother's room.

He could specify the position of every object and paint a sort of miniature in his mind. Alas, nothing remained of it. The walls were entirely bare; the beautiful vases had been removed, and there was nothing in their place but two bunches of desiccated flowers. The modest furniture had vanished along with the pictures; the moldings of the wooden bedstead, devoid of mattress or curtains, were obscured by dust.

There was nothing left, alas—nothing but the crucifix, which had doubtless seen service during poor Filhol's last hours, and which had been left there, in the dust on the floor.

Etienne knelt down. He lifted up the crucifix and studied the image of Christ—which had touched the lips of the dying Treguern—through his tears. This testament, left there since the fatal hour, spelled out for him, one by one, the agonies of his brother's final anguish. The solitude of the room was populated, the shadows cleared, and at the four corners of the bed on which Treguern was lying, utterly pale, stood four candles. Marianne was there, composing her features, little sister Laurence rubbing eyes bathed in tears, and distraught Geneviève, mad with sorrow, veiling features even paler than those of the dying man beneath her scattered tresses. Further away, by the door, a few common folk and pious women counted their rosaries devotedly. Then Geneviève brought the crib in which the infant Olympe was sleeping in her swaddling-clothes; a smile was born on the livid lips of the young father, who tried in vain to extend his arms towards the sweet treasure that he had to leave behind forever.

He spoke—and how changed his voice was! He blessed his young sister, his wife and his daughter, Geneviève, Laurence and Olympe de Treguern. A priest came. Every knee flexed while a prayer rose up in the silence. Filhol had the crucifix on his bosom, and was no longer moving. In her little crib, the infant smiled again. She did not know, poor little Olympe, that that mournful hour had rendered her an orphan.

But Geneviève—my God, Geneviève! Geneviève was in despair. Was it possible, what they said about her—that a few weeks had been sufficient to make such a difference? Cal-

umny is cowardly, and always attacks the weak. No, no—
Geneviève had not cast aside the dear aureole that had
formerly crowned the forehead of an angel. Just a few steps
more, and Etienne would find her watching over her
daughter's crib. Etienne got up in order to take the few steps
that separated him from the truth. He kissed the crucifix and
quit Filhol's room.

The next two rooms had belonged to the good Comtesse.
They were still empty and abandoned. As he passed through
them, he pricked up his ears, afraid of catching some noise in
the silence. One sound, one voice, might perhaps be
Geneviève's condemnation. On the other hand, silence and
respite would plead her cause.

Etienne heard nothing. He knew from experience what
phantoms imagination invokes in the fearful Breton peasant,
and he began, in his own mind, to deny the existence of that
mysterious person who had entered into the manor, according
to poor Claude's story. As he came to the doorway of the second room, which had served as the Comtesse's bedchamber,
he heard a soft and monotonous song of the kind with which
young mothers rock their children to sleep; he stopped, more
emotional than if he had suddenly found himself in
Geneviève's presence. Poor beautiful saint! She was there,
lavishing upon the daughter of Treguern the pious care of
motherly love. Had she the least suspicion of the lying rumors
that were running around the excited countryside?

That was Etienne's first thought. But the tender smile did
not remain long on his lips. It was not only Dowager Le Brec,
not only the people at the dinner-party... Treguern himself had
quit his tomb to speak to him about Geneviève!

Beyond the room where Etienne found himself there was
a corridor closed off by a windowed door. Etienne could see a
light through the panes; he extinguished his resin-lamp and
went forward. His heart beat faster; the lullaby continued—but
was that really Geneviève's voice? Etienne was no more than
a couple of strides from the windowed door; his eyes lowered

involuntarily, as if he had taken fright at the moment when he would finally discover the key to the mystery.

When he lifted his gaze again, he saw through window-panes veiled with tatters of muslin, that there was a huge room before him, almost bare of furniture, just like all the rest. There was, however, a bed, a crib and a few chairs. In the crib, little Olympe was asleep. Laurence de Treguern, Filhol's young sister, was rocking it and singing in a tremulous voice; her child's face, admirably beautiful but already veiled by precocious sadness, was fully illuminated by the lamp.

Etienne tried to make out what it was that Laurence's frightened eyes were continually searching for, but the back of the room was steeped in shadows. At first, Etienne could not see anyone except the two children. Then, by following the fearful gaze, he perceived a man dressed entirely in black sitting in an upholstered armchair by the chimney. He was immobile, and seemed to be waiting. As a slight movement exposed his features to the light, Etienne recognized the first of the two travelers who had arrived in the twilight at the inn where he and Mathurin had stopped to rest: the Englishman, since Mathurin—who knew whereof he spoke—had thus identified him. Doubtless he was also the "Man in Black" of the Orlan villagers' dinner-party.

At that moment, when appearances seemed so strongly to confirm the village rumors, Etienne was surprised to find more curiosity within himself than indignation. As he came through the manor's apartments, he had said to himself: "If that man is really there, I shall be convinced."

The man was there—Etienne could see him with his own eyes—but he was not convinced. Facts are only worth as much as the appearances under which they present themselves to us. The fact existed; the man was there—but he was in the room where little Olympe was asleep, soothed by Laurence's lullaby. There was a mystery; the young man's heart rebelled, and its accomplice, his reason, cried: "It's impossible!"

But in that case, what business did this man have in the house of Treguern? Etienne's train of thought was lost in a maze of conjectures when a door opened behind the bed, and Geneviève—Geneviève herself—came in. She had changed so much that Etienne could scarcely recognize her. She was dressed in widow's mourning. At the sight of her, little Laurence let out a cry of joy, and ran towards her; it was obvious that Geneviève's presence had put an end to her terrors.

Had the stranger frightened her so terribly? She must be unaccustomed to seeing strangers. That rationale sprang immediately to Etienne's mind. At the same time, though, a question occurred to him: who, then, in the absence of old Claude and Geneviève, had pulled back the heavy bolts of the main door to let the stranger into the manor?

Laurence whispered a few words in her sister's ear. Geneviève was unsteady on her tremulous legs, and seemed to be on the brink of fainting, but she turned excitedly towards the stranger, whom she had not noticed when she came in.

The stranger came towards her and bowed to her politely. "Are you the widow of Comte Filhol de Treguern?" he asked, in the guttural accent that Etienne had already heard at the suburban inn.

"Widow?" Geneviève repeated, with an obvious hesitation. Then she collected herself, and added, while lowering her eyes: "Yes, Monsieur; I am the widow of Comte Filhol de Treguern."

Etienne drew closer to the glazed door and put his eye to the panel. The commencement of this scene was so completely different from anything he had feared or foreseen that every sentiment within him yielded to surprise.

The stranger was a middle-aged man, with a stern and cold face. He said, straightforwardly: "I disembarked yesterday across from Sarzeau. The coastguards took me for a Chouan, and chased me as far as La Roche-Bernard—but I knew that I was risking my life when I left London to come here. Madame, when an Englishman has given his word, there is no force on Earth that can prevent him from keeping it."

Little Laurence had turned back to the crib, but her astonished eyes followed the stranger's movements.

"Have you proof of your husband's death?" the latter asked.

Etienne searched in vain for a tear in the corner of Geneviève's eye. Save for the physical suffering that was evidently afflicting her, what possessed her was not pain but anxiety, extended to the point of anguish. "I have such proof," she murmured. Her hand went to her faltering heart.

"Will you pardon me, Madame," the Englishman went on, in the sincere belief that he was the cause of her distress, "I have awakened your sad memories—but the Company has put its trust in me, and I must fulfill my duty."

Geneviève dragged herself, rather than walking, to the head of her bed. From beneath the pillow, she took a portfolio that Etienne immediately recognized as one that had belonged to Filhol. She opened it and selected several sheets of paper, which she held out to the Englishman. He read them with the attentiveness of a businessman.

"You have the insurance policy?" he asked afterwards.

Geneviève handed him another sheet of paper. The Englishman made a gesture of approval after having read it, then added: "The only other item I need is your marriage certificate."

The marriage certificate was extracted like the rest. When the stranger had taken cognizance of it, he bowed once again to Geneviève, who was as pale and motionless as an alabaster statue; then he turned around and went back to the spot he had formerly occupied beside the chimney. In that interval, when Geneviève thought that she was hidden from every gaze, Etienne saw her pass her hand across her forehead, throw the portfolio aside with a sort of horror, and lift her beautiful eyes towards Heaven as if she were imploring the Lord's forgiveness.

The Englishman returned, drawing along the floor a heavy object that had previously escaped Etienne's attention. As he moved, the Englishman said: "This would have given the coastguards a good return. I shall return more briskly than I came. Our banknotes are no longer valid on the continent because of the war; I was obliged to bring gold to pay the contracted amount."

He placed his burden at Geneviève's feet, and Etienne recognized the leather valise that the foreigner had put on his shoulder when he changed horses at the inn in Redon.

The Englishman opened the valise and overturned it. A veritable river of gold streamed across the floor. Etienne rubbed his eyes, for all this surpassed the limits of credibility; he had to interrogate himself with each passing instant to make sure that he was not dreaming. In the face of that pool of gold, scattered on the floor, Geneviève remained cold and sad. Little Laurence, on the other hand, smiled—but that was only because the lovely gold sparkled prettily in the gloom; the very *naiveté* of her smile testified that she had not the least suspicion of the value of what she saw.

As Olympe, awakened by the noise, stirred in her swaddling-clothes, Laurence set herself to rocking the cradle and resumed her monotonous lullaby. Etienne said to himself: "There must be ten thousand *écus* there!"—but it was a poor estimate.

The Englishman looked around for a table on which he could align his piles of sovereigns. When he did not find one, he sat down on the empty valise and set to work. The money was counted on the floor. The Englishman divided the heap of gold into stacks of 40 pounds sterling, each one worth 1000 francs; when he got up again, there were 100 such stacks, laid out in a line one after the other.

"Would you like to count it, Madame?" he said.

Geneviève leant on her bedpost for support.

"I'll wait, if necessary," the Englishman said, resignedly, "but the skipper who brought me across from London will sail tomorrow from the mouth of the Vilaine, and the least delay might be fatal."

Geneviève took one last sheet of paper from the portfolio. "I've prepared the receipt, Monsieur," she said. "Here it is. If you care to accept the hospitality of Treguern tonight, you are welcome to stay. If you are pressed for time, I shall not hold you back. May the Lord be with you!"

The Englishman took the receipt, bowed and made for the door. Before crossing the threshold, he paused. "When I came in," he said, "I heard someone replace the bars behind me."

"He who replaced the bars will withdraw them," Geneviève murmured. Etienne took note of the fact that her voice struggled to make that simple reply.

The Englishman went out. Little Laurence threw herself towards the piles of gold and began playing with the glittering sovereigns. "Is all this yours, then, sister?" she asked.

Geneviève crossed the room, supporting herself on the chairs she passed them by; she leaned over Olympe's crib, weeping. From outside, the noise of the main door opening and closing was audible; then the heavy bars fell back into place and there was the sound of muffled hoofbeats on the grass in the avenue. Almost immediately afterwards, someone knocked softly on the door by which the stranger had gone out. Geneviève shivered and stood upright.

"Go to bed, Laurence," she said. "You need your sleep. I'll watch over Olympe for the rest of the night."

Laurence did not make haste to obey. "You seem to be very ill, sister!" she replied. "If you knew how pale you are! I'd rather stay with you."

"Little fool," murmured Geneviève, trying to smile. "I'm not ill, and it's not good for children to be up so late. Go to bed."

Laurence came to present her forehead for a kiss, then she went meekly away.

During the minute that followed, cold sweat penetrated Etienne's hair. He had understood Geneviève's stratagem; the ordeal was not over, and he stared in dread at the door whose opening would reveal the key to the mystery.

Geneviève waited until Laurence's light footsteps had faded away in the corridor; then she said, in a low and discouraged voice: "You can come in. I'm alone."

90

A gleam lit up in Etienne's eye. This was the answer that he had dreaded! But his wrath scarcely had time to be born before it died as he saw the person that appeared on the threshold. It was the apparition that he had already seen once that night, at the *Pierre-des-Païens*.

It was Filhol de Treguern.

Filhol came to kneel before the piles that the Englishman had lined up, and his trembling hands dispersed them in order to reformulate a single heap of gold. Geneviève say down next to the crib and hid her face between her hands. Filhol left the gold in order to plant a kiss on the forehead of the sleeping Olympe. "You shall be happy," he murmured.

Etienne saw tears streaming between Geneviève's fingers.

Filhol took her in his arms and repeated, with a delirious intoxication: "You shall be happy! You shall be happy!"

"God can see us!" the young woman muttered.

"And our little Tanneguy, who would have been born into poverty," Filhol went on, "now has the wealth that he needs to bear the name of Treguern!"

Pressing both hands to his feverish forehead, Etienne said to himself: "I'm dreaming, or I'm mad!" He saw Filhol thrown himself towards the heap of gold for a second time and scoop it by the handful into the valise that the Englishman had left behind on the floor.

Filhol lifted the valise onto his shoulder and hurried away, saying: "The treasure of Treguern isn't safe in the manor. I'm going to put it somewhere that Gabriel will never find it! Think of tomorrow, Geneviève. Tanneguy will be baptized tomorrow: Tanneguy, the happy and rich child!"

Geneviève made an effort to answer him, and perhaps to hold him back, but her voice died in her throat and Filhol was already gone.

Geneviève, vanquished at last, collapsed and lost consciousness. Etienne thought at first of going to her aid, but when he heard little Laurence's furtive footsteps in the corridor, brought back by her anxiety, he took the same route as

Filhol, deciding to follow him until the adventure was concluded.

Dead men can certainly show themselves in the moonlight on Breton nights, at Druid altars or amid ruins—but even in Brittany, they cannot lift heavy satchels of gold on to their shoulders. Etienne wanted to know, now, what was going on.

Shortly before the dinner-party at worthy Marion's house broke up, a man on foot leading a horse by the bridle became stuck in the mud on the sunken path that led directly from the *Grand'Lande* to Château-le-Brec. The storm had died down an hour before, but it had left so much water in the hollowed-out path that it was like an elongated lake of liquid mud from one end to the other. The man whipped his poor horse cruelly to make it go forward; he cursed in a voice replete with anger, but which nevertheless resembled a woman's voice in its lightness and peevishness.

Despite the profound gloom, one could have divined that he was little more than a child. He had lost his hat en route, and thick masses of blond hair fell to his shoulders.

"What a night!" he murmured. "I'd have done better to come on foot. I'd have arrived much quicker—but if I'd gone astray in the forest or on the heath, even though I'm from these parts, the Englishman would have stayed on the road!"

He turned around to deal the horse a blow on the head with a holly-branch that he held in his hand.

"My star!" he went on, pressing forward as if the idea had shocked him out of his lassitude. "At the height of the storm, I looked up at the sky and I saw my star, shining between two clouds!"

The mud in the road yielded beneath his footfalls; he sank into a rut up to his knees.

"A hundred thousand francs!" he said, laughing, his thoughts changing direction like a weathervane. "Last winter, I would have thought that a fortune. Show yourself, my star, and tell us if I shall be a prince! A hundred thousand francs—that's nothing!"

The sound of his voice and the crazy energy of his gestures were indicative of a kind of drunkenness. The ancient oaks on either side of the path interlaced their crows above his head. It was like a dome, but the dome was broken here and there, and the young man, who had lifted his head, let loose a cry of joy. Through one of the gaps in the foliage he saw a beautiful diamond in the blue of the sky.

"Hello, hello my star!" he said, in a burst of enthusiasm. "Those hundred thousand francs are merely a stake, are they not? Should I not risk them on a single play? I'm a fine player—I want millions!"

He had taken another stride, and could no longer see the star; his head fell pensively toward his bosom.

"Those hundred thousand francs," he went on, "that I haven't got yet. Let's go! Ignoble and accursed beast, will you stop me on the road to my fortune?"

He took the holly-branch by the thin end in both hands and belabored his horse; it broke into a trot with its head between its legs. The sunken path widened out. A somber mass in the shape of a large house appeared, vaguely silhouetted against the night sky. To the right of the house a tall tower—entirely enveloped, as the farmhand Mathelin had said, in ragged ivy—stood out like a giant sentinel. The house was Château-le-Brec, and that somber mass of granite flanking its gable-end—the ancient debris of an edifice that no one in the country had ever seen—was the Tour-de-Kervoz.

The closed shutters of Château-le-Brec did not allow a glimmer of light to escape; nothing showed in the loopholes of the tower. The traveler frowned as he left the sunken path to go on to the common, planted with willows, that extended in front of the farm.

"They're already asleep here!" he muttered. "Is it so very late?"

He did not take the trouble to tether his horse, certain that the poor beast was not in any mood to run away. He merely released the bridle, in order to arrive at the door of the house sooner.

"Hey, Mathelin!" he shouted, knocking with his stick with each hand in turn. "Open up for me quickly, my lad. It's imperative that I see Dowager Le Brec right now!"

Mathelin the farmhand made no response, being still at the feast. The traveler knocked harder. After shouting for Mathelin, he shouted for the Dowager herself. But Dowager Le Brec made no more response than Mathelin. The traveler then did what he should doubtless have done to start with. He tried the door-latch, which yielded to his first effort. The door opened.

"So you're fast asleep, mother Françoise," the young man said, as he went in.

The farm's watchdog barked in the yard, but all was still silent in the interior. The traveler knew what to do. He went directly to the chimney, avoiding the table that stood in the middle of the room, and put his hand into the flint-hole. The steel grated on the stone; a shower of sparks shot out, and the kindling caught fire. A few moments later a lighted resin-lamp illuminated the traveler's features.

His face resembled his voice: there was something soft, almost feminine, about it: a prominent white forehead with two traceries of blue veins at the temples; abundant blond hair, light and silky, which the rain had gathered into sparkling curls; fine eyebrows, boldly drawn upon the trenchant arch of the frontal bone; blue eyes that concealed some indefinable mixture of audacious effrontery and virginal timidity, beneath lids fringed with long lashes.

You would have had to go a long way to find an adolescent endowed with a beauty that was both as symmetrical and as intelligent. Why did the *cloarec* Gabriel inspire in the good folk of Orlan a sentiment very different from affection?

Why? The tonsure would have suited that Cherubim's face very well. The affection that the last Treguern, who was so strong and serious, had conceived for this delicate and timid child was understandable. The tenderness of Dowager Le Brec was understandable. Any sympathy would have been understandable—but the fear and hatred of the people of Orlan was incomprehensible.

Only the religious sentiment that permeates the souls of the people so profoundly could explain that revulsion, because

Gabriel, although he wore the garb of the seminary, manifested neither the conduct nor the faith of those destined for the service of God. Having said that, though, he had not accepted any appointment within the Church, and he still had plenty of time to say to himself: I have mistaken my vocation.

If you had interrogated the good people of Orlan on the subject, the good people of Orlan would, in all probability, have kept silent. If you had been able to plunge a curious glance into their conscience, however, this is what you might have seen:

First of all, the Breton does not want anyone to touch priestly vestments carelessly—inadvertently, as it were. He reveres priestly robes above all else, and he does not tolerate anyone trying to playing games therewith. Secondly, Gabriel had not been born in the environs of Orlan; the early years of his life were a mystery. In the third place, Gabriel reeked of Le Brec, as the lads of the district put it. Finally, the general opinion was that he had put a spell on the last Treguern; those who had known Filhol before Gabriel's arrival could tell how much Filhol had changed before dying. Those who loved him had not been able to recognize him in his last days. And the death of the last descendant of knights, premature and unfortunate as it was, had been accompanied by circumstances that were sufficient in themselves to motivate the dread inspired by the handsome Gabriel.

We have not counted among our motives for hatred the rumors that were circulating of a mysterious and perhaps sacrilegious marriage contracted under the auspices of the Dowager—who was a pagan, or, at the very least, a heretic—between Gabriel and Marianne, Filhol's half-sister. The half-sister was named Treguern, but she was the daughter of a Le Brec—which is to say, a cousin of the Devil, whose instrument the good folk were willing to grant that she was. They were mildly anxious for her.

One thing that was certain, though, was that the aversion of the local people hardly bothered the blond Gabriel at all. He had his star, and the flight of his ambitious dreams lifted him so high that he no longer saw those who remained down there beneath his feet. There are idle dreamers, but Gabriel worked as he dreamed, and the contemplation of his star never prevented him from action.

When he had lit the resin-lamp, he drew aside the curtains of the Dowager's bed; it was empty. Gabriel's forehead darkened again. He opened the door to the hole that served as Mathelin's retreat and found that Mathelin, too, was absent.

"No one!" he thought, aloud. "I won't know what's happening! Will this be an unlucky day?"

He returned to the Dowager's bed and went into the space separating it from the wall. Bracing himself against the wall, he used his back to shove the massive bed sideways, uncovering a trapdoor set in the floor. He placed his resin-lamp on the floor. The trap was lifted by means of a thick ring of rope secured within a molding in the wood. Gabriel set to work valiantly; he seized the rope in both hands and pulled with all his might. He had taken off his cloak and rolled up his sleeves. As he hauled on the trapdoor, muscles of steel were visible, standing out beneath the white satiny skin of his arms; the veins in his neck swelled up, and a surge of blood reddened the delicate pallor of his cheeks. As the Morbihan expression would have it, he had inner strength.

Because the trapdoor was secured from beneath, though, and because the weight of the heavy wooden bars surpassed the young *cloarec*'s might, he was obliged to let go in order to mop his brow, which was already bathed in sweat. He tapped the planks with his heel irritably.

"Must I go all the way back to the *Pierre-des-Païens*?" he murmured.

He glanced at the clock, whose creaky pendulum was making a racket in the depths of its box, and his face took on a duller pallor. "It's getting late," he murmured, pushing the Dowager's bed back towards the wall. "I haven't time to go all the way to the *Pierre-des-Païens*."

An idea sprang into his mind. He left the farm in a hurry and made for the tangled undergrowth at the base of the Tour-de-Kervoz. He obviously knew about the crevice about which the farmhand Mathelin had spoken earlier that evening, because he rummaged around in the brambles with his stick until he had located the hole.

"If anyone's there," he thought, aloud, "I'll see the light." The sentence was punctuated by an oath that seemed too coarse to pass his lips. Gabriel knelt down on the damp ground. His head was now touching the opening.

"Treguern!" he called, in a restrained voice. "Answer me, Filhol—are you there?"

There was no sound in the mysterious hall into which the farmhand Mathelin had intruded his gaze the previous evening. On the upper floor, though, Gabriel could hear a sort of extended murmur. At the same time, there was a movement in the bushes; their rain-charged branches shook.

Gabriel sprang to his feet; there was a horse nearby that was not his own, browsing the outermost brambles. The horse's bones were protruding through its skin; one might have thought it a skeleton. Gabriel immediately looked up at the tower's loopholes, having recognized Commander Malo's mount. One of the loopholes was now illuminated.

Gabriel shivered. The murmur grew in volume and became more distinct. What was said—or what Gabriel thought he heard—was: "*Treguern will die three times!*"

The light shining from the loophole shifted its position and lit up a larger breach that some ancient war had made in the tower's wall. Against the lighted background a dark face stood out, surrounded by bristling wisps of grey hair. The voice was raised again, to say: "Why are you looking for the deceased Treguern, Le Brec?"

Gabriel made no rely. He eyes remained fixed on that strange face and his breath caught in his chest. He had iron in his soul, that boy, but his soul also had a vulnerable component.

The Commander went on, as if speaking to himself: "The night's black; I can't see a thing—but I know that Le Brec is here. The hour is nigh!" Then, suddenly, he cried, as if it were a kind of challenge: "Le Brec! Le Brec! Turncoat! Have you seen the uprooted cross that lies upon Treguern's grave? It was me who did that! The cross can wait—Treguern has died but once."

Gabriel attempted to slide out of the brambles, but, whichever way he turned, the skeletal horse was always there to bar his way.

"A curse be upon you, Le Brec!" the Commander's raucous and quavering voice went on. "Since the time of the great knights, Treguern has never told a lie. You have bought, for a handful of gold, the first falsehood of Treguern! You intend to have it, that gold—at this very moment it runs upon the heath. Fool that you are! Work your wiles—yet it is thanks to you that the name of Treguern will rise again!"

Gabriel shot between the horse's legs and crawled out of the brambles. The Commander had taken hold of the lamp behind him and was now thrusting it outside; the wind seized the flame, which grew fainter as it flickered. The emaciated, seemingly petrified, features of Malo de Treguern were vaguely perceptible.

"You are young and I am old," he said, throwing back the stiff tufts of his hair. "I am poor and you shall be rich, but you shall die before me, and poorer than me, for it is God's will that I shall live until I have recovered the Broken Stone missing from the Tomb of Tanneguy!" He paused, as if he were pricking up his ears. "I hear the sound of gold!" he murmured. "I want that gold to be yours, Le Brec! Go quickly, turncoat, go quickly—for once the hole is dug, you shall never find it, so vast is the heath!"

Gabriel shivered, and cold sweat chilled his temples. There were people who said that Commander Malo had lost his reason; there were others who credited him with supernatural powers. Gabriel, whom Dowager Le Brec had made into an atheist, who defied God every day on the altar steps, still believed in some mysterious supernatural power. His delirious ambition was pregnant with superstition; he had the faith of an infidel and the religion of those devoid of love. He knew that he dared; therefore he could. His was an aristocratic spirit that age would deepen and ripe, His was a strangely-tempered soul, weak and strong at the same time, which knew how to counter its own terrors and capable of any audacity—but great as his knowledge would one day be, and his strength too, Gabriel would always remain enslaved to some extent by his infantile impressions. No matter how high his star might lift him, the legacy of Dowager Le Brec's tutelage—the distilled spirit of the village—would remain within him like those imprints that hot iron and gunpowder trace upon the skin, which people carry with them to the grave.

To Gabriel, every word that fell from the Commander's lips was an oracle. He trembled, but he did not stop—and the vague terror that gripped his breast only increased the passion that impelled him to the struggle.

"The gold has been delivered," he said to himself. "Filhol did not wait for me! Damn him!" He found his horse on the common. His tremulous hands took out the pistols that were in the saddle-bags and thrust them into his belt.

There was no longer a light in the breach, but, as Gabriel crossed the common on foot to take the sunken path, he could still hear the Commander's voice, like an indistinct echo, saying: "Go, Le Brec! Go, pagan, make haste! Blood will expiate the lie. The tempest will not prevent your harvest; the child will grow up! Make haste! Make haste! The night will be good..."

Gabriel made haste. He hurried across the fields in the direction of Treguern Manor. Preoccupied with a single thought, he said to himself: "There's been time to count the gold! Filhol has betrayed me! The old man's right—the heath is vast; once the hole is dug, how shall the treasure be found?"

He increased his pace. He cut straight across the cultivated enclosures, leaping the hedges and fences. But where should he go? To the manor? The Englishman must have got there before him. Perhaps the Englishman had already left...

This adventure, which has presented itself to us in such a bizarre fashion—the arrival of a stranger carrying 4000 pounds sterling at the poor house of Treguern, falling down and almost stripped bare—Gabriel could explain quite naturally. There was an intrigue therein, of which Gabriel was the prime mover. Gabriel had left for La Roche-Bernard in order to meet the Englishman and serve as his guide to Treguern Manor, but he had missed his man because the other had gone into the fields to avoid the coastguards.

Treguern—for it is necessary to put a name to the person who was playing the role of Comte Filhol, whether it be Comte Filhol himself, or his specter, or an audacious impostor—ought to have waited for Gabriel, all night if necessary, in the subterranean room beneath the Tour-de-Kervoz. Since Treguern was not at the rendezvous, there had been treason; Commander Malo's mystical speech left no doubt on that score.

Gabriel was not one of those who try to put their conscience to sleep; he spoke frankly to himself. He admitted, without shame or remorse, that if he had met the Englishman that night, the valise would never have passed through the door of the manor. He had counted on that, absolutely and mathematically: he had to have the hundred thousand francs this very day.

A hundred thousand francs for that frail, pretty child, unwelcome guest at the poor presbytery of Orlan! A hundred thousand francs for a man whose gaze had never extended beyond the dreary horizon of the heathlands! Had he any idea, as he ate his black bread, of the true value of that sum? If he had, what excesses must his fevered imagination be anticipating! Goodbye school, stale bread and humble loft beneath the timbers of the church! Hello endless pleasure: everything that had been denied; everything that was obtainable; everything to intoxicate and everything to procure damnation! A hundred thousand francs! Could one ever see the end of such a treasure as that?

Well, it was not along those lines that Gabriel was thinking. No, he was possessed by other thoughts—thoughts that also emanated from Hell, for desire can only grow in us according to the tailoring of our science, and Gabriel's desires were as vast as the unknown.

It was not to plunge himself into the midst of the joys that intoxicate young imaginations that Gabriel had need of the Englishman's 100,000 francs. He was more corrupt than that. His was a dream of our era, devoid of poetry and entirely concerned with business; it had for its base that which stirs the very heart of our epoch: covetousness and ambition. He wanted possessions and power.

In the entire parish of Orlan, you could not have found a man who could estimate in material terms the worth of the enormous sum of a hundred thousand francs. Gabriel, who had not seen the world from any closer range than the peasants of the parish, regarded that sum with the coolness of a calculating-machine—and, as he had said himself, it was no more to him than a stake: a first installment.

There are destinies. The great vulture is entirely contained in an egg that weighs a few ounces, and the acorn that serves as an infant's plaything contains the seed of an enormous oak. The vulture will break its shell; the oak will sprout from the acorn. What does the humbleness of the point of departure matter?

From the depths of his narrow solitude, Gabriel had seen a world through the sins and hatred of an old woman: a world for him alone. He had sometimes estimated it well, sometimes badly; he had sometimes calculated falsely, sometimes accurately. The clairvoyance of his mind, obscured by that species of pagan mysticism that rested upon his eyes like a blindfold, had shown him the universe in an odious aspect, but which was not entirely lacking in verity. He had seen society as an immense crowd in which everyone armed himself as best he could to overwhelm and dispossess his neighbors—but he had never seen sovereign Justice above the crowd, and he sought arms, believing that his every action must strike a blow.

The first weapon was gold—that is as obvious in the village as in Paris. At the outset of his calculation, gold, for Gabriel—who had never seen 100 six-*livre* coins—was

doubtless a modest amount: perhaps what was needed to purchase to purchase a piece of land, Guillaume's mill or old
Michelan's farm. But once the first term is in place, a progres-
sion makes rapid and extensive progress in the mind of a logi-
cian.

Once, during a trip he had made to Redon, chance had
delivered into his hands an English newspaper in which there
was a long article with a French translation underneath. That
article was headlined: *Life Insurance*. Gabriel had read it once,
then 20 times.

He thought about it for two long months. By the end of
that time, he had put together, all by himself, a plan that would
bring to Treguern Manor the famous sum of 100,000 francs.
He needed an accomplice; he chose Filhol de Treguern. In the
beginning, perhaps, his sincere intention was to share, but his
ambition soon grew and he had to have the entire sum. Then,
that sum itself came to seem a mere drop in the ocean, and he
said to himself: "to be a man of true substance, it will have to
be multiplied a hundred times over."

And he had set about making the calculations that would
multiply 100,000 francs a hundred times over. The English
newspaper furnished him with the precise basis of the calculation. The calculation was made with a cold precision that is
not entirely exclusive of passion. Certain natures, which are
the most dangerous, retain the lucidity that promotes calmness
even in the midst of exaltation. According to the English
newspaper, to multiply 100,000 a hundred times required 20
years and an annual input of 100,000 francs. Now, one could
acquire such an input in several ways: by hard work, com-
bined with unusual good fortune, or by crime.

Gabriel said to himself: "In 20 years, I shall be nearly 40
years old; that is the prime of life; I would certainly give 20
years and my soul to be richer than a king!"

His pact with himself was concluded.

Assuming that your rationality will not admit the merit of
these calculations in millions made by a petty *cloarec* in his
dusty loft—assuming that you regard him as a hollow and

wicked dreamer, or as an odious madman—it is necessary to assure you, at least, that in our present epoch, his fantasy castle in Spain was not entirely devoid of foundations. That child, from the depths of his poverty, had had the inexplicable power to cause a man to leave London at the height of a war, and to draw that man to Treguern Manor: that you have seen.

In the gigantic game that he wanted to play, was it not the first stake that was the most difficult to find for those who wanted to take their chances? He had found that, contrary to all probability: the other stakes would likewise come. But now his inestimable conquest was about to escape him—the man he had intended to deceive had deceived him!

For the first time in his life, Gabriel experienced a poignant and mortal anguish. He felt his fortune slipping through his fingers. He no longer had the coolness necessary for reflection; he simply said to himself: "I shall get it back! I shall get it back, if it is necessary to go into the bowels of the Earth!" And he accelerated his pace with every passing moment.

He could not have said exactly where he was when a woman's voice, tremulous and full of emotion, called out his name. His eyes opened; he saw before him a large open door and an illuminated room. His first impulse was to flee, but Dowager Le Brec had already caught hold of him with both arms. The lighted room was the ground-floor room in Guillaume Féru's mill.

"Here you are at last, Gabriel!" said the old woman. "We've been waiting for you for a long time—do you know how your wife, poor Marianne, has suffered to give you a son?"

"A son!" the young man repeated. "Marianne! My wife!" He did not seem to be able to get these notions into his head. "Let me go!" he added, trying to break free.

Dowager Le Brec looked at him, by the light that emerged from he doorway. "How pale you are!" she murmured, anxiously. "Are you falling ill?"

"I told you to let me go!" repeated Gabriel, whose lips were pursed with anger.

"But of course, you must see her, child!" cried the old woman, "She's here! They're both here—your wife and your son!"

A feeble voice called out from inside the windmill: "Gabriel! Gabriel!"

The *cloarec* recoiled. "Time's running out!" he murmured. "The heath is vast. Once the hole is dug..."

"Are you delirious with fever?" Dowager Le Brec put in, drawing him towards the mill.

She was strong. Gabriel wilted in her arms.

"A wife! A child!" he said. "A curse on her, and on him! I don't want that! I no longer want that!" Dowager Le Brec halted, as if petrified. Gabriel seemed to wake up suddenly, and his voice changed: "Yes, Yes," he said, passing his hands across his forehead—"it's the delirium of a fever. Is it not for them that I work, for her and for him? So, mother, you don't want me to build a palace to put them in: a palace for Le Brec on the very spot where the house of Treguern was built?"

The old woman's eyes glittered.

"Let me go," the *cloarec* repeated for the third time. "This is the hour that will decide between the two families. Have you now found a love that is stronger than your hate?"

"No!" said the old woman, releasing her hold, lowering her somber gaze to the ground.

The feeble voice was still calling out within the windmill: "Gabriel! Gabriel!"

"One word of consolation!" murmured the old woman. "One kiss, one minute..."

"Who can tell what minutes are worth?" cried Gabriel, resuming his course toward the manor. "Console her for me—I'm seeking my destiny!"

Dowager Le Brec remained motionless for a moment, listening to the dwindling noise of retreating footsteps. "What does he have in that breast of his?" she murmured. Then she went back into the mill and hugged Marianne to her bosom, saying: "I was mistaken, my daughter—it wasn't our Gabriel."

The story of the secret marriage between the deceased Filhol de Treguern's half-sister and Gabriel Le Brec was a singular one. Many people have said that some ferment of ancient Druidism persists in the superficially Christian Breton lands, and that this aftertaste of paganism perpetuates heresy and revolt in the dark recesses of a few secret hidey-holes. These closet pagans became Huguenots in the 16th century, Jansenists in the 17th, atheists under the Republic.

Françoise Le Brec had denounced priests in 1793 and knitted at the foot of the scaffold in Redon. She loved the Revolution that cut off noble heads, in keeping with the ancient hatred of Le Brec for Treguern. She had consented to make a cleric of Gabriel, after the fall of the Revolutionary tyrants, simply to save him from conscription, but she had said to him: "You shall not be a priest. There is no God; it's the demon Bel who rules the Earth.[22] You shall wed the half-Treguern who is the daughter of a Le Brec, and you shall have all the wealth of the old Communes."

It was also said that one night, at the *Croix-qui-Marche* on the *Grand'Lande*, the blasphemer-priest known as the *Janséneux*,[23] who had followed the cart of the goddess Reason to Vannes, had come at midnight with Françoise Le Brec, Marianne and Gabriel, plus two witnesses that they had collected while passing the cemetery. Candles had been lit on the pedestal of the cross and a Black Mass had been said, dedicated to evil and to marriage.

It was also said that the voice of the dead Filhol had protested in the night, and that in the distance, on the *Grand'Lande*, Commander Malo's phantom horse had been heard galloping, neighing thunderously...

X. The Double Baptism

We have already mentioned the place to which we shall now conduct the reader; it was called the *Trou-de-la-Dette*. It was a ravine that set a limit to the *Grand'Lande* between Guillaume Féru's mill and Treguern Manor. The path that ended at the avenue of the manor passed along the very rim of the ravine; a few privets had been planted along the road to secure the ground. In the thankless soil, the privets had grown poorly and very black; they formed a little hedge, about the height of a man, which descended halfway down the slope. At the place where the privets ended one could see the stony carcase of the heath through the dwarfish bushes; a calcareous rock that the least touch might reduce to bluish powder. At the very bottom of the ravine, there was a narrow pool, which contained nothing in summer but shallow mire covered in lentils. Withered willows, living on their sturdy bark and extending their new branches in bunches, surrounded the pool. To get down there, one had to use one's hands as well as one's feet; there was no trace of any artificial track.

When one was at the edge of the lake, under the willows, one could see nothing but the near-circular slope all around; nothing else could be seen but a circular patch of sky that seemed to be the lid of the vase.[24]

In the region, this ravine was thought to be haunted; those who had the right went down to the edge of the lake every two years to prune the willows, which vegetated with astonishing vigor. The rest of the time, no human foot intruded upon the deserted spot. When the peasants of the neighborhood were obliged to follow the path above the privets after nightfall, they quickened their paces, closed their eyes, and made the sign of the cross.

Tonight, stormwater had filled the lake that bordered and bathed the trunks of the willows. Rainwater was still dripping from the moist foliage. It was about half an hour before dawn, at the moment when the deepest darkness draws its veil uniformly over everything.

There was a man at the bottom of the ravine. The man was leaning on a pickaxe and staring at the waters of the lake, which the modified soil was slowly drinking. He seemed to be waiting for the level to decline to a certain limit. From time to time, he would raise his eyes to interrogate the starry sky.

"I have the time," he murmured at such moments. Then he would resume his study of the movement of the water, which was slowly declining. When the bottom of the stoutest of the willows was uncovered, the man lifted his pick and plunged it into the damp ground for the first time. The pickaxe was scarcely able to get a grip on the inert soil. The man redoubled his effort, his blows succeeding one another rapidly. After a few minutes, he stopped to draw breath. With half as much work, he could have made a good hole in agricultural terrain, but here his efforts had only succeeded in cutting into the soil.

"The valise will be safe here," he thought aloud, "when I have made its nest. I'm sure that no one will come looking for it here."

He took up his pick again, in two hands. It rebounded again from ground that was both damp and hard—but he only struck one blow, because he heard a noise of hoofbeats above his head, on the privet-bordered path. He listened hard; the noise ceased; there was silence all around. He told himself that his ears were ringing and set himself valiantly to work again.

His ears had not been ringing, though; it was indeed the sound of footsteps he had heard on the road. A man was running at full tilt over the heath, coming from Guillaume's windmill and heading for the manor.

On arriving at the edge of the ravine, the man on the road had done exactly what the man digging the hole at the foot of the willow had done. He had been stopped by the dull sound of the nearby pick; then, when the sound stopped at the same instant, he too had told himself that his ears were ringing, and he had continued on his way.

It happened that the man in the ravine, having scarcely returned to his work, heard footsteps again, and that the walker, as soon as he had taken his first step, heard the sound of the pickaxe again. They stopped at the same time and pricked up their ears, one on high and the other down below. The more patient of the two would have the key to the mystery.

The more patient was not the man with the pick, who was doubtless pressed for time. He resumed his task after a few seconds. After that, he heard no more. He had such a strong heart that, even though the soil was intractable, he had soon hollowed out a hole big enough to bury the little valise that was on the ground beside him. He took hold of the valise and shoved it into the hole, to see if it would fit there easily. The result seemed favorable to him, and he stood up quite contentedly.

As he got up, though, he saw a man standing in front of him—the man from on high, who had just been walking along the privet path.

"Gabriel!" murmured the digger, taking a few steps backwards.

The newcomer remained immobile, his arms folded across his chest. "So you didn't wait for me, Filhol, my worthy brother?" he said, in a soft and mocking voice.

The man who had been digging with the pickaxe took up his instrument, instinctively gripping it with both hands as if it were a weapon. "No, Gabriel," he replied. "I didn't wait for you."

"Doubtless you grew weary of waiting for me at the Tour-de-Kervoz," the young *cloarec* continued, his voice becoming more mocking.

"I didn't wait at the Tour-de-Kervoz," Treguern replied.

"No? And why is that, my brother?"

"Because it would pain me to break the head of a man who has been my friend."

There was a silence after that reply, which was made in a rude and menacing tone. Gabriel still remained motionless and seemingly calm. By contrast, the man he had called Filhol de Treguern was shaking the shaft of his pickaxe.

Gabriel took a step forward. The man with the pick said: "Don't come any closer."

Gabriel took one more step, making a show of courage. "Do you have something against me, brother?" he said, in a soft voice that no longer retained any hint of mockery.

"On my honor, Gabriel," Filhol said, turning his head aside, "you would do better not to stay here."

"What have I to fear?"

"Gabriel, Gabriel!" Filhol cried, his tone replete with sorrow. "I put my trust in you. To you, the door of my father's house was never closed. Gabriel, I was at the *Croix-qui-Marche* that night when Dowager Le Brec, Treguern's enemy, brought the evil priest. You know quite well that I could neither show myself nor protest. I was at the *Pierre-des-Païens* yesterday, when Marianne passed by with Dowager Le Brec on the way to Guillaume's mill. Gabriel, that marriage is a lie and a crime. What have you made of the honor of my sister Marianne, Gabriel?"

"Oh, you know about that," murmured the *cloarec*, whose voice changed abruptly. "And you said to yourself: I ought to give 50,000 francs to Gabriel, but instead, I shall keep them for myself; that shall be the price of the honor of Treguern?"

Filhol raised his pickaxe. Gabriel put his hand to his waist. Filhol threw himself towards him, and aimed a blow at him, which Gabriel—as supple as a serpent—avoided. With a single bound, Gabriel took refuge behind the willow. "You've struck first," he said. "I'm only defending myself!"

Filhol heard the dry sound of a pistol being cocked. The ravine lit up with the flash of a detonation, and Filhol collapsed, a bullet passing through his breast. The slanted walls of the ravine prolonged and magnified the detonation. A great cry mingled with the echoes. In the initial moment of confusion, Gabriel thought that it was his victim that had released it.

Filhol, was lying at the foot of the willow, his hair dangling in the lake; he did not move again.

For a second, Gabriel stood there as if stunned; his hand released the pistol instinctively, in order to touch his own bosom, where the heart was set. "It beats, it beats!" he murmured. "My head's swimming. The first time you look into a precipice, vertigo takes hold of you... then you get used to it. That's worth 100,000 francs!"

A second cry reverberated from the walls of the ravine. Gabriel listened, his whole body shivering; this time, he could not be mistaken. The stupefaction that accompanied the crime had had time to calm down; the echoes of the detonation had ceased. The meager foliage of the privet hedge shook; someone was coming down the steepest part of the ravine, pronouncing Filhol's name.

Gabriel took his other pistol from his belt. A branch cracked and broke. Gabriel thought that he would have no need of his weapon, because the newcomer, losing his balance, was rolling down the calcareous rock-face. He arrived at the bottom of the ravine in this manner, and rebounded to his feet, saying: "Filhol! Filhol!"

Miraculously, the fall had left him unharmed. The first light of dawn was blanching the sky. Gabriel could make out a tall man dressed in military costume, who had only one arm. At the same moment, Etienne, in his turn, perceived him in the darkness and threw himself towards him.

"You're not Filhol! he cried. "What have you done to Filhol?"

Gabriel had already cocked his second pistol.

"Where have you come from, friend?" he said, coldly, "if you don't know that Filhol de Treguern died of marsh-fever in September last year?"

Etienne's foot bumped into the valise, which yielded a metallic sound. "Ah!" he said. "God sees to the bottom of this mystery! Here is a witness. I've followed Treguern to this place from the manor; he had this valise on his shoulder.

You're the *cloarec* Gabriel, and you've just murdered Treguern!"

Gabriel saw then that his adversary was holding a slender curved saber in the one hand that remained to him. He had recovered all his coolness. Etienne was so close to him that the point of the saber could reach his breast before he could lift his arm to discharge his second pistol. The resources of his quick and fertile mind furnished him with a stratagem on which he might now stake his all.

"Look down at your feet," he said, "and see whether that is your Filhol's head dangling in the lake."

Etienne turned abruptly; the pale light of dawn showed him the cadaver stretched out on the other side of the willow. He only spared him a single glance, and the muscles of his arm were braced to lift his saber. Gabriel was doomed—but Gabriel had had time to set his pistol against the trunk of the willow, in order to avoid the tremor inseparable from emotion. At the moment when Etienne turned back towards him, a new detonation awakened the ravine's echoes.

The young sergeant's breast yielded a plaint. His left arm, broken at the shoulder, fell inert by his side. His spirit was not broken, though, and he hurled himself upon Gabriel, perhaps without yet comprehending the full extent of his powerlessness. Twice, in spite of the atrocious pain he felt, he tried to lift the arm that no longer possessed any elasticity. Twice, the butt of Gabriel's pistol came down on his forehead, which had no protection at all.

At the first blow, Etienne's face was inundated with blood; at the second, his eyes closed and he fell backwards, next to Filhol's body.

Gabriel washed the butt of his pistol in the lake-water and passed his moistened handkerchief over his temples. The half-light brightened enough to allow objects to be made out more distinctly. Gabriel stared at the two corpses. He was pale, but he held his head high. The breath emerged forcefully from his inflated chest. He lifted the valise on to his shoulders and set about climbing the slope of the ravine with a firm step.

It was during the night of August 14 to 15 [25] in the year 1800 that the *Trou-de-la-Dette* witnessed that double murder. The next day was the feast of the Assumption. Early in the morning, the natives of Orlan assembled, according to custom, in the cemetery that served the parish. There was a great deal of movement among them; a kind of apprehension was visible on every face, but curiosity showed behind that anxiety.

They stood in groups, talking in low voices, the whispering woman very pale, holding the children back from playing in the tall grass surrounding the graves. The bell sounded for the first mass but no one except for a few pious women left the cemetery to go into the church.

The largest group was composed of the friends who had gathered to celebrate Assumption's Eve at worthy Marion Lécuyer's house. The farmers' wives wore neatly-folded cloth headpieces mounted on top with a cockade reminiscent of the crest on a helmet. The farmers were smoking their short-stemmed pipes beneath the brims of straw hats beaten down into the form of umbrellas. The young women displayed their shining silver crosses outside their jupe chemisettes, and the young men had their badges of red wool, won at rifle-shooting or sack-racing.

All of this was for the day of the feast. But all of it seemed melancholy and awkward in association with the worried faces. The group was gathered at the foot of the crucifix.

"In that regard," said Pelo the basket-maker, "last night was unlike any other nights!"

"Damn it!" said someone in the circle. "Since yesterday, everyone's felt that something terrible was about to happen."

"What time did Dowager Le Brec get home?" asked the skeptic Vincent Féru, who was almost as restrained as the others. The question was addressed to Mathelin.

"On my sworn faith," the farmhand replied, "it was already broad daylight when I heard her. But you don't all know, do you? When I came back, after the party, I found a black horse on the common. The door of the house was wide open; there were muddy shoeprints and the Dowager's bed had been shifted a foot and a half from its normal position."

Heads shook, silently and gravely.

"There was a candle lit in the Commander's lair," Mathelin went on.

"Ah!" voices said. "He sensed it!"

"But what are they saying over in the forest, Pelo?" asked one of the wives.

"Sergeant Mathurin returned to his mother's house," the basket-maker replied, "and Sergeant Etienne to his sister's."

"What?" the cry went up. "Perhaps that was him sleeping under the chimney-mantel yesterday evening."

"It was him—but he didn't sleep at the farmhouse, and he was abroad when the two gunshots were heard from the direction of the heath."

The members of the group looked at one another repeating "What? What?"

"Someone saw him this morning," the basket-maker went on, "as he was going up the avenue of the manor. He had blood steaming down over his eyes and his left sleeve—the right one is empty, as you know—was all red and black with blood, from the shoulder to the cuff."

"My Lord! My Lord!" the murmur went around the cross. "What on Earth is going on here?"

"Good day to you, Père Michelan!" cried several voices. The old farmer was coming over the slate stile that secured the cemetery. He came at a slow and halting pace, and everyone was able to take note of his livid face beneath the thin wisps of his grey hair.

"Good day to you, and God bless you, my children," he said, taking off his hat to sign himself in front of the church door. "Who lives long shall see plenty, that's for sure—but have you ever seen a time when dead bodies rise up to deny themselves a sepulture?"

The group stirred restlessly, sensing something terrible in the enigmatic quality of that statement. More than one cried:

"You've found out something else, Père Michelan. What is it? What is it?"

The old man left a pause before speaking. "Since Comte Filhol died," he said, eventually, "no one has been hunting in the forest or on the heath. It wasn't a hunter who fired those two shots last night."

"No, no!" said voices in the group, "That's true, for sure—it wasn't a hunter."

"But who was it?" added the most curious.

"I wanted to cut my second crop before Mass was sung," the old man went on, "because there's no fodder in the cow-shed and one's allowed to work until the first of the three Masses sounds. At daybreak, I sent my nephew Jean-Marie to the village to look for the others who were to work with me. He came back after a quarter of an hour, white as linen, the poor little chap, unable to speak. I gave him a bowl of strong cider to untie his tongue, and this is what he told me, as true as the Lord is the Lord and we are fishermen."

Père Michelan recovered his breath and the group drew more closely around him. He continued: "This is what Jean-Marie told me: 'When I was going along the privet path, above the ravine that borders the *Grand'Lande*, I heard some-one moaning in the depths of the hole. I'm too small to see over the privets, so I slipped through the bushes, going down as far as the edge of the thicket. There was a trail already made, as if someone had gone down before me. At the far end, I found a bush broken in two and a landslide that had scattered soil over the rocks. The lake was full to its edges. Next to the water, I saw two bodies lying in blood.' "

"Two bodies!" The words were repeated in muffled tones within the group.

"One for each gunshot!" added Pelo the basket-maker.

"I asked the little fellow," Père Michelan continued, "what they looked like, these bodies. He said to me: 'The first was a soldier who only had one arm...' "

"Etienne!" The name was repeated on every side. "Worthy Marion's brother!"

115

"The other," old Michelan continued, relentlessly, "had his head dangling in the lake, and he was dressed in a black velvet jacket, just like the one young Comte Filhol wore when he went hunting..."

Michelan fell silent. Headscarves and straw hats bobbed up and down while an extended murmur was raised around the cross.

"And you haven't been to see for yourself?" cried Vincent Féru. "You aren't curious, Père Michelan!"

"I did go to see for myself," the old man replied, "because I thought that there might be Christians in need of help. But when I got to the edge of the lake, there was nothing there."

"Ah!" sighed the disappointed group. "The little boy had lied?"

"Not at all, you wretches! When I say 'nothing,' I'm talking about bodies. There were traces of a struggle in the mud, and the blood hadn't had time to dry."

"But what about the bodies? Who took them away, then?"

"I was asking myself the same question," old Michelan retorted, "when all at once I saw a man close beside me, with his back to the trunk of a willow, dressed in a long black robe with embroidered designs, like those representing the instruments of the passion: the cross, the scourges and the crown of thorns. He was as thin as a skeleton and his grey hair hung down over his hollow cheeks. How had he got so close to me without me being able to see or hear him? I don't know. It's been years since I last saw Commander Malo, but I recognized him straight away..."

The breath was coming out hot from many a bosom. At that moment, in the depths of the church—whose door was open—the attendant's bell signaled the elevation of the Host. Men and women got down on their knees in the grass, and bowed their heads.

"Commander Malo," Michelan went on, when they had all risen to their feet again, "was looking at the bloodstains,

116

and didn't seem to see me. He was murmuring between his teeth—those strange words that he alone pronounces and that no one else understands. He said, or at least I thought I heard him say: '*Treguern shall die three times!*' Then, he suddenly looked me in the face.

" 'Why are you not at the baptism?' he asked me, sharply. 'Your father and grandfather were Treguern's men. It's not every day that a descendant of knights is carried to the font!'

"While I stood there open-mouthed, without replying, he knelt down at the foot of the willow, and he studied some footprints full of blood.

" 'This is the blood of Treguern,' he murmured. 'That's the way of things. The new growth sprouts over the felled trunk of the old tree! Go, vassal! Go to your master's baptism! Me, I have something to do here.'

"His imperious finger pointed in the direction I had to go.

"There was a half-dug hole at the foot of the willow, with a pickaxe in it. The Commander had a hatchet under his arm. Once I was on the path to the heath, doing exactly what he had told me to do, I turned to look back, as you might imagine. I saw the Commander turning over the soil with his pickaxe everywhere there were bloodstains, as if he were making a little grave. Then, I saw him take the hatchet, cut a young willow, and make a cross, which he planted in the overturned Earth." Old Michelan paused to ask: "But who among you can tell me what baptism Commander Malo was talking about? I've heard no bells as I crossed the heath, and I see no new-born child at the door of the church."

As he finished, the women who had attended the first Mass came out of the church, and the bells immediately began to sound, as for a baptism. In the path that ran alongside the cemetery, they saw the midwife Fanchette [26] approaching, dressed in her best clothes and bearing an infant in each arm. Dowager Le Brec was behind her, carrying her curved white

117

staff, costumed in black silk in the regional fashion, with a great headpiece in black lace.

As the midwife and Dowager Le Brec climbed over one of the cemetery stiles, another group of people appeared at the second stile. It included worthy Marion Lécuyer, weeping copiously, and Sergeant Mathurin; they were supporting, as best they could, the staggering Etienne, who seemed so weak as to be on the point of death. Etienne had two large wounds on his forehead and his left arm, swathed in bandages, was extended by his side, hanging as limply as his right sleeve, which was empty.

The two parties came slowly across the funereal lawn while the local inhabitants remained silent, rendered mute by sentiment and surprise. They met at the door of the church, where the *cloarec* Gabriel was waiting for them.

The midwife Fanchette went in first. She immediately headed for the little chapel where the font was, to lay down her double burden. The parish priest was in his ceremonial garb next to the polished granite vase containing the baptismal water. When the two aforementioned parties had gone in behind Fanchette, the crowd erupted into the church. Everyone in it had a strong feeling that something extraordinary was about to happen. The entire village gathered around the baptismal chapel.

"Have these two children been taken to the commune?" the parish priest asked, before beginning the ceremony.[27]

Fanchette replied without hesitation, like a bride who has learned her lines in advance: "There are poor innocents who have died without receiving holy baptism, because they were brought to the commune before being brought to the church."

The parish priest nodded in approval, and then asked: "Who are these children?"

You could have heard an insect flying in the church, so complete was the silence that question contrived.

Fanchette lowered her eyes, and did not reply immediately. She half-turned towards Dowager Le Brec, who fixed her with an imperious stare.

"This one," said Fanchette, whose voice was trembling slightly, indicating the child she held in her right arm, "is the son of a woman I do not know."

A murmur went up. The curate took the parish register from a lectern next to the window. He opened it.

"And his father?" the parish priest asked.

Fanchette bowed her head and said nothing. Gabriel never moved a muscle.

"Let the godfather and godmother step forward," said the parish priest.

Dowager Le Brec and Gabriel advanced toward the font simultaneously. The Dowager's head was held high, arrogantly. Gabriel seemed impassive. "I have mistaken my vocation," he said, in a calm and distinct voice. "I shall never belong to the Church."

The parish priest turned away from him sadly. "And the other child?" he went on, continuing to interrogate Fanchette while the murmur swelled.

"This one," the midwife replied, "is the son of Filhol-Aimé-Tanneguy Le Mâdre, knight, Comte de Treguern, and his wife, Geneviève Le Hir."

There was a great stir beneath the vault of Orlan's church. It was a mute but general protest. The priest seemed to take no notice of it, and said as he had before: "Let the godfather and godmother step forward."

Marion Lécuyer, Etienne and Mathurin stepped forward.

"Which of you is the godfather?" asked the old priest.

"It's me," Etienne replied. "But as I lost my second arm last night, Mathurin is here to hold the infant at the font in my place."

The crowd was moved by this statement; the young sergeant was handsome, in spite of his pallor, and beneath the thick linen of the head-dresses more than one eye moistened tenderly.

The priest opened his missal.

Since the commencement of the scene, Etienne's face had worn an expression of doubt and disquiet. He had ob-

119

served Fanchette's hesitation when the priest asked his first question; he had seen the imperious glance that Dowager Le Brec had cast upon the midwife. Now, it seemed that there was an indefinable air of triumph beneath the *cloarec*'s affected calm; there was triumph, too, and an even greater measure of sarcasm, in Dowager Le Brec's bitter smile.

"Woman," he said, brusquely, turning towards Fanchette. "Would you dare to lie in the sanctuary of the Lord?"

Gabriel shivered. Dowager Le Brec's eyebrows knitted as she clasped her staff with both hands. Fanchette changed color, and could not find words to reply.

"She lied!" said Etienne, firmly.

"She lied!" repeated Marion Lécuyer, pointing a finger at her. "Lied before the altar!"

The crowd, avidly welcoming the new turn of the drama that was being played out before them, set up a muttering refrain from one end of the church to the other: "She lied! She lied!"

The terrified Fanchette burst into tears.

"And that's not all," Marion went on, darting a glance of dolorous tenderness at her brother. "Gabriel, and you, Françoise Le Brec, must answer for spilled blood!"

"Be patient, Marion," murmured the Dowager. "There will be time for everything, and we are not afraid!"

Gabriel smiled disdainfully.

At that moment, voices were raised in the doorway. "Make way! Make way!" they cried. "Here's someone who will tell you the truth!"

"Make way!" other voices joined in. "Make way for Commander Malo, who will recognize his nephew!"

There was no trace of mockery in these words. The presence of Malo de Treguern imposed a supernatural impression on everything. No one was bothering any longer to count the months that had passed between the death of the father and the birth of the son. Had not the history of the house of Treguern been a web of mysteries ever since the great knight Tanneguy, whose austere and proud tomb stood next to the altar? They made way for Commander Malo—who, after kneeling piously on the first step of the church, came towards the baptismal font.

Gabriel's face had finally gone pale, and Dowager Le Brec had great difficulty in maintaining the defiant smile grimacing amid her wrinkles. On arriving at the center of the chapel, Commander Malo immediately went to the fatherless child whom the midwife had presented first; he put his hands upon him and looked at him for a long time.

"See! See!" murmured the crowd. "The Le Brecs have paid Fanchette Féru to lie!"

"Not that Commander Malo can't make a mistake!" old Michelan added. "At the lakeside, he said: 'This is the blood of Treguern.'"

The Commander finally left the fatherless child to turn towards the one who had been presented second, as being the son of Comte Filhol's widow. He gave that one no more than an indifferent glance. His mouth opened. Everyone thought that he would pronounce judgment. It seemed, though, that he changed his mind. He looked at Gabriel, at Dowager Le Brec and then at the two children, the furrows in his forehead deepening beneath the thick strands of his grey hair. He kissed the crucifix that hung upon his breast. His entire attitude testified to the labor of profound meditation. Finally, his lips moved. Etienne was the only one who heard him murmur: "It must be so. Thus will the name of Treguern be reborn."

His extended hand posed above the forehead of the child he had formerly disdained, and he said in a loud voice: "This one is the son of my nephew and lord, Filhol, Comte de Treguern."

Gabriel and the Dowager Le Brec breathed as if a crushing weight had been lifted from their bosoms.

The two children were baptized, the one who had no father, curtly, under the name Stéphane, and the other under the name of Tanneguy-Filhol de Treguern.

At the exit from the church, the villagers saw four gendarmes in the cemetery. When Etienne's turn came to go out,

121

supported by Sergeant Mathurin and his sister Marion, Gabriel—who had preceded him—pointed him out to the gendarmes, saying: "That's the one who spilled the blood!"

Dowager Le Brec's eyes challenged Marion, who was mute with astonishment, as she repeated: "That's him!"

Is it possible, though, to arrest someone for killing a dead man for a second time? The people of the parish asked one another that question.

This was the explanation that emerged: A stranger had stopped the previous evening at the inn on the outskirts of Redon where Mathurin and Etienne had stopped to rest. The stranger was carrying a valise full of gold. Someone had accosted him on the heath during the night, near the privet path. A fight had taken place at the bottom of the ravine on the edge of the *Grand'Lande*, and that fight had left obvious marks on Etienne's body. The stranger had vanished, along with his valise. Etienne had been accused of murdering the stranger.

That same day, at nightfall, Gabriel took the road to Redon. He went on foot, carrying a burden. At Redon, exhausted as he was by fatigue, he presented himself at the house of one of those merchant adventurers who were continuing to trade with London despite the war. He counted out 100,000 francs on the merchant's desk, and the merchant gave him a receipt by which he undertook to transmit that sum to London, to the head office of Campbell Life, the foremost of the companies speculating on human mortality.

Having done that, Gabriel said to himself: "That's my premium. I've got it once; I shall have it 19 times more! I believe in my star!"

As for the 20 years of his life it would require, Gabriel had not the slightest doubt. He was a good player. He bought a piece of bread with the last *sou* he had in his pocket, and went back to Orlan on foot, to put himself to bed in his loft.

Part Two
The Man Who Died Three Times

XI. The Vampire

We are in Paris. The by-ways of the Bois de Boulogne were beginning to fill up with carriages. The sun, less ardent now, was descending towards the horizon. It was the day of the feast of the Assumption in the year 1820—20 years, to the day, therefore, after the events that we have described.

Newly-planted hedges were extending their shoots and leaves prodigiously. The last pruning in the Bois de Boulogne had not been done in the regulation manner, and had been carried out by Cossack sabers. The Cossacks had crossed the frontier never to return, thank the Lord, and the Bois de Boulogne, with a vigorous effort, hid beneath a more opulent verdure the outrage of those healed wounds. The shade was still somewhat lacking, because the principal boughs had not had the time to put out branches, but the verdure was so lush that everyone was patient, and Parisian fashion had returned to the Bois already, if only to watch it grow. It was five o'clock in the evening. In the lane that led from Madrid to Bagatelle,[28] the sunbeams slanted through the powdery mist. On every side, in the neighboring avenues, the rolling of carriage-wheels was audible.

Three horsemen appeared at the corner of a hunting-path. They were three contemporary men-about-town, mounted and carefully dressed according to the prevailing fashion: hip-length frock-coats—worn open to display waistcoats tailored in the shape of a clarinet's mouthpiece—rounded and crimped at the back, pleated from sleeve to thigh; tight nankeen trousers, secured beneath rounded boots with the aid of undersoles as narrow as laces; cravats held in place by whalebone collars, overblown trinkets; hats widened at the top, whose brims curled above the ears like the volutes crowning Doric columns.

One of them was stout, another thin, and one was of medium size. The fat one was Baron Brocard; the medium-sized one was Monsieur de Champeaux; they were from the provinces. The thin one was the Chevalier de Noisy, nicknamed *le Sec* because of the absence of corpulence that characterized his person.[29] Chevaliers still existed until 1825 or thereabouts.

As they emerged from the hunting-path to enter the avenue, Monsieur de Champeaux, the provincial, said: "The Three Rooks! Valérie-*la-Morte*! What next? They're tales of Mother Goose! [30] There you go. Does anyone ever talk about anything other than ghosts at your tiresome Marquise du Castellat's house?"

"Strange things happen," replied the Chevalier de Noisy earnestly. "Things that you should not mock!"

"The fact is," said Champeaux, "that my aunt often used to tell me tales of devilry that gave me goose-pimples. Do you know that when she was young, she met a white ram..."

The stout Baron Brocard shrugged his shoulders. He had a strong mind. The three riders were now moving forward at a walk. The Chevalier de Noisy came to a halt as Champeaux started to continue, and pointed towards a covered path that curved around towards the little pheasantry of Madrid.

"These people aren't like everyone else, I tell you!" he murmured. "Seeing is believing..."

"And have you seen anything there, Chevalier?" asked Champeaux, pointing at the covered path.

"The Three Rooks of Brittany?" added Baron Brocard, teasingly. "Or even Valérie-*la-Morte*?"

The Chevalier shook his head slowly. "The Three Rooks and Valérie-la-Morte are more-or-less true stories that are told in Madame la Marquise's house, because Madame la Marquise is like me—she believes in such stories. I don't mind that others are less credulous, but when I've seen something with my own eyes and I swear that I've seen it..."

Champeaux interrupted him. "Chevalier," he said, "you haven't sworn anything at all!"

Noisy had turned the head of his horse towards the covered path. "Do you remember," he asked, lowering his voice reflexively, "that lovely young girl who was the younger sister of the Marquise, called Laurence?"

"Laurence de Treguern, who was to marry Gabriel de Feuillans?" said Brocard. "Of course, I remember her."

"Very early one morning, last year," the Chevalier de Noisy went on, "I came here, to this very spot, to meet Monsieur de Saint-Julien, who had called me *le Sec*. I hadn't slept all night—not because I was afraid, but because it irritates me to be obliged, from time to time, to kill some honest young man on account of that stale joke. I had set out too early, and it was not yet dawn when I arrived all alone in the Bois. I went for a walk to pass the time. I heard a horse trotting along the path that you see there. Dawn began to break. I soon saw a horse's head emerging from the darkness, then an amazon whose face was hidden behind a thick veil...[31] I should tell you, at this point, that I had been, along with many others, a contender for the hand of the beautiful Laurence, and that her unfortunate death had cast me into a listless malady. When the amazon passed close to me, her veil lifted up, and it seemed to me that she greeted me with a smile. I fell to my knees in the middle of the avenue, for I had definitely recognized Laurence de Treguern!

"It was more than six months after her death, and I took it for a premonition. I presented myself at the dueling-ground certain that I would remain there..."

"It didn't prevent poor Saint-Julien from departing to the other world in your stead," said Champeaux. "They told the tale of that diabolical sword-thrust from here to Romorantin."

"That doesn't detract from the fact of the apparition," replied the Chevalier. "I've never seen the Three Rooks, as they're called, nor the shade of Valérie that everyone's talking about, but since that's connected with Treguern, there must be

125

some truth in it. Treguern is a phantom name; all Treguerns have one foot in the other world."

As Monsieur de Noisy pronounced the two phrases "the Three Rooks" and "the shade of Valérie"—which cannot have any precise significance for us, and which related to certain legends that were current in one of the most fashionable salons in Paris—Champeaux cried out, half-laughing and half-astonished: "Well, I'm damned! Here come three truly fantastic individuals, who could easily be the Three Rooks!"

At the same time, Brocard said: "Isn't that the impalpable Valérie?"

A young woman, dressed as an amazon in black cloth and mounted on a magnificent steed of the same color, hurtled out of the covered path, crossed the avenue more rapidly than an arrow, and disappeared up the hunting-path that our companions had just quit. Her face was covered by a veil. No cavalier accompanied her.

A heavy old-fashioned fiacre rolled heavily through the dust of the avenue; it contained three men whose expressionless faces had attracted Champeaux's attention and motivated his exclamation.

Rapid as the young woman's transit was, she had time to exchange a nod of the head with the three men in the fiacre—upon which they pulled down their red-tinted blinds. The heavy vehicle, which now resembled a closed box, continued on its laborious way.

Our three friends exchanged glances, and the Chevalier de Noisy said, as if speaking to himself: "That's her!"

"Who?" asked Champeux and Brocard, at the same time.

"I told you those people aren't like everyone else!" murmured Noisy, instead of answering them. Then he urged his horse forwards.

Behind the fiacre, which was reminiscent of an ugly caterpillar strayed into the midst of a swarm of butterflies—for they were lighter and brighter than butterflies, those carriages skimming over the ground behind handsome trotting horses with a spring in their step, proud to be carrying their cargoes of females and flowers—came an elegant uncovered *calèche* which gathered as it rolled an ample moss of smiles and bows. It contained a single female passenger—very good-looking, admittedly, but who seemed already to have exceeded the limits of youth. The panels of her *calèche* bore a bizarre and rather ominous coat-of-arms which was thus blazoned: *sable sewn with tears of argent*. It was stamped with the crown of a Comte.

To judge by the attention she excited, she had to be a fashionable woman. Her costume was both simple and re-markable; her blonde hair, the most beautiful in the world, framed a pale face whose proud features were a trifle care-worn, which spoke of suffering—except for the gaze of her large blue eyes, which was as clear and insouciant as a young girl's.

This young woman had a foreign name: Comtesse Gin-evra Torquati.

One the cushion beside her was a prayer-book with clasps of guilloched gold.[32] She responded smilingly to the greetings and smiles that came from every direction. Our three horsemen followed the example of everyone else, and bowed their heads sincerely as she passed by.

At that every moment, another *calèche*, approaching at a right-angle, crossed the fiacre's path and turned on to the other side of the avenue. This one too carried a single female pas-senger, whom everyone similarly saluted eagerly. Her name has already made its début beneath our pen; she was Madame la Marquise du Castellat. Her costume was a trifle overbur-dened, her figure too full, her pretensions left over from an era when pretensions were tolerated—vague reminiscences of a beauty that had undoubtedly had its flower and had left for its fruit an indefinable bourgeois bloom with a faint odor of ego-ism. As the two *calèches* approached one another, the beauti-ful Comtesse's gaze fixed itself calmly and coldly on Madame la Marquise, who looked the other way, caressing the plump lap-dog [33] that was on the cushion beside her.

Whether by virtue of some clumsiness on the part of the coachman, or a whim of its unwilling team, the rude fiacre containing the three unknown men veered sideways across the road. As it did so, the Marquise du Castellat's *calèche* was forced to draw away, and the Comtesse Torquati's two dashing horses hurled themselves at a fast trot into the inadequate space that remained between the *calèche* and the fiacre. Our three horsemen were caught in the bottleneck. Horses and carriages were coming at them from every side, increasing the confusion. The stout Marquise was already sniffing fearfully at her smelling-salts.

Comtesse Torquati hardly seemed to see what was happening around her. There was a moment when her extended arm would have been able to reach into the fiacre all the way to the elbow if the red-colored blind had been raised just a little. A voice within said: "This evening, August 15!"

The beautiful Comtesse changed color, and her eyes lowered.

"Did you see that?" said Champeaux, as the calèche, freed from the tangle, headed drew away along the sand of the avenue. "The fellows inside there are lucky chaps! Comtesse Ginevra gave them a nod of the head just like the charming amazon a moment ago. I believe the three fellows slipped her some compliment underneath their tattered blind."

"I'm sure of it myself," Brocard replied. "They're ambassadors in disguise or princes going about incognito. Noisy must have heard what hey said, because he was between them and the Comtesse."

The Chevalier was following the increasingly distant calèche with a pensive eye. "I didn't hear anything," he replied.

The circulation was restored and the traffic was moving smoothly on both sides of the avenue. "Good day, Stéphane!" cried Brocard, raising his hand to greet a handsome young man who was mounted, with a remarkable elegance, on the finest horse in the Bois.

This was one of the privileged few who knew how to counter the incurable ridiculousness of fashion—one of the happy few who wear their youth so bravely that the inventions of tailors cannot contrive to deprive them of their native gracefulness. You might have thought, as he passed by, with his blond hair blowing in the wind and a cheerful smile in his eyes and on his lips, that this was the sole gentleman in the midst of a herd of human cattle [34] in their Sunday best. He raised a hand to Baron Brocard and the Chevalier de Noisy, then he bowed to Monsieur de Champeaux, with whom he was unacquainted.

"Messieurs," he said, "you've freed me from a great torment. What one isn't used to is wearisome, and I, though it hardly seems possible, was occupied in deep thought."

"You, Stéphane!" cried Brocard, laughing.

"And what were you thinking about, fortune's darling?" asked the Chevalier de Noisy, in a sincerely amicable manner.

"Before anything else, Messieurs," Stéphane replied, "Have you seen the play that's on at the new Théâtre de la Porte Saint-Martin, called *The Vampire*?"[35]

Everyone had seen *The Vampire*. In 1820, *The Vampire* was a runaway success. When he had received an affirmative response, Stéphane struck a serious pose, seemingly quite carried away, and directed an oblique glance towards the end of the avenue. As chance would have it, the crowd was less dense at that moment; at the spot on which Stéphane's gaze was directed, there was a large empty space. Through this void, a man was approaching, at his horse's own pace, his head bowed and his fist on his hip. Behind the man rode a black servant who must, before quitting his native land, have been the ugliest man on the Guinea coast.

Stéphane pointed towards this group.

"I beg you to look attentively at my illustrious friend, Gabriel de Feuillans, and his familiar spirit, Congo," he said, in a half-mocking tone beneath which a certain fascination was discernible.

"We're looking at them," Brocard replied. "Now what?"

"Don't you find anything extraordinary about him?"

"Nothing, except that he's wearing black, like everyone else."

"The fact is," Noisy added, "that he's a marvel, this Gabriel de Feuillans! It's said that he ties his cravat like the Devil—look at that knot: how classic it is! It's said that he's never had a garment altered—look at that outfit: what cut, what style and what severity! Brummell,[36] who made a vocation of that sort of thing, was nothing but a little boy compared to him!"

Stéphane shook his curly head. "It's not for his cravat, nor for his suit that I ask you to look at him, Messieurs," he said.

"Why, then?"

"Solely to know whether you don't find, as I do, a resemblance to the Vampire of the Porte Saint-Martin."

Baron Brocard burst out laughing, and even Noisy— whom one had never to call *Noisy-le Sec* to his face, lest one receive a bullet in the head or a sword-thrust in the breast—became more cheerful.

"If you don't find a resemblance," Stéphane continued, trying to join in with the laughter, "that's because I've gone mad, without a doubt. For several days now, this Feuillans has produced in me an effect that is truly teasing.[37] I can't help but like him. He attracts me, he seduces me, he fascinates me— and yet there's some sort of mysterious voice within me that cries: '*Beware!*' "

"Exactly like the drama of *The Vampire*!" said Baron Brocard.

Noisy had already stopped laughing, and his gaze attached itself to Stéphane, interest mingled with curiosity. "Are you being serious?" he murmured.

"On my honor!" the young man replied. His charming face was slightly constrained. "I'd rather be joking, but I can't."

Gabriel de Feuillans approached slowly, followed by his black servant. Stéphane looked at him for a second time, and they were all able to see him shiver. "He's stronger than I am," he added. "I don't know why I like him, but still less do I know why I have this crazy idea that he is bound to kill me!"

"Kill you!" exclaimed Brocard. "Nonsense!"

The Chevalier interrupted him, taking Stéphane's hand and whispering: "Myself, I never laugh at things I don't understand." He added, lowering his voice even further: "Trust me—avoid Gabriel de Feuillans. And if your course in life should present the opportunity of one of those romantic adventures that young people of your age are too often drawn into, believe me—stay out of it!"

Stéphane was in that state of mind in which one listens willingly to a warning. As he set out to reply, he saw Baron Brocard exchange a greeting with someone on the other side of the road. He turned round reflexively. That someone was Gabriel de Feuillans, in person.

It was very difficult to estimate Monsieur de Feuillans' age by his features or his figure. Those who admired him solely for the elegant rigor of his outfit were really quite niggardly. He was handsome; his bearing had a certain nobility; he had a good seat. If one could not say that he was a young man, it was only because of the firm and earnest maturity that were etched on his forehead. Around that forehead curled blond hair, already thinning slightly and very fine, worn longer than was fashionable. His prominent temples had a bluish tint beneath the whiteness of the skin. A layer of indifference veiled his piercing and profound gaze. I do not know whether he really resembled the Vampire of the Porte Saint-Martin, but theatrical vampires generally have spitefully sarcastic mouths, while Monsieur de Feuillans' lips offered nothing but calm and pure lines.

The Chevalier de Noisy, who was examining him attentively at that moment, found another resemblance altogether. He compared these features with those of the charming young man Stéphane Gontier, whom he had called "fortune's darling" a few moments before. He found certain differences: more thinness and pallor in Monsieur de Feuillans, as well as a greater trenchancy in the bony ridges and more *hauteur* in the overall design of the face, while Stéphane, on the other hand, possessed more grace and harmony, and also more physical strength. Apart from that, however, the Chevalier de Noisy found numerous and striking similarities between them.

Monsieur de Feuillans passed very close to the group, and raised his hat as he said: "Messieurs, I hope to have the pleasure of seeing you again this evening *chez* Madame la Marquise?"

Brocard and Noisy nodded. Stéphane lowered his eyes. Monsieur de Feuillans widened the smile on his lips—but before he had completely overtaken the group, his eyes met Stéphane's, who had looked up again involuntarily.

"Until this evening!" Monsieur de Feuillans said, in a tone so soft as to be almost caressing.

Stéphane blushed, and replied in a low voice: "Until this evening."

Much later—after events had unfolded—Monsieur de Noisy claimed that he had seen Congo's thick lips open to display a full set of wolf's teeth. Be that as it may, at the very moment when Congo, following his master, was lost in the crowd, a young boy, whom you might easily have taken for a girl in disguise, hurtled out of the hunting-path into which the amazon had disappeared a few minutes before, recklessly running through the confusion of speeding carriages to catch up with our four horsemen.

Noisy was in the process of asking Stéphane whether he had a specific arrangement to meet Monsieur de Feuillans that evening. Following the young man's response, the Chevalier was just about to follow his disposition to preach, when the boy planted himself directly in front of the riders and held out a folded piece of paper to Stéphane.

Stéphane took the piece of paper. The boy crossed the roadway again, and vanished into the bushes.

XII. Comtesse Torquati

Baron Brocard, because he was a Parisian, and Monsieur de Champeaux, because he was from the provinces, were thinking the same thing and wearing the same smile. "Good!" they cried, simultaneously. "Monsieur Stéphane will have to part company with us!"

"That's what speaks louder than presentiments!" muttered the Chevalier de Noisy. "That's how these wretched adventures start!"

Stéphane had changed color after opening the note; joy sparkled in his eyes. "Excuse me, Messieurs," he said, half-heartedly—and without saying anything more, he pricked his horse, which leapt forward. Three seconds later, he had disappeared around the corner.

"Dear me!" said Champeaux. "You must have pity on me, since I have just arrived from Normandy and the simplest things present themselves to me as insoluble enigmas. What does this Stéphane do, and what sort of man is this Gabriel de Feuillans?"

Brocard and Noisy looked at one another, as if each of them were passing responsibility for replying to the double question to the other.

"Whatever profession they follow," Champeaux said, still under the spell of his admiration, "they're both dashed [38] well turned out!"

"To explain to you in detail what Feuillans is," the Chevalier de Noisy said, after a pause, "would require a session of several hours... and still you would not know what society says about him. Briefly, Feuillans is a man very much *à la mode*, who appears at present—although he used to possess very little—to have an absolutely colossal fortune, or so it's said. No one knows where he comes from, but he's accepted at Court. His name is one of those that are not discussed, because it sounds well in profane ears while believers have no hesitation in consigning it to the realm of fantasy.[39] A few idle gossips have taken the trouble to embroider a romance around the mystery of his existence. He has, it's said, a star, like Caesar or Napoleon. Far away in Brittany—I don't know exactly where, in the depths of some forgotten *canton* full of phantasmagoria and legends—he has constructed a palace fit for the habitation of the fairies. He doesn't own an inch of the land around his palace, but he's only waiting for a gigantic fortune to which he'll soon be the heir to purchase an estate 20 leagues square..."

"Is he a madman?" Champeaux put in, his eyes growing wide.

"No, certainly not."

"Is he a captain of industry?"

"Never repeat that phrase unless you want to be stoned to death by the prettiest hands in Paris."

"In what category do you put him, then?"

"I put him," Noisy replied, quite seriously, "in the category of individuals who have a familiar demon. No one knows anything of any fortune, but in the full sight and knowledge of the world, he has accomplished a veritable financial *tour de force*. He had always had whatever he wishes, and it's said that he's the one who will marry Olympe de Treguern, the queen of beauty of the Parisian salons—and who is one of the richest heiresses in the world, by virtue of the will of the late Marquis du Castellat."

"But what is this financial *tour de force*?"

"He has been insured for 20 years at Campbell Life for an annual premium of 100,000 francs. He has always paid it, and the policy is approaching maturity."

Champeaux filled his cheeks with air and then emptied them, in a manner that said: "*Damn! I'd certainly like to be in his place!*" Then he asked: "And Stéphane?"

"Oh, Stéphane!" said Baron Brocard. "That's another thing altogether. We were talking just now about *The Vampire*, and supposing that Feuillans has something of the Vampire about him. Well, Stéphane is the blond youth, handsome as Eros, endowed with an innocent and generous nature, who arrives in the fifth act to save the victim on the brink of the precipice. That blond youth is most cruelly killed—two or three times over if necessary—for the requirements of the plot, but he is always revived in order that virtue might triumph in the *dénouement*. I believe I saw, at the Marquise's last *soirée*, the eyes of the beautiful Olympe—Feuillans' fiancée—fixed upon Stéphane..."

Noisy *le Sec* interrupted him gravely. "Baron, he said, "I don't know why, but the entire flow of your thoughts rings false in my ear today. There is a threat hanging over that young man. I can't say how I know it, but I sense it."

"Well, Chevalier, to please you, I shall close the lock-gates on the flow of my thoughts. In addition, Stéphane is a charming fellow that I like as much as you do. I can complete his story in a couple of sentences. It's some 18 months since he arrived in Paris from Brittany. He had the pretty face that you've seen and 100 *louis* in his wallet. A letter of recommendation that he carried with him gave him entry to the Hôtel du Castellat. I remember very well having seen him in a corner of the salon, immobile and utterly embarrassed, contemplating the beautiful Olympe from afar with timid admiration.

"One evening, the beautiful Olympe did not come to a ball held by the Marquise, her aunt. That happens some-times—and the beautiful Olympe, be it said in passing, isn't one of the less piquant mysteries of the Hôtel du Castellat, which is full of mysteries. Our Stéphane, that evening, al-lowed himself to be drawn to the gaming-table—the stakes are high at the Castellat house—and won, without taking over-much account of it, some fabulous sum.

"The following day, the losers demanded a return match; Stéphane gave it to them gallantly; he won twice as much as the night before. Take note that there is a voice here to testify that he never touched cards of his own accord save for that one time. After a whole series of return matches, though, he is to be found in a charming town house on the Champs-Elysées, with a well-furnished stable, 50,000 *écus* in his desk, a suitable household staff and a reputation as a natural player worthy of the hero of a novel, which sets him apart in our society—and that's it!"

Baron Brocard set that phrase in place in the manner of a final point, and the horsemen resumed trotting, bowing to the right and to the left, inhaling the dust wholeheartedly—in sum, conducting themselves like true gentlemen.

It is certain that Stéphane's ears were not burning while they spoke about him thus. Stéphane had forgotten his three companions as completely as if he had not seen them for a hundred years. Stéphane was galloping like a madman through the transverse lanes to expose his feverish brow to the wind. His hand still clutched the note that he had read at a glance. The note said: *Take care, you are under threat. My brother and the Breton lawyer arrive this evening at 8 p.m. at the Post Office in the Rue de Bouloy.* Beneath the inscription was a name: *VALÉRIE.* Baron Brocard had only made mention of the beautiful Olympe, though. What was there in these few lines that made Stéphane so joyful?

Since Champeaux was in the process of interrogation, he might as well also have asked, it seems, who the blonde Comtesse was who had an Italian name but whose hair had certainly not acquired its sheen under the ardent Italian Sun. That was another puzzle, worth at least as much as that of Monsieur de Feuillans or young Stéphane.

Her *calèche* continued to follow the road to Bagatelle, She caused a sensation; everywhere, as she passed by, one saw women whispering. Whenever some provincial, more curious than Champeaux, asked about that solitary woman, proudly attired in her simplicity, the response was always the same: "That's the stepsister of the Marquise du Castellat, the widow of the last Treguern; her second marriage was to Comte Torquati."

"And Comte Torquati?"

"No one has ever seen him."

Then the idler noticed the somber attire of her team and the gloomy enameling of the coat-of-arms stamped on the panels of the *calèche*. He noticed that the blonde woman had a black girdle around her white dress, and a jet cross on her chemisette. Among all that sparkle, beneath that elegance, there was a manifest hint of mourning.

Comtesse Torquati seemed quite unaware of the attention whose object she was. Her eyes were half-closed; her beautiful face seemed to be languishing in a reverie. At the moment when her horses crossed the roundabout, a young boy that we would be able to recognize, by virtue of having seen him deliver another message, came running towards her and said to her: "She's waiting for you by the ditches at La Muette."[40]

Comtesse Torquati sat up straight and her large blue eyes lit up. "To La Muette! At the gallop!" she said to her coachman.

The two black horses, touched by the whip, leapt forwards. The dust they threw up left a lingering cloud at the roundabout, and the dedicated idlers looked around something else to stare at, for the Comtesse's carriage was already no more than a confused dot in the distance.

It is well-known that the caprice of Parisian society only ever adopts one little corner at a time to serve as places designed for pleasure. The Bois de Boulogne is vast; fashion traces its limits according to the times. In 1820, the Allée de Longchamps was the frontier of fashion's empire. No one strayed to the southwest part of the Bois, because everyone knew perfectly that one could walk there at one's ease. La Muette would have its reign, but for the moment it was as far from the Bagatelle as Pézenas or Quimper-Corentin.[41] If the beautiful Comtesse Torquati's whim was to wander into these exotic latitudes, the crowd could not follow her by that route.

Ten minutes later, the calèche was skimming over the sand of a deserted lane. Without having quit the Bois de Boulogne, the Comtesse was 20 leagues from Paris. Through the light foliage of acacias, she saw the opulent plumes of the flowers that overhang the ditches of La Muette. A young woman, dressed in amazon costume, whom we would have had no difficulty in recognizing, came galloping across the grass, waving the handkerchief that she was holding in her hand. She went into the grove to the left of La Muette's enclosure. Comtesse Torquati ordered her coachman to stop, and got down to the ground.

The driver asked if he should follow Madame la Comtesse. He was answered in the negative. Madame la Comtesse headed for the ditches, whose floral crests she admired momentarily before slowly crossing the grass and going into the grove into which the young woman had disappeared. A moment later, they were to be found together, the Comtesse and the young woman, on the green fringe at the foot of a large tree. The Comtesse was sitting down, the young woman kneeling before her and offering a smiling forehead to her kisses.

The Comtesse said, in a voice tremulous with emotion: "Olympe! Olympe! How I love you—and how long the hours seem when you are absent!"

The young woman had thrown back the veil that had covered her face, displaying the exquisite beauty of her features. She appeared to be scarcely 20 years of age. She was a brunette, and the deep blue of her eyes seemed black when her half-closed eyelids lowered the long fringe of their lashes. She held the Comtesse's two hands pressed to her lips.

"Look at me! I see you as often as I can!" murmured the one who had tears in her eyes. "God did not wish that I should have the joys of a mother, although I think of nothing but my children!"

"If you could only see him," said the young woman, lending herself happily to the other's caresses, "how you would thank Heaven!"

"That's true, you've come from Brittany. You've seen him yourself. Tell me about him straight away. Is he handsome?"

"He resembles you."

"Is he good?"

"I told you that he resembles you—he has your face and your heart. He is good, he is straightforward, he is candid. He is as brave as a lion, and the rustling of a leaf makes him shiver in the dark. All the terrors of superstition have floated above his crib! Many a time he has heard *the voice that speaks beneath the Tour-de-Kervoz!*"

"Will he be strong enough to bear his father's name?" asked the Comtesse, whose expression filled with disquiet.

Olympe was smiling. "Today," she replied, "he's only a poor little country boy. Tomorrow, if you wish hard enough, he'll be a knight."

The Comtesse rose to her feet and placed her hands on the young woman's shoulders in order to look her in the face.

"But you speak to me of *him*," she said, "as if there were no longer any doubt or mystery. Are you perfectly certain, then, that it's *him*?"

"I'm sure of it," Olympe said, lowering her eyes.

"And the other one?" the Comtesse murmured.

Olympe's cheeks took on a shade of pink.

"The other one? Stéphane?" she said, in a restrained voice. "Stéphane is good and brave too. Once, when someone spoke ill of Geneviève de Treguern—for there are wretches who speak ill of you, mother—he set himself, alone, against everyone, and imposed silence on the slanderers. But Stéphane is not your son. No, no—it's Tanneguy who is my brother!"

Words hovered on Comtesse Torquati's lips, but she did not pronounce them. "Olympe," she said, to change the subject, "did you know that the three men—the Comte, the Diamond Merchant and the Doctor—are in Paris?"

"I've seen them, mother."

"In the fiacre?"

"In the fiacre."

"Were they in Orlan while you were there?"

"Yes—then they went to Germany, to Cologne."

"And what have you being doing all this time, since I last saw you?"

"I've obeyed the three men. On the day of my arrival at Redon, I found Commander Malo waiting for me on the *Grand'Lande*, as if he had been forewarned. He took me to an old woman named Marion Lécuyer. When he told her my name, she kissed my hands, weeping—but her intelligence, tempered by suffering, revealed her good will, and I couldn't deny her anything, since she had had the great honor in her life of being godmother to a Treguern. While I was talking to her, the Commander whispered in my ear. 'Hurry, for you shall see her but once. The Veil is here!' "

"The Veil!" repeated the Comtesse, shivering. "The old woman died, didn't she?"

"She died before the night was out."

The Comtesse passed the back of her hand over her forehead. "Marion Lécuyer," she murmured, "was the older sister of a servant we loved very much."

"The man with no arms?" Olympe asked.

The Comtesse looked at her in astonishment. "I thought I'd never told you about that!" she said.

"His name is Etienne," Olympe went on, seemingly following the thread of her reverie. "He was accused of a murder committed in the *Trou-de-la-Dette* on the night of August 15, 1800. I've looked for him. If he hasn't rendered his soul to the Lord, I'll find him—take my word for it."

"But he was innocent!" cried the Comtesse, mistaking the import of the statement.

"Were he anything but innocent," the young woman said, in a whisper, "the great families would be reconciled. I suppose you remember everything that this Etienne has done for Treguern."

The Comtesse remained silent for a moment, then she lowered her eyes and replied: "I remember, daughter."

"You, my dear mother," cried Olympe, covering her hands with kisses, "it is necessary to love on both knees, and it's you who have reconciled me to my lot in life! I know only too well how good and saintly you are. I know only too well that you have set yourself between me and evil. But have you not a blindfold over your eyes, mother? Do you know what plans these three men have, in whose hands you've placed me as a docile instrument?"

The Comtesse's forehead darkened. "God moves in mysterious ways, child," she murmured. "There are instruments that Providence chooses, to secure the ends of justice."

Olympe shook her head. "When Etienne was accused of murder in 1800," she said, "there was a young advocate who generously defended him, when everyone else had abandoned him. That advocate has grown old, but he remembers that he once swore that he would get to the bottom of the mystery before he dies."

"Ah!" said the Comtesse, excitedly. "Take care, Olympe, poor child! You too are avid to know! You too want to get to the bottom of the mystery!"

"That's right," Olympe replied. "I intend to do it."

"But to get there, daughter, will you set yourself up as an adversary of those to whom you owe respect?"

"Monsieur Privat," Olympe said, instead of answering, "has nothing but hatred for deceit and crime."

"So you've seen him, too—Etienne's old advocate."

"Yes, mother."

"You've spoken to him?"

"Often, and at length."

"Take care!" repeated the Comtesse, who had become even paler.

One might have thought that Olympe's gaze sought to penetrate the depths of her mother's heart. "Comte Torquati is not my father, is he?" she asked, abruptly.

"No," the Comtesse replied, after a pause. "You are a Treguern." Then, placing her head in her hands, she added: "A child who loves her mother does not doubt her thus."

Olympe threw herself on her mother's neck, weeping. For a few moments there was nothing but tears and caresses; then the Comtesse continued: "And the register of births?"

"Monsieur Privat took me to the presbytery at Orlan," Olympe replied. "I looked through the register of births. The page dated August 15, 1800 has been torn out."

The Comtesse crossed her arms upon her bosom.

"At the town hall," Olympe went on, "the only birth entered in the register on August 16 is that of Stéphane, father and mother unknown. They say out there... but tell me, mother, is it true that the Marquise du Castellat, my aunt, with whom you wish me to live, was once the wife of Monsieur de Feuillans?"

"That's true," said the Comtesse, with disgust.

"How, then, could she marry Monsieur le Marquis du Castellat?"

"The first marriage was annulled."

"And how, then," Olympe followed up, "could Madame la Marquise consent to the proposed marriage between that same Gabriel and our beloved Laurence?"

The Comtesse hesitated, then said: "Marianne is an unhappy soul who is no longer her own mistress. She doesn't have an evil heart, but she has been lifted up by Dowager Le Brec, a woman who does not believe in God." She shook her head and added: "I've been told about the torn-out page already. Dowager Le Brec must be very old; as the years take their toll, repentance sometimes comes. If you've questioned her..."

"I've questioned Dowager Le Brec," Olympe said. "That one will never repent. But it's not her that I accuse, mother. At that time, in the presbytery of Orlan, there was a man..."

"Gabriel!" the Comtesse put in. "The one you hate."

"Gabriel," repeated Olympe, whose eyes were flashing. "Gabriel, whose friends surround him with a mysterious protection. Gabriel, for whom the road is cleared of obstacles. Gabriel—Monsieur de Feillans!—to whom I shall be instructed, perhaps imminently, to give my hand. Must I still be obedient?"

The Comtesse set her cheek against Olympe's lips, rendering her mute. "Reckless and rebellious!" she said, trying to smile. "There are those who watch over you. Don't you want to contribute anything to the hope of seeing the glory of your forefathers renewed? Can't you close your eyes and let yourself be guided by those who love you?"

"Who love me!" Olympe repeated, bitterly. "I'm the slave of those three men whom you have ordered me to obey. If they had to set their feet on me in order to pass, they would crush me without remorse." She got up suddenly. "It's late," she said. "Mother, have you anything more to ask me?"

"Nothing," replied the Comtesse. "Love me, and think of me!"

Olympe gave her forehead to her mother's lips, and while her mother gave her a long kiss, she said to her: "If you have nothing more to ask me, I have something else to tell you, mother. Prepare to be happy—the one you love more than anything in the world is very close to you!"

"The one I love more than anything in the world!" repeated the Comtesse, trembling with emotion. "My son! My Tanneguy!"

"In a few hours you shall see him, mother."

Olympe withdrew from the Comtesse's arms, leapt on to her horse and galloped away towards the Champs-Elysées, where she turned into the Allée des Veuves.

A quarter of an hour later, she was to be found in the room that she occupied in the Hôtel du Castellat, where a girl with a jaunty air was briskly unhooking the spencer jacket of her amazon costume. This girl resembled, feature for feature, the little boy who had given the note to Stéphane and who had sent the Comtesse Torquati towards the ditches of the Muette.

A dark-colored dress replaced Olympe's amazon costume. "Vevette," she said, "I'll return in an hour. Everything must be ready: my flowers, my dress and my jewels; we'll only have a quarter of an hour to dress."

Olympe went out by a door that led to the garden, through which she passed. She soon found herself in a narrow lane leading to the Allée des Veuves, where she found a carriage for hire.

Olympe got into the carriage and said to the coachman: "The Post Office in the Rue du Bouloy!"

Dusk was beginning to fall.

143

XIII. Tanneguy's Entry into Paris

A diligence of small and humble appearance shaved the boundary-marker as it turned into the courtyard of the head-quarters of the French Post Office, which was then situated in the Rue du Bouloy. Three horses running with sweat and stained grey with dust were pulling it. It had two compart-ments, one of which was enclosed and the other a *coupé*.[42] The daylight was fading; the evening was hot.

While the three horses panted on the bare pavement of the courtyard, the conductor descended from his uncomfort-able throne beneath the extension of the awning. As he touched the ground, he muttered: "Broken down twice! That old cart is bedeviled—it's finished. I'd rather beg for my bread than get back in there." The fact was that the little diligence did bear a certain illusory resemblance to a hearse. The doors of both compartments opened at the same time. From the *coupé*, a person emerged whose costume was slightly reminis-cent of a monk's. He had an elongated face, pale and sorrow-ful.

"When one thinks of what becomes of heads like that..." murmured the conductor. He never finished.

A liveried servant threw himself at the *coupé* traveler to welcome him. "Bonjour, Monsieur le Commander!" he said, with an eagerness in which respect and dread were mixed in equal proportions. "Madame la Marquise sent me here to wait for you. Have you any luggage?"

The man he had called the Commander pointed to two large square boxes, which the unloaders were just uncovering.

"I don't know if we'll be able to get that in the *calèche*," the servant objected.

"There's a gentleman who has more luggage than me!" pronounced a young and cheerful voice, outside the door to the enclosed compartment. The voice belonged to a tall young man, marvelously well-built, who was shaking the dust off his

144

traveling-coat. His gaze fell upon the Commander and his mouth fell open. "Ah!" he thought aloud, as his face suddenly lost its good-humored expression. "Are these visions to follow me to the ends of the Earth?"

He turned towards the interior of the diligence, where a piping voice was saying: "It's ridiculous to set a footboard as high as that. Lend me your hand, would you, Monsieur Tanneguy?" Monsieur Tanneguy was our handsome strapping fellow, freshly arrived from his village—where, it seemed, he had experienced some visions of an ominous sort.

Anyone who had heard the sharp voice speaking in the interior would certainly have said to himself: that's an old woman. He would have been mistaken, as to both sex and age. A small, gaunt hand emerged from the interior to lean on Tanneguy's strong and sturdy hand, then a chestnut-colored peaked cap. Beneath the cap there was a face as gross as a fist, bony, angular and excessively colorful, of the sort that popular gaiety characterizes by the word "nutcracker." The little man who owned this face carefully came down the two steps of the footboard and shook himself quite vigorously as he touched the pavement.

The Post Office employees looked at him as they would have looked at a pretended brother they did not know, and the little man certainly had something about him that was even more fantastic than the grave and slender person. The general opinion was that the diligence that looked like a hearse had been bound to break down twice *en route*: once for the man in the black monastic habit, once for that lively grimace grinning beneath the broad brim of the peaked cap.

One singular thing was that the tall person with the monastic mien, for whom the Marquise's valets were waiting with a *calèche*, bowed to the man in the peaked cap, and that the man in peaked cap, who reeked of provincial guttersnipe, showed the nape of his neck in returning a respectful, almost protective bow.

"Do you know that gentleman?" Tanneguy whispered in his ear.

"Yes," replied the little man. "I know everyone, slightly—but you know that I don't much like questions, comrade."

A question rose to Tanneguy's lips, but he was one of those brave lads who would confront an army but who are as timid as a girl; he did not dare voice it. "In this respect," he said to himself, "the courtyard of the Post Office is still partly the country. Once out of here, I shall be 100 leagues from all my devilries! In Paris, there are no longer any phantoms. Tomorrow I shall have forgotten the Tour-de-Kervoz, the *Trou-de-la-Dette* and that old round room where I almost went mad!"

"Are you planning on sleeping here?" the squeaky voice of the little man said to him, awakening him with a start—for Tanneguy was very apt to wander off into the land of dreams.

As he returned to his senses, he saw a newcomer standing immobile next to his traveling companion, who, at first glance, appeared to have his arms crossed tightly across his chest. On looking harder, he saw that the man was actually devoid of arms. A hook was secured by straps to each of his mutilated shoulders. Tanneguy did not remember ever having seen such a bleak face before. It was like a block of sculpted granite.

"Ah," said Tanneguy to his traveling companion. "You've someone waiting for you? It's only me that no one's waiting for."

The Commander left, followed by the Marquise's valet and three porters carrying his square boxes. A fourth porter was next to the man in the peaked cap, unloading his trunk.

"Have you nothing to reclaim, Monsieur?" an employee asked Tanneguy.

Tanneguy lifted his slender package, at the end of his stick, and the employee went back into the office, blowing into his cheeks.

"Help me load my beast of burden," said the man in the peaked cap, expressionlessly, pointing to his trunk with one hand and the man with no arms with the other.

Tanneguy frowned at what seemed to him a cruel joke. The man with no arms lost none of his impassivity. Tanneguy lifted up the trunk and placed it on the hooks. The man with no arms immediately started walking. "Wait!" the little traveler said to him, in the manner of a military command.

The mutilated man stopped short, his foot half-raised in mid-stride. The little man used the time thus gained to offer his hand to the handsome young man. "My young comrade," he said, "let's not worry too much about this honest mule; he'll carry many more of them yet. The arms are no longer there and the head's slightly gone, but the trunk is solid. Oh well, we need to say our farewells, we two. I only observed one defect in you while we were on the road, and that was asking too many questions. One learns nothing that way, you see, because human nature is perverse."

"So, if I hadn't questioned you," Tanneguy put in, naively, "you would have told me the name of the young woman..."

"Perhaps," replied the nutcracker, chuckling softly.

Tanneguy looked at him with a supplicatory expression so eloquent that the little man had to turn away in order not to weaken, lowering the peak of his monumental cap. The mutilated man took that as an order and took a step forwards.

"Wait!" the little man ordered, again. He raised his eyes again, fixing Tanneguy with a piercing gaze, in whose expression the Breton thought he could read a certain regret.

"Listen!" Tanneguy exclaimed. "I'll accompany you to your house, if you wish..."

"You're not going that way, comrade."

"How do you know where I'm going?"

"It's a long way from my quarter to the Allée des Veuves," the little man said, smiling behind his spectacles. We have forgotten to mention that he was wearing spectacles, with lenses as large and round as six-*livre* coins.

Tanneguy took a step back, as he would have done in his native land had he seen the shaggy head of a witch behind him in the moonlight.

The little man's smile lost its mocking quality. "Have you known Stéphane for a long time?" he asked.

"Did I tell you that I know Stéphane?" cried Tanneguy, indignantly.

At that twice-pronounced name, the mutilated man opened his eyes wide and breathed heavily. Instead of answering Tanneguy, the little man continued in a slow and earnest voice: "Stéphane was handsome, Stéphane was strong, Stéphane was rich..." The man with no arms seemed to understand now; at each word he moved his head gravely in a sign of approbation.

"You speak of him as if he were dead!" the Breton stammered, growing pale.

The little man went on, careless of the emotion that he had aroused: "Dowager Le Brec gave you some lines of writing; look after Dowager Le Brec's writing very carefully."

In the midst of the astonishment he felt—for every word spoken by his interlocutor was a mystery to him—Tanneguy perceived the nutcracker's gaze turn suddenly towards the other end of the courtyard. He followed the direction of the glance and an exclamation caught in his throat.

He had caught sight, during a single moment of rationality, of the figure of a young woman. He recognized—or thought that he recognized—that figure, and he would have raised his fists, like the true rustic knight that he was, against anyone who affected to pretend that the figure in question as not the most perfect in the universe. The young woman had turned the corner of the main gate and disappeared into the street before Tanneguy had seen her face.

"It's her!" he murmured, seizing the arm of his traveling companion.

The other shrugged his shoulders.

"I tell you that you made a signal to her!" Tanneguy cried, his manner almost threatening. He dragged his companion as far as the gate and looked along the length of the street.

The mutilated man had followed them, step for step; he went as far as the middle of the road in order that he might see further. A singular emotion had replaced the apathy painted on his face. "Valérie!" he whispered, softly and tenderly. "*La Morte!*"

"Valérie!" repeated Tanneguy, who had heard nothing but the name. The mutilated man looked at him, and his eyelids fluttered.

The nutcracker set himself between them. "Valérie, then!" he muttered. "Now you know her name—much good may it do you!" Then he added, in a trenchant and sententious tone: "In Paris, one rarely finds what one is looking for, but one often finds what one isn't looking for. Before long, comrade, you will perhaps remember what I've just said to you."

Tanneguy was not listening. "I've seen her twice," he murmured. "Once as she glided beneath the chestnut-trees at the Orlan presbytery, once as she prayed at Comte Filhol's tomb. On one other occasion, I heard her as she knelt in the old church, and I was certain that she was saying to God: 'It's Tanneguy who is my brother...' "

"Now that you've nothing more to ask," the nutcracker went on, raising himself up to his full height, "I'll tell you something. My name is Monsieur Privat—remember that! I'm an advocate without any cases. I live in the seven-story house in the Rue Saint-Denis, opposite the *Fontaine des Innocents*. The pigeon-loft on the roof is mine. If you need advice, comrade—and you will, before long—pay me a visit. My pigeon-loft has a good view. Anyway, we shall meet again, perhaps sooner than either of us imagines."

He shook Tanneguy's hand lightly, and shoved his "beast of burden"—as he called the man with no arms—crying: "Giddy-up!"

Tanneguy had not much knowledge of the world and had no pretensions to the title of observer; nevertheless, during the journey, he had been able to assess his companion's character. He had seen that he was obstinate, willful and cantankerous, a pleasant fellow at certain times and under certain conditions, original more than anything else, by nature and in the part he played.

Until he attained the age of 20, Tanneguy had scarcely been out of sight of the broken and ivy-clad tower of Château-le-Brec, where he had been brought up by an old woman named Dowager Le Brec, whom he addressed as "grandmother." There was, strictly speaking, no mystery about his life, but a host of mysteries surrounded him. Since the age of reason had opened his eyes, he had lost count of the frightening—or at least inexplicable—things that seemed to throw him out of the real world incessantly, making his existence a phantasmagoria.

You would have sworn, on no more evidence than the sight of this handsome Tanneguy, with his deep blue eyes full of gentleness and fire, that he was brave—and in truth, when he had an ash-bough staff or a sword in his hand, Tanneguy was not afraid of any living soul. By night, though, when he was all alone, the handsome Tanneguy often broke out into a cold sweat, and his pale lips trembled in spite of himself, at the memory of what he had seen out on the heath at Orlan, by moonlight.

Monsieur Privat, with his round lenses and his peaked cap, had nothing about him that was precisely reminiscent of the terrible poetry of Breton nights—and yet, Tanneguy had felt a tremor at the sight of him, as if the little man had brought the entire apparatus of Armorican superstition with him in that Paris-bound diligence.

Monsieur Privat had not said a single word concerning otherworldly matters, even remotely, but Tanneguy's heart had experienced once again the same oppression that the livid rays of moonlight passing through the cracks of the Tour-de-Kervoz used to impose upon it.

It had been half-way along the route from Brittany to Paris that the little man in the peaked cap had arrived to take his place inside the diligence. Tanneguy did not know him, but the vague terrors of his childhood, from which he was fleeing and which he had already succeeded in putting out of his mind in the new atmosphere, had suddenly made his skin crawl again. This unknown man was like the country raised up like a rump behind him. Merely at the sight of him, Tanneguy had heard the plaint of the wind on the heath and had seen the spirits dancing around the *Pierres-Plantées*. The crowns of the willow that grew on Treguern common had suddenly loomed up before him, displaying the three black men that he had once followed into the darkness, beneath whose feet the earth seemed to open up: the Three Rooks, as the fear of the good people of Orlan had named the mysterious trio.

Why were all these memories coming back to him? Because, just as Monsieur Privat had closed the door of the diligence, the head of a young woman had appeared.

Among all the terrible visions that darkened Tanneguy's memories, there was one radiant one. The young woman had only shown herself for an instant; for him, she had then no name, but the good people of Orlan called her *la Morte*: the dead woman. The young woman had done nothing but pass in front of the window in the door, and had said no more than two words, which seemed to be addressed to Monsieur Privat, but a strange circumstance had engraved those two words in Tanneguy's memory in letters of fire. Those two words evoked in him a whole world of terrors. They were, however, perfectly simple. As she had glided past like a shadow, the young woman had said: "August 15!"

This had taken place a few leagues from the town of Laval. At that time, it took two full days to get from Laval to Paris. During those 48 hours, Tanneguy had questioned Monsieur Privat insistently but had not been able to ascertain the name of the young woman or the significance of the mysterious date. Now, the name had slipped by chance from the lips of the poor creature who no longer had arms—Monsieur Privat's "mule"—but what about the date?

Tanneguy remained for a full three minutes, planted like a maypole at the Post Office gate, always watching the corner of the Rue Coquillière. At the end of the three minutes, a passing dandy bumped into him. Tanneguy woke up and sincerely begged his pardon. The dandy brushed himself down ostentatiously, as if contact with the young man had soiled his frock-coat—then, seeing that the other seemed unconcerned, he became surly and muttered the word "lout" while raising his swagger-stick. Tanneguy was still unconcerned, but he deposited the dandy in the gutter. After that, he went contentedly down the Rue de Bouloy.

From then on, he was in possession of himself; punishing the dandy had woken him up and he was frankly delighted by the sight of the Palais-Royal. This time, the Breton fog had been well and truly dissipated. How could one persist in funereal thoughts amid these dazzling lights, which illuminated so much gold and so many flowers?

XIV. August 15: Allée des Veuves

Tanneguy was uncertain in his own mind as to whether the stiff and dried-up farmer of Château-le-Brec was actually his grandmother. In Orlan, the people sometimes called him Tanneguy Le Brec, sometimes *the little Monsieur*. Why the latter name, if he was the son of a farmer? He had not neglected to ask the question of anyone and everyone, but the people of the parish did not know any more than he did.

Dowager Le Brec was not, in any case, a farmer like any other; her local costume was made in silken cloth. Tanneguy had never been dressed like his childhood companions. In the environs of the Palais-Royal, full of trinket-sporters, fingers hooked into the double pockets of smart nankeen trousers, florid side-whiskers and enormous pairs of dangling eyeglasses, Tanneguy certainly could not pass for a dandy, but he had a pair of unbleached linen trousers floating above his neatly-laced gaiters, a velvet jacket tailored to fit his graceful and robust figure, and a woolen ribbon tied like a cravat securing a white shirt embroidered with fine blue piping. For a headpiece he had a large straw hat tilted sideways across the thick curls of his hair. Be assured that Tanneguy's costume was worth as much as the outfit of any ornamented blockhead.

The largest mirror at Château-le-Brec was scarcely more than six inches square. Tanneguy paused in front of one of the looking-glasses that decorated the frontage of the Café de Valois and studied himself from top to toe at his ease. He found himself well-built and nicely-poised—and a small surge of pride made him walk a little taller as he overheard, for the first time, some passer-by say: "What a handsome fellow!" Had it not been for the hospitable glass that had unexpectedly acquainted him with himself, he would never have dreamed that the flattering exclamation applied to him, and as soon as he had taken it thus his modesty was abruptly reawakened. In his naive embarrassment, he dared not look any longer into the glass that made him so handsome, nor at the women who were passing by. *What would they say, then*, he thought, *if they were to see my brother Stéphane?*

He resumed walking, his eyes lowered and very pensive. The name of Stéphane altered the current of his reverie; that was his best and dearest memory. When Tanneguy looked back on his sad childhood full of bizarre terrors, he saw no smiles save for two rosy faces crowned with curly fair hair: the frank and friendly face of his friend Stéphane, who had bid him adieu one day while calling him his brother, and the gently face of Marcelle, the little girl with the patience of an angel who looked after Dowager Le Brec and tolerated her harsh whims.

Alas, Marcelle! Would he ever see her again?

Like Tanneguy, Stéphane was an orphan with neither father nor mother. He had been brought up in Guillaume Féru's windmill. Everyone in the village loved him. There is a mysterious attraction that Paris exerts upon those who have no family. Stéphane sometimes received a little money from an unknown hand. One morning, he had set off for Paris. "If I make my fortune," he said to his brother Tanneguy, "you shall be rich."

A few months afterwards, Tanneguy had received a letter from Stéphane, which said: *I have become rich! Come keep me company: I don't want to be happy all alone.*

What a coincidence! When he received that letter, Tanneguy had just started packing his little bundle to quit Château-le-Brec, because a mad impulse had entered into his head. He wanted to go out into the world to find the woman he had heard, saying to God as she knelt in the old church: *It is Tanneguy who is my brother!*

When Tanneguy had packed his bundle, Dowager Le Brec had said to him: "If you want to stay, stay; if you want to go, go." In the 20 years he had lived, Tanneguy had never seen a smile on the stony face of the old farmer. He called her grandmother, and yet, when he looked into the depths of his heart, he—so good, so young, so ardent for love!—could find no trace of filial affection.

At the hour of his departure, when the farm-laborers came to bid him adieu, Dowager Le Brec sent them away rudely. When Marcelle wept, Dowager Le Brec threatened her with her white staff. "Why does everyone love him?" she cried. "Who among you will weep when I go?"

They left her alone with Tanneguy. She put ten gold coins in his hand, and a sealed letter, which bore the address of Marquise Marianne du Castellat, Allée des Veuves, Paris. "If you come back, I shan't chase you away," she said, showing him the door. "But if you never come back, so much the better!"

That was all. Tanneguy departed with his little bundle at the end of his stick. He only turned back once, in the middle of the heath, to see the Tour-de-Kervoz still raising the unequal teeth of its crenellations above the tall willows. His heart had skipped a beat; tears had come to his eyes; then he had set off at a determined pace, with a firm tread, giving the curls of his hair to the wind as if to salute the unbounded route and the unknown future. Adieu, Marcelle!

Now, four days after leaving Château-le-Brec, adventure seemed to be pressing hard on his heels. He had already seen the woman who might be his sister—since she had mentioned him to God in her prayer—twice more. She was in Paris! Paris was as beautiful as it was vast. Tanneguy no longer felt the sorrow of loneliness.

While dreaming thus he had passed through the garden and found himself in front of the Arcades Montpensier. In the crowd he heard a voice that made him start; the voice had said: "Look! There he is!"

Tanneguy gave a cry of joy and turned around, for he was certain that he had recognized Stéphane's voice. He looked straight ahead, to the left and the right, but saw only people that he did not know. Three of these people, standing still and grouped beneath the arcade, seemed to be looking at him attentively. The light was behind them, and Tanneguy could not make out their features because it was so dazzling, but his blood ran cold nevertheless.

"Have the Three Rooks left the Tour-de-Kervoz?" he murmured.

He lowered his gaze involuntarily. When he raised his eyes again to the arcade, whose arch had framed the silhouettes of the three unknowns, it was empty. Tanneguy ran towards the gallery, for he was ashamed of the reflexive sensation whose chill still lingered in his veins. Superstitious terrors did not belong in a place like the Palais-Royal, so full of movement, noise and light.

Tanneguy expected to find the three men, who could not have gone far, behind one of the pillars of the arcade. He had no idea what he wanted to say or do to them, but the opportunity was there and instinct commanded him to seize it.

It appeared that Breton phantoms that made the journey to Paris did not lose the faculty of melting into the ground as they pleased. In the gallery, Tanneguy found nothing but the bustling crowd. This was the point at which Tanneguy rebuked his imagination and decided that he had been dreaming.

In this case, the dream persisted; just as he was taking pity on himself and shrugging his shoulders he distinctly heard the three syllables of his name whispered in his ear. He stopped, as if a hand had seized him by the collar. The people passing by must have been astonished to see the handsome youth standing stock still in the middle of the gallery, his eyes staring, his cheeks pale and his head shrinking into his shoulders as if he had been struck by lightning.

A soft voice had pronounced his name. Valérie was there—Tanneguy knew it; when he turned round, it was in the certainty of seeing the white vision of the church at Orlan.

He was not entirely mistaken; nevertheless, it must be said that visions lose something of their poetry in the capital of the civilized world. Instead of the white undine that Tanneguy had seen kneeling at the tomb of Treguern, he saw through the crowd a black mantilla that half-concealed the figure of the sylphide, whose face disappeared entirely behind the brim of her hat.

She was walking next to a tall young man who had a fine and handsome head, richly coiffed in blond hair.

"Stéphane!" Tanneguy cried, extending his hands toward them. "Valérie! My brother and my sister!"

The young couple were going into one of the narrow passages that led from the gallery to the Rue de Montpensier. Tanneguy hurled himself toward them like a madman. The passage was already empty, but Tanneguy could still hear the echo of the last words spoken at the corner of the street. The words were: *August 15, Allée des Veuves.*

Tanneguy crossed the Rue de Montpensier at a run, mounted the steps to the Rue Richelieu four at a time, and arrived on the pavement just in time to see an elegant closed carriage departing at the gallop. Tanneguy had good legs; because he was convinced that the carriage contained those he sought, he set off after it.

The carriage burned up the road along the Rue Saint-Honoré; it was all that Tanneguy could do not to lose sight of it. After going three-quarters of a league, the carriage stopped somewhere in the Pépinière *quartier*, in front of a well-kept town house. Tanneguy made a final effort, and arrived at the carriage entrance just as a servant in livery was lowering the footboard. His soul was in his eyes. He saw a stout woman get down, carrying a lap-dog in her arms.

Tanneguy almost fell over; the first thought that sprang into his mind was that there had been a diabolical transformation. Perhaps the old lady was Stéphane, and the lap dog the mysterious belle of the willows. While he was wiping the sweat from his brow, the stout woman said to the servant: "Allée des Veuves! Monsieur de Feuillans will bring me."

The door of the house closed on the lap dog and its mistress; the carriage went off at a modest pace.

"Allée des Veuves!" the Breton repeated, trying to set his thoughts in order. Then he added: "That's where I have to take Dowager Le Brec's letter."

157

Mechanically, his gaze fixed itself on the walls of the town house; there was a billboard attached to it, carrying theatre bills. Tanneguy did not see it right away, but his eyes, which were pinned without his being aware of it to the ten or 12 pieces of paper, finally assembled the letters. Suddenly, the same date, inscribed at the head of all the bills, struck his gaze ten or 12 times over:

August 15! August 15! August 15!

Every theatre had produced a handsome bill for Assumption Day, but Tanneguy was unacquainted with the customs of theatres, and that date, fluttering before his eyes in all directions, afflicted him with a kind of vertigo.

He asked a passer-by for directions to the Allée des Veuves, and continued on his way.

Half an hour later, he was wandering under the trees of the Champs-Elysées. He had gone past the entrance to the Allée des Veuves without realizing it, and now found himself among the groves in the vicinity of the Cours-la-Reine. In those days, once night had fallen, it was a veritable desert. Nothing of what is there today existed then: no English gardens, no musical cafés, no Panorama, none of the houses of the *quartier* François I. Even the Allée d'Antin was little more than a tree-planted avenue, bordered by gardens and villas. Along the Cours-la Reine and in the Avenue de l'Etoile, smoky street-lights hung here and there, seemingly augmenting the profound obscurity that reigned in the groves.

Tanneguy was taking long strides. Fever already had him in its grip, for the shadows around were strangely astir. In the very center of great Paris, where 800,000 breasts were already drawing breath at that time, a frisson was running through his flesh—as it had in the hours when the echo of his own past had formerly frightened him on the lonely heath, and as it had in the hours when cold sweat bathed his brow while he was abed, when he heard those three superhuman voices through the thick wall of Château-le-Brec, which seemed to rise from the depths of the Tour-de-Kervoz, speaking of past murder and future vengeance.

Suddenly, he stopped, stupefied.

"It's almost August 15," said a voice in the night.

"Today has no more than two hours to run," added another voice.

A third took up the refrain: "The money must be at the Englishman's before midnight."

Tanneguy knew all these voices, having heard them in Orlan. They were the nocturnal terrors of his childhood, which dogged his paces. His eyes tried in vain to pierce the darkness.

"The Englishman will have all of it," the first voice went on, "for it's necessary that the child shall be as rich as a prince!"

"He will have the whole price of a murder!" the second voice continued.

"As always!" the third finished, indistinctly.

Tanneguy thought that he saw a confused movement under the trees. Almost at the same moment, a mysterious password, which seemed to descend from Heaven to announce the presence of an angel, resonated softly in his ear. He heard his name pronounced murmurously: "Tanneguy! Tanneguy! Tanneguy!"

A woman ran past in the nearby roadway; she was bareheaded and her wavy hair floated on the wind. She said: "Come on!" There were tears in her voice. Tanneguy made an effort to follow her, but his legs turned to jelly beneath the weight of his body.

The young woman disappeared into a sort of dark alleyway that opened on to the plane of the Avenue d'Antin, a little above the present opening of the Rue Jean Goujon. Tanneguy lost sight of her. Nevertheless, he went into the alleyway in his turn; it was tortuous, and bordered by gardens. He still seemed to hear a sort of echo that repeated: "Come on! Come on! Tanneguy! Tanneguy!"

At the same time, there was a soft but lively sound of music in the distance, behind the groves of lilac. There was a bend in the alleyway. As Tanneguy moved forward, a glimmer of light appeared in front of him, and he saw a bright flash between the branches of the trees. The music was drawing nearer. As he turned the corner, Tanneguy's eyes were suddenly dazzled by a sort of luminous ramp. The music was very close at hand, behind a wall; the musicians were playing a waltz. A concert of joyful conversations and bursts of laughter was audible.

The place in which Tanneguy found himself was a small triangular space at the end of the alleyway. One of the triangle's sides, seemingly devoid of an exit, was formed by a garden wall covered by firepots and Chinese lanterns; this wall supported a terrace, which was deserted at present because all the couples at the party were dancing. The second side of the triangle was the entrance to the alleyway. The third side, closed by a wrought-iron gate furnished with shutters, had a double door in the middle, which was shut. Behind that enclosure, the light of the Chinese lanterns displayed a genteel country-house, which was not the one where the party was being held.

Tanneguy scarcely paid any heed to all of this, however. Where had Valérie gone? There was no exit. How had Valérie got out?

Tanneguy's eyes interrogated by turns the illuminated wall of the large garden and the shuttered enclosure of the white villa. As his eyes turned in the latter direction, he saw the door come slowly ajar. A man appeared on the threshold, coming out backwards.

Was this still a dream? There was a strong black hand holding this man by the collar. The hand let go and was abruptly withdrawn. The door was closed, and the man fell backwards like a dead weight. As he fell, the cloak that had been disposed to hide his face fell away. The light from the ramp struck a full face inundated with blond hair. It was a handsome young man, who seemed scarcely to have reached his twentieth year.

"Stéphane! My brother Stéphane!" stammered Tanneguy, his knees buckling. He intended to put his hand on his

160

friend's heart, but drew it back red with blood. A cry of horror was stifled in his bosom.

In the neighboring garden, the thousand noises of the party burst forth in sheaves: joyful voices, hectic laughter, smooth harmonies. Tanneguy made a supreme effort to retain his reason, which was in full flight. His eyes clouded. He fell, deprived of consciousness, next to Stéphane's inanimate body.

Everyone in Madame la Marquise du Castellat's circle believed in ghosts.

In 1820, nobility made certain concessions to nascent liberalism. The Marquise was intoxicated by the young liberalism, while the king of her salons and lion of her parties, Monsieur Gabriel de Feuillans, was a very advanced liberal— a strong-minded man, a philosopher, almost an atheist, although he believed in ghosts. The handsome Gabriel de Feuillans was very highly ranked in Madame la Marquise's circle; to win his affection, people willingly extended skepticism as far as denying the existence of God—but they believed in ghosts. That was the fashion.

The Marquise du Castellat lived in an isolated house of melancholy appearance on the Allée des Veuves, near the present-day location of the Rue Bayard. The Marquise's house did not face directly on to the Allée des Veuves; it was set between two gardens, the first of which served as a courtyard. A monumental iron railing extended its gilded flanks to either side of a Louis XV gate. Between the gate and the house a labyrinth cleverly extended its winding alleys, displaying white statues here and there, which seemed to be playing hide-and-seek behind the hornbeam hedges. The house was also in the Louis XV style, but bare and unornamented. There was something sad in the appearance of the great pallid edifice standing alone amid ancient trees, showing off its shuttered casement-windows to distant observers.

On the other side of the house, an immense flower-bed, punctuated by clumps of trees planted in the French style, rounded out at its extremity into a large enclosed lawn. Around the enclosed lawn were shady arches, ruined cottages copied from paintings by Watteau [43] and grottoes—yes, grottoes!—with superb stalactites. The whole ensemble was terminated by a terrace which looked out on to the deserted triangular space where the catastrophe that terminated our last chapter took place.

There were magnificent parties at the Hôtel du Castellat, especially in summer. The fashionable set had adopted these parties. The Marquise—and it was not the least part of her glory—was known to be the intimate confidante of Gabriel de Feuillans, a man who was both sparkling and serious, profound and supremely seductive, who wore the aureole of a "friend of the people," as they put it in those days, in passing for one of the moguls of Carbonarism,[44] and whose fortunate daring would soon make him richer than a fairy-tale prince. Despite the splendor of the Marquise's parties, however, and in spite of the fashionability that Feuillans conferred on her salons, there was a something indefinably gloomy about her house: a sorrow or a threat.

It was an era of vaporous things. Lamartine was tuning his melancholy lyre; Chateaubriand was singing the mortal agony of René; Byron was sculpting his inconsolable heroes out of storm-clouds. Black was triumphant.[45] Some people even said, laughing from the sides of their mouths, but pensively, that there was a mysterious element of mourning in that dwelling. Chance, it has to be admitted, became the accomplice of these rumors, and hardly a season passed without some tragedy or other interrupting the pleasures of the Marquise's house. The Marquise's young sister, Laurence de Treguern, had died suddenly on Assumption Day in 1817, a week before the date fixed for her wedding, August 22. The Marquise du Castellat had, it was said, put diamonds worth more than 100,000 francs into the wedding-chest, which were never recovered.

There were certain strange features concerning the demise of the Marquis du Castellat himself. The old gentleman had had no dearer friend than Monsieur de Feuillans. One evening, the following year—it was August 15—Monsieur le Marquis had roused his entire household, because an important theft had been committed in his office. He was heard several times to repeat: "I know who did it." The next day, Monsieur le Marquis got up early and gave orders that he was to be driven to the law-court, where he would make his complaint—but he never completed that plan, because he was struck down *en route* within the carriage, by a fatal stroke the cause of which the physicians could not identify.

There were many other stories surrounding the Hôtel du Castellat. The present Marquise belonged to the old Treguern family, whose name was legendary in Brittany and was the subject of nocturnal village conversations from Vannes to Roche-Bernard. It is by no means rare for the origins of these chivalric houses to be lost in Faerie. Everyone is familiar with the siren of Lusignan and Rieux's wanton spirit.[46] The supernatural idea awakened in the natives of Morbihan by the name Treguern was of a less gracious sort. It was not a mildly capricious fairy that frolicked in the armorial bearings of Treguern, nor a lively sprite stirring the waters of a large pool at midnight; it was the frightful fever of dead men who could not sleep in their coffins, and the sinister second sight that permits the hour of death to be read in advance upon the face of the future victim.

There was no marble heavy enough to retain a Treguern in his tomb, and Treguerns had the redoubtable gift of seeing death as it crept up on its unsuspecting victims, whether at a ball or in the church, in the forest when the joyous horn sent its fanfares echoing, or around a festive table—everywhere! That was well-known, and many a strong man trembled whenever the prophetic gaze of a Treguern fell upon him. But that second sight operated in a very strange way. When a Treguern found himself confronted by someone who was about to die, a black veil sprinkled with white tears would spread out between the two of them. This extraordinary circumstance was consecrated by the very design of the Treguern coat-of-arms—a coat-of-arms that the Marquise du Castellat had never had the least desire to set on her carriages beside the arms of her former spouse. Le Mâdre de Treguern [47] bore *sable sewn with silver tears*—"which is the mortuary flag," as the armorial of Pontivy adds.

A gentleman of bizarre habits was often to be encountered at the Hôtel du Castellat, who appeared to be a trifle weak in the head, and who was the last surviving male of the Treguern family. This was Commander Malo, whom we have seen arriving from Brittany in the same carriage as Tanneguy and Monsieur Privat, along with three large boxes. Some people regarded Commander Malo as a harmless madman; others were afraid of him. He studied a great deal, after his fashion, and possessed the best collection of *grimoires* imaginable. He had traveled a great deal. Hungary, Moravia, Silesia and Poland had shown him their vampires; he was familiar with the cemetery of Kadam in Bohemia,[48] where one is obliged to put cadavers in chains to prevent them hurling themselves upon the living. In Belgrade, he had seen cock's eggs containing serpents. He was familiar with chiromancy, alectromancy,[49] hydromancy and divination by means of silver alloy. He knew everything; he had seen everything—but he said that he had never seen anything to match the spectacle of an All Souls' Night spent on the heath of Carnac in Brittany.[50]

In the course of his travels, the Commander had assembled a collection of fragments of tombstones. The apartment he occupied in the Castellat house was overflowing with these riches, now further augmented by the three boxes from Brittany. He was already a man of advanced years, extremely gentle by nature; he was more timid than a child, and it was very difficult to get him to open his mouth in front of a numerous assembly—but when he spoke, it was terrible. The Marquise had a superstitious fear of him.

If, among the guests at the Hôtel du Castellat, we have spoken first of poor Commander Malo, it is because of the tradition of the Black Veil sprinkled with white tears, and the Treguern coat-of-arms. The traditional gift of second sight had, indeed, played a role in the Commander's life.

Thirty-five years before the epoch in which our drama is unfolding, the Commander had been a cheerful young man, who scarcely dreamed of withdrawing from the world. One autumn evening, in the large half-ruined farmhouse that we have already encountered under the name of Château-le-Brec, a modest and frugal banquet was held at the farmhouse to celebrate an engagement. The fiancée was a beautiful young woman named Catherine Le Brec de Kervoz; the young and happy fiancé was Malo Le Mâdre, the younger brother of Treguern. The latter would have laughed wholeheartedly had anyone told him that he would take a vow of celibacy and enter the Order of Malta within a fortnight.

When that dinner finished, there was dancing in the open air. Catherine and Malo were together; suddenly, Malo was seen to shiver. He moved away from his fiancée abruptly.

"Where are you going?" he was asked.

"To seek God," he replied.

And he crept to the parish church, weeping.

"Father," he said to the priest. "Light candles for Catherine Le Brec, who is about to die!"

He went back to the farm, where Catherine was waiting, annoyed by his absence. "Catherine! Catherine!" he cried, taking off his ceremonial clothing. "You have time to make your confession and give your soul to your master."

The joys of the engagement party were banished. After the first moment of astonishment, a murmur ran through the assembly of relatives and friends. It said: "Malo has seen the Veil of Treguern!"

Catherine, who was very pale, came to take him by the hands. "Is it true, Malo?" she asked, all a-tremble. "Is it true that you've seen the Veil of Treguern, which presages death between us?"

The priest arrived on the threshold.

"Quickly! Quickly!" cried the young man, instead of replying. "Make your confession, my beloved Catherine! Death does not wait!"

Catherine knelt down beside the priest. When she had finished her confession, her lip was reddened by a drop of blood. She turned toward her fiancé and said "Thank you!"— then she died of an aneurysm that had ruptured.

The Order of Malta was still receiving professions. Malo wore the mourning-dress of his happiness under his novice's robe. When the Order was dispersed, Malo was a Commander. He had not desired liberation; liberty weighed upon him like a burden. He returned to Brittany, where his family was battling against adversity. Dowager Le Brec allowed him to prepare himself a shelter in the Tour-de-Kervoz. Malo spent several years there; his new dwelling was not designed to cure the exaltation of his spirit. He became a total recluse, immersing himself more and more deeply in the spaces of the world of imagination. The local people had almost forgotten what he looked like, for he never went out by day—but sometimes, on the heath of Orlan, under the willows of Treguern common or alongside the cemetery wall, whenever someone saw a large black shadow gliding slowly and silently through the moon-less night, everyone knew that it was Commander Malo. Dowager Le Brec, who was not afraid of anyone, would have fasted all day rather than fail to carry something to eat to her tower.

On the night of August 15 in the first year of the century, gunshots were heard on the heath. From sunset to dawn, a feeble light was seen glimmering in the loopholes of the Tour-de-Kervoz. For some time before, the local people had been saying that Commander Malo was not alone in his tower,

The first people who crossed the Orlan heath the next day found a pool of blood at the bottom of the ravine. Commander Malo, braving the daylight on this occasion, came as far as the edge of the wood, with a hatchet on his shoulder, and cut down a young tree. From the tree, as the reader knows, he fabricated a stout cross, which he planted in the middle of the pool of blood. From that day onwards, no glimmer of light showed in the loopholes that let air and daylight into Commander Malo's retreat.

That was 20 years before, when Madame la Marquise du Castellat had been Marianne de Treguern.

XVI. Commander Malo

In the days when Commander Malo lived like a were-wolf in the Tour-de-Kervoz, Filhol de Treguern was a young man, strong in body and serious in mind. The misfortunes of his house had left him with none of the gaiety of youth. He had married a woman from a noble family, ruined like his own, and his wife had already made him a father. Filhol often said that he would give half his blood to bring comfort back to Treguern Manor, which soon became little more than a heap of debris, but those were words; he did nothing to get out of his predicament and awaited the hour of ruination draped in his discouragement.

Suddenly, a change in his tread became visible; the *cloarec* Gabriel had arrived in the vicinity. Filhol became friends with him, and crossed the threshold of the Château-le-Brec, where the enemy of his family dwelt, for the first time because of him.

Until that moment, Filhol had loved his wife Geneviève dearly. No misery is complete within the peaceful haven of the family; in a little corner of his heart, Filhol was happy. One day, Geneviève, the poor devoted child, warned Filhol of what was being said in the parish regarding Gabriel and Marianne. For the first time in his life, Filhol became angry and scolded his wife. Soon, Gabriel was more the master of the manor than he was. When they went walking together, they were seen in animated conversation, always debating heatedly and examining large sheets of printed paper, which they laid out on the grass in order to read them at their ease. One morning, the sacristan found one of these sheets, forgotten on the heath. Only two words, printed in large characters at the foot of the torn-off sheet, remained comprehensible:

Life Insurance

We recognize that sheet, brought from Redon by Gabriel. We know that it contained the Campbell Life prospectus. At

168

the end of the last century, J. F. Campbell, Esquire, a Scottish philanthropist, had invented the game of life and death that now fills the coffers of opulent companies throughout Europe, under the name of *Regulated Annuities on Survivorship* (regulated tontines).[51] J. F. Campbell died a millionaire 30 times over.

While the sacristan was reading, he heard Filhol and Gabriel behind the hedge, who were doubtless discussing a brilliant future and an immense fortune, the poor young fools.

Gabriel's future was to be a curate in some country parish, if the clairvoyant Church did not chase him from her bosom; Filhol's was to die of hunger in his noble hovel. The sacristan knew that—and they were talking about 100,000 francs!

That same day, Filhol went to Redon and pledged his last piece of land in order to raise a small sum of money. When he had the money, instead of returning to the manor, he boarded a three-master bound for the English coast. Before it sailed, he wrote a letter to his wife, which seemed to be dictated by drunkenness:

I want to be rich, it said. *I shall be; when I return we shall be happy. Have confidence in Gabriel, my friend and our benefactor...*

Geneviève turned her tearful eyes towards the crib in which little Olympe was asleep. Marianne, by contrast, clapped her hands, already intoxicated with joy. Laurence, Filhol's little sister, began rocking Olympe's cradle, laughing and saying: "When we're rich, Olympe shall have a new vest."

One morning, while Filhol was away, Commander Malo left his tower and came to the manor. He put both hands on Gabriel's shoulders and looked at him for a long time. "Oh!" he said, in surprise. "So, young man, it's you who have done all this." It was never easy to grasp the meaning of the Commander's statements. He went on: "Good day, my nieces! Last night, I saw my nephew Filhol running after happiness."

"Last night!" Geneviève repeated, tremulous with hope. "Is he close by, then?"

The Commander's gaze seemed to be wandering in the void. "He's very far away!" he replied. "Over there, beyond the sea! He's doing something that no Treguern has ever done before—he's lying!"

He released Gabriel in order to go to Geneviève and take her hand. She was weeping. "You are the best, Madame la Comtesse de Treguern," he said, in a serious and affectionate tone. "You will never cease loving... When your son sees the light of day, look hard at his features, in order to be sure of recognizing him!"

"My son," repeated Geneviève, astonished.

Instead of continuing, the Commander caressed little Olympe in her crib, adding in a whisper: "Beautiful and happy..." Then he bowed ceremoniously to Marianne. "Mademoiselle my niece," he went on, "Are you a Le Brec or are you a Treguern? I'm looking for the color of your heart. You shall be rich!"

Laurence was listening. He leaned towards her and kissed her on the forehead, while pronouncing these words: "Unhappy and beautiful!"[52]

Then he went back towards Gabriel, who made an effort to keep his face straight. "You," he said, "have watched the snake change its skin. Son of a witch, traitor to God, the habit of the Saints is burning you. Woe betide the one who opened the door of Treguern Manor to you! Filhol is a man; if he kills you before August 15 of next year, he will see his daughter grow up and will know his son!"

Gabriel was utterly pale, although he tried to smile. Commander Malo looked at him again, then turned his back and marched out of the door without saying another word.

Following Malo's departure, Gabriel did not stay at the manor. He went back to the presbytery, taking the long way around, and as he wandered randomly through fallow fields and coppices he repeated to himself:

"Over there! Very far away! A thing that no Treguern ever did before! So that man's sight can cross the sea and pierce the envelope around the heart!" He shivered, adding:

"And me! And me! Did he not speak as if his eye had sounded my consciousness?"

He paused at the summit of the hill that overlooked the parish of Orlan. It was a beautiful spring day. The outstretched landscape was smiling beneath the Sun's rays: a Breton landscape, of horizons veiled by diaphanous vapor, of great dark forests advancing into the plain like promontories into the sea, of heaths trimmed like felt, their pink and blue tints fading in the distance.

Gabriel wiped sweat from his brow and breathed heavily, for his bosom was constricted. His gaze embraced the landscape; he saw the forests on the mountain slopes, the green meadows in the depths of the valleys, where the silver ribbons of 20 streams followed their meandering courses; he saw the mills deploying their long sails in the wind, the farms with thatched roofs, which launched the joyful smoke of their hearths towards Heaven; he saw the rich fields and the large herds of livestock searching for the freshest grass at the waterside, making moving fringes along the streams.

Then his eyes fell back to his worn-out vestments.

"Nature is very beautiful!" he thought aloud. He added, as a skeptical smile was born on his anxious face: "Very beautiful to the one who can say: *It is mine; I am its master!* Those majestic forests belong to me; I alone can run after the red deer and chase the roe deer! Those mills that animate the landscape pay tribute to me; those fields are ripening their harvests for me; all those streams are irrigating my lands and providing drinking-water to my herds. My sight is piercing and the horizon is vast; all that I see, as far as my sight extends, to the horizon's limits, is my domain!"

His head was raised and there was a glitter in his eye. "But what of God?" he murmured, while his forehead darkened again. His gaze slipped involuntarily towards the little church of Orlan, whose modest bell-tower seemed to be protecting the village. Around the church, the cemetery extended its green girdle.

"God!" the *cloarec* repeated, pressing his cold hands against his feverish temples. "And death!"

He remained immobile for a moment; then his rebellious head shook the curls of his long hair.

"Eternity is longer than life," he said, taking out the missal that he held under his arm, "but life comes before eternity!"

There was now a kind of fever in him, and he opened the book with a convulsive gesture. "The right for eternity, the left for life!" he cried, as children do when playing a game.

He was obliged to look twice, for his vision was clouded. To the right there was the word *Requiem*; to the left there was the word *Laetare*.[53]

"Life has won twice over!" cried the seminarian. "L against R! Joy and feasting against repose and death! Thank you, my prayer-book."

He closed the book again and went down the hill at a run. Behind a furze-hedge, a few paces from the place that he had just left, a strange head rose into view. It was an old woman, wearing a local costume in black silk. She watched Gabriel racing down the hill. She pointed after him with the crozier-like white staff she held in her hand.

"Joy and feasting," she repeated, "to you who are my blood, Le Brec! To Treguern, repose and death."

When Filhol de Treguern returned to the manor, he did not appear to have made a fortune. His clothes were a little more threadbare than before his departure, his complexion was paler, his face thinner. The Lord knows that Geneviève, his wife, found him handsome as he was—but his half-sister, Marianne, asked him as soon as he arrived: "Well, brother, are we rich?" Filhol replied "Patience!"—and when Gabriel came to the manor, he cried out to him through the window while he was still some way off: "All goes well!"

Filhol and Gabriel shut themselves in and stayed together until the middle of the night. Marianne tried hard to hear a little of what they were saying, for she was as curious as a

172

little girl destined to become a Parisian Marquise, but Filhol and Gabriel were talking in whispers.

We shall now relate what happened, simply and without commentary. Scarcely a week had gone by since Filhol's return when he suddenly fell dangerously ill. After three days, the illness had progressed to the point at which all hope of a cure was gone. The local physician, who was not at the height of his powers, having employed leeches and emetics, declared that human art was powerless against fate. Filhol, well and truly condemned, asked to be left alone with his friend Gabriel.

That could have been the last request of a Christian, since Gabriel was committed to the Church. Marianne and Laurence withdrew; poor Geneviève followed them, suffocated by sobbing. An hour later, Gabriel came out of the room holding a handkerchief to his eyes, saying: "My poor friend has yielded his last sigh!"

Geneviève fainted dead away, for she loved her husband tenderly. Laurence stood as if struck by lightning. Even Marianne shed a few tears, though not many.

It is the custom in Orlan, as elsewhere in Brittany, to hold a public wake in a dead man's room, but Filhol de Treguern was not a peasant and his ancestors had done enough good in the parish of Orlan to permit a representative of the presbytery to undertake the vigil. The parish priest was away, the curate was ill; Gabriel replaced them both to the extent that he could. Gabriel kept vigil next to Treguern's body, not only as his friend but also in an official capacity.

Some rather remarkable particulars of that funereal night were recounted in the village. Firstly, the vase of holy water and the aspergillum remained outside the door. No one was given permission to enter the room to sprinkle holy water over the deceased, as custom and duty required. Those who came heard nothing but the *cloarec* Gabriel loudly reciting the prayer for the dead in the funerary chamber.

As for Geneviève, the widow, Marianne and Laurence, they were all in the anteroom: Geneviève, motionless and stupefied, her eyes devoid of tears, holding her baby in her cold hands, Marianne leaning back against the window and Laurence crouching in the dust. People guessed, or took the inference, that they had not been given permission to approach the bed where the dead Treguern was laid out.

Towards morning, Marianne and a charitable neighbor went to the town hall to register the death, which had already been entered in the parish records, thanks to Gabriel. He was admirable, that Gabriel! He buried his friend with his own hands; he nailed the coffin shut himself. The curate got up from his sickbed to say the burial Mass, but it was Gabriel again who did what was necessary at the cemetery.

Commander Malo came when it was all over. Only a handful of local people still remained by the side of the freshly filled-in grave. The people of Brittany stay there as long as they can; they are immeasurably fond of the emotions they feel after deaths. Commander Malo approached the grave, but he did not kneel down.

"Treguern, Treguern, Treguern!" he said, distinctly repeating the word three times—and while the audience shivered fearfully, he leaned his ear towards the ground, as if he were awaiting a reply.

Geneviève came forward, carrying a meager cross on which the name of her husband, Filhol, was inscribed. Commander Malo took the cross and laid it flat on the damp ground. The local people wanted to stand it upright, but the commander pushed them away and said: "Wait! I saw Treguern yesterday, and I have not seen the Veil. I came to call Treguern, and Treguern has not replied. Treguern shall die three times, and his tomb shall be marble, like that of the great knight Tanneguy!"

Towards the end of that same year, people sometimes encountered Geneviève with little Olympe in her arms and a smile on her lips. Geneviève no longer went to the cemetery, where she had wept so many tears! The people of Orlan said in low voices that the poor young woman had gone mad.

Where did she go, when Laurence saw her going out at night, carrying little Olympe at her breast? A mother who is up to no good leaves her baby in its crib, and Geneviève had always been so saintly! Geneviève could not be doing anything wrong.

She certainly did not go where the half-sister Marianne went.

Some had met Geneviève in the vicinity of the Tour-de-Kervoz. There was talk of a dark-clad unknown man wandering, around midnight, between Treguern Manor and the *Pierre-des-Païens*.

On the ground floor of the tower, under the redoubt where Commander Malo lived in his fantastic solitude, there was the opening of a ventilation-shaft. Laborers returning late from the fields sometimes thought they perceived, through the brambles, a faint glimmer of light through the opening of that ventilation shaft. A few of them even claimed to have heard voices that seemed to emerge from the bowels of the Earth; they specified—for those who told these stories were never short of details that gave them countenance and truth—that one of these voices was Gabriel's and the other belonged to Geneviève de Treguern, and that when they fell silent, one could hear the joyful babbling of little Olympe.

But there was also another voice—and here the raconteurs hesitated. Cold sweat sometimes broke out on their temples, because the other voice that emerged from the air-hole resembled Filhol's.

Was it still possible to believe, in this day and age, that the dead became revenants at the Tour-de-Kervoz?

That lasted until the night of August 15, 1800. That night, there was a great storm. Two sergeants crossed the heath, coming from Redon, then a foreigner carrying a valise.

Two gunshots resounded near the privet path and traces of blood were found in the *Trou-de-la-Dette*, to which Commander Malo came the following day in order to plant a cross.

Then the Tour-de-Kervoz remained mute and dark; neither noise nor light passed any longer through the ventilation

175

shaft. The *cloarec* Gabriel had quit the presbytery; Geneviève de Treguern did not return to the manor, and the voice of the deceased Filhol was no longer heard by frightened passers-by.

XVII. The First Apparition

It was 11 years before that terrible night, during the last days of the Empire. Marianne de Treguern was living in Paris with one of her relatives, who had made her as welcome as her young sister Laurence.

Marianne de Treguern could still pass for a pretty woman even though she was over 30. She was in an environment where the blade did not stay long in the scabbard. The Faubourg Saint-Germain was coming together again, little by little; a few petty rose-water conspiracies were born and died in the boudoirs while the Emperor turned Europe into a vast battlefield. Monsieur le Marquis du Castellat was a conspirator; it was politics that put him in touch with a young man of great ambition who, it was said, had connections with the German secret societies and had appointed himself as personal enemy of Napoleon. This young man was named Gabriel de Feuillans. Those who judged that the Emperor's defeat was probable set no limits upon the young man's potential.

One evening, there was a reception at the home of the relative who had taken over a maternal role in respect of Marianne and Laurence de Treguern. Gabriel chatted to Marianne alone in the embrasure of a bay window. Laurence. hidden among the crowd of her young companions, watched them attentively. Laurence had attained her 18th year. No one was close enough to Gabriel and Marianne to hear what they were saying, but indiscreet eyes translate speech, and Marianne's spoke of anger.

Monsieur le Marquis du Castellat was announced. Gabriel de Feuillans wore a singular smile. He whispered a few words in Marianne's ear, and the contagious smile passed from his lips to the young woman's. Monsieur le Marquis du Castellat, an honest middle-aged nobleman, neat and balding, who was playing his role as a gentleman conspirator very seriously, probably had no idea that Gabriel de Feuillans and

177

Mademoiselle de Treguern were talking about him. History does not say whether he had even noticed Marianne.

Instead of answering Gabriel, Marianne squinted to inspect the Marquis more carefully. Then she made an affirmative nod of the head.

After that, Gabriel, without losing his smile, kissed her hand with respectful gallantry, saying: "Farewell, then, Madame la Marquise!"

He withdrew. While he was crossing the room, his eyes met those of Laurence, and his expression changed completely, becoming clouded. He went over to her, as if to invite her to dance, and said to her in a low voice: "Laurence, I'm going to marry off your sister."

Laurence de Treguern possessed a rare beauty, but the delicate and charming pallor of her features already bore the traces of suffering. It was to her that poor Commander Malo had said: "Unhappy and beautiful."

A month later, the noble gossips of the Parisian *monde* had a story to tell: the Marquis du Castellat had run off with the elder of the demoiselles de Treguern, a dowerless orphan of excessive maturity. Why the elopement? The Marquis could not marry like anyone else! A few malicious tongues spoke of a certain petty romance whose hero was the handsome Gabriel; according to this version, the Marquis had eloped with Marianne because Marianne was engaged to Monsieur de Feuillans. Everyone, however, had noticed the attentions devoted by Monsieur de Feuillans to Laurence de Treguern, and everyone knew that he was a good friend of Monsieur du Castellat's. Be that as it may, the Marquis soon reappeared, radiant and glorious, with his young woman on his arm, like a trophy. The Hôtel du Castellat opened its brilliant salons, and Laurence went to live with her sister.

One evening in 1812, Laurence and Marianne found themselves alone in the latter's bedroom. The Marquis was conspiring somewhere, and Feuillans was in England. It had been a warm day; the Marquise, as was her habit, had put on fresh clothes, while Laurence was wearing a black dress, as if

178

she were in mourning. Laurence was responding to the Marquise's babble with a melancholy distraction.

"You're sad, sister," the Marquise observed.

"It was 12 years ago today," Laurence relied, "that our brother Filhol died."

The Marquise looked away with a shiver; she was the kind of person who avoided unhappy memories like the plague.

"He loved us dearly!" Laurence went on, with tears in her eyes. "And Geneviève, our poor sister, is doubtless dead too, since we have not heard mention of her for so many years."

Marianne shifted position in her winged armchair, fidgeting beneath the weight that oppressed her heart.

"And little Olympe!" Laurence went on. "Do you remember how she resembled Filhol, and how pretty she was in her crib?"

Marianne remained silent. Laurence got up and went to embrace her. "Goodnight, sister," she said, as she left, feeling the need to be alone in order to remember and to pray. Laurence de Treguern was a noble and beautiful soul.

The Marquise remained alone. When her chambermaid came in to light the candles, she sent her away rudely. The Marquise was in a bad mood.

Marianne's bedroom was a moderately large room on the top floor, decorated in a style that was a trifle austere for the first wife of a Marquis. There were two principal doors, one of which gave out into the antechamber while the other connected to Monsieur du Castellat's apartment. The windows overlooked the garden.

The Marquise, more sulky than sad, sank into the yielding cushions of her armchair. She blamed Laurence, who had called forth somber visions of the past at exactly the wrong moment. Whatever she did, those visions were obstinate in their persistence: her brother, laid out palely on his bed; her sister-in-law in tears with the baby in her arms... and mixed with all that, the strange face of the *cloarec* Gabriel.

179

The Marquise shut her eyes as she tried hard to take refuge in sleep. She did not know whether she was already asleep or still awake when she heard a voice, which whispered in her ear: "Marianne de Treguern!"

The Moon pierced the foliage of tall linden-trees and blanched the curtains at the windows. The Marquise saw Commander Malo standing next to her, holding by the hand a young girl scarcely out of infancy, whom the Marquise immediately recognized, by virtue of family resemblance, as her niece Olympe, the daughter of her brother Filhol. The Marquise had not seen her since she was in her crib. She tried to believe that she was dreaming; a kind of numbness enchained her senses.

"Hasn't she grown well?" said Commander Malo, a smile on his lived face.

Marianne heard herself reply, rebelling against the evidence: "I don't recognize her. It's not her!"

The girl's long eyelashes lowed over her large blue supplicant eyes. The Commander murmured: "Marianne, do you need Filhol and Geneviève to say to you: *This is our daughter*?"

"They're dead! They're dead!" cried the Marquise, shivering. "The dead don't come back!"

She saw the Commander extend his arm toward the part of the room where the canopied bed was concealed by its velvet curtains.

"Turn around, Marianne," he said, "and look!"

The bed-curtains were lifted up. The Marquise saw two beams of moonlight passing through the window converge and renew one another, striking the bed like the light of an enormous lantern: the bed on which Filhol and Geneviève were laid out side by side, their hands crossed upon their breasts. You would have been put in mind of one of those ancient tombs on which the ostentatious piety of families laid their male and female ancestors upon a mattress carved in stone. Filhol's colorless lips never moved, and nor did Geneviève's, but two feeble voices pronounced in unison: "This is our daughter!"

The Marquise tried to get up in order to flee, but she fell back in a faint...

When she woke up, her room was fully lit; the heavy folds of the closed curtains were draped around her bed. While the servants retired from the room in dismay, the young girl of her dream was holding a vial of smelling-salts under her nose, and Commander Malo, very white in his great black cloak, put out his bony hand to take her pulse.

She looked at the young girl, who was smiling at her timidly, and said as a chill sank into her bones: "Welcome to you, my niece!"

It was in this manner that Olympe de Treguern made her entry into the Hôtel du Castellat.

We have finished with the past; let us return to the present—which is to say, to the year 1820. It was about the time that the little diligence, reminiscent of a hearse, came into the courtyard of the Post Office in the Rue de Bouloy, carrying Commander Malo, Monsieur Privat and our friend Tanneguy. Dusk was falling; a line of lights was already running from window to window along the facade of the Hôtel du Castellat. Inside and outside, the preparations for the *fête* were being completed—for Madame la Marquise was giving a big party that evening.

From the groves and pathways of the magnificent garden to the summit of the terrace, an army of valets was busy setting out the carpet that covered the orchestra platform, placing bowls of flowers in the amphitheater, arranging the rustic chairs around the enclosed garden. Here and there, in the depths of the arbors, a few yew-trees were lit up, while the last garlands were hooked on to columns of foliage flourishing with their festoons.

The illumination of the Marquise's gardens was no trivial business; effects had to be arranged as in a theatre; it was necessary to extend clarity to the edges of the ballroom, while casting mysterious shadows into the grottoes. At the end of a proud avenue of lindens, there was a certain Louis V pavilion which it was extremely important to light up as brightly as by day. This pavilion marked the boundary of the Marquise's property on the side of the nameless sprawling village—then composed of workshops and shanties—that has since become the *quartier* François I. The weather had beaten down the branches of neighboring trees to the level of the terrace roof; it was as if the genteel pavilion was lost in the midst of a chaotic mass of verdure.

In a collector's display-cases, among the rare and valuable items, you often find some favorite curiosity that is worth as much as the rest of the museum. This was the Louis XV pavilion in the rich and gracious garden of the Hôtel du Castellat: it was the master-gem of the jewel-box, and no one ever came to the Marquise's parties without declaring that the pavilion was a small marvel. They only saw its exterior, though; what was behind those delicate walls decorated with sculptures, no one knew. Marble vases bearing enormous sheaves of red geraniums stood on the steps leading up to the door. The Marquise's hospitality stopped at the top step. More than one person asked themselves, occasionally, what the Marquise hid in that charming redoubt.

A young domestic servant and a serving girl, armed with long poles, were lighting the lanterns artfully disposed under the lindens. The serving girl had a Morbihan accent. Her eyes shone with intelligence; she laughed as others breathed, incessantly and without pause. The houseboy had not merely the accent but also the fine figure of a lad from the region between Vannes and Redon. He was called Josille;[54] we already know Vevette's name.

It seemed that she was ready for anything, this amiable Vevette, and that she was not at all lazy, for she spent her time as she should while awaiting the return of her mistress. She was, to be sure, perfectly ready and fully dressed for the party; she was wearing a smart costume that was, properly speaking, neither Parisian nor Breton, but recalled the simplicity fashionable among comic-opera villagers. It fit her like a glove, and Josille liked it so much that he was grilling the branches of the lindens instead of lighting the lanterns.

Josille was as plump as a quail, a ruddy-faced and rather good-looking lad. He was awkward, and stammered slightly when talking, but chattered more than a magpie. In Orlan, his native parish, he was considered a shrewd fellow.

"Damn it, Vevette!" he said, "we didn't need this many candles to amuse ourselves back home in Orlan. With the money that all these lanterns cost, we could practically set up home together!"

"A fine husband you'd make, Josille!" the girl replied, shrugging her shoulders. "You don't even know how to light a wick—your pole's been fumbling around that lantern for a quarter of an hour."

Admittedly, the boy had no aptitude for the work; if all the lighters had been like him, the Marquise's garden would not have been lit up till the following morning.

"Listen here, Vevette," he murmured, with a certain emotion, "you weren't as brave as this in the country—I'm always looking at you to see how beautiful you've become."

Vevette obviously had no intention of letting the conversation stray on to this sentimental terrain, for she asked: "Have you seen them yourself, the Three Rooks?"

Josille almost dropped his rod. "It's getting too dark for talking about them!" he stammered.

"Bah!" said Vevette. "We're a long way from the *Grand'Lande*, and the Three Rooks won't come as far as Paris to look for you."

"How do you know?" said Josille, casting an anxious glance into the grove.

"By damn, my lad," Vevette cried, laughing all the more loudly at her companion's seriousness, "if you're afraid of your own shadow, you've done badly to land up in Madame la Marquise's household. This is a house of revenants—they talk of nothing but devilries, and there's a sorcerer living in that pavilion you see over there."

"A sorcerer?" Josille repeated.

"A true sorcerer! But I'll protect you against him, if you'll tell me how Valérie-*la-Morte* is."

"It's funny, all the same," the boy murmured, "to be talking about the Three Rooks of Orlan and Valérie-*la-Morte* like this, in the big city."

"I'll bet," said Vevette, "that Madame la Marquise, the Chevalier de Noisy and the all the keepers of the Sabbath who are gossiping while the others dance will be harping on about that story all night long!"

"Is that how they spent their time at parties here?"

"Light it, Josille, light it, or we'll be late! Is she young, Valérie?"

Josille presented the tip of his pole to a recalcitrant lantern for the tenth time, but the klanten appeared not to notice. "I don't know if she's young or old," he replied. "Anyway, spirits don't have ages the way we do."

"Where did you see her?"

"Behind the church, in the sunken path that passes by the cemetery."

"Are you absolutely sure that it was her?"

"Am I sure? Ah, Vevette, I still have a chill in my spine! When you left the neighborhood, I was so upset I caught a fever. To cure myself, I was paying court to Scholastique, who has a bit of pasture and two cows—nice cows! So, one day, coming out of church after Mass, she hit me in the eye, playfully, with a rock and I paid her back by ducking her neck-deep in Menain Pond. How I laughed! She had mud up to her ears and the lads who pulled her out were holding their noses—you have to laugh, don't you? Anyway, she got back into my good books, as they say, in due course, and in the end, everyone said to me: 'Josille, my lad, marry her or you'll be the death of her!' "

Vevette, as nimble as a fairy, continued lighting up. Josille followed her, telling his story in a lachrymose fashion.

"Oh, what a bold fellow you are!" Vevette cried. "Did she finally get a taste for you, this Scholastique who has a bit of pasture and two cows?"

"Nice cows!" Josille went on. "So Scholastique said to me: 'Come at dusk so that we can arrange the wedding.' I did. There was no Moon; the three of them were chatting at the end of the old Avenue de Treguern, in front of the *Château-sans-Terre*..."

"The Three Rooks?" put in Vevette, who had stopped to listen.

"Absolutely and truly, my Vevette: the Three Rooks, black as moles. They were looking at Monsieur Gabriel's new château and saying: 'That will come to us with the rest when the hour sounds!' I put my head down, covering my ears so as not to hear their voices, for their words bring misfortune to everyone who listens to them. Near the *Pierre-des-Païens*, I saw a woman running in front of me and I ran after her, thinking that it was Scholastique—but it wasn't Scholastique at all, and I'd rather have found myself facing Dowager Le Brec herself on a Sunday night! The woman stopped on the sunken path to wait for me. I'm certain that I saw her eyes glowing like charcoal in the middle of her white face. The wind set her black hair afloat, as Mam'selle Olympe's curls are said to do. Her figure was so slender that one could tell that she had no flesh under her belt, although our demoiselle Olympe—who's alive, thank God—has a figure every bit as fine!"

"Did she speak to you?" Vevette asked then.

"She told me to go away," Josille replied. "And when I heard Mam'selle Olympe's voice, afterwards..."

"Go on—you're mad!" cried Vevette. She was still laughing, but a more skillful observer than little Josille would have been able to see that she was now very uneasy.

"There it is!" he went on. "Our demoiselle Olympe can't be in Paris and Orlan at the same time, that's the truth—and then again, why would our demoiselle be climbing over the cemetery wall?"

"Ah!" said Vevette. "*La Morte* climbed over the cemetery wall?"

"Yes indeed. When she told me to go away, I only did half what I was told. I hid behind the hedge. I saw her, as clearly as I see you, slipping between the graves and jumping into the church through a window that someone had left open because of the heat."

"And what did she do in the church?"

"That's something I didn't dare to watch, Vevette. I saw light escaping through the sacristy windows and I took myself off home smartly. Would you have gone closer?"

"Of course," the girl replied, bravely. "Let's go, Josille. You don't need your pole—climb up the steps and light the lanterns up there!"

They were at the end of the avenue of lindens, and the graceful facade of the Louis XV pavilion was in front of them.

Josille started to go up the staircase. Vevette heard him cry out loudly. "There! There!" he yelped, letting himself fall on the sand. "They're inside there!"

Pale light was shining through the windows of the pavilion. Vevette launched herself forwards intrepidly, climbing the first steps. Josille repeated: "There! There! Three of them! I saw them—and the Tomb of Tanneguy too!" He went on, weeping profusely: "Ah, Lord God, when spirits get hold of you, it's all over! I've left the country, I've lost Scholastique, her bit of pasture and two cows... such nice cows. I've covered leagues and leagues so as not to see all that any more, and here's the Tomb of Tanneguy, followed me all the way from the choir at Orlan to Paris! And the Three Rooks too!"

"There's nothing there," said little Vevette, from the top of the steps. "You're dreaming while wide awake!"

Footsteps were heard at the other end of the path. The light that had shone for an instant inside the pavilion was abruptly extinguished. Josille was cowering at the foot of the staircase; he was trembling so strongly that Vevette felt the steps shake. "You can't see anything?" he stammered. "Then it's me they want! They were there, beside the Tomb, all three standing, and there was something like a huge skeleton behind them, leaning against the wall." He interrupted himself to let out a stifled exclamation. Then he said: "Hold on!"

He could not speak immediately. His mouth opened convulsively and his extended finger pointed at the bushes which hid the wall girdling the garden, to the right of the pavilion. That whole section of the Marquise's little park was plunged in complete darkness. The lights stopped at the linden avenue. To the left of the path, from the pavilion to the ballroom, all was already resplendent; the festooned garlands of flowers stood out as far as the eye could see, but the nearness of this brightness only served to render the darkness more profound in the unilluminated part of the garden.

From the top of the staircase, Vevette followed Josille's pointing finger. She thought that she could, indeed, see a confused movement in the bushes, but the lanterns of the facade, which were in the process of being lit, hampered her view.

"Who goes there?" she cried, boldly—for little Vevette was not afraid of anything.

Josille picked himself up, thinking that the voices of the Rooks of Orlan's cemetery were about to burst forth like three thunderclaps.

It was a soft female voice that replied: "It's me, Vevette. I'm waiting for you."

Josille, however, was perfectly sure that he had seen the three men from the pavilion, be they living men or shades, gliding silently between the tree-trunks.

Vevette leapt down the staircase and threw herself into the bushes, as lightly as a hind.

In the path through the lindens, the distant footsteps they had heard before were drawing closer. Josille's stricken mind had already lost its equilibrium; he thought he must be dreaming when he saw a kind of procession approaching, composed of a valet in livery carrying a lantern that was rendered all-but-useless by the illuminations, a thin, pale and stiff figure dressed in black from head to toe, and three Post Office porters, each one loaded down by a large white pinewood box.

There was no one in the parish of Orlan who did not know the redoubtable silhouette of Commander Malo; evening conversations often turned to the subject of the man who only had to hear someone mentioned, let alone look at him, to know whether he would lie or die. Even the least superstitious shivered at the thought of the fatal Veil that fell before the eyes of a Treguern when death lay in wait for its designated prey— and little Josille was by no means the least superstitious.

Vevette had been right to say that the pavilion was inhabited by a sorcerer: Josille saw that only too well, now! He ran into a clump of trees to leave the way clear for the terrible

Commander. The latter came to a halt before the door of his pavilion; he ordered the porters to deposit the boxes on the steps.

"It's heavy!" one of them said. "While we're here, you'd better let us take them inside."

Having put a key into the lock on the door, the Commander turned back and made a sign to the servant in livery. "Put them down!" the latter said, dryly.

The three porters set down their burdens and wiped their sweaty brows. The valet paid them and sent them away. When they had gone, not without darting curious glances at the door, Josille noticed that the valet did not offer to help Commander Malo take the boxes inside; instead, he said: "Madame la Marquise hopes that Monsieur will do her the honor of attending her celebration."

Malo de Treguern turned his gaze—which was firm but slightly haggard—towards the valet. "Her celebration!" he repeated, while a bleak smile strayed across his lips. "There will be more than one celebration tonight! Leave me."

The valet bowed respectfully and withdrew. As he heard the sound of the servant's footsteps fading away on the sand of the pathway, poor Josille felt his anxiety growing, for there was no longer anyone else there, and he was all alone with the sorcerer.

The door of the pavilion opened; the interior was utterly dark. Malo de Treguern came down the steps as far as the first box and pronounced a few mysterious words over it, whose meaning Josille could not make out. Malo tried to lift the box, but he was weak and the box was heavy; his efforts were unavailing. "Will the person who is hiding in the bushes come to my aid?" he said.

Josille would have run 100 leagues if his will had been free, but an unknown power pushed him forward and he crossed the path without knowing what he was doing. Commander Malo knotted a handkerchief around his eyes as a blindfold.

One of the boxes was lifted. Josille climbed up the steps; he heard Commander Malo breathing effortfully in front of him. Josille's blood ran cold in his veins once he had passed over the threshold and felt the cold, stale air of the interior. It was here that he had seen the Tomb of Tanneguy, the skeleton, the powdered bones and the three phantoms.

"Now the second!" the Commander said.

They made two further journeys; then Josille found himself on the steps in front of the closed door. The blindfold was no longer covering his eyes; he rubbed his swollen eyelids and looked around, dazzled by the illuminations embracing the garden. A reddish light appeared at the windows of the pavilion, then went out, as if someone had drawn thick curtains over the casements.

Josille would not have stayed in that spot for an empire, but his legs were numb beneath the weight of his body, and the sense of being abandoned was crushing. What would he not have given to hear the joyful voice of Vevette?

He thought he could see her, Vevette, in the shadow-filled clump of bushes where he had hidden himself a few minutes before. Something white appeared there, in the darkness. Josille's fear gave him courage, and he got under way, calling out to the young girl. The white object made a sudden movement and fled, gliding between the trees like mist. At the same time, Vevette came out, laughing and singing like the most cheerful person in the world.

As he opened his mouth to interrogate her, Vevette put her hand on his lips, saying: "Shh! Listen!"

In the darkness, the dull sound of a door-knocker rapping on its plaque was audible.

A knocker! A plaque! A door! In the midst of that vegetation, under those huge trees, in that sort of little virgin forest where there was no trace of any habitation. It had to be a dream.

"Wait for me in the avenue," the young girl said, blithely, plunging with a will into the thickest of the undergrowth.

Josille distinctly heard the groaning of hinges nearby—but what does it matter what one can hear, once has once strayed into the land of chimeras? After a minute, Josille saw Vevette reappear, as she had promised. She was accompanied by a short man, decently dressed and wearing spectacles, who had absolutely nothing supernatural about him.

"Josille," said Vevette, who seemed to be having difficulty repressing a mischievous smile, "take this gentleman to the house, where Madame la Marquise is waiting for him. Announce him as Monsieur Privat."

XIX. The Marquise's Boudoir

Madame la Marquise du Castellat was getting ready for the party—a serious business, for Marianne de Treguern was already over 40. Her hair was thinning. her figure was filling out, and a certain fatigue was evident in her puffy features. There was obviously a struggle going on within her between present anxiety, augmented by the ineradicable sorrow of memory, and her determination to numb herself with forgetfulness.

The boudoir in which she was ensconced was a small room, furnished in the fashion of the last years of the Empire. On the same evening when Olympe de Treguern, still a child, had been introduced into the house in the mysterious fashion that we have related, the Marquise had abandoned her bedroom for another apartment. Since then, she had never wanted to set eyes on the place where the frightful vision had appeared to her.

Four portraits encased in similar frames hung from the walls of the boudoir. Firstly, there was the bewigged Marquis du Castellat: an honest face, polite, slightly lacking in intelligence, maintaining about his thin lips the eternal smile of society portraits. Facing him, the Marquise, in a white satin dress, breathed in the perfume of a bouquet of roses. To the left of the chimney, Laurence de Treguern, accurately rendered—which is to say, perfectly beautiful—fixed her melancholy gaze upon the fourth portrait, which was that of Gabriel de Feuillans.

Gabriel, in this portrait, did not look any older than 30. A black cloak was draped over his shoulders, and his white hand, delicately veined, held an open book. His was a pensive and austere figure; his hair was positioned high on his head; the contours of his face were compressed near the temples but swelled out at the cheeks and described an exceptionally harmonious oval around the chin. His eyes were narrow, bordered by large lids, their gaze possessed of a great pride. His nose and mouth seemed to be sculpted in bronze.

At the time when Madame la Marquise du Castellat had been painted, she could still be referred to as "pretty Marianne." Beneath her pretentious coiffure her features—regular, but rounded and characterless—were reminiscent of the noble beauty of Laurence. Laurence had been painted in the same year that she died, and those who had known her found something almost celestial—the vague sadness of her last days—in the soft but penetrating gaze of her likeness.

It had been a long time since Madame la Marquise had borne any resemblance to that white and pink portrait smiling from the wainscot, but tonight she appeared to have put on ten years more, so somber and anxious was she. She was sitting at her dressing-table, and her chambermaid was sewing her impoverished tresses with a superabundance of flowers.

"There is a milord," said the maid, continuing a conversation already commenced, "who wanted the little house with the green shutters over the way, but Monsieur Stéphane has paid I don't know how many thousands of francs to get it."

"So he's rich, this Monsieur Stéphane?" asked the Marquise, pronouncing the name with an affectation of profound indifference.

"I should think so!" replied the maid. "He broke the bank at Frascati's.[55] Does Madame la Marquise know that the windows of the little house face the casements of Mademoiselle Olympe's apartment?"

"No," said Marianne de Treguern, turning her head. "I never noticed that.

"Directly opposite! And not a single tree in between! Now, I think, Monsieur Stéphane will come to his town house more often."

The Marquise put on a show of taking a close look at the work of her coiffure, and pointed out a few faults, as if to put a stop to the conversation—but it appeared that the maid, Juliette, was given to speaking her mind.

"Such a near neighbor!" she went on, while her skilled hands made corrections according to her mistress' instructions. "And a young man who moves in high society! I'm sure that won't displease Madame la Marquise. Monsieur de Feuillans knows him—knows him well, and often goes to see him."

"Monsieur de Feuillans does what he wants," the Marquise said, dryly. Then, testing her coiffure with both hands, she added: "That will do, Juliette, I'll call you to put on my jewels."

Juliette immediately went to the door, but before going out a malicious glance darted from beneath her eyelids. Many a philosopher has wondered why every woman has an intimate enemy in her personal maid.

As soon as she was alone, Marianne de Treguern, Marquise du Castellat got up and began pacing slowly back and forth. A darker cloud had fallen upon her face, and wrinkles were creasing her forehead.

"Stéphane!" she murmured. "Why does Gabriel leave me in such uncertainty?"

Juliette had taken away the candelabra that had been on her dressing-table; the room was no longer illuminated by anything more than a globular lamp placed on a small bureau, whose light fell on scattered letters. All the letters were still sealed; as the Marquise passed close beside her little bureau, she turned her eyes away, as if a secret repugnance had prevented her from opening her mail this evening.

For some unknown reason, the uncertain glow of the lamp gave the elegant bureau an appearance of desolation. The four portraits gazed at one another sadly in the half-light. The Marquise let herself fall into an armchair and put her head between her hands, at the risk of spoiling her freshly made-up hair. The lap-dog drowsing in a corner got up, stretched its obese loins, and came to roll at its mistress' feet, growling plaintively.

"Stéphane!" murmured the Marquise for a second time, sighing deeply. "What good does it do to rack my brains? Can a young man of 20 resemble the infant that one carries to a baptism? Besides, I know that the young man is at Château-le-Brec..."

As she pronounced the words *young man*, her voice altered slightly. She plucked a letter from the table at random and opened it mechanically. It was a blue-tinted paper with a printed heading; the writing was in the firm and full hand that practice gives to lawyers.

The late Marquis du Castellat, having no children, the letter said, *was at liberty to dispose of the totality of his wealth in favor of a stranger. The legacy in favor of Mademoiselle Olympe de Treguern is regular and perfectly legal; the document appears to me to be in order, and there are no grounds for litigation.*

The Marquise crumpled the letter.

"She knows that!" she murmured. "How long shall I be mistress here? Perhaps as long as I pay due recognition to her generosity in letting me stay in her house!"

She took another letter, and held it in her hands without raising it to her eyes.

"Who knows?" she thought, aloud, while a mocking smile was born on her lips. "Gabriel married me once, as well, and I call myself the Marquise du Castellat. Gabriel wanted to marry Laurence, and Laurence is dead. Now Gabriel wants to marry this one—who knows?"

The letter she was holding in her hand was a thick greyish-brown sheet, folded ineptly; the large letters of the address were spidery. When the Marquise's gaze finally fell upon this missive, strayed by some mysterious means into her elegant boudoir, she shivered and went white.

"The Dowager!" she stammered. "The Dowager has written to me!"

She broke the seal with a feeble hand and read:

Marianne, you did well to run away; my nights are terrible, and I often see those who are dead. What I did, I did for you and for Gabriel; you have both abandoned me. Perhaps there is a Providence. Malo de Treguern has slept in his

195

tower; he says that the hour has come when the old tree will put forth new growth. May I be dead when Treguern rises again!

This is to warn you that you will see the child; he wanted to leave, as the other left some time ago. It isn't me that chased him away. For a long time, though, I've had my doubts; they were born so close to one another, those two. We deceived the priest; Fanchette could have deceived us. The child does not have the face of a Le Brec. When you see him, look at him closely. Gabriel looked at him, the last time he was here, but said nothing to me. But why should a man love his child, when he does not love his mother?

The hour of the last battle is nigh. The voices that used to talk to me in the silence of the night have fallen silent; my blind eyes no longer see the future. You are still young enough to suffer in this life; adieu, Marianne, we have built on sand, and my tenderness has been your misfortune.

Françoise Le Brec de Kervoz.

Postscriptum: The Three Rooks have vanished; La Morte *is no longer seen. The locals have found the Treguern coat-of-arms nailed to the main door of the* 'Château-sans-Terre,' *as they call the palace that Gabriel has ordered to be built on the place where Filhol's manor was; everyone says that Treguern will return. Privat, the advocate who defended Etienne 20 years ago, has left for Paris. Take care—and warn Gabriel, if you have not separated your fortunes from his.*

Terror and dismay were painted on the Marquise's features; every word of this letter was, for her, a threat. While she closed it again, she noticed a little square-folded sheet on the table whose address was in an unknown handwriting.

This sheet contained but two lines, and said:

I shall have the honor of presenting myself today at the home of Madame la Marquise du Castellat at eight o'clock precisely.

It was signed with the name of Privat.

The Marquise turned to the clock with a start; the hands were just approaching eight o'clock.

"It's him!" she cried. "It's the man who undertook Etienne's defense. Why is he coming to my house? I don't want to see him."

She sounded her handbell violently, and said to Juliette, who came running: "Warn the concierge immediately! I am not at home to a Monsieur Privat, who will arrive at eight o'clock."

As Juliette turned to obey, she found herself face to face on the threshold with a short man, decently dressed, who smiled and took off his hat to her politely. He stood aside to let the maid pass, and advanced towards the Marquise with aplomb, saying: "Exact to the minute, as you see, Madame! Monsieur Privat, advocate, who has covered 100 leagues to have the honor of presenting you with his respects." He bowed, turned about-face and went to close the door in Juliette's face.

The Marquise stared at him in astonishment.

Monsieur Privat was much better dressed than he had been in the courtyard of the Post Office; he wore black trousers that were almost new, creased above stout well-polished shoes, a very proper black coat that was slightly too large, a black waistcoat cut in a old-fashioned way, and a beautiful white cravat formed into a rosette that would have been the envy of a country bridegroom. His nose was pointed, his mouth wide and smiling; his small eyes were peering over enormous spectacles whose lenses were as round as coins. His thin and colorful cheeks moved up and down as he spoke; his improbably high forehead terminated in a bald peak, and the hair at his temples, artistically swept back, tried in vain to darken the nudity of his mountainous skull.

All of that might have been rather ugly, but it was all content with itself: carefree, lively, feverish even, and enlivened by a small measure of rather spiritual jollity.

"My dear lady," he said, coming back toward the Marquise and adopting a tone of benevolent bonhomie, "I don't suppose you can place me. We have both grown old. For myself, I confess that I would have had great difficulty recognizing you."

Marianne de Treguern darted a glance at the cord of her bell, but she did not touch it. "Would you care to tell me, Monsieur," she murmured "to what I owe the honor of your visit?"

Instead of answering, Monsieur Privat continued cheerfully: "It's a fair distance, you know, from the Marché des Innocents, where I live, to the Allée des Veuves! My means don't permit me to hire carriages to any parts of the field; I've come on foot. If Madame la Marquise will permit me..."

Marianne de Treguern did not wait for him finish; she gestured towards a chair with her hand. It appeared, however, that Monsieur Privat preferred armchairs; he pushed back the proffered chair and rolled a wing-chair to face the Marquise. Having done that, he sat down, released a joyful sigh and caressed his old-fashioned waistcoat like those great lords of comedy who wear a ruff so that they may crumple it knowingly.

"I know your young neighbor Stéphane Gontier very well," he said, without preamble, still peering at the Marquise over his round spectacles. "If he had wanted to, I could have made a lawyer of him."

"I rarely receive Monsieur Stéphane Gontier," Marianne Treguern put in.

"Bah!" said the little man. "That's the way it is in Paris, it seems. One lives next door, and one scarcely sees one another. I would be pleased to bring the young man to you more often; he has honest principles and good manners."

The Marquise tried to smile.

"Is that the reason you came, Monsieur?" she asked.

"I love legal cases," replied Monsieur Privat, pushing up his spectacles with a thrust of his stiff and precise finger. "My father was a court usher with the Seneschal of Redon. I was born into it; my crib was surrounded by lists and my breast opens out to breathe the air of cases—that's my native atmosphere!"

198

Monsieur Privat's voice became animated, and his little eyes shone behind his blue-tinted spectacles. The Marquise had folded her arms on her bosom. An instinctive fear told her that the bizarrerie of these preliminaries masked a serious attack. She waited.

"In my father's office," the little man went on, in an emotional tone, "there was a set of piegeonholes, extending from the floor to the ceiling, filled with green folders that could no longer be closed, so full were they; there were bundles squeezed into corners and thrown in heaps like sheaves of ripe corn; there were piles of dusty papers whose rebellious corners were dog-eared, and whose margins were covered in tiny handwriting, cramped, mixed-up and illegible. Why, your family's file—the Treguern dossier—would have filled this boudoir all on its own! Ah, that's what I call a beautiful dossier. Enough papers to ruin a King, or to give a beggar a princely fortune, as fate might dictate! Well, Madame, you may believe, if you will, that—child though I was—I deciphered all of that! And all of that was not yet enough for me!"

He sat up straight in his wing-chair. "I want more!" he cried, with a rush of pride. "I've dreamed of a case... a case whose like has never been seen! Something complicated, inextricable: an imbroglio with a thousand characters, a kind of *danse macabre* wheeling deliriously around a mountain of gold!"

The little man did not have the air of a poet, however. Marianne de Treguern hoped for a moment that he might be mad. We say that she hoped because, involuntarily, the vague sensation of dread of which we have spoken was growing in her mind.

Monsieur Privat had retreated into the depths of his wing-chair. "Interests in conflict," he went on, savoring his dream, "which become divided and confused, like a tangled skein. People who change their names, lost birth certificates, false testimonies; living men who pretend to be dead and dead men who return; long-past murders... what a case, Madame la Marquise: a heroic and splendid affair! A nocturnal and pitiless struggle such as is fought, it's said, between the Indians of the North American forests! An unremitting battle in Limbo, an Ann Radcliffe romance, a Miltonic epic! Insensate efforts, atrocious betrayals, the Civil Code sharpened like a sword-blade, the Penal Code slashed as by an axe! Insane sums shoveled hither and yon, impossible phantasmagorias in the midst of our incredulous world! And me, alone—me, you understand—in that profound darkness, penetrating the shadows—I don't know how—with the eyes of a short-eared owl, lifting the veils, unraveling the mysteries, bringing together all the strands of that gigantic intrigue in this hand here!"

He stretched out his hand before him, as stiff and wrinkled as an old woman's. "Do you understand?" he added, mopping the sweat from his brow.

"No," murmured Madame la Marquise du Castellat, perhaps dishonestly.

The little man half-closed his eyes and stared at her. All the enthusiasm that had possessed him a few moments before had gone, as if by magic. "No?" he repeated, abruptly changing his tone. "Well, everyone can't have the same tastes as me. What I said was in response to the question Madame la Marquise did me the honor of addressing to me on the subject of the motive for my visit. One fine day, when I'm no longer searching, I shall find that immense case of which I dreamed in my youth. Chance has given me a role to play here, and if I have crossed the threshold of this house, it is because Madame la Marquise is involved in the same case as me."

Marianne de Treguern made a forceful gesture of negation.

"It is August 15!" the little man went on, taking no notice of the gesture, "And it's 20 years, to the day, since your young neighbor Stéphane Gontier was baptized in the parish of Orlan. Another child was brought to the font at the same time. I made the journey from Brittany to Paris with that other child—who is a handsome lad, I give you my word! I have come to see you, Madame la Marquise, because I need to know which of these two young people is your son, and which is Tanneguy, the last heir to the house of Treguern."

The little man had moved his wing-chair back slightly to put himself in a position to see the effect these last words produced on the Marquise. The Marquise kept her eyes firmly fixed on the floor. As if it had understood that its mistress's sentiments had become hostile or apprehensive, the lap-dog set itself in front of her, and shook its fleecy fur valiantly.

"Good day, *bichon*," said the little man, stroking it. "So you don't know the friends of the house? I have a dog of my own, but it's a barbet."[56] He removed his spectacles and began cleaning them carefully, with the aid of a silk scarf that he took from the side pocket of his coat. His weary eyes were blinking in the lamplight.

"You must think that you are strongly armed against me, Monsieur," the Marquise said, after a silence, "to be so bold as to speak to me thus."

When Monsieur Privat made no response, she stood up angrily and cried: "But before anything else—how do you come to be here?"

"In the capacity of a dancer, for the party," Monsieur Privat replied, simply. "In the country, the ladies are generous enough to find that I do not spoil a quadrille."

The Marquise looked directly at him. In any other circumstances, she would doubtless have had great difficulty preventing herself from laughing, for the little man replaced his spectacles with minute care and, with a conceited gesture, replaced the two tufts of hair that formed a Gothic arch over the top of his skull—but it seemed that the Marquise was not in a good humor this evening.

"We're talking at cross purposes," she said, dryly. "I want to know under whose auspices..."

"I present myself to you?" the little man finished, as he saw the Marquise hesitate. "That's quite understandable." He looked at one of the portraits hanging on the wall. "But how these Parisian artists capture a resemblance!" he went on. "One might think that one were looking at Monsieur de Feuillans himself!"

"You know Monsieur de Feuillans?"

"I have that honor, Madame."

"And it was Monsieur de Feuillans...?"

"Dear Lord, no!" said Monsieur Privat. "Had I needed a guarantor, I could have chosen one within your own household."

"Ah!" said the Marquise.

"I could, for example," the little man went on, "have selected Commander Malo, or better still..."

The little man stopped. Except for the Commander, there was only Olympe de Treguern in the Hôtel du Castellat. While the Marquise's curious gaze fixed itself upon her guest, she slowly repeated: "Or better still?"

Monsieur Privat plunged a hand into his coat pocket and pulled out a thick wad of papers; from among these papers he chose one, which he presented politely to the Marquise. It was simply a formal letter of invitation.

At bottom, there was nothing very extraordinary about it. Everyone knows that letters of invitation to grand houses sometimes go astray. Nevertheless, the Marquise lowered her eyes again, her unease redoubled. The little man was taking on fantastic proportions in her eyes.

"Although I was born in a provincial town," Monsieur Privat went on, refolding his letter carefully, "I am no stranger to the customs of high society. I know what the duties are of the mistress of a house on a day like this, and I do not want to take up too much of your time, Madame la Marquise. The quickest way, it seems to me, would be to answer my questions frankly."

"And if I don't want to answer your questions, Monsieur?"

"As you said just now, Madame, I am strong! Not armed against you, exactly; at the end of the day, I wish you neither good nor ill. But I am very strong. And as I have a direct interest to instruct me, I shall use all my strength to obtain from you all the information I need." He coughed lightly, and went on: "Well, is it Stéphane, or is it Tanneguy?"

As Marianne de Treguern remained silent, he extended a finger towards Dowager Le Brec's letter, which was half-open on the table.

"I know that handwriting!" he said.

The Marquise made a reflexive gesture, as if she wanted to snatch the letter out of his sight.

"I know what's in it," the little man said, placidly.

Suddenly, real fear was manifest in the Marquise's eyes.

Monsieur Privat leaned over to stroke the dog, which shook its fleece and showed the double row of tiny white teeth mounted in pink satin. "Pull yourself together, my dear lady," he murmured. "Time's passing; if we can only talk briefly, all the more reason for talking straight. Twenty years have passed since I put my foot across the threshold of this labyrinth; for 20 years I have been wandering inside it without a moment's rest. You should not forget that my first step on the path I have taken was the defense of Sergeant Etienne, presented by me before the assize court at Vannes. I know, therefore, *a priori*, everything that Etienne knows himself. Now, Etienne's opinion is that a fraud was perpetrated at the baptism, and that each of the children received the name intended for the other."

"The midwife, Fanchette, is dead," murmured Marianne de Treguern, giving up the struggle.

"The midwife Fanchette made no revelation before dying?"

"Nothing."

"And the midwife Fanchette was the only one who knew the secret?"

"The only one."

"Then, you do not know yourself...?"

"I have doubts."

Monsieur Privat made a face, in which it was impossible to read a complimentary meaning.

"Damn!" he muttered. "You've had those doubts for 20 years, Madame la Marquise! That's skepticism unbridled! As one grows old, one learns something new every day, but I still don't understand the workings of maternal love."

The Marquise pursed her lips.

"Let's leave that," Monsieur Privat continued, abruptly. "The famous *cloarec* was named Gabriel, isn't that so?"

Marianne de Treguern nodded her head affirmatively.

"And Monsieur de Feuillans is also named Gabriel," the little man continued. "Is it not possible that Monsieur de Feuillans knows the midwife's secret?"

"He doesn't know it," the Marquise replied.

"And his own secret?" he said, slowly. "Do you know that? Why, on August 16, 1800, he sent 100,000 francs to London? And why, every year since then, on the same date, he pays an unknown creditor the enormous sum of 4,000 pounds sterling? Always 100,000 francs!"

"No," said Marianne de Treguern, fanning herself with her embroidered handkerchief. "I don't know anything about any of that."

"Myself, I've done well on that road!" murmured Monsieur Privat, as if talking to himself. "I know many things. But the labyrinth is so vast! I'm not at the end. From 1800 to 1804, so far as I am concerned, there is a void—and yet the annuities were paid regularly. In 1804, there was the story of Jérôme Clément..." He stopped to observe the Marquise. "Did you hear, Madame?" he went on. "I said Jérôme Clément."

"Jérôme Clément?" repeated Mariane de Treguern.

"The rich physician of Laval."

"It's the first time I've heard the name," the Marquise said, more calmly.

The little man sat back against the back of his armchair and scrutinized her more intently; there was profound surprise in his eyes. *Is that lack of conscience?* he thought, *or is it true ignorance? Well, a lap-dog is a peevish, egotistic, intolerable animal, but it is not aggressive. Perhaps this good woman has*

closed her eyes so determinedly that she really has seen noth-
ing. It's improbable, but it's possible.

"From 1804 to 1810," he went on, aloud, "another la-
cuna, until the affair of Johann-Maria Worms, a diamond merchant of Cologne. I dare say you have some knowledge of
that?"

"None," replied the Marquise. "I don't understand any of
your questions, which seem to me increasingly strange."

"Even in speaking to me thus, my dear lady," Monsieur
Privat said, emotionlessly, "you are still teaching me something. I beg you to believe that I have excellent reasons for
subjecting you to this annoying interrogation. Besides, these
two affairs are only episodes—tragic ones, it's true. I've been
to Laval and I've been to Cologne; to tell the truth, I didn't
think that you could tell me anything new about them. It's
understood, then, that Monsieur de Feuillans has spared you
the excessively dramatic part of his confidences, and has only
acquainted you with those intrigues that constitute the lighter
side of his work."

Marianne de Treguern opened her eyes wide, and the little man could see that he was speaking a language that was
unintelligible to her.

"And yet," he repeated, furrowing his brows in spite of
himself, "you know that Monsieur de Feuillans has made
plans to acquire the ancient Treguern domains—all the land
between the Vilaine and the Oust? You know that Monsieur
de Feuillans had built the insolent palace they call the *Château-sans-Terre* on the site of the old Treguern Manor? You
know that Monsieur de Feuillans has taken steps to obtain the
right to wear the Treguern name and coat-of-arms?"

"Those projects were initiated," the Marquise replied, "in
the days when Monsieur de Feuillans was to marry my
younger sister Laurence. I supported them because the name
of Treguern no longer had a male representative."

"At that time, was that your sincere belief?"

"Yes, Monsieur."

"And now?"

"My belief is unchanged."

"And the projects continue," the little man went on, with a bitter smile, "because Monsieur de Feuillans desires to marry your niece Olympe, the daughter of the last Treguern. Well, Madame, if it had pleased God to leave only one arm to that poor boy of our acquaintance, all this would have been finished a long time ago!"

The clock chimed nine; the little man got up and walked around the room, stopping briefly in front of each portrait.

"Filhol's is not here," he muttered between clenched teeth, "and neither is Geneviève's." He turned abruptly to face the Marquise, whose sly gaze was following him. *What difference is there*, he thought, *between a woman who knows everything and a woman who tells herself that she does not want to know?* "When do you think your sister-in-law Geneviève died?" he went on, aloud.

"She left the manor on the day of the baptism," the Marquise replied. "Since then, I have not seen her again."

"Living... but otherwise?"

The Marquise started, and lowered her eyes. Monsieur Privat paused for a longer interval, meditative and almost melancholy, before the portrait of Laurence de Treguern, whose angelic gaze seemed to look down on him. From Laurence's portrait, his eyes went towards the canvas where the proud face of Gabriel de Feuillans was brought to life. He shook his head slowly, turned about-face and went to stand behind the back of his wing-chair.

The Marquise was now trying in vain to conquer her unease; she would gladly have given a handful of *louis* or two to anyone who had come to interrupt this tête-à-tête. Even though he came from the rustic environs of Redon, Monsieur Privat had chosen his time with particular tact, as if he were familiar with the intimate customs of Parisian society. The moment that precedes the opening of a salon is one of perfect and absolute solitude; during that solemn interval, the most intractable visitors absent themselves. Save for the sort of violation of the domicile of which only country cousins are capable, the mistress of the house is sheltered from all importunity during the sacred hour of preparation.

The Allée des Veuves was still deserted and the carriage that would draw up first at the gate of the Hôtel du Castellat had not yet been hitched up. The little man adopted the half-mocking, half-wheedling Norman accent that is no stranger to the court-ushers of rural Brittany. "What of the revenants, my dear lady?" he cried, suddenly.

Marianne de Treguern shivered in her armchair.

The little man went on, with a satisfied smile: "It appears that these rascally revenants torment you in a very particular manner."

The Marquise bit down on the embroidery of her handkerchief. "Monsieur," she stammered, "there are things of which one should not speak lightly."

"As a general rule, Madame," Monsieur Privat replied, striking an oratorical pose and leaning his elbows on the back of the wing-chair like a tribune, "I force myself to speak respectfully about all things. Don't think that I am one of those skeptical and boastful people who take a playful attitude to the mysteries of the other world. Stories of revenants are the order of the day in your circle: I see no harm in that. You talk about the Three Rooks and Valérie-*la-Morte*—that's all very well... but have you ever frightened your noble guests, avid for the marvelous, by telling them about one of the visits that your brother Filhol paid you after his death?"

Marianne de Treguern put her feverish forehead between her hands.

"You don't answer, Madame la Marquise," Monsieur Privat went on, And yet, you have seen your brother Filhol, have you not? You've seen him more than once?"

"Yes," Marianne stammered. "It's true... I've seen him."

"In Brittany?"

"In Brittany."

"And in Paris?"

Marianne's whole body shivered. She kept silent, as if she were afraid that her words would only summon the specters that might perhaps be roaming under the large trees in the garden or in the darkness of the corridors,

"And your husband, the late Monsieur le Marquis du Castellat," Monsieur Privat went on. "Have you seen him?"

Marianne de Treguern shook her head negatively.

"And Laurence, your younger sister?"

"Nor her," said the Marquise in a whisper.

"Which tends to suggest," said the little man, who seemed to be treating the matter lightly despite his protestations, "that there are dead people who come back, and dead people who don't come back..." He looked at the Marquise incisively. "Well, Madame," he continued, in a sharp and trenchant tone, while pointing his finger at the portrait of Laurence de Treguern, "what if I told you that I myself encountered that beautiful young woman, this evening, as I came through the garden of your house!"

"My sister!" cried the Marquise. "This evening!"

Monsieur Privat passed the back of his hand across his forehead. One might have thought that his words had ended up making an impression on his own mind. "It's not the first time that I've seen family portraits get up and walk," he said, in a slightly altered voice. "I regret, Madame la Marquise, that you don't know the story of Johann-Maria Worms, the jeweler of Cologne, or the story of Jérôme Clément, the physician of Laval. It's getting late, and I don't have time to relate them to you in detail. It may be as well to tell you, however, that Jérôme Clément died a violent death in a meager cabin in the forest of Montigné, a few leagues from Laval, on August 15, 1804."

"August 15!" repeated the Marquise.

"And that Johann-Maria Worms was assassinated in his beautiful schloss on the banks of the Rhine on the night of August 15, 1810."

"Strange!" stammered the Marquise, who heard all this as if in a dream.

"Well, my dear lady", the little man went on, simply and deliberately, in a tone that demanded credence, "I have often

209

seen the portrait of Jérôme Clément, who was so rich when he was alive, in his widow's room in Laval—she never wanted to sell it, despite her poverty! In the environs of Cologne, in the beautiful schloss whose foot is caressed by the blue waves of the Rhine, I've seen the portrait of Johann-Maria Worms When one looks at the portrait of an assassinated man like that, while listening to the story of his murder, one could live to be 100 and not forget it!" At this point Monsieur Privat paused, and asked, parenthetically: "Madame, did you ever own a portrait of your brother Filhol?"

"At the time of his death," the Marquise replied, "we were very poor, and we lived in a little village in Brittany where there was no painter."

Monsieur Privat nodded, and went on: "That's plausible... I asked you that, Madame la Marquise, in consequence of the mental labor that one undertakes in the school of the association of ideas. It occurred to me, in fact, that Filhol de Treguern also died on the night of August 15..."

"We lost our brother," the Marquise replied, in all sincerity, "in the month of September, in broad daylight, and he died in his bed."

"*The first time...*" said the little man. Marianne thought that he was about to go on, but he stopped abruptly. "One night," he resumed, after a further pause, "when I was in Orlan's cemetery, I saw the portrait of Jérôme Clément and the portrait of Johann-Maria Worms walking in the moonlight, swinging their arms. They had a third person with them—also a specter, presumably, if the first two were not alive. And it's because of that, Madame la Marquise, that I did myself the honor of asking whether or not you possessed a portrait of the late Filhol de Treguern, your brother. I would have been able, with certainty, to put a name to the third specter, if you had had a portrait."

Marianne de Treguern seemed to be on the point of becoming ill.

"They are the ones," continued Monsieur Privat, magnified in the Marquise's eyes by her distress, "of which there is sometimes talk in your salons: the Three Rooks of Orlan. But which of the two of us, Madame la Marquise, will pronounce the true name of the one they call Valérie-*la-Morte*? Is it Geneviève? Is it Laurence...?"

XXI. Olympe de Treguern

Never had the salons and gardens of the Hôtel du Castellat been more magnificently embellished. Beneath the garlands of flowers and lights, the glittering crowd was eager for pleasure. It was one of those fine crushes that Paris alone, in all the world, can bring together and infect with joyful fever. There was a veritable swarm of charming women. There was already an effervescent sparkle in a thousand conversations contrived by chance; Tolbecque's orchestra [57] tuned up in a lively and graceful manner. There was a sort of palpable dazzle, the precursor of happy intoxication, in the embalmed warmth of the atmosphere.

It must be admitted that the Marquise du Castellat's parties were even better than their reputation. The Hôtel du Castellat, constructed in an era when parties were grand affairs, had become a Stradivarius beneath the fingers of a virtuoso in Marianne de Treguern's hands. She threw an excellent party; it was her vocation and her passion. Immeasurably frivolous, having no knowledge of work, reflective thought, or even conversation—in the true sense of the word—the Marquise devoted her entire intelligence to the labor of being mistress of a house and paying insane sums for the privilege of having her salons well-filled.

She was there that evening, giving everything to everyone, modestly proud of the great success of her work, not retaining the slightest evident trace of the distress she had felt a short while before, during her interview with Monsieur Privat.

Monsieur Privat had not left her until the threshold of the salons, and now he was walking in the ballroom, his nose in the air and hands behind his back, casting an approving eye over the magnificence of the *fête*.

The lion of these sumptuous gatherings, Gabriel de Feuillans, had just made his entrance. When he had kissed the

Marquise's hand, she had said to him in a low voice: "Take care! There's news."

A constrained emotion, concealed with great difficulty, was perceptible beneath the proud gravity that was Feuillans' habitual mask.

"Marianne," he murmured, "do you know the names of all the people who have obtained entry to your house this evening?"

The Marquise opened her mouth to reply, but she encountered the piercing gaze of Monsieur Privat, fixed upon her above his spectacles.

"We're being watched," she said, summoning a cheerful smile to her lips. "I can only repeat: Take care!"

Analyzing that smile, Monsieur Privat asked himself: *Is that a stout woman, petrified by egotism and insignificance, or the most perfect actress in the universe?*

A rumor spread through the crowd; the groups stirred and the crowd grew thicker beside the path through the lindens where Josille and little Vevette had made every effort to light the lanterns a short while before. The Marquise squeezed Feuillans' arm; he bowed and withdrew.

In the linden path, a couple was coming forward slowly. There was a tall old man with a bleak and sad face, wearing a bizarre costume that one could readily have taken for a carnival disguise. The principal element of this costume consisted of a ground-length black cloak, on which were embroidered in gold the symbols of the passion of Our Lord. A large Maltese cross hung about his neck. Leaning on his arm was a young woman whose evening dress was primarily remarkable for its elegant simplicity. As they passed by, the names of Commander Malo and Mademoiselle de Treguern were murmured.

Everyone wanted to look, and when they had looked, curiosity extended into admiration. Such strange rumors circulated around that beautiful young woman, who was Monsieur de Feuillans' fiancée, and whose life was enveloped by a mysterious veil.

Soon, everyone was talking about her. Olympe de Treguern had too many admirers not to have enemies. Her absence drew comment; people asked themselves why she was not by the side of the Marquise who played the part of her mother.

There were people who claimed to be aware of an icy coldness between the Marquise and her niece. Olympe was the sole heir of the late Monsieur le Marquis du Castellat, who had made a will in her favor—but that was not the *casus belli*, for the aunt and the niece never talked about matters of financial interest. On the other hand, Olympe certainly could not complain about the Marquise's severity; she was allowed absolute freedom of action—and, so certain rumors alleged, made full use of that liberty.

The rumors that run through the *monde* have sources as undiscoverable as that of the Nile. The *monde* leveled no positive accusation against Olympe; the *monde* itself, confronted with the child's angelic pride, was afraid that it might both be the stronger. But the *monde* whispered, with a thousand insinuating voices, that there was a secret in Olympe's existence. Only the Chevalier de Noisy, Laurence de Treguern's former respectful admirer, denied it strenuously. It was supposed that the Chevalier de Noisy knew a little more about it than the others.

There were sudden and unexpected absences—eclipses, one might say, since the favorite expression of poets represented Olympe as a star. These eclipses had been known to occur even in the middle of a party. Sometimes they lasted no more than an hour; at other times, Olympe would not reappear for a whole week. On one recent occasion, those who kept a close eye on the small mystery had searched for her in vain for the best part of a month.

Where did she go? Did her fiancé, Gabriel de Feuillans, know? For some time, Gabriel de Feuillans had been more often in London than in Paris, in connection with his great tontine. Where did she go? On these occasions, the Marquise du Castellat invariably limited herself to answering that her niece was indisposed. But when a rich heiress is ill, physicians are not found wanting, and physicians have never been accused of mutism. When Olympe was mentioned, the Marquise's physician twiddled his thumbs and shook his head to indicate ignorance. Once, when he was pressed, he admitted that he had not once been called to attend Mademoiselle de Treguern; he had nothing to occupy him but the Marquise's nerves. It must have been true, with regard to visits, the doctor was incapable of lying for distraction's sake.

There are maladies so unfortunate and so terrible that one conceals them out of shame. The patient hides away to suffer them; daylight is prevented from penetrating into his retreat, as if he does not wish the Sun to witness the horror of his convulsions. He shuts off every sound, as if he were afraid that a door standing ajar might reveal the secrets of his howling or his death-rattle. But there was such a sweet freshness in Olympe's cheeks, such a lithe vigor in her figure, such a lightness in her step, so much youthful and valiant life in her smile! How could one believe it? And yet, there was talk of certain days when pallor replaced the incarnadine of that dazzling complexion, when mortal sorrow drowned that beautiful smile.

In sum, if it was not that, what was it? Where did she go? It often happened that those people who, like Monsieur de Noisy, wanted to explain it all naturally, said: "She's a young girl, who shuts herself away to dream; she's a spoiled child who has her whims."

But these sages, far from stifling debate, irritated and inflamed it. Whims have bounds, and reverie does not extend as far as somnambulism. Explain then, since you want to explain everything away, why, one evening when Mademoiselle de Treguern was indisposed, a young woman similar in every respect to Mademoiselle de Treguern—either her or her double—had been seen climbing over the shuttered gate of the little house situated behind the gardens of the Hôtel du Castellat: the little house that gave out into the triangular space to which the Breton Tanneguy's course had ultimately led him, where he fainted next to the body of Stéphane Gontier, his friend and his brother. That was Stéphane's house.

There are resemblances. Mistakes can be made. But the story was also told of some gentleman or other who had come across a broken-down *poste-chaise* on the road to Brittany, some 50 or 60 leagues from Paris, during the time of the indisposition or eclipse that lasted longer than the others, which had deprived Olympe's admirers of the sight of her star for at least a fortnight. The gentleman had come forward to offer his services. A young woman had appeared at the carriage-door of the broken-down *chaise* and, on catching sight the gentleman, had moved more rapidly than lightning to bring down her veil. There is, however, no movement of the hand rapid enough to overtake a glance, and the gentleman said that, in the *chaise* that had broken down on the highway, in the middle of lower Normandy, he thought he had recognized Mademoiselle Olympe de Treguern.

Noisy-*le-Sec* had struck that gentleman with his sword, but a sword-thrust proves nothing. Before closing the chapter on Olympe,[58] however, everyone made quite certain that Noisy-*le-Sec* was not within earshot.

She was a brunette, delicate and decisive at the same time, pensive but also full of smiles—but graceful, above all, bearing her poetic crown of beauty with a naive pride. She might have been 20; all the joys and hopes of youth were radiant in her face. In the depths of her limpid gaze, a treasure of courage, tenderness and purity was divinable.

Paris, the immense treasure-house of pearls of beauty, the spangled flowerbed of animated blooms, possessed no pearl more perfect, no blossom more delicately opened. The poets said that the delightful Olympe, the noble, proud and blissful beauty of beauties—whose dark hair extended in a stream over her nacreous temples, whose blue eyes glided their soft rays between long lashes curing beneath the ebony arcs of her proudly-defined eyebrows, and whose serious mouth released, when the coral of her lips parted, an angelic smile—was a Heavenly dream.

Commandeer Malo returned Olympe to the Marquise's hands, while Monsieur Privat, abruptly going up to Gabriel de Feuillans, said to him: "In answer to your question, Monsieur, no—Marianne de Treguern does not know the names of all the people who have obtained entry to her house this evening."

There was a place in the shadow of the great hornbeam hedge that the Marquise had long since chosen to hold her little court. The dazzling clarity of the ballroom was visible through the verdure, but the strains of the orchestra were muffled and somewhat quieted before reaching it. It was lit solely by beams of light extending from the yew-trees planted behind bushes. These glimmers were quite adequate to illuminate the bower where the Marquise sat, surrounded by her intimate circle, but the opposite side, which gave out into the grove next to the Louis XV pavilion, remained plunged in shadow. In fact, the Commander had extinguished the lanterns surrounding his mysterious dwelling with his own hand.

The Commander was there, standing with his back against a tree.

"And you, Feuillans," someone asked—for the conversation was revolving, as usual, around otherworldly matters— "will you finally tell us whether you believe in revenants?"

"I have never seen a revenant," the handsome Gabriel replied.

"Madame," Champeaux said to his neighbor, "I had an aunt who knew heaps of tales to send one to sleep standing up. I'm annoyed to have forgotten them; it would have given me pleasure to narrate them in detail."

"I would have wagered," Baron Brocard murmured in Noisy's ear as he looked at Olympe, "that she was our amazon of the Avenue de Madrid."

"You would have lost," the Chevalier retorted, dryly.

"In my part of the world," said Monsieur Privat, with feigned or real timidity, "—and if I take the liberty of referring to my part of the world, it's because I have the honor of being a compatriot of Madame la Marquise—they talk of revenants who never show themselves and whose voices alone are heard in the night."

"You're from somewhere near Orlan?" exclaimed someone in the circle.

Monsieur Privat nodded modestly. Twenty voices speaking at the same time pronounced the name of the Three Rooks, of whom there had so often been talk at the Hôtel du Castellat, and the circle re-formed around the little man. Gabriel de Feuillans was a dozen paces from Commander Malo; Olympe de Treguern had just sat down facing them, after the quadrille.

"Mesdames," said Monsieur Privat, simply, "I don't know what freak of chance has carried the renown of the triple apparition that frightens the good people of Orlan as far as here. If anything has astonished me in this brilliant society, where everything is new to a poor village advocate like me, it is certainly hearing mention of our rustic specters, who would surely be very flattered by the honor."

He darted a glance towards Olympe de Treguern.

"Once," he continued, addressing himself directly to her, "there was a manor that bore the name of your illustrious family, Mademoiselle." Bowing to Gabriel, he added: "Monsieur de Feuillans will no doubt give that name to the château that he has had built, when he becomes your husband. It's to the environs of the brand-new walls of that palace that the Three Rooks come at midnight. Monsieur de Treguern knows very well that there is a prophecy warning that the last Comte de Treguern must die *three times*. The people of the *Grand'Lande* think that this apparition, known as the Three Rooks, is none other than Treguern three times dead, desirous of visiting the place where his father's house used to be."

Monsieur Privat had addressed himself successively to Olympe, Monsieur de Feuillans and the commander, but all three of them remained silent. The Marquise was fidgeting with her fan; contrary to her habit, a skeptical smile was playing upon her lips. Baron Brocard shrugged his shoulders frankly; Noisy was listening intently.

"As for Valérie-*la-Morte*," Monsieur Privat went on, "people began to see her beneath the willows that surround the Tour-de-Kervoz at the time when Comte Filhol's young sister unfortunately departed this life."

"Laurence!" murmured the Chevalier de Noisy, squeezing Baron Brocard's arm unwittingly.

"Nonsense," muttered the latter.

A convulsive tremor had stirred Feuillans' lips.

Behind the hornbeam hedge, Josille and little Vevette were coming along the path, carrying plates of refreshments towards the ballroom.

"I told you that I'd seen her!" Josille said, impatiently. "As I see you, Vevette! Perhaps better than with my eyes!"

"I told you that you were seeing things!" the girl riposted.

"She went along the base of the wall while I was lighting up the terrace," Josille went on. "Her hair was messy, falling over her mantle."

"While you were lighting up the terrace, Mademoiselle was just getting dressed!"

"Then she has a double, or I'm *fainé*."[59]

"You're innocent, that's all," the young girl exclaimed, pushing him forwards.

But Josille resisted "You're like Baron Brocard," he said, "who doesn't believe in anything."

"And you," Vevette retorted, "are like the Chevalier de Noisy, who tries to persuade people that black is white, and who spends his mornings reporting what he dreamed the night before, without laughing."

"Listen: I wasn't dreaming. The proof is that I slid down to the base of the wall to see where our demoiselle had disappeared. When I was in the path that runs along the foot of the terrace I couldn't see anything, but you know the house with the green door and a little iron gate close by?"

"Well?" said Vevette, gripped by curiosity despite herself.

"Well, I heard someone talking behind the bars. Guess who! Stéphane Gontier—the one we knew in the country..."

"Since he lives there!" said Vevette.

"And Monsieur Gabriel," Josille finished.

"Ah!" murmured the girl, drawing closer. "And what were they saying?"

"Monsieur Gabriel was saying this: '*You have funds; lend me 100,000 francs for three days*.'"

"Is that so? And what was Stéphane's answer?"

"He said that he didn't want to—and Monsieur Gabriel tried to make him believe that he'd be as rich as Croesus, and that he'd share it with him. But Stéphane still said: '*No, no, thank you very much! I don't trust you*.'"

At that moment, they found themselves on the other side of the hedge forming the verdant enclosure where the Marquise and her circle were gathered. Vevette deposited her platter on the ground and took Josille's arm. With her other hand, she parted a few branches, in order to look into the enclosure.

"Look!" she said in a soft voice. "That's Monsieur Gabriel de Feuillans, and that's Mademoiselle Olympe de Treguern."

Josille put his head forwards and looked.

"Do you see them?" the girl asked.

"I see them," Josille replied.

"Well?"

"Hand on heart," Josille repeated, almost solemnly, "It was definitely him, and it was definitely her!"

XXII. The Enclosed Garden

Little Vevette remained pensive for a moment, then picked up her platter and said: "Poor Josille, you were always a silly boy!"

Within the enclosed garden, Monsieur Privat, who was definitely the orator of the moment, was saying: "It must be admitted that the setting is all-important in these dramas of revenants. If you had seen Treguern Common, where the old ruin they call the Tour-de-Kervoz stands, the triple circle of the *Pierres-Plantées*, and the ravine overhung by the privet path, you would understand all this much better." He looked around him. "We're not so badly placed here, though. Those clumps of bushes are vast, these shadows impenetrable. Somewhere over there, I passed grottoes as dark as the entrance to Hell. And didn't someone tell me that the paths running round this enclosure have served as a theater to more than one tragic adventure?"

There was a silence.

"It's all here," Monsieur Privat continued, slowly. "The large and ancient battlements, the long corridors, profound isolation, the abandoned rooms where the memory remains of those who are no more. Allowing for the differences between Brittany, the land of shadows, and Paris, the fatherland of light, I believe that a connoisseur could still place some beautiful apparitions here."

Commander Malo stirred, and seemed to sniff the air, like a bloodhound scenting distant smoke. "Treguern is close by!" he murmured. Then, raising his voice for he first time, he said: "Advocate! Where is the young man who was with you inside the diligence?"

"Monsieur le Commandeur," Monsieur Privat replied, "the city is vast and the youth appeared to have good legs; if he's still on the move, he must be far away."

221

Malo folded his arms across his bosom. "The hour's drawing near," he muttered between his teeth, "but the one who must die isn't here, for I don't see the Veil."

Monsieur Privat's gaze, active and piercing, moved incessantly between the Marquise and Gabriel de Feuillans. The Marquise had recovered an appearance of calm; Feuillans, evidently, did not deign to enter into the conversation. The circle, on the other hand, was of an excellent disposition to listen to stories; the vague yet emphatic speech of Monsieur Privat had awakened its curious appetite without giving it the least pasture, and the Commander's presence put into everyone's mind the fine preliminary *frisson* that doubles the value of stories told in the dark.

The dance was, to be sure, quite close at hand, with its luminous nimbus and joyful noises—but who does not know the power of contrasts? The flash of the ballroom only added to the somber aspect of the enclosed garden.

"Is nothing more known about these three supernatural beings, the Three Rooks?" asked a pretty Vicomtesse.

"Lovely lady, one knows from the start that they don't exist!" cried Baron Brocard, impelled to establish his strong-mindedness."

"I've just remembered my aunt's story!" Champeaux said, clapping his hands triumphantly. "When she was young, she always saw a white sheep... no, a black sheep... at any rate, a white or black sheep. The important thing is that it was a sheep. This sheep..."

"Actually, Madame," Monsieur Privat replied, meanwhile, "it's believed that more is known, and there must something real at the bottom of all that phantasmagoria, for there are certain details that the poor people of the *Grand'Lande* certainly could not have invented. If I were not afraid of abusing..."

"Speak, Monsieur, speak!" they cried from every side.

"Whether one asserts that the apparition is only the triple form of the last Treguern," the little man went on, "or whether one admits three different specters bound together by a mystic

222

chain—for they are never separated—the common belief is that they come to Earth to avenge spilled blood... one murder, or three. Valérie-*la-Morte*, according to the same theory, is their servant, their sentinel or their courier. Commander Malo could tell you as well as I that they have had the object of their vengeance in their power more than once..."

"They have," Malo pronounced, coldly, "and they will have."

"But they did not strike him," continued the little man. "On the contrary, they have protected him, so well that he, looking back pridefully—for he has come up from the depths—and measuring the distance he has covered, sometimes says to himself: '*Where is the obstacle that can bring me down?*' "

Feuillans' posture changed; he fixed his severe stare upon Monsieur Privat, who did not appear to notice.

"That man," he went on, "gets up every morning to find his work done and his road smooth. He does not even see the hand that aids him, and he only feels the power that surrounds and presses upon him on occasions when he desires to halt his terrible descent. In those moments of remorse and doubt, he must sense that the voice which says to him: '*Go on! Go on!*' is his damnation."

Monsieur Privat paused, and Champeaux's voice became audible, saying: "Now that it's coming back to me, the sheep was a goat that walked upright on its hind legs. My aunt was tempted to enter a convent..."

"It is known, then, who it is that they pursue on Earth?" queried the pretty Vicomtesse.

"I know him," Monsieur Privat replied.

There was, as they say in our Parliamentary times, a prolonged sensation in the circle. Feuillans smiled disdainfully.

"Won't you tell us what your three revenants look like?"

"Two old men and one who is still young, but whose hair and beard are as white as snow."

He was interrupted by a faint cry, and everyone saw the Marquise, white with terror, move sharply backwards.

"There they are! There they are!" stammered the Vicomtesse, at the same time, hiding her pretty face behind her fluttering fan.

The Marquise's mouth was wide open and both her hands were trembling as they pointed, involuntarily, to a gap in the wall of vegetation that happened to be behind Gabriel de Feuillans. Every avid gaze followed the direction of the gesture. Some saw nothing but a black hole in the foliage; some thought they could make out a confused movement in the darkness; others—among whom Noisy-*le-Sec* was in the vanguard—swore that they had perceived three bodiless faces: two of them the heads of old men and the third a face that retained the appearance of youth although it was framed with white hair.

Gabriel de Feuillans had turned around like everyone else; he was one of those who saw nothing.

"My word!" murmured the stout Baron Brocard, "I believe that the Marquise will end up by installing contrivances in her garden like those at the Théâtre de l'Opéra, to give her guests pleasant thrills!"

Olympe de Treguern left the place that she occupied facing de Feuillans, silently crossed the enclosed garden and went out through the same gap in which the three supposed specters had shown themselves. There was a murmur of astonishment. For a few seconds, Olympe's white dress was visible among the trees; then the Vicomtesse, still thunderstruck, stammered in a faint voice: "There are two of them!"

For a moment, those who were facing the gap could, indeed, see two white dresses; then, there was only darkness.

A few minutes afterwards, the Marquise's intimate circle had left the enclosed garden. Believers and skeptics alike withdrew, under the impression of a vague malaise; the most deeply affected took refuge beneath the chandeliers in the ballroom.

Commander Malo and Gabriel de Feuillans remained alone, ten paces apart, in the enclosed garden. The Commander was still standing, leaning against his tree. Feuillans, seated at the far end of the bower, was holding his pale face in his hands.

"False priest!" the Commander said, suddenly. "When you're as rich as a king, what will you give me for my silence? And what will you give me for the pronouncement I made in the church at Orlan, on the day when the two infants were brought to baptism?"

"Do you mean what you say, Malo de Treguern?" Monsieur de Feuillans asked, in a low voice. "Can your friendship be bought?"

The Commander stood up straight. "I was standing here," he said, "and the Marquis du Castellat was sitting where you are, on the eve of his death. The Veil fell *there*." He pointed to the center of the bower. "False priest!" he continued, "I watch you always, waiting for the Veil to fall. On the site of the old manor, there is already a young palace. Patience! Patience!"

The Commander moved towards the exit that led to the ballroom. As he passed close to Feuillans, he added: "You, buy me, Le Brec! I said it to you 20 years ago, and I repeat it now, as the hour draws nigh: you shall die before me, and you shall die poorer than me!"

At the very moment when the Commander disappeared around the corner of the hedge, a voice was raised in the darkness of the bushes that extended to the Louis XV pavilion. "What does the impotent bravado of an old man matter?" it said. "Your star is in the sky, ever brighter and prouder. Go on!"

Two other voices replied: "Go on! Go on!"

Feuillans lifted his had slightly. "Go on! Go on!" he murmured, as if in a dream. "Yes, yes... the dead have opened the way and have pushed me forwards!"

"There is only one more step!" said the voice that had spoken first.

Feuillans got up immediately; his hair was standing up on his head.

"Dead souls!" he said, controlling the tremor in his voice. "What lies beyond the hours, so brief, that one calls life?"

An indistinct murmur, which seemed to descend from foliage caressed by the breeze, said: "Sleep!"

"Annihilation!" Feuillans said, his head coming proudly upright. "But then—where do they come from, those who speak to me?"

The voices in the covert were silent; nothing was audible but the cheerful strains of the orchestra. Feuillans looked up at the sky through the verdant vault.

"My star!" he said. "There it is, reaching its zenith. Only one more step, that's true: *Go on! Go on!* My calculations are well made, now as before... a hundred witnesses could establish, if need be, my presence at Madame la Marquise's ball. To accuse me of murder would be madness!"

"Madness!" repeated a faint echo.

Feuillans' hands were convulsively clenched. *That child, Stéphane*, he thought, *is handsome, young, happy...* Instead of completing the thought, he said: "But time's running out—in a few minutes, it will be too late."

Feuillans passed both his hands over his sweat-bathed brow. He took a step toward the bushes; he stopped, struggled against himself for a moment, then resumed his march impetuously. Nothing was audible within the thicket.

After a few seconds, there was a slight sound. The distant lanterns of the *fête* illuminated an indistinct, almost diaphanous form gliding beneath the slanting branches. You might have thought that it was one of the daughters of the air: an incorporeal soul transported through the void by the night-breeze. She came into the bower. It was a young woman. Her unpinned tresses fell loosely about a face that was whiter than her white dress. There are no words to paint the exquisite melancholy of her beauty.

She resembled the portrait of the young girl hanging in the Marquise's boudoir—the portrait of Laurence de Treguern—as a vague and fugitive memory resembles a happy reality.

She paused for a moment, her back turned to the lights in the ballroom, her head tilted and attentive, looking sideways at the place where Feuillans had disappeared. Then she turned round, and her face, suddenly illuminated, exposed her large timid eyes, in which some mysterious veil seemed to mask her thoughts. Her lips opened slightly, and let out a few verses of the lullaby that young Breton mothers murmur next to the cribs of their sleeping angels: the song with which Laurence de Treguern had once rocked little Olympe to sleep on the occasions that she remained alone by night in the abandoned manor.

Was this a poor soul in torment? She went to place herself on the spot formerly occupied by Gabriel de Feuillans, and leaned on her elbows on the back of the bench, as if it were a balcony from which she could watch the joyful movement of the party. She lowered her eyes, dazzled by the bright lights. When she raised them again, a vague smile shone in her eyes. There was dancing; her charming head began to move in time to the music. A sound passed between her lips. She murmured: "Unhappy and beautiful... was I beautiful?"

Two tears rolled down her cheeks.

At that moment, a terrible cry was heard in the vicinity of the terrace. The orchestra fell silent. The Marquise's guests ran towards the terrace. At the foot of the wall, in the triangular space, in front of the wrought iron gate with the green shutters, there were two men lying on the ground, both apparently dead. The young Breton, Tanneguy, had just fallen unconscious upon the body of his friend Stéphane.

When Tanneguy awoke from his faint, the small triangular space that separated the Marquise's garden from the house rented by Stéphane Gontier was crowded with curious people. At midnight as at noon, Paris is always ready for per-

227

formances of these kinds. By the bright light of lanterns, one could see the terrace of the Hôtel du Castellat full of women in evening dress.

Tanneguy looked around. In that first moment, he had not the slightest idea what had happened. He wondered why the crowd was moving so agitatedly and crying out tumultuously. He heard words repeated on every side:

"He was assassinated right here!"

"At the door of his own house!"

A vague anxiety gripped Tanneguy's heart as he began to recover the thread of his thoughts. He saw people pointing at him, saying: "That man was found lying across the corpse!"

The corpse? Tanneguy remembered. It was Stéphane who had been assassinated!

But where was Stéphane, or what was left of him? Tanneguy searched in vain; the body was no longer there. As he searched, he saw three people dressed in black standing in front of the shuttered door, who formed a separate group: there were two old men and one who was still young, whose hair was as white as snow.

A chill ran through Tanneguy's veins; he had seen those men before, more than once. He recalled the menacing words he had heard beneath the trees of the Champs-Elysées a short while before. But he did not have time for reflection, because a voice was raised on the illuminated terrace, which pronounced his name distinctly. Tanneguy shivered and raised his eyes. He saw his little traveling companion, Monsieur Privat, who was leaning on his elbows on the balustrade of the terrace and carefully polishing his round lenses. Monsieur Privat was no longer wearing his peaked cap; he too was in evening dress.

Next to him, Tanneguy recognized, with inexpressible stupefaction, the young woman who had guided him to the very spot where he now was: the beautiful, cherished vision of his nights in Brittany; the one whom Monsieur Privat had called Valérie, and whom the good people of Orlan called *la Morte*. She was wearing a white dress; a few eglantine flowers

228

hung among the curls of her dark hair. She was beautiful and calm; her serene gaze was fixed on Tanneguy. Tanneguy lay still, as if struck by lightning.

He heard Monsieur Privat ask, while pointing a finger at him: "What do you think they'll do with that big lad there, Monsieur de Feuillans?"

Monsieur de Feuillans, whom Tanneguy recognized as the master of the *Château-sans-Terre*, replied: "I think they'll hold on to him until the authorities arrive."

Privat described a pirouette and fixed his polished spectacles in place. "And you, Monsieur le Commander?" he asked.

Malo's pale and sad head looked over the gallery. He was seen to smile strangely when his gaze fell upon the young Breton. "It is necessary," he murmured, so quietly that no one could hear him, "in order that the name of Treguern shall rise again!"

"My friends," said the Marquise, addressing the crowd. "Seize the murderer!"

Tanneguy looked at her, and recognized her as the stout woman he had seen getting out of the *calèche*, with a lap-dog, in the deserted street where that fatal date *August 15* was inscribed in giant letters on every wall. There was a movement in the crowd, while Monsieur Privat, bowing to the stout woman and smiling, said to her: "Madame la Marquise, I have covered 100 leagues with that young fellow, of whose imminent arrival Dowager Le Brec warned you in her letter, and I warn you that they will find another letter in his portfolio, recommending him to you."

Mariane de Treguern hid her pallor behind her fan. "That's him!" she stammered, fearfully.

"In the flesh!" Monsieur Privat replied, tranquilly.

XXIII. Comte de Treguern

No one was dancing any longer in the Marquise's garden. The orchestra had been given permission to leave. The sinister episode that had just taken place did not permit further enjoyment; the *fête* had changed its character. But the party was not over; it had merely beaten a retreat before the odor of blood, and had taken refuge indoors.

Oddly enough, the noble crowd was not thinning out to any great extent. Ordinarily, the least catastrophe is sufficient to disperse these frivolous assemblies. As soon as one can no longer enjoy oneself, one leaves—that is the rule. Why had the Marquise's party survived the extinction of pleasure? Was it to allow talk of the recent drama, to mull over every detail and circumstance at leisure? Not in the least; scarcely a handful of drunken dotards persisted in talking about that ancient history, which had grown old in an hour. There was something else: there was another drama in performance. Vague rumors circulated here and there, spread from who knows where, and Madame la Marquise's guests stayed where they were in order to see what happened.

The romance that was now the focus of concern bore little resemblance to the brutal tragedy that had unfolded a little while before in the neighboring covert. This was a novel of intrigue, a high comedy full of elegant mysteries and gilded changes of fortune. Its hero was Gabriel de Feuillans, its heroine Olympe de Treguern; there was talk of marriage and there was talk of millions.

The *monde* had been preoccupied for some time with vague rumors concerning the handsome Gabriel. The story of the English tontine with the 100,000-franc annuity and the 15 or 20 millions that it would produce was so familiar that it had attained the status of a children's tale: no one believed in it any longer—or, at least, it was said that Feuillans would run aground, that he had reached the limit of his resources, and that money-lenders, profiting from his dire necessity, were demanding half of his 20 millions in return for the last 100,000 francs!

This evening, however, the rumors were changing their tone. Despite the doubts, the thundercloud of gold had burst. Feuillans had found his 100,000 francs; he had won the immense sum pledged. He was a multimillionaire. How could anyone could still be bothered about a poor fellow with his throat cut in a hole? What's a murder worth? There are hundreds of them every year. But 20 millions, perhaps more, won in a gambling coup—that's an event! That's a mine of emotions! Merely thinking about it makes the heart leap in one's breast. Listen! It's the force of an earthquake—no murder can hold its ground. I don't believe that an entire quarter on fire, or an entire town inundated by a flood, is more interesting than that—because every man is a gambler; because every man has had the extravagant dream that seeks to calculate the delirium that would seize him in the face of impossible good luck!

Can you imagine the face of a man who has won 20 million? A million in annual income at 5%! 83,333 francs and 33 centimes to spend every month, without eating into his capital! Must his face not be as radiant as the Sun? Can his feet still touch the ground?

Then again, millions were much more common in those days than they are today.

It was for this reason that everyone wanted to contemplate the illustrious Gabriel. One would not see a similar transfiguration twice in a lifetime. The Marquise's guests—excited, collected, mollified—were searching for the handsome Gabriel; even the least expansive felt the urge to carry him in triumph.

Gabriel was almost as imperturbable as usual, though perhaps a little paler. The little advocate, Privat, on the other hand, was radiant. On seeing him, you would have taken him for Monsieur de Feuillans' heir presumptive. He was restless; that was his nature. He had been seen chatting quietly with the Marquise, slipping a word into the Commander's ear, exchanging glances with Olympe de Treguern. He had monopolized the demigod, taking Feuillans into the embrasure of a window and speaking to him volubly. When he left Feuillans, people crowded around him as if he were a celebrity. He struck a pose, and—among other remarkable things—said: "Although I do not have the honor of belonging to the family, whose confidence is more than sufficient honor for me, Monsieur le Comte de Treguern and Madame la Marquise have given me permission to speak as I do."

"The Comte de Treguern!" they repeated.

"Who are you calling the Comte de Treguern?" asked Noisy-*le-Sec*.

"The man who has the right to bear the name, obviously," Monsieur Privat replied, self-importantly.

Those who knew even a little of the history of the house of Treguern looked at one another in astonishment. Then all eyes turned interrogatively to Commander Malo, who was sitting apart in a corner of the room. The Commander was listening to Monsieur Privat, and did not seem disposed to contradict him.

"We have experienced many difficulties," Monsieur Privat went on, shaking his head slowly. "There was a subterranean opposition that gave us a great deal of trouble! But His Majesty has deigned to intervene, and I can announce to you officially that, upon marrying Mademoiselle Olympe de Treguern, Monsieur Gabriel de Feuillans will take the name of his wife, with the title of Comte, which has belonged to the family since Tanneguy VII, who died in 1614."

The Commander extended his hands on the arms of his armchair and raised his eyes to the ceiling. His lips moved, but he said nothing. It was not the Commander who interested the Marquise's guests; curious eyes sought out Olympe. She was discovered, sitting next to Madame du Castellat, in the next room. It was assumed that the Marquise was imparting to her little circle of intimates a communication analogous to that of Monsieur Privat.

There was not a single young woman in the rooms of the Hôtel du Castellat who would not have traded her destiny for Olympe's—for Feuillans was one of those men who seize the imagination and the heart at the same time. He did not need all those millions to be attractive, but the millions did him no harm. It annoyed those demoiselles to see Olympe's cold and almost disdainful attitude. From their viewpoint, although Olympe's happiness must be boundless, she affected to despise her triumph as if it were a disaster! Everyone had noticed that Olympe's gaze had not once moved towards her fiancé. There were sympathetic souls who were already saying to themselves: "Poor Monsieur de Feuillans! He won't be happy!"

The Chevalier de Noisy could not determine the species of the coldness, tainted with bitterness, which was inscribed in Mademoiselle de Treguern's features. This Noisy-*le-Sec* was a romantic. His friends accused him, not without reason, of importing a mysterious aspect to the simplest incidents of everyday life. He had something of the character of the good Chevalier de la Mancha, who took sheep for Moors and windmills for giants.[60]

As he looked at Olympe de Treguern, Noisy-*le-Sec* was vividly reminded of the beautiful Laurence, who had also been the fiancée of Gabriel de Feuillans. He recalled the singular words spoken by poor Stéphane that very morning, in the Bois de Boulogne. Stéphane, comparing Gabriel to a Vampire, had let slip his inexplicable fear of being killed by Gabriel.

And Stéphane had died in the dark, violently; Noisy had seen his corpse.

It was quite impossible to make any connection whatsoever between that death and Gabriel de Feuillans, and Noisy made none, but he mulled over everything that had been said in the Bois; the meeting arranged by Feuillans; the note given to Stéphane by an unknown boy; and, above all, that voice from the fiacre, at the moment when the beautiful Comtesse Torquati was passing by, which had murmured: "*This evening!*"

As an unexpected consequence of all this, the Chevalier felt a conviction growing within him that Olympe was a human sacrifice. Why did he think so? He could not have said—but from that moment on, he could think of nothing but approaching Olympe to relieve her supposed distress, and to offer her the loyal support of his arm should the need arise.

"Laurence loved that beautiful child," he said to himself. "Laurence is looking down on us. Laurence will thank me in Heaven!"

"Well!" cried the stout Baron Brocard at that moment, "It's very interesting to see Monsieur de Feuillans become a Comte and call himself Treguern, but nothing's been said about the 15 or 20 millions that is also very much in his interest."

Silence fell so that they might listen to Monsieur Privat's reply. The latter blew into his cheeks and took a pause, as they say in the theater. "You mention a precise figure," he replied, eventually. "I cannot, but I believe it's more than that. It's said that the benefits of Campbell Life's class of 1800 are extremely handsome!"

"More than 20 millions!" The exclamation came from all sides.

There was, in truth, a certain hatred brooding now in the sly sideways glances that the dancing-girls directed as Olympe de Treguern. As Feuillans' lips brushed the young woman's hand, Noisy thought he saw her entire body shiver. He swore to himself that he would know the truth before leaving the house.

"The ceremony will take place at the Château de Treguern," Monsieur Privat went on. "I do not think that I am being indiscreet in saying that everyone here will receive invitations to the celebration. You shall see, Mesdames, what the domains of the great families of olden times were like; you will be able to walk all day, and quickly, without reaching the limits of the lands that the Comte de Treguern will repurchase." He paused, and a slight smile came to his lips as he added: "When all Paris descends thus on the parish of Orlan, I am perfectly certain that the Three Rooks and *La Morte* will seek their fortune elsewhere!"

At that moment, Gabriel de Feuillans offered his arm to the Marquise to lead her to her apartment. Only princes are accustomed to treat their hostesses thus, but when one has more than 20 millions, it is surely permissible to do a little of what princes do.

Noisy launched himself into the second drawing-room, where Olympe de Treguern remained alone, and went straight up to her. The larger room was also beginning to empty, because Monsieur Privat had finally concluded his discourse.

"I belong, body and soul, to those whom Laurence loved," Noisy said. "Mademoiselle, have you no orders to give me?"

He expected to be understood, for his mind had been working, and in his eyes, Olympe was a condemned victim. A heavy step sounded on the tiled floor. Noisy turned around and saw Commander Malo coming forward. "Since you cannot answer me here, Mademoiselle," he said, in a soft and rapid voice, "I shall wait in the grounds, in the enclosed garden. Do not hesitate before that frivolous barrier that is called convention. For you, I shall be as an older brother, or a father."

He bowed and went out. There was no one in the garden; the only audible sound, coming from beyond the hedge of the courtyard, was the tumultuous noise of the carriages packing the Allée des Veuves, in front of the railings. That lasted a quarter of an hour, after which nothing more could be heard.

The lanterns distributed beneath the foliage were going out one by one. Noisy strode back and forth, bare-headed. He had already gone into the enclosed garden twice and found it empty. The third time, he saw a white form sitting on a bank of grass. It was Olympe—he recognized her ball-gown and her long dark hair... except that her hair was let down, and there were no longer any eglantine flowers in her ringlets.

"What must be done, Mademoiselle?" Noisy cried. "I am ready for anything."

The young woman did not move. Noisy could scarcely see her face, inundated as it was by her hair.

"Beautiful and unhappy!" she murmured.

Noisy's heart skipped a beat.

"Is that you, Olympe?" he asked.

The young woman pushed back her hair and turned her eyes towards him. He sank to his knees, releasing a loud cry. His hands came together.

"Laurence!" he said. "Laurence, it was for you that I wanted to save her!"

The young woman smiled sadly. "Who will save me?" she said. Then she added, in an indistinct murmur: "Unhappy! Unhappy!"

The last light burning in the neighboring grove went out. A sigh escaped Laurence's bosom. Noisy reached out for her; he seized nothing but impalpable air. The white dress slipped behind the trees—and beneath their foliage, already fading into the distance, a Breton lullaby was audible...

It was a very large room, high-ceilinged and vaulted like a chapel. There were windows to either side, in the longer dimension. The dusty walls still retained a few scattered traces of delicate frescoes, whose pastel colors were trying to render themselves visible beneath the cobwebs hanging from the friezes like rags of clothing.

Between the windows, vestiges of sculpture were visible; in two or three places one could even make out the flirtatious contours of the scrollwork which framed portraits or coats-of-arms of the era of Louis XV. But time and the dust had been aided in their work of destruction here; hammers had pitted the reliefs, and it seemed that some vandal had attacked the garland of nymphs that ran around the cornice with a mallet.

Once, when these sculptures had been smiling, when these enamels, shiny and new, had sparkled in reflecting the light spread by crystal chandeliers, this place had been like a little temple of pleasure. Now that it was redolent with the odor of the cellar and the sepulchre, though, a few souvenirs remained of its original purpose. A lugubrious fantasy had accumulated in this place every emblem of mourning, every object that recalled the idea of death, without being able to erase entirely the traces of the gracious past. In one place, in the midst of the debris of the frieze, the hammer had forgotten a floating sash, which offered its floating drapery to the wind; in another, a scrap of painted canvas smiled vaguely beneath the folds of a mortuary cloth; in a third, roses were lost behind the head of a skeleton.

But we have said enough about the appearance offered by this place, which surpassed the limits of the bizarre, for the reader not to have the least shred of doubt that it could only serve as the retreat of a visionary or a madman.

Even though the room was large, any movement therein was hampered at every step by a profusion of objects scattered in disorder, every one of which made its contribution to the strangest and most sinister ensemble. At the back, opposite the main door—at the place where a chimney is normally found—there was a granite tomb which must have been transported piece by piece and then patiently reconstructed. On the tomb, a knight clad in armor was lying, his arms crossed on his bosom, his feet resting against the belly of a large greyhound.

The wall-panel forming the backcloth of this monument was almost entirely occupied by a colossal coat-of-arms of the House of Treguern, enameled in black and silver, whose supports were two ancient mourners with faces veiled in white, bearing the device: *Sub Morte Vita*.

To the right and the left of the tomb was a pell-mell of shapeless fragments bearing scraps of inscriptions, funeral urns, worm-eaten bones and crosses wrenched from the soil of cemeteries. On each of these crosses the name of a member of the Treguern family was legible.

That was all of the furniture, save for a narrow camp-bed bearing a plain mattress, and a huge table charged with compasses, astrolabes, parchments and vials of every sort, which rested on a decrepit old trunk. The trunk was stuffed with old books, and its ill-fitting panels were displayed a series of cabalistic sculptures.

The room was lit by two of those black candlesticks, as tall as a man, that are used at funerals. Two church candles, fixed in points of iron, were burning in a melancholy fashion, scarcely rendering the darkness visible. A man was standing before the tomb, with his back to the door, showing nothing but his large bald skull. He was dressed in a black robe with open sleeves, like the magicians of olden times; in front of him, on the tomb itself, stood three big pinewood boxes, whose lids had just been prised loose.

The reader will have recognized these three boxes, and cannot have forgotten the grave, gentle and modest face of the traveler who arrived from Brittany in the coupé of the carriage whose interior had been occupied by Monsieur Privat and

Tanneguy, whom the Marquise's domestic servant called "Monsieur le Commandeur."

This was his home. This huge room in mourning-dress formed the only story of the Louis XV pavilion, whose exterior created such a cheerful and graceful effect in the Marquise's gardens.

The three boxes brought from Brittany were full of fragments of stone similar to those already crowding the pavilion's floor. Among the stones, there were a few old books and scraps of parchment. The Commander was deeply engrossed in his work; his work consisted of taking pieces of granite at random from one or other of the boxes and setting them against one of the corners of the mausoleum, which was broken.

The Commander has already done that with numerous pieces of stone, but none had fitted the fissure in the tomb— but the boxes were still nearly full, and every time the Commander selected a new fragment a spark illuminated in his eye. It was easy to see that this work was vitally important to him, and that it was not merely a matter of effecting a material repair to the ancient mausoleum.

"I've been searching for a long time," he murmured, "and I still haven't found it. A great many stones must have been lost when Gabriel had the foundations of the manor moved, but all things are written in Heaven; if I am destined to find it, I shall find it."

He stopped, releasing a cry of joy, and a hint of blood reddened the pallor of his cheeks. The angles of the stone that he held in his hand fitted almost exactly into the worn cavity of the funerary tablet.

He knelt down to get a better view. The beating of his heart was distinctly audible. His hand shook violently. For an instant, his entire soul entered into his gaze. But the light in his eye died away and the pallor returned to his cheeks. The stone went to join those already heaped up in the dust.

"It's not even the same granite!" murmured the Commander, crossing his arms. Then he added, as if to rebuke his discouragement: *Sub morte vita!* Life is beneath death! The days of ordeal are over. Will not tomorrow complete the 20th year?"

He remained pensive for a moment. Two o'clock sounded on the hoarse clock whose weights hung against the wall. The gardens had already been deserted for some time, for the tragic incident to which the Marquise's guests had been witnesses had, in spite of everything, abbreviated the last phase of the party. A profound silence reigned without, and nothing could be heard but the nocturnal voice of the city. The light of the two candles fell upon the Commander's face, as white and polished as antique ivory. His eyes were lowered and spoken words slipped slowly from his lips.

"We other Treguerns," he said, "are the children of the Tomb; our arms are an emblem of mourning; our destiny is bound to the Tomb... but all sins are expiated by the mercy of God, and if science is not futile, I have read our name inscribed in shining letters in the book of the future."

He cocked an ear as a distant sound reached him.

"There are people watching out," he went on, in a strangely emphatic tone, "for the restoration of the old tower! The fields still bear their gilded harvest; the river runs between meadows populated with livestock; the mills turn in the wind that blows from the sea; and the trees of the forest are grown. The land awaits its master!"

He paused to listen again; then he went to one of the casements and lifted a sheet of grey serge that served as a curtain. In front of the window a long line of lindens extended into the distance; the moonlight passing through the rounded branches lit up marble statues here and there, which seemed whiter still in the midst of darkness. Everything was still and silent. The Commander passed his hands, one by one, over his forehead.

"If that child were destined to die," he thought, "I would have seen the Veil!"

He let the curtain fall back and went to sit down next to the table, whose robust antiquity buckled beneath the weight of the debris that encumbered it.

The Commander pushed away an octant corroded by verdigris, which grated against an alembic furnished with its retort.[61] He finished clearing a space by moving two three iron handles to the right or the left, and sat down on the table, beside a tall pyramid of books. There were the 12 tomes *in folio* composed by Albert of Lauringen, in Swabia, better known as Albertus Magnus, Cornelius Agrippa's *Treatise on Occult Philosophy*, Gaufridi's *Mirror of Apparitions*, the Spanish *Hexameron* and Bartholomaeus Holzhauser's *Infernal Voyage*.[62]

The Commander picked a volume from this sinister library at random, and began riffling through it distractedly.

"Comte de Treguern!" he said, abruptly, covering the open page with his hand. "A Le Brec! Is that not the final outrage? Treguern, Treguern, Treguern! Are you not dead enough to live?"

He resumed reading, but it was obvious that his mind was elsewhere, and that he was expecting to be interrupted at any moment. Sure enough, after a few minutes, the main door opened very quietly, and without anyone knocking. Olympe de Treguern slid, rather than merely entering, into the room. She was still wearing her ball-gown, but her hair fell loosely about her shoulders. She crossed the room without saying a word.

"I've been waiting for you," said the Commander, closing his ancient book and coming to his feet. "Will they come?"

The young woman went past him without stopping and made an affirmative nod of the head. At the far end of the room a noise was heard, to the left of the huge Treguern escutcheon that was behind the Tomb. Olympe forced a path through the midst of the broken weapons, fragments of stone and worm-eaten crosses to the place from which the noise seemed to be coming. She touched a button hidden behind the antique canvas, and the black field sewn with silver tears of the large Treguern coat-of-arms swung upwards like the decking of a drawbridge to reveal a large gaping hole, from which a damp, cold draught spread into the interior of the pavilion.

A human figure emerged from the darkness of the opening and came into the room. Then two other men came forth in their turn, carrying a stretcher draped with a cloth. "Thank you, Valérie," they said.

Olympe had stood aside to let them pass; the first to arrive came around the mausoleum and bowed silently to the Commander. He gestured towards the table, where his two companions, bearing their burden with difficulty, set the litter down. Olympe set her hands against her bosom to contain the beating of her heart; she went to stand behind the Tomb and remained there, immobile.

The three men who had come in with the stretcher differed in age, figure and face. The first appeared to be still young, despite his hair and beard, which were dazzlingly white. The two others were old men. All three were dressed in dark clothes. The one that held the head of the litter was tall, strongly built, and his long face terminated in an enormous jaw covered by a forest of greying hair. The one holding the foot of the litter was, by contrast, short, bald and puny in appearance. The man with the white beard had regular and handsome features; his figure conserved an air of nobility, and he could well have been the leader of the mysterious trio.

Despite the physical differences between them, some indefinable stigma marked the three beings with a uniform stamp. Perhaps it was just that they had devoted their lives to the same endeavor, and shared the passion brooding beneath the frosty pallor of their faces. These men must have been engaged in a terrible task; they must all have endured the same difficulty and attempted the same labor, for the same sign of bleak resolve was etched in their expressions, which no longer seemed human.

They were grave, obdurate, inflexible; it was obvious that their hearts, dulled by their own suffering, could no longer hear cries of pain uttered by others. None of them had a name. The man with the white beard was known was the Comte; the tallest of the three was the Diamond Merchant; the little bald one was the Doctor.

The Commander looked at the cloth draped over the stretcher with trepidation. Olympe, by contrast, turned her eyes away and made an effort to restrain the tears that were eager to spring forth.

"He's not dead!" pronounced the Commander, in a strained voice. "He can't be dead! I haven't seen the Veil!"

The Comte wore a cruelly mocking smile. "Treguern has fallen very low!" he said, through pursed lips. "The Devil won't take any more trouble to pull him through this fine adventure!" He lifted the cloth that covered the litter, and they could all see Stéphane's body, with his livid face and his bloodstained shirt. A plaintive groan escaped Olympe's breast, while the Commander repeated, in a kind of stupefaction: "He's not dead! He can't be dead!"

The unfortunate young man's appearance only served to contradict these words.

"Daylight comes quickly at this time of year," the Comte said, calmly, "and he must be in the ground before daylight."

"Here's Commander Malo," added the Doctor, "who will show us the place where Madame la Marquise du Castellat's gardener keeps his spade and pickaxe."

Olympe became weak at the knees and propped herself up on the corner of the table. The Commander took a step forward before putting his hand on Stéphane's heart; the young woman's breath caught in her throat.

"Well?" said the Diamond Merchant to the Commander. "What do you say?"

"I can't feel his heartbeat," the other replied, in a low voice, "but he isn't dead." Addressing himself to the Doctor, he added: "You're a physician—you could save him, if you wished."

Olympe's hands came together involuntarily, while her lovely pleading eyes turned to the Doctor. The gesture and the gaze were futile. The Doctor said, coldly: "The knife went in under the fourth rib; an organ was punctured and the bleeding has determined his death. It wasn't the negro who struck that blow!"

"If Gabriel killed the young man himself," the Comte murmured, "God's judgment begins on Earth!"

"At midnight," the Diamond Merchant said, "Gabriel was in the Marquise's drawing-room."

"A quarter of an hour before," added the Doctor, "he got down from his carriage at the Englishman's door with the last 100,000 francs of the tontine."

"At half-past eleven," the Commander said, "Gabriel Le Brec went back into his victim's house. I saw him!"

"The house was already surrounded!" said the Comte, anxiously. "How was he able to get out?"

As he finished this speech, someone knocked three times in quick succession on the back of the Treguern coat-of-arms. The three unknowns cocked their ears and looked at one another. Only the Comte remained calm.

"Put out the lights!" he ordered.

The Diamond Merchant went one way, the Doctor the other, to snuff out the candles at the two corners of the mausoleum. The room was now illuminated solely by the moonlight, whose slanting rays struck the windows looking out over the garden.

"Hide!" the Comte said then, seizing Malo by the arm and drawing him behind the trunk. The other two crouched down between the granite tomb and the embrasure of the first window. Outside, the knocking was repeated, more loudly— and the person responsible, doubtless believing that the interior of the pavilion was deserted, tried to force an entry.

A profound silence now reigned within the Commander's retreat. All the objects it contained had a changed appearance, and the moonlight, sifted by the serge of the curtains, threw great shadows everywhere, among which those of the mausoleum, the urns and the cross seemed to stand out, blurred by sallow gleams. Here and there, capacious draperies seemed to hang over the mutilated heads of statues. Theater scenery executed by a bold and energetic paintbrush could never have produced such sinister and mysterious effects.

The door hidden by the Treguern escutcheon, by which the Comte and his two companions had entered, had a lock that dated from the time of Louis XV. In those days, the new lock had been strong; once closed, it would have required a battering-ram to break it. But three-quarters of a century and the damp of a subterranean staircase are sufficient to rust even steel. After a few minutes, the Treguern coat-of-arms swung upwards again, and a man wearing a long cloak over an evening suit of irreproachable elegance came into the room. He looked around him then he put the coat-of-arms back in place.

"No one!" he murmured, having pricked up his ear. "I've always had the same good luck. God won't punish me in this life!"

He shuddered, because his eyes, habituated to the gloom, saw clearly in the lugubrious chaos. *If the dead return*, he thought, *it's surely here that I'll see the dead again!*

He came around the mausoleum and headed for the main door, next to which he could make out Commander Malo's meager camp-bed. A cloud passed in front of the Moon, and the room was suddenly plunged into darkness.

The newcomer took a few paces at hazard; his foot tripped two or three times, and he felt lost in the midst of all the debris cluttering the floor. Was that an illusion? It seemed to him that he could hear restrained breathing in the night that surrounded him.

He groped about, trying to get his bearings; his extended hands sounded the darkness. He encountered the corner of the sculpted table, then let out a cry, because his fingers had touched a cold hand.

The Moon slid out from behind the cloud, illuminating both the face of the newcomer and Stéphane's corpse. The man was almost as pale as the cadaver; if an eye could have been certain of its impressions in that darkness, an observer might have been struck by a strange and striking resemblance between the man and the corpse.

The dead man's head was tilted back. The face was young amid curls of blond hair; it was also blond hair that crowned the high and proud forehead of Gabriel de Feuillans. The latter let out a second stifled cry and took a step back; his knees trembled; his fearful gaze made another tour of the room.

"Why here?" he stammered. "Who brought him here?"

His hands came together and his head bowed like that of an accused man suddenly and unexpectedly confronted with proof.

"The police are at the scene of the murder," he said. "They're following a trail of blood, looking for a cadaver. The assassin did not have time to hide the corpse. Who, then, has come to the assassin's aid, this time as always?"

He raised his head, and his eye had a glint of distrust. It was obvious, despite his audacity, that this man believed in supernatural beings.

"I accept!" he announced, slowly, extending his arms into the void, as if he were making a pact with those who were not of this world. "I accept your help! I made my choice between life and eternity a long time ago!"

An indistinct murmur followed these words. Gabriel tapped the floor with his foot, confidently, and raised his voice to say: "Show yourselves, then! I'm waiting for you!"

His intrepid and calm eyes searched the darkness. No one showed himself, but an indistinct voice that came from who knew where pronounced one word: "Later!"

"Later, then!" Gabriel replied, draping his cloak about his shoulders and making for the door. "Until then, thank you and *au revoir*!"

He crossed the room at a rapid pace, opened the door and disappeared.

The Commander was the first to emerge from his hiding-place; he was even paler than usual.

"The Prophecy," he murmured, as though speaking to himself, "says: *When the damned calls out to the avenger; when the Stone missing from the Tomb of Tanneguy is found again, Treguern, three times dead, will be resurrected.* Has not the damned called out the avenger?"

Olympe lifted up the curtain behind which she had hidden and went back to the Tomb.

"Did you see," the Comte said, "how the dead man resembled the living one?"

"That's true," replied the Diamond Merchant and the Doctor simultaneously.

The Commander went on: "The Stone is still missing, and Treguern has died but twice."

"Let's go," said the Doctor. "It's the spade and pickaxe we need at present. Even if we weren't night-birds, work like that can't be carried out in broad daylight."

"Who will keep a vigil with the corpse?" the Commander asked. "I'm a Breton and a Christian. I've given hospitality to the dead; it's necessary for a prayer to be said before the descent into the tomb."

The Comte turned towards Olympe. "Valérie," he said, "would you like to watch and pray?"

Olympe replied in a low voice: "I will watch and I will pray."

They went out. Olympe heard their footsteps fade away on the sand of the pathway; she saw them pass like shadows between the trunks of the great lindens, then vanish into the thicket. She knelt down next to Stéphane's corpse. She wanted to pray, as she had promised, but the words of the prayer could not find their way to her lips; their route was choked by sobs.

She stood up and put her elbows on the granite table; her hair and her tears inundated the dead man's face.

"Stéphane," she said, "can't you hear me any more? I don't know this master whom my mother has ordered me to obey. I love no one in the world but my mother and you... and the Comtesse said to me this morning: 'If it's necessary to choose between the one you want for a husband and me, your mother, what will you do?' "

She leaned closer. She was as beautiful as the angel of pain.

She went on: "Stéphane, I chose between you and my mother! Despite her wishes, I warned you of the danger threatening you. Why didn't you want to believe me?"

XXV. The Grave

Olympe de Treguern remained in that position for a long time, immobile and lost in anguished meditation. She did not speak again. The heat of her eyes had dried her tears. She contemplated poor Stéphane's pale face, to which the movements of the light sometimes gave an appearance of life—but the lie did not deceive her. Stéphane was dead. He was just 20 years old.

Alas, danger is appealing and attractive at that age. Stéphane had not wanted to believe it when he had been told: *Death is nigh!* He had closed his ears to his fiancée's voice, and to the voice of his own presentiments.

Do you remember how handsome and happy he was just a few hours ago? How well he wore his proud and smiling youth? How he pushed his frisky horse in answer to the call of that note signed with the name *Valérie*—the name by which Olympe was known in Orlan, whence Stéphane came?

Now, Valérie called again, but she called in vain.

Out there in Brittany, this blond Stéphane had loved no once but his brother Tanneguy. Once, someone had told him: "Fanchette Féru is not your mother. You are the son of a great lady who lives in the city of Paris." Fanchette wept when he left. Tanneguy had gone with him as far as Redon, and the two of them had embraced, with their hearts full.

"We shall see one another again," Stéphane said. "The big city is the place where everyone seeks his fortune. When I have made a fortune, you'll come to join me."

Ordinarily, the wind carries away such childish words, but the wind did not carry away Stéphane's words. He made his fortune and he remembered his promise. We know where and how his brother Tanneguy found him, Both of them— Tanneguy in Brittany, Stéphane in Paris—knew Olympe under her mysterious name of Valérie-*la-Morte*. Tanneguy had seen her mixed up with strange things that frightened the inhabitants of the old Treguern estates, but he did not know

249

the old Treguern estates, but he did not know that she was his sister.

Stéphane and Olympe had met in the Marquise du Castellat's salons at the time when Laurence de Treguern—"beautiful and unhappy," according to the horoscope drawn by Commander Malo—had died just as she was about to marry Gabriel de Feuillans. Olympe had a great secret that did not belong to her. Stéphane did not know this secret, even though he had offered Olympe his hand and his heart and she had not refused him. But Olympe had once said to him: "A danger threatens you. If you receive a letter signed *Valérie*, think of me and do as you are bid." Much later, Olympe had said to him: "The world is mistaken; I shall never be the wife of Gabriel de Feuillans."

Instead of praying, Olympe lost herself in memories of those bygone days. A noise that came from outside, in the garden, not far from the pavilion, woke her up with a start. It was the sound of a pickaxe, attacking the ground with discretion.

"His grave!" she murmured, seized by anguish. "They're digging his grave!"

She got up right away. The sounds continued: slow, regular and implacable.

She dragged herself to the window and lifted up the serge curtain. In the moonlight she saw the Comte and the Doctor standing in the nearby grove, leaning on their spades. The Commander was leaning against a tree and the Diamond Merchant was breaking the soil with his pick. She collapsed on the floor, stammering with horror: "There! There, where I said to him, at a party one evening: 'I am your fiancée...' "

The Diamond Merchant paused to wipe the sweat from his brow. The Comte and the Doctor worked in their turn, using the spades to clear the loosened soil out of the pit. Olympe covered her face with her hands, and went back to the table where Stéphane was stretched out. She sank down there, as if crushed—but she came upright again at the first blow of the pick-axe, which began to sound again.

"Stéphane! Stéphane!" she cried, madly. "Malo de Treguern has not seen the Veil! You are not dead!"

There was a fragment of a mirror among the debris cluttering the table. Olympe seized it, and presented it to the discolored lips of the young man. No vestige of breath clouded the polished glass.

Olympe threw herself to her knees and kissed the ground, praying ardently. Then she attempted the mirror test for a second time—and released a cry as she saw the glass fog. She doubted the evidence of her eyes. She had not wanted to believe that Stéphane was dead, but she dared not believe in his resurrection.

And yet, the clouded glass had spoken: Stéphane had exhaled. A few moments later, he opened his eyes slightly and tried to smile as he awoke, recognizing the gaze of his fiancée, who was kneeling beside his bed of stone.

"Valérie!" he said. "Where are we? And what's that noise?"—for they were continuing to dig up the ground in the grove.

Olympe warmed his hands in hers. Stéphane touched his breast, and his memory came back to him in a sudden rush. "Ah!" he said. "I remember. I found my house empty—someone had sent away my servants. Feuillans' negro was hiding in my study... then Feuillans himself came up behind me... but is it possible? Gabriel? Gabriel de Feuillans—an assassin!"

As Olympe was about to reply, the door, which the three unknown men had left ajar, turned softly on its hinges. A man appeared on the threshold. His face was haggard, but retained among its profound traces of suffering a frank and generous character. Above the man's forehead was a forest of black tresses, in which a few curling white hairs showed here and there. His eyes made a rapid tour of the room. He started with surprise as he perceived Stéphane half-lying on the table—but when his eyes met Olympe's he nodded his head in a satisfied manner.

He took a step forward, and then it became evident that his broad shoulders had no arms.

"Have you come on behalf of Monsieur Privat, Etienne, my friend?" Olympe asked, in an affectionate tone.[63] At the same time, she exchanged a glance with Stéphane, as if to say to him: *We have nothing to fear from this man.*

The man with no arms, whom we have already seen in the court of diligences, and who was indeed the little advocate's beast of burden, smiled mysteriously. Instead of replying, he crossed the room at a deliberate pace and headed directly towards the Tomb of Tanneguy. A shapeless object was hanging around his neck, which Stéphane could not quite make out. When he came closer, they saw that it was a fragment of stone, retained on his shoulders by a cord. Having arrived in front of the mausoleum, he examined the tablet attentively, looking for the broken corner.

"Here's the crack!" he said.

Deprived as he was of both his hands, he made futile efforts with his body, his neck and his head to bring the stone he carried at his breast to the funereal tablet.

"Would you like me to help you, Etienne, my friend?" said Olympe, in a low voice.

The man with no arms still made no reply. He had finally contrived to take the stone beneath his teeth. He brought it to the broken corner. Necessity had taught him to make up as best he could for the limbs he had lost. The stone was presented with a certain dexterity; it slotted so perfectly into the fissure in the tablet at the first attempt that the man with no arms was able to let go of it without it falling. It fitted snugly in place, and the thin line between the two sections of manifestly homogeneous granite was scarcely perceptible.

The man with no arms stood up straight again. His ample torso filled with air. By the proud smile that suddenly lit up his face, one could divine that in the time when the hand of God had not yet weighed upon him he had been a handsome and gallant man. He looked scornfully at the fragments of stone heaped up around him and the three boxes recently brought in by the Commander.

"I only had one stone, myself," he said, with child-like glee, "but it was the right one!" He added, as he withdrew it: "I'm the one that will fulfill the Prophecy. Provided that it falls from a great enough height, the stone is heavy enough to crush the misfortune of Treguern!"

He went back to the door, as if the only reason he had come was to confront the tablet of the mausoleum with his piece of granite. As he passed the young woman again, his gaze was impregnated with caressing tenderness.

"It's a good day!" he murmured. "I've seen the father, the son and the daughter!" He added, as if thinking aloud rather than speaking: "Filhol's hair has gone white, but how handsome the child is, and how he resembles the portraits of knights in the hall of the manor!"

"Who is that?" Stéphane asked, when the mutilated man had passed over the threshold.

Olympe put a finger to her lips; footsteps were audible on the path through the lindens.

"They're coming back," she murmured.

"Who?" Stéphane asked again.

"The time is approaching when you shall know everything," Olympe replied. "The man whose wife I shall be must not be ignorant of anything that concerns me, and I don't want even the shadow of a mystery to come between us—but it would take hours, and we don't have a minute. Consent to remain ignorant tonight, and let yourself be guided by me, as if I were your mother."

"Command," said the young man, smiling. "You shall see whether I am a docile son."

"Are you strong enough to get up!" Olympe asked.

Stéphane tried; his wound drew a groan from him, but he contrived to be get to his feet. As he did so, a voice outside was heard, saying: "The grave is dug; let's make haste—it's almost dawn."

The Diamond Merchant and the Doctor appeared in the doorway. They both took a step back at the sight of the man they had left lying lifeless on the table, who was now standing in the middle of the room.

"What is it?" asked the Comte, the third to arrive. The Diamond Merchant and the Doctor moved to the right and to the left to let him see or pass through, according to his whim.

The Comte looked, and halted in his turn. His eyebrows, which seemed darker beneath his snowy hair, came together forcefully. While the three companions hesitated, seeming to consult one another, Olympe advanced towards them, taking Stéphane by the hand.

"As you have done on other occasions," she said, in a firm and measured tone, "this man has cheated the assassin's weapon today. If he follows the same rules as you, he shall have the same rights as you. That's the agreement."

"That's the agreement," repeated the Comte

And the other two repeated after him, with a kind of regret: "That's the agreement!"

Stéphane remained silent and still; he did not understand what was happening, but had only to keep his promise of obedience. The Commander pushed past the men blocking the door, came forward and placed his hands on Stéphane's shoulders.

"I told you that the grave would remain empty," he murmured, without turning around. "Treguern has lost none of its power, and death must always take account of its secrets."

"Is the young man ready to swear the oath?" asked the Comte.

Olympe squeezed Stéphane's arm, and he replied: "I am ready."

"Half Le Brec, half Treguern," murmured the Commander, who was still looking at him intently.

The three companions came forward, but Malo set himself in front of them.

"You," he said, raising his voice, his eyes glued to Stéphane's face. "I forbid you to take the oath. Le Brec has stuck you down and Treguern has saved you—but a child does not have the right to judge his father!"

XXVI. The Four O'Clock Bell

The church bell at Saint-Eustache had sounded three o'clock in the morning. Although Paris was still asleep, a great bustle and hubbub began around the marketplace. From the Marché des Prouvaries to the Fontaine des Innocents, a rustic population unknown to the idle towndweller swarmed restlessly. This is the bourse of fishmongers, market-gardeners and all manner of other brokers with iron-capped shoes and callous hands, always armed with whips, who take it upon themselves to satisfy Parisian appetites. Around the fountain, the pavements disappeared beneath huge baskets of fruit, which covered the ground all the way to the footpath of the Rue aux Fers.

The countryfolk were standing there calmly, guarding their merchandise, letting the crowd of buyers move back and forth. If you have seen the runners at Longchamps racecourse pawing the ground and champing at the bit, impatient for the signal for which they are waiting, you will have some idea of what goes on among the hucksters, victims of the rigors of regulation. They suffer the torment of Tantalus, placed there in the middle of so many fruits, beautiful melons and fresh vegetables without the power to reach out and seize them. No one can begin before the designated time of four o'clock; it is necessary that the first chime of the municipal clock has sounded before the purchases commence. Before then, one may cry out, haggle and argue, but one cannot complete a deal and place one's marker on the coveted basket.

But as soon as the clock sounds—what a party and what a battle! The moral chain is broken, the wave breaks and the tide surges forward, invading the scarcely-defended shore; everyone joins in the stampede, jostling for position in the crush. Long ribbons are passed around the baskets with prodigious velocity—ribbons that mean don't touch! The ribbon is a sacred thing; it is like the frail seal that the law places on the

255

strong-box of a deceased person, which is worth more than all the locks in the world. The countryman, imperturbable in the midst of this fever, smokes his pipe calmly and looks on incessantly. The color of the ribbons is of little importance; he will be paid in cash and he has stated his price in advance; one man's money is as good as another's.

After a minute or so, the tempest eases; all the baskets are marked and nothing remains but to pour the price of the lovely creamy fish, vermilion grapes and aromatic pears into the leather purses of the Normans. Norman is the generic name of the rustic courtiers who buy up goods in country markets and trade them on in the Paris markets.

But that is only the space that surrounds the Fontaine des Innocents. Paris would go lamentably hungry if it only had these trifles to nibble on. The neighboring streets are cluttered, and while carts wait along the riverside, on the bridges, and even in the Place du Châtelet, veritable mountains of vegetables are heaped up on the pavements, from Saint-Eustache to the Pont Neuf, and from the Pont Neuf to Saint-Denis. In the shelter of these hills of cabbages, leeks and lettuces, barbarous women lie about—in the dust, if it is fine; in the mud, if the weather is wet. They sleep there as they do elsewhere. Those who prefer to chat require brandy—and there is no lack of brandy in this neighborhood, where Paul Niquet,[64] like an ancient river, empties his inexhaustible urn by night and by day.

In the Rue de la Ferronnerie, not far from the monumental arch that gives entry to the market, facing the fountain, no one was sleeping for 100 paces around. The guardians of the various mountains of vegetables whose chain extended along the pavement had formed a conventicle and were holding a discussion in front of the arch. The buyers who had been crowding around since three o'clock were making their choices, but they had difficulty finding anyone to talk to because the club of village-women were concerned with a matter of more immediate interest—to such an extent that the buyers, having tried in vain to negotiate their impending purchases, joined the group in their turn and listened in.

256

The discussion concerned a murder committed that same night, in very extraordinary circumstances—and who wouldn't forget everything else to talk about a murder?

"Quite young, I tell you, quite young!" cried a woman whose ruddy face was half-hidden by her ample headscarf. "And handsome as a cherub!"

"Have you seen him, then, Madame Michel?" the question came from all sides.

"I didn't have the chance," the good woman replied, bitterly. "I arrived a quarter of a hour too late—but the Norman who lodges with us saw him, and said that he was a fine figure of a lad, with eyes as blue as love!"

"What had he done to the other one, then?" asked a voice in the crowd. "Was it a fight?"

"No one knows," Madame Michel retorted, "And I can only tell you what was told to me. It was behind the Allée des Veuves; there's a Marquise's house here, let's say where Madame Mathieu's heap is, and another, smaller house across the way, about where Madame Richard's heap is. Between the two houses, here where we are, they found them lying one atop the other... and the most amazing thing is that three civilians came to take the cadaver, pretending to help, and spirited it away like some vanishing trick!"

"You can't hide a corpse under a blade of grass," observed Madame Richard, incredulously.

"That's what happened! I'm just telling you what was told to me. And God knows that everyone from the Allée des Veuves to the Invalides is talking about the business!"

"Have they searched the houses?" someone asked.

"They searched the house on the right, which belonged to the young deceased. And guess what they found?" Madame Michel paused; every ear was straining. "They found a big ugly negro, dead drunk at the back of a cellar."

There was a murmur in the group; the mention of negroes have that effect.

"But I've forgotten something," Madame Michel said then, "because things don't all come back to me at the same

257

time. He had servants, you understand, this young man. Well, the police found the house empty—not a soul! And when the servants came back, after midnight, they said that they'd been sent away—one here, one there—by someone. Who? Probably the other young man—the one who got away from the guardsmen..."

"The villain escaped, then!" cried those who had not heard the beginning of the story.

Madame Michel looked at them askew. "As I said," she replied, "he'd already escaped when I brought my cart past the guardroom at the Esplanade! The soldiers were running about looking for him. And the people gathered there didn't hesitate in saying that it was a mistake to have left him on his own in the room with the worthless grille at the back, which gives out on to the Esplanade."

"Ah!" said a short woman under the arch. "You mean the youngster who did the dirty deed?"

"Monsieur Monnerot! Monsieur Monnerot!" cried the assembly, in chorus.

Monsieur Monnerot was "the Norman who lodges with us" cited by Madame Michel. He came forward, with the chin-strap of his bonnet over his ears, a pipe in his mouth and his hands inside his blouse. The circle opened to let him through.

"It's true, isn't it, Monsieur Monnerot, that you've seen him?" Madame Michel said.

"As clear as I see you, with no more inconvenience," the Norman replied. "My cart was passing the Pont des Invalides at the moment when the soldiers were bringing him out of the Champs-Elysées. As good-looking fellows go, he's a good-looking fellow!"

"There are so many like that—deceptive faces!" observed Madame Mathieu, the proprietress of the right-hand heap, to Madame Richard, the proprietress of the left-hand heap."

"It caused an immediate traffic jam along the riverside," Monsieur Monnerot went on, "and we had plenty of time to find out the ins and outs of it. When the youngster was in the guardhouse, a young lad of 15 or 16 came in wanting to see him, saying: 'I'm his brother.' I've a keen eye, me, though it might not appear so, and I twigged right away that it was a filly in disguise."

"And she was let in?" cried the crowds, whose curiosity had grown more lively.

With every minute that passed the crowd had grown; it occupied almost the entire width of the street.

"It's down to the man in charge of the post," said Monsieur Monnerot, "And he'll be punished—if he was at fault. About ten minutes after the so-called *gamin* went in, the alarm was given inside the guardhouse and all the square-bashers came out with their rifles, as if they were about to lay waste to the quarter. No use, though—the night was black. They beat the Esplanade thoroughly, but the bird had flown!"

"And the *gamin* who was a girl?"

"Gone! No more *gamin* than there is on the end of my nose. After a while, the carts got under way again, and I left the rubbernecks gossiping in front of the guardhouse door."

"Then you don't know what happened next, Monsieur Monneret?" asked Madame Michel in an insinuating tone.

"I don't think anything's happened since," replied the Norman.

Madame Michel, immediately recovering her self-importance, turned her back on him to address the public directly.

"Well," she said, "that's probably the most amazing thing of all. When our cart, in its turn, passed the guardhouse, the soldiers were there, dumbfounded. It turns out that this assassin, since he is an assassin, is a young man from a great family..."

The Norman shrugged his shoulders. "Straw hat," he muttered, "thick velvet jacket and canvas trousers!"

"Clothes have nothing to do with it," said the good woman. "No common young man would have been asked for like that by a Marquise, a Comtesse and a Comte!"

This coup was almost tumultuous.

"What Marquise?" he cried. "What Comtesse? What Comte?"

Madame Michel struck a dignified pose and put her plump hands under her apron, "I can only tell you what was told to me, my children," she replied. "Who told me this? The soldiers at the post themselves. As regards the names of the Marquise and the Comte, you're asking too much of me. What's certain is that I'll be reading the *Journal du Commerce* tomorrow to get all the details."

The inevitable moment when the crowd broke up into a number of petty clubs, in which the story, embroidered in a thousand various ways, was repeated for the edification of latecomers. Monsieur Monnerot, left alone with a few acolytes, affirmed that if the youngster ever crossed his path he would certainly recognize him and put his hand on his collar without hesitation.

From the direction of the Rue Saint-Honoré, they heard the heavy tread of a fiacre, making progress as best it could amid the obstacles accumulated in its path. The women appointed to guard the piles of vegetables exchanged glances, as if the Rue de la Ferronnerie were their personal property. They disapproved strongly when the people of the quarter came home in carriages—cabbages were crushed by the dozen, in no time at all!

When they heard the fiacre, the groups began to disband, and each sentinel went to watch over her heap. The carriage, wandering through that immense boutique of vegetation, reaped a rich harvest of invective during its passage. The coachman, who presumably knew from experience the somewhat barbaric mores of these latitudes, turned a deaf ear and patiently followed his course.

When it arrived opposite the fountain, the lantern placed under the arch cast its beams into the interior of the fiacre. A small and rather pale face sculpted like a nutcracker was suddenly illuminated; then the light fell on another face. Monsieur Monnerot let out a cry of astonishment; he pointed at the fiacre, and the gossips surrounding him could see a handsome young man with a straw hat, dressed in a velvet jacket.

"Stop that fiacre!" commanded Monsieur Monnerot, in a thunderous voice.

The nutcracker stuck his head out of the carriage door and said: "At the gallop!"

The coachman whipped his horses, and the blinds were immediately closed. The crowd, however, had already begun to move. Monsieur Monnerot, who seemed to be a man of determination, threw himself after the fiacre, crying: "It's him! I'll swear that it's him!"

The two skinny hacks pulling the fiacre went into the Rue de l'Aiguillerie at a trot. The result of the pursuit was never in doubt for an instant, for the crowd was already gaining ground and the coachman would not have been able to press his beasts any harder if it were a matter of making a fortune. Anticipating an easy triumph, Monnerot was already saying: "He's ours! We've got him!"

At that moment, however, the sound of the four o'clock chimes threw out its magical call. It was like the flourish of a magic wand. Monnerot stopped with his foot in mid-air and turned around impetuously. Rustics and merchants alike copied him. The fiacre no longer existed; there was no thought of anything except abandoned baskets and heaps of vegetables, defenseless against pillage. Monnerot was knocked down twice in that frenetic scramble, and there were many who came off worse than he did.

At the first chime of the bell, the coachman—who knew his business—eased his hacks down to a gentle trot. He turned the corner of the Rue Saint-Denis at his leisure, and came to a halt in the very center of the market, in front of a six-story house with a pigeon-loft at its summit.[65]

The commercial storm was at its height. People were buying and selling furiously, with fists and cash. The area had the appearance of a desperate skirmish. All the murderers in the universe could have passed by at that moment without anyone taking any notice of them.

The fiacre's door opened; the nutcracker got down cautiously and rang the bell of the six-story house. After him came the handsome young man in the straw hat and velvet jacket.

"Come in, my traveling-companion," Monsieur Privat said to him, after paying the coachman. "What I predicted has happened, point by point. We have met again sooner than you anticipated; you haven't found what you were looking for; and you have found what you weren't looking for. In Paris, more than anywhere else, life is a lottery: who knows whether you have the winning ticket in your pocket now?"

He closed the door behind Tanneguy, who was stupefied by surprise, while the empty fiacre went down towards the riverbank.

XXVII. The Man With No Arms

On the top floor of the six-story house facing the Fontaine des Innocents in the Rue Saint-Denis there was a little apartment of meager and paltry appearance, poorly furnished, consisting of a kitchen and three rooms. The kitchen was separated from the rest by a corridor, in the middle of the corridor's ceiling was a skylight that gave access to the famous pigeon-loft of which Monsieur Privat had spoken so complacently.

An iron bedstead was wedged in between the stovepipe and the wall; its only utensils were two or three earthenware pans. Facing the bed, a table wobbled on its unequal legs. On the table was the stone that the man with no arms had carried around his neck the night before, when he had gone into Commander Malo's retreat. The man with no arms was there, clad only in a shirt that covered his mutilated shoulders. He was sitting on the floor, on a bundle of straw, in front of the table, working hard.

What work could this unfortunate possibly do? It was 20 years since Sergeant Etienne, deprived of his right arm, had lost his left arm at the *Trou-de-la-Dette*. At that time, he had been a proud young man, as brave and generous as a lion. What had he been doing since then? Into what depths had his decline and misery dragged him? Etienne could not have told you himself. The candle burning on the table shone directly upon his ravaged temples and a face in which intelligence sometimes seemed to be dead.

It is true that, on occasion, a vivid spark of intelligence suddenly lit up in his eyes. At other times, when his gaze happened to encounter certain objects hanging on the wall above his bed, his head sank, heavily and sadly upon his breast. There was a curved saber, linen epaulettes, and a military jacket whose sleeves bore a sergeant's stripes: poor trophies

263

that reminded him of his youth; cherished memories that broke his heart, but which he did not have the courage to put away.

There are lives made thus: long martyrdoms that are irrefutable proof of another and better existence. Since the day when Etienne had lost his second arm, he did not remember having experienced a single moment of joy. We know his story up to the point of the double baptism the day after Assumption. After the baptism, he had been put in prison. The surgeons had given him hope that the amputation of his second arm might kill him, but he had survived. A year later, the prison gates had opened and he had been thrown out, impotent as he was in body and mind, on to the streets of the town of Vannes. Have no fear that this biography will drag on; we know of only one further detail. Etienne had become the beast of burden of the little advocate who had defended him in court and saved him. This was pure charity on Monsieur Privat's part, for Etienne was the least useful of servants.

To what mysterious work was he devoted that night—he, whom his master was obliged to serve every day? He had a cord in his teeth, which terminated in a slip-knot. With his head and shoulders, by any means available, he got the stone—the stone that fitted into the broken corner of the Tomb of Tanneguy—into the slip-knot; then he shook it, and the stone fell out. Ten, or perhaps 20 times, he began the trial again; then he got up and wiped sweat from his forehead on to his bed-linen.

"It will fall from on high!" he murmured, looking at his stone with affectionate and satisfied eyes. "It fits—and the Prophecy cannot lie!"

As he came back to the table to attempt the movement one last time, he heard the noise of the bell at the street-door. His face changed; he made haste to hide the cord and the stone, and hastened to throw himself on his bed, after extinguishing his candle. Almost at the same moment, someone knocked on the door to the landing. Etienne hooked his toe into a ring at the foot of his bed and pulled a ribbon. The door opened.

"Don't disturb yourself," said Monsieur Privat's voice in the corridor. "I have everything I need: stay where you are."

Etienne heard the little advocate draw a bolt on the outside of his door; he pricked up his ears. "Who's that with him?" he murmured. Ordinarily, it was not Monsieur Privat's custom to bring strangers to his lodgings. Etienne got out of bed and moved silently to the door—but Monsieur Privat was no longer in the corridor. He had ushered our friend Tanneguy into a fairly large room, full of dusty piles of old papers and redolent with stuffiness. Between two sets of pinewood bookshelves there was a moderately large bed, for which Monsieur Privat immediately headed.

"My traveling companion," he said, cheerfully, "tomorrow, when it is light, I shall show you my pigeons, and the other treasures of my home. We have a magnificent view and an excellent atmosphere, ceaselessly purified by the fresh vegetables brought to us as tributes from the provinces. For the present, what you need most is a nap. Without flattery, I've never seen a brave lad as perfectly stupefied as you are!"

Tanneguy looked at him dumbfoundedly, as if he had taken it upon himself to confirm the observation.

"Help me," Monsieur Privat continued, unable to stop himself laughing. He removed the blanket and sheets from his bed—carefully, for he was a very orderly man—then grabbed the upper mattress at one end and instructed Tanneguy with a nod of his head to take the other. Tanneguy obeyed. Monsieur Privat went out of the room, went along the corridor, and pushed the door of a little room entirely bare of furniture, on whose floorboards he set the mattress down. This room situated directly across from the windowed door of the kitchen.

"Lie down on that, fully dressed, my traveling companion," Monsieur Privat said. "At 20, one doesn't need a featherbed. I shall say 'sleep well,' and go about my business."

"Monsieur!" Tanneguy protested, immediately recovering his presence of mind. "I beg you, tell me..."

The little man interrupted him. "Not one treacherous word! I've already wasted too much time with you. Your servant, with all my heart!" He went out of the room in a hurry and closed the door on Tanneguy, The latter remained alone in profound darkness. He pressed his hands to his forehead; in the first moment of his abandonment he felt that he was going mad.

From the moment when he had woken up in the middle of that curious and hostile crowd, in the very place where he had seen the inanimate body of his brother Stéphane, unexpected adventures had followed in such strangely rapid succession that he had remained in a kind of drunken stupor. The illuminated ramp of the Marquise's garden, the strains of the joyful music, the magnificently-dressed women—with the beautiful young woman from Orlan, Valérie-*la-Morte*, among them—Commander Malo and Monsieur de Feuillans, the master of the *Château-sans-Terre*... then, the soldiers who had suddenly appeared and seized him, the insulting gazes of the people gathered on the route... a young boy unexpectedly introduced into his prison, who saved him, as if he were possessed of a fairy's magic wand... a rapid flight beneath tall trees in the company of the boy—who seemed to be a girl in disguise, and who spoke in a familiar voice, with a familiar accent... a fiacre waiting behind a great edifice surmounted by a dome, with Monsieur Privat in attendance...

All of this whirled around in his head, tangled in a web of confusion.

"Hurry up!" Monsieur Privat had said, in his piping voice, as he opened the carriage door.

When the boy had lifted his helmet, exposing the curly strands of abundant hair, had Tanneguy not recognized the sharp face of little Vevette, whose old mother lived in Orlan, on the far side of the presbytery orchard? There had been no light, except for the smoky lanterns of the fiacre; he could have been mistaken.

"What should I say to Mademoiselle?" the boy or girl had asked, on leaving Monsieur Privat.

"To warn Madame la Comtesse," Privat had replied. "I'll take this fellow to my pigeon-loft."

The fiacre had got under way, and from the Invalides to the marketplace, Monsieur Privat had not unclenched his teeth. Now Tanneguy felt as if he were imprisoned in this closed room, whose thick air weighed upon his bosom. He wanted to move; he wanted to run—but at the first step he took in the midst of that profound obscurity, he stopped, discouraged.

He let himself fall upon the mattress. The thought of his brother Stéphane came back to him, and his eyes filled with tears. The radiant vision that had drawn him away from his village could not help appearing to him in that feverish hour, and indeed it did, but it was like one of those diamantine fires shining in the vault of Heaven, which sparkle in the night without lighting it up, rendering the shadows darker by contrast.

Tanneguy's heart came under greater stress; the thought of Valérie was now linked within him to some indefinable fatal horror. Had he not seen her, white and cold, among the women staying at the place where Stéphane was covered in blood?

His eyes, weighed down by fatigue, closed. He was only 20 years old. At that age, all sorrow has the privilege of taking refuge in sleep. At the moment when his limbs became numb, as his consciousness vacillated before extinction, it was not the image of Valérie that floated in front of his eyes. He saw Treguern Common, with its ancient willows and its cropped grass, strewn with dwarf chamomiles. On the far side of a ditch, a young girl was sitting: a child in the white headscarf of a Morbihan peasant; an almost angelic figure with large, sad and gentle eyes, which seemed to be speaking to God.

As he drifted off to sleep, Tanneguy pronounced the name of Marcelle, the companion of his infancy: he saw her picking the petals from a daisy and heard her asking the meadow-flower: "Does he remember me? A little? A lot? Sometimes? Never?"

267

XXVIII. Monsieur Privat's Bundles of Paper

Here is a man who was not dreaming about daisies, and for whose sake no one was consulting any petty wild flower oracle: Monsieur Privat, praise the Lord! Boxwood sawdust sprinkled on the fresh ink and the old ink on yellowed paper were as pretty and sweet-smelling as daisies to him. He was in his study. He had taken off his dress suit, more for reasons of economy than to make himself more comfortable; a grey dressing-gown, which had served him faithfully since the days of his youth, was wrapped around his meager torso, and the peaked cap had resumed its post atop his skull.

He was seated at a large table, under the reflective shade of the lamp. Bundles of papers were heaped up around him as the cabbages had recently been on the pavements of the neighboring streets. He was in his element; his blinking gaze caressed confusion of dusty scribbles, passing from one to another with greater contentment than a miser washing his hands in his coffers full of gold.

"There would have been a way," he said to himself as he pushed his spectacles up to his forehead in order to rub his weary eyes. "If my comrade Tanneguy had been left in the hands of the law, it would have been necessary, this time, to bring it out into the open. And, when all's said and done, I'm not the slave of that enchantress and I don't believe in ghosts. If the beautiful Olympe doesn't tell me what I need to know, I still have time in hand. There's still time to retrace our steps—unfortunately for my traveling companion."

He took an imposing ledger—old, soiled and shiny—from the table, and began riffling through it rapidly.

"Twenty years of notes!" he murmured. "What gropings! What mad hypotheses! But I've followed the thread, and I'm now very close to the exit from the labyrinth."

He dipped his pen in the ink, and on the last half-filled page he wrote a dozen lines, doubtless a summary of what he had learned during the day. Then he pushed the ledger back, stretched his legs out under the table and crossed his arms.

"Let's recapitulate," he said to himself. "Towards the end of the last century, an English company—which was to have many imitators—was formed to exploit two common sentiments at the same time: a father's concern for his family, and ambitious egotism. The company, which adopted the name of Campbell Life, General Insurance, Annuities on Survivorship in honor of its founder, offered to some a combination of insurance in the event of death, and to others the exciting hazards of the tontine. To the first it said: 'If you die, I shall put bread in your children's mouths.' To the others, it cried: 'Only live, and you shall be rich!' A young boy named Gabriel, a *cloarec* preparing his studies for the Church, brought an English newspaper to the poor parish of Orlan, which contained a pompous advertisement for this enterprise. That young man was the friend of the last Treguern; the last Treguern went to London one day in order to insure himself in the event of death for the sum of 100,000 francs. While he was away, the *cloarec* Gabriel made contact with an international agent, and took out a subscription to the tontine for 20 annual payments of 100,000 francs each, no less!"

Monsieur Privat paused, blowing into his cheeks. "He had scarcely come of age, this Gabriel," he muttered, "When he had that idea. A headstrong rogue!"

He continued his summary, with the aid of notes that he consulted one by one: "Gabriel hadn't a *sou* to his name, and the first payment was due on August 16, 1800. Filhol de Treguern came back home and did something that might seem incredible in our era of tranquillity, but which was not so very difficult in the midst of the troubles to which our western provinces were so long subject following the fall of the Monarchy. Thanks to Gabriel, who lived at the presbytery in Orlan, and who could assist him in more ways than one, Filhol feigned a mortal illness in the month of September 1799. Gabriel recorded his death in the parish register and Filhol, legally deceased, hid in the environs of Treguern Manor, to wait for the English company to pay the insurance due in the event of death.

"It took a long time, because the war made relations between the two countries very difficult. Finally, in response to legal proceedings launched by Gabriel, the executor of Comte Filhol's estate, an agent of Campbell Life risked the Channel crossing and arrived in the town of Redon on August 14, 1800.

"Ten months had passed since the empty coffin that was generally believed to contain the remains of the last Treguern had been put into the ground. During that interval, Geneviève Le Hir, Comte Filhol's wife, had been visiting him in his retreat. She became a mother on that same night of August 14 to 15, brought into the world a child of the male sex.

"All that is as clear as daylight! Gabriel assassinated Filhol de Treguern to get the Englishman's 100,000 francs to pay his first annual premium. The double baptism followed, and the exchange of children, as if Gabriel wanted to remove every chance of a future from the race of Treguern, which he had robbed in the present and in the past. The trial of Etienne, accused of murder, introduced me to these infamies, and since then, I've followed the trail of this former *cloarec* Gabriel. Filhol was Gabriel's friend; he died a violent death. Jérôme Clément, the physician of Laval, was Gabriel's friend; he met the same fate as Filhol. Johann-Maria Worms, the diamond-merchant of Cologne, was also Gabriel's friend, as was the Marquis du Castellat. Laurence de Treguern was Gabriel's fiancée... all rich, all dead on the same deadly date. And Gabriel, who had no known resources, always paid that heavy annuity of 100,000 francs on time!

"A child could deduce the implications of that, But there is something else, which not only requires more than the intelligence of a child, but which goes beyond the limits of human reason. The dead live on! Some of them, at least. Why do they not claim what is rightfully theirs? And if they are ghosts—for the mind weakens before these nameless bizarreries—why do they not take their revenge? Why does Commander Malo de Treguern, who knows everything, remain silent? Why does

270

that strange young woman who seems ignorant of nothing, Olympe de Treguern—Valérie-*la-Morte*—keep her mouth shut?"

Monsieur Privat was going over these questions, which he could not resolve, again and again, when he shivered as he felt a hand fall lightly upon his shoulder. The lamp was beginning to pale before the first light of day. He returned around and saw Olympe de Treguern standing next to him.

"Valérie!" he exclaimed. "I wished for your presence!"

"Shh!" said the young woman, putting a finger to her lips. "Comtesse Torquati is there."

"Geneviève... in Tanneguy's room?"

"I had no need to show her the way," Olympe replied, with a melancholy smile that made her even more beautiful. When Monsieur Privat began to speak again, she stopped him with a gesture and said: "I heard you. You want to ask me why the victims have forgotten to attend to their vengeance. You don't know, then, that they have done more than that? The murderer's path was full of obstacles; these obstacles vanished from his path."

"Indeed!" stammered the little man.

"And after each crime was committed, has there ever been any trace of it? Has there not always been a mysterious hand that has removed the cadaver and washed away every trace of blood?"

"That's true!" the little man said, again.

"Be they living or dead," she said, "they are working towards an end, and woe betide anyone who gets in their way! They said to me once: 'Choose between your brother Tanneguy and your fiancé Stéphane.' My heart rebelled, and in my pride, I refused. I wanted to save both of them, the one by means of the other. By bringing them together, I almost lost them both!"

"I, who have neither fiancé nor brother..." Monsieur Privat began.

Valérie stepped forward and put her hand on his shoulder. "You have loved us," she said, slowly. "Beneath the whim of your curiosity, there is some sort of chivalric devotion. But without being aware it, you have already hampered the plans of those whom you serve more than once. If you get in their way again, I shall not be able to save you."

"Do you think I'm afraid?" cried the little man, quick to take offense.

"And you?" Olympe asked, without losing her composure. "Do you want to prevent justice being done? You know enough to believe me when I tell you that, in certain circumstances, far removed from the ruts of everyday life, ordinary means of redress—legal means—are closed. Monsieur de Feuillans might perhaps emerge the victor from a judiciary battle in which no material proof could be marshaled against him."

"Perhaps!" said the little man, who relished the thought of that battle. "You don't know."

Olympe's eyes were shining. "They have not fought and suffered for 20 years to finish up saying to themselves: 'Perhaps!' It's not probability they need now; it's certainty." After a pause, while Monsieur Privat reflected, she went on: "I am a Treguern. My brother Tanneguy, who is here and whom I love, does not know what hands have built that splendid palace, in which the grandeur of our name will be renewed in him. Others can hide their sadness in retreat, but he, our Tanneguy, will be happy and glorious. Listen to me..."

When she spoke thus, her beautiful face became so proud that Monsieur Privat, subjugated, looked at her with admiration and respect.

"Listen: if I have done wrong, God shall be my judge. The gaze of human justice would dispel the magnificence of our dream like the breath of a malign spirit. I do not want human justice!"

"But you're very young, Valérie," objected Monsieur Privat, hesitantly. "You might have been deceived."

"They are four, now," Olympe de Treguern replied, speaking as if her interlocutor had got to the bottom of the mystery. "Four, since last night. These four men have made a pact; each of them wants vengeance for himself, and for their leader—for Treguern—they want the great power that wealth alone can give upon the Earth. The day after their victory, their interests might make them enemies; today, I shall make ready for the struggle. In the meantime, are you with us or are you against us?"

Monsieur Privat reflected for a moment, then said: "What must I do?"

Olympe de Treguern offered him her hand. "In getting hold of the enormous sum to which Monsieur de Feuillans is entitled by his contract," she replied, "there will be difficulties of more than one sort. We have no lack of protection, and the government itself will support us if need be, but you can serve our purpose better than anyone else, having been in contact with the English company for such a long time. The first thing to do is to put in Monsieur de Feuillans' hands the 20 millions owing to him. That's absolutely necessary!"

Monsieur Privat shook his head. "One can do nothing more against a man who had 20 millions!" he said. "Take care!"

"With human means, that's true," murmured Olympe de Treguern. "But those who are no longer of this world have other weapons..."

The first rays of sunlight crept into the small bare room where Tanneguy was sleeping on his poor mattress. Comtesse Torquati, made more beautiful by her emotion and the immensity of maternal joy, was leaning over his bed, contemplating Tanneguy meditatively and lovingly. From time to time, her eyes turned heavenwards, with passionate gratitude.

She thought that she was alone, but on the other side of the windowed door that led to the kitchen, the crippled Etienne was kneeling in the dust, gazing through the tears that filled his eyes. One might have thought that his soul was reaching out through his gaze towards the woman leaning over the face of the sleeping Tanneguy.

Etienne's trembling voice was murmuring words, among which a name recurred incessantly, pronounced with tender veneration: "Geneviève! Geneviève!"

In Paris, now, it takes a year or more to settle a life in-surance payment. That is progress. In London, in 1820, it re-quired no more than a day. The art was in its infancy then.

Within a week, 200 workmen from Nantes and Rennes were working night and day on the *Château-sans-Terre*. Every morning, according to what the good people of Orlan were saying, fully-laden carts were seen to arrive, bearing velvet draperies beautifully fringed in silk, furniture made in gold, and more crystal chandeliers that it would have needed to light up the whole of the *Grand'Lande*. One would never have imagined that there were so many beautiful things in the uni-verse. And all of it went into the palace that had replaced the ancient manor. When anyone questioned the carters or the upholsterers, they invariably replied, as if they were retelling the story of the Marquis de Carabas [67] with another name: "It's for Monsieur le Comte Gabriel de Treguern."

The good people of the parish of Orlan did not ask who this Comte Gabriel was; they returned home addressing something very different from blessings to the skill of the former *cloarec*, who had crowned his work of spoliation by going so far as to steal the name of his victims. But as they passed in front of the open door of Château-le-Brec, where the Dowager trembled with the fever of old age, they changed their faces and struck a cheerful pose, for that is how the good people of Brittany are made: fear subdues them, and often leads them to caress the Devil.

The Dowager had had her large bed with the brown serge curtains rolled to the doorway, so that she could enjoy a little sunlight. She had been bedridden for a long time, her arms crossed on the coverlet, as motionless as a block of stone. Her coarse and malevolent face stood out beneath the whiteness of her headscarf, and everyone knew perfectly well that they were not prayers that were falling from her tremulous lips.

Once, the saintly parish priest of Orlan had come to talk to her about Heaven; she had forbidden him to cross her threshold. By now, her groom, her chambermaid and all her laborers had abandoned her, for all of them sensed that she already had two feet in the Inferno. By now, even Mathelin, the farmhand, who had been in her service for 25 years, had knotted his bundle on the end of a stick, shaken the dust from his gaiters, and fled. There was no longer any place for a Christian in the house of that reprobate.

Even though she was still rich, even though she still owned Guillaume Féru's windmill on the heath, the pasture-land beside the river—rich and fecund meadows—enclosures, woodlands and her own farm at Château-le-Brec, the Dowager would have had no one to close her eyes without Marcelle, the poor little girl who had grown up with Tanneguy.

Marcelle had not saved herself, even though she was as good a Christian as the groom, the chambermaid, the laborers and Mathelin the farmhand. Marcelle stayed, as strong as her own piety. Marcelle looked after the old woman with angelic devotion, and the idea had never entered her head that God might punish her for her charitable labor. The Dowager paid her in invective and sarcasm. Half-dead as she was, she knew how to strike the heart of the poor child in its vulnerable spot, and her paralyzed lips often found the strength to open in order to hurl these pitiless words at Marcelle: "Your friend Tanneguy has gone forever. He has forgotten you, and you will never see him again!"

Marcelle went to pray in her little room, then, at the foot of a little image of the Virgin, which Dowager Le Brec did not know she had.

It was the octave of the feast of the Assumption. As they made their way home after vespers, the inhabitants of the parish of Orlan saw a veritable procession of carriages coming along the road that crossed the *Grand'Lande*. It extended all the way from Guillaume's mill to the privet path. They set themselves on both sides of the road to watch it. Those who asked what was happening received the reply:

"Monsieur le Comte Gabriel de Treguern will arrive to-morrow to take up residence in his château, and has sent his carriages in advance."

So he was richer than the King, this Comte Gabriel de Treguern!

Yes, certainly, and richer by far! He was everyone's master. All the land between the Oust and the Vilaine belonged to him. He had bought all the lands comprising the domain of the great knight Tanneguy, at whatever price was asked. It was to him, now, that all the farmers in Orlan must pay rent. They had to be prudent in talking about him, for it was necessary to live and keep bread on the family's table.

While the carriages passed by, Père Michelan, winking and nodding his white head, said: "That, my lads, is good weather for making the buckwheat grow, by damn!"

"As to that, yes," relied Mathelin, with the same mysterious air, "Although a little rain doesn't hurt the apple-trees that grow on high ground."

"Nor the meadows, for sure," added Toinette Maréchal, his wife. "Dry weather makes for a pitiful second crop."

"Ah, lady, lady," said Michelan the patriarch, taking the stopper from his ox-horn snuffbox, "one can't expect the seasons of yesteryear today. Everything withers away, and one must be content only to endure hardship by halves. The kind of apples we press nowadays, no more than pips and skin, we'd have thrown on the fire the year I got married!"

Everyone over 50 nodded in assent; the young people consoled themselves by thinking that the world might perhaps cure itself of its languid illness, and that they would see apples as plump as those of former years again before they died.

The last carriage turned the corner of the road; the local people came together again and the masks fell back upon every face. There was now a general and visible discontent: a vague need to rebel, with the consequent obligation of superstitious terror.

"If that's not a crying shame!" said Mathelin, clenching his powerful fists.

"Shh!" said Père Michelan, who heard the sound of wheels drawing closer again—but the housewives had held their tongues long enough.

"It's shameful!" they cried, in chorus.

"A nameless boy!"

"A defrocked priest!"

"A vagabond that we've seen running along these roads in clogs!"

Père Michelan sat down beside the road, in the heather, and the company gathered around him. Dusk was beginning to fall.

"We were speaking of seasons that change," the old man said, in a dreamy tone, "and men likewise! Do you remember the fellow they called the good advocate of Redon?"

"Privat! Monsieur Privat!" the chorus cried.

"Who defended poor armless Etienne for the love of God!" a few voices added.

The former Sergeant Mathurin said as he approached: "A worthy soul, uncle, or I don't know anything!"

"Well, Mathurin, my nephew, you don't know much," the old man went on, bitterly. "I told you that men change. This Privat is now Gabriel's *factotum*."[68]

The crowd uttered a collective cry of protest.

"What's more," the old farmer went on, animatedly, "it's this Privat who has bought—on the false priest's behalf—all the land comprising the ancient Treguern domain."

"Is that really possible?" the murmur went around.

"Why not?" said Vincent Féru, who had become increasingly philosophical as he had grown older. "Since there are no more Treguerns."

Old Michelan looked him in the face. "Fanchette was your sister-in-law," he murmured. "If Fanchette were still alive, she'd tell you that you're lying, or mistaken."

Vincent Féru shrugged his shoulders and retorted: "Fanchette couldn't tell her right hand from her left, man. I

278

know what you're talking about—that's what ruined Fanchette. Treguern has always brought bad luck to those close to it."

"You, Vincent Féru," said the former Sergeant Mathurin, "should shut up."

"Or say what you mean!" added Mathelin the farmhand, putting a large hand on his shoulder.

The wives' choir raised their voices in support of this double execution. From every side, repeated by the old and young alike, one heard: "Treguern was a good master!"

"And those two children who lived among us before they left," added Père Michelan. "At least one of them was a Treguern!"

"Which one?" demanded Vincent Féru, in a provocative tone.

"The one that will one day live in that beautiful house over there," the old farmer replied, pointing towards the forest. "It needs noblemen to live in châteaux, and the air breathed within the walls of Treguern Manor will choke the nephew of that witch Dowager Le Brec."

There was a silence, and an emotional *frisson* ran through the group, for the old man had said this in a prophetic tone. He sensed it himself and perhaps regretted, in a fit of prudence, that he had not continued to discuss the ripening buckwheat or the decadence of apples. But the spirit had been imparted; it would have been impossible now suddenly to change the course of the conversation.

The famous Breton fidelity exists. In addition to the honorable sentiment that national poets might have exaggerated, the local people of Orlan also had a robust superstitious faith in the future of Treguern. Were there not prophecies on the subject?

There was also something else. Rightly or wrongly, the Breton peasant abhors the middle class; he recognizes no one above him but the aristocrat. To the newcomers living in the towns, he is indifferent, but he finds the newcomer who buys a château odious. He sees in that a kind of divine punishment striking the entire country, and sees himself as having fallen from grace in consequence. A manor usurped by a bourgeois is, for him, a manor accursed.

The generalization is too broad; instinct is perhaps not always just. The Breton peasant does not believe in exceptions; he sees brutal vanity in the place of legitimate pride, the avarice of the merchant in the place of grandeur. Even bourgeois piety seems to him to be hypocrisy. The luxury that he admires in his lord, he detests in the newcomer. For the local people of Orlan, the so-called Comte Gabriel was nothing but a perjured priest, representative of the detested victory of money over nobility.

At any rate, there were not ten individuals there on the *Grand'Lande*, who would not have been ready, if the need arose, to take up the scythe and the pitchfork to defend the ancient rights of Treguern. Hostile words met with opposition, and tenacious hopes were brought into the light.

"Can it be chance, then?" demanded Mathelin the farmhand, gesticulating like a man possessed. "Can it be chance that nails the Treguern coat-of-arms to the door of the *Château-sans-Terre* every night? There's no lack of watchmen, I think! There are 200 workmen there who watch all night—but the coup has not failed once. When the Sun comes up, the black veil sprinkled with white tears is always there, swinging above the gateway!"

"Yesterday, at dusk," Toinette Maréchal said, "I was going to confession, and I had to pass in front of Dowager Le Brec's door. She had the *grolet*.[69] I went on my way, crossing myself without looking at her, but I couldn't help hearing her saying, among her groans: 'He'll come back! He'll come back!' "

"He'll come back! He'll come back!" repeated the young man and women. "Voices have been heard at the *Pierre-des-Païens*!"

"And I've seen the red light through the cracks in the Tour-de-Kervoz," Mathelin added.

"All that's nothing, children," said old Michelan, adopting a more serious tone and uncovering his bald head. "Do you know what's behind the planks that are hiding part of the choir in the church?"

"No," was the reply. "What is it?"

The old man pointed across the distant heath, at the place where the druidic monument known as the *Pierres-Plantées* stood. "It was no human hand that stood those rocks on end," he said slowly. "While we're asleep, the spirits are awake. You remember the Tomb of Tanneguy, which we saw transported away, stone by stone? It took nine weeks to take the Tomb of Tanneguy apart—and on the ninth Sunday, there was nothing left on the spot it occupied behind the altar but a hole full of dirt."

"We remember that," the murmur went around, although the women were crossing themselves.

The darkness was deepening. Within the assembly there was already more than one man and woman who would rather have been safe in their own hearth, sheltered by a closed door.

"Well," old Michelan went on, "what took nine weeks to take apart has been put back together in a single night. Instead of the hole full of dirt, the tomb of the great knight is standing as it did before."

"And who rebuilt it?" asked a few timid voices.

"Who demolished it?" murmured the old man, instead of answering.

"And the missing corner?"

"Is still missing."

A noise was heard in the tall undergrowth on the other side of the Redon road. The idea of flight came to everyone, but no one had the time, for the flowering furze-bushes stirred and one of those vague forms that haunt Breton nights slid between their branches. Scarcely had they caught sight of it when it was on the road, ten paces away from the good people.

It was a young woman, clad in a loosely-fitting white dress with a waistband. "Which one of you," she said, in a voice so soft and so sad that one might have thought that one was listening to the angel of tears, "knows where I might find the man who is presently known by the name of Comte Gabriel?"

No one had the courage to reply.

"I need to talk to him on the Lord's behalf," the young woman went on, "and I must find him, for time is pressing!"

She continued on her way, and as the floating pleats of her white dress were already disappearing into the gloom, a voice began to sing the mournful lullaby of Breton mothers.

Old Michelan crossed himself. "Did you recognize her?" he stammered.

"God has her soul!" said Mathelin. "She's dead!"

And the name of Laurence de Treguern ran from mouth to mouth, while someone said: "Unhappy and beautiful..."

They had, however, to get back to the village. What had happened had chilled every heart; they huddled close together; you might have thought that they were the remnant of an army attempting a perilous retreat.

Mathelin the farmhand and the former Sergeant Mathurin led the march, with their round-tipped staffs; then came the fearful battalion of housewives. Boys and girls followed, without attempting any pincer movements, and without giving one another those vigorous thumps on the back that are the evidence of affection. Old Michelan formed the rearguard, with the Mayor's Deputy and a Churchwarden who was reputed to be the bravest man in Orlan.

The advance guard took the long way round to avoid the *Pierre-des-Païens*, where the souls would certainly by holding council on that terrible night.

As they were turning into the sunken path that the *cloarec* Gabriel had taken on the night of August 15, 1800, to go down to Château-le-Brec, they saw four horsemen racing across the fields, devouring the space like a whirlwind.

The Moon rose into the sky behind the trees of the forest; its uncertain light silhouetted the four riders. The one who was galloping in front had a crown of hair whiter than snow. They passed silently to the right, heading in the direction of the former home of the Treguerns.

The good people of Orlan arrived in front of the open door of Château-le-Brec. By the light of a resin lamp, those who dared could see Dowager Le Brec, as fleshless as a cadaver, sitting in her bed, her arms extended towards the section of the road where the four horsemen had disappeared.

"It's them! It's them!" she cried, hoarsely. "I recognized Treguern! May Treguern be accursed!"

On the other side of the bed, little Marcelle was kneeling at prayer. Among the good people of Orlan, there was not one who retained a drop of warm blood in his or her veins.

Beyond the common, the cemetery wall extended like a white girdle around the church, half-hidden by the dark foliage of the yews. The Moon climbed higher and the stone cross was outlined here and there on the grass. Suddenly, lights appeared in the window of the church. The bell rang out a slow and triumphant carillon.

Mathelin the farmhand and the former sergeant stopped. Footsteps could be heard at the other end of the path. A man came forward and said: "Make way for Treguern!"

The good people arranged themselves on the two sides of the path, as docile as automata. They were living in a dream now, and their deceived eyes were the audience at a pageant of the impossible. The man who came forward had no arms.

"Etienne! Etienne, is that you?" stammered the former Sergeant Mathurin.

Instead of answering, the man with no arms said, imperiously: "Hats off to salute Treguern!"

Young and old alike uncovered their heads, even though no one could be seen—but at that moment, by the moonlight passing over the crowns of the trees, they saw a handsome young man in the middle of the road, riding proudly on a vigorous horse. The horse was walking, and a very old man dressed in a cloak embroidered in gold was leading it by the bridle.

The people of the parish immediately recognized Malo Le Mâdre de Treguern.

Every knee was flexed and every head bowed as the handsome young man passed between the two hedges. When they got up again, the bells fell silent and darkness reigned behind the windows of the church. The Moon illuminated the full extent of the solitary and silent road. Nothing could be heard, save for the echo of the Dowager Le Brec's voice, repeating: "Treguern! A curse upon Treguern!

XXX. The Stone from the Tomb of Tanneguy

Was this the realization of the dream that Tanneguy had had on his poor mattress in the six-story house in the Rue Saint-Denis?

Behind an embankment, under the willows of Treguern common, the young woman he had seen that night was lying on her elbow in the tall grass. Her poor weary eyes retained the traces of tears. She was pale, and her sadness was mingled with a sort of inexpressible fear. From time to time, her gaze turned toward the wide open door of Château-Le-Brec, which was visible through gaps in the foliage of the willows. At these moments, her entire body shuddered.

Within the doorway, very close to the threshold, there was one of those enormous country beds whose two stages serve to accommodate an entire family. The bed was empty, and the rays of the Sun, which had already passed its zenith, were striking the crumpled and twisted bedclothes.

Between those bedclothes, Dowager Le Brec had passed the entire night. Poor little Marcelle's blood still ran cold at the memory of those frightful hours. From dusk to dawn, the witch had struggled against an invisible hand that weighed upon her throat and took her breath away. During all that time, she had blasphemed, denying everything that Christianity adores and appealing to the forces of evil for help. Every time Marcelle wanted to pray, a fire had lit up in the reprobate's eyes which said: "Child, you're burning me! What have I done to you that you should torment me thus!"

Her clenched hands tried to tear her bed-linen. She pronounced the names of Gabriel and Marianne, sometimes in a tone of passionate tenderness, sometimes with hate-filled bitterness. Then she collapsed back on to her sweat-bathed pillow, babbling: "I've seen them! I've seen the friends of the resurrected Treguern passing by. The bells of Orlan have rung

285

out unaided. Shall I die soon enough to avoid hearing their songs of triumph?"

As daylight approached, her agitation increased. She tried to raise herself up in the paroxysms of her furious fever, but her strength let her down.

"Help me!" she said, in a voice that the young girl could no longer recognize.

"Where do you want to go, Dowager?" Marcelle asked, trembling.

"Help me!" the old woman repeated.

And the submissive Marcelle could do nothing but obey. She was convinced that the Dowager could get out of bed, even with her help, but that was not the case. The Dowager contrived to set herself on her tottering and fleshless legs.

"Give me my staff!" she commanded.

And when she had her large white staff, like a crozier, in her hand, she suddenly stood upright. The speechless and stupefied Marcelle saw her cross the threshold of the farm and march into the road. She wanted to rush out, to guide or support her, but the old woman turned round and pointed the end of the staff at her. Marcelle felt her feet nailed to the ground.

"I'm going a long way from here," the Dowager said. "You'll never see me again. I forbid you to pray for me."

The early morning light was still feeble; after taking a few paces the Dowager was lost in the shadows of the sunken path that led to the *Grand'Lande*.

That morning, the noise of the great Sabbath held at the *Pierres-Plantées* could be heard as far away as Bains.

And since that hour when the Dowager had quit her bed, little Marcelle had been all alone, wandering around the abandoned farm. The animals were bellowing in the cowshed, the dogs were howling in the yard; Marcelle, in despair, lay down on the grass of the common and wept.

She had no other refuge but that huge accursed house, but to take shelter there it would be necessary to climb over the bed placed across the doorway, and go all alone into that place so full of fears. That was impossible, alas. If only Tanneguy had still been there! But Dowager Le Brec's cruel words were still engraved in the depths of the poor girl's heart, and were often repeated amid her sobs: "Tanneguy has gone forever!"

In the tall grass, next to Marcelle, the stems of the white and pink daisies swayed in the breeze. Marcelle picked one without thinking and her hands slowly stripped its petals, equally unconsciously. She no longer did so, alas, to consult the oracle. What good would it do? Tanneguy was no longer there.

The petals fell, one by one, and Marcelle remained silent; but as her tear-stained face grew heavy and hot, her ears began to hear strange noises. Marcelle thought she could hear something like a voice, an echo of her own thoughts, pronouncing the sacred words as each petal fell: "A little... a lot... passionately... not at all!" And as the last petal fell, that echo of her soul burst forth like a triumphant cry as it said once again: "*A lot!*"

She lifted her eyes, all a-quiver, for that was definitely a voice, which had spoken close at hand.

"Marcelle! My poor Marcelle!" said Tanneguy, who was there, laughing and weeping.

Marcelle buried her head in the bosom of her childhood companion and murmured; "If you go away again now, I shall die!"

In constructing his magnificent château, Gabriel de Feuillans had conserved the west wing of the old Treguern Manor, which had a handsome appearance. That wing comprised the hall—where we once saw the Englishman at Geneviève's feet, counting the gold from his valise on the floorboards—the late Comtesse's apartment, and Filhol's and Etienne's bedrooms. Beyond the last-named room, there was the secret corridor leading to the farm of the late Marion Lécuyer, by which her brother Etienne had introduced himself into the manor on the night of August 15, 1800.

The interior of the building's shell, which we have seen sad and desolate, was much changed now. Gabriel had accumulated there all the magnificences that made his château worthy of the title of palace. The hall, in particular, which he had reserved for his own use, could pass for a masterpiece of luxury and excellent taste.

On the day after the octave of the Assumption, Comte Gabriel was sitting at his desk, which was covered in title-deeds and papers of every sort. Nowadays, immense wealth no longer has the stunning aspect of antique treasures; a few scraps of paper suffice to represent many millions. At any rate, we will not have any trouble describing Comte Gabriel's treasures, which would have fitted easily enough into the pockets of your frock-coat. There were bundles of English banknotes and a rather voluminous packet composed of contracts of sale. That packet made Gabriel the richest landowner in Brittany.

In the embrasure of a widow, Madame la Marquise du Castellat was lying on the cushions of a chaise-longue, cradling her lap-dog in her plump arms. She seemed to be worried. Gabriel, on the other hand, was tranquil in his victory, as a strong man may be who has left nothing to chance and has merely brought the rigor of his calculations to the point of realization. The Marquise darted distracted glances through the window-panes at the gardens and the park, where an elegant crowd was already gathered. No one had refused the invitation of Feuillans, 20 times a millionaire; as he himself had put it, all Paris had mounted an invasion into the solitudes of the *Grand'Lande*.

Preparations had been made to treat Paris according to its tastes; a splendid ballroom had been raised, as if by enchantment, in the center of the flowerbeds, and on the edge of the park the frail framework of a firework display could be seen, which promised marvels.

"Are you quite certain of this Monsieur Privat?" Marianne de Treguern asked, abruptly.

"I pay him," Feuillans replied, disinterestedly.

"In your place," the Marquise went on, "I'd be more worried about his relationship with Olympe."

"I'm not worried about anything," said Comte Gabriel. "Olympe is intelligent; she must be ambitious, and I have 20 millions."

The Marquise looked at him, astonished; this was not how Gabriel talked ordinarily.

"If I were the kind of man to fear anything," the latter continued, "I'd have many other things to worry about. The phantoms that have tormented you for such a long time, Marianne, have finally got to me."

"Ah!" said the Marquise, changing color. "Do you believe in that now, Gabriel?"

"I've believed in it since childhood, Marianne—but I also believe in my star, which is stronger than phantoms!"

"Ah!" the Marquise said, again.

"Twenty years have passed," Gabriel went on, "since I took the first step on the road that I've traveled. Since then, an occult power has always surrounded me and pressed upon me from every direction. I have never spent a single day without the presence of that invisible force making itself felt around me—not to stop me in my course, but to push me forward and break the barriers that rose up in my path."

"On the evening of the last party I gave in Paris," the Marquise murmured, "this Monsieur Privat told me what you have just told me."

"I heard him, and I understand, Marianne. It was to me that those words were addressed. Since then, I have bought Monsieur Privat as I shall buy every instrument that is not worth taking the trouble to break violently. But I had no need to wait for Monsieur Privat to know that my star had tamed the phantoms and that the phantoms were my slaves."

"And yet, Gabriel, you have obeyed these slaves at least once," said the Marquise, whose smile had a hint of mockery in it.

Monsieur de Feuillans lifted the piece of paper that was in his hand. "What are you talking about?" he said.

"I'm talking about your will," she said.

Feuillans put the piece of paper down again. "Here's the duplicate," he said. "It was on that occasion that I saw for the first time the three fantastic beings who are bound so tightly to my life. The English company seemed disposed to enter into a conflict; as I was about to lay my hands on the stake, I saw my hopes dwindle, if not vanish. It was night; fatigue had ended up closing my eyes. I awoke with a start; the lamp had gone out, leaving my room in profound darkness. I heard a voice, which said: 'Gabriel, you shall receive the whole of the contracted sum tomorrow if you will leave all your wealth to the child who was baptized under the name of Tanneguy de Treguern on August 15, 1800.' "

"Our son!" cried Marianne, excitedly, sitting up on her chaise-longue.

"I divined their error," Gabriel continued, instead of replying, "and I accepted, after having asked my mysterious visitors their names. To that question, three voices replied in turn: 'Filhol de Treguern; Jérôme Clément; Johann-Maria Worms.' "

The Marquise put her head in her hands, murmuring: "Those names! Monsieur Privat mentioned all three of them to me! But the other child—the one that we substituted for our son? Stéphane?"

"He's dead," Feuillans said, without any change of expression. Then he continued: "To finish the story, the Englishman's money was at my house the following day."

"These men must be very powerful!" Marianne thought aloud.

"They will be feeble against me," Feuillans said, confidently. "If they are specters, I have my star; if they are alive, I have 20 millions!"

In the bedroom of the late Comtesse, Filhol's mother—which was separated from the hall by the corridor in which Etienne, 20 years before, had listened to the conversation of the Englishman and Geneviève—seven people were gathered.

They had not come in by the main door of the château, and Comte Gabriel had not the least suspicion of their presence.

First, there were the three individuals we have seen in the Louis XV pavilion: the Comte, the Doctor and the Diamond Merchant. Then there was Stéphane Gontier, still very pale from his wound, leaning on Tanneguy's strong arm. Lastly, Olympe Treguern and Commander Malo were standing upright.

Doctor Jérôme Clément and the jeweler Johann-Maria Worms were saying: "Provided that we get our share, the rest is unimportant. Take care of your family business; we shall help you, in accordance with the agreement, if possible."

The Comte looked gravely at Tanneguy and Stéphane, in their turn. "Which one is he?" he murmured. "I don't believe in the voice of the blood."

The door that communicated with Filhol's old room suddenly opened, and a woman appeared, whose long blonde hair fell in disarray upon her traveling-cloak.

"Mother!" Olympe exclaimed, throwing herself into the newcomer's arms.

The Doctor and the Diamond Merchant pronounced the name of Comtesse Torquati and bowed to her. She only paused to brush Olympe's forehead with a kiss before throwing herself towards Tanneguy, who pressed her passionately to his heart.

"See!" said Malo de Treguern.

The Comte shook his white-crowned head. "I don't believe in maternal instinct," he said, coldly. As the Comtesse shot him a reproachful glance, he went on more gently: "Don't blame me, Geneviève. I'll believe it when I have one further item of proof."

Stéphane and Tanneguy clasped hands. "Whatever happens," they said, as one, "we shall still be brothers!"

Olympe's eyes filled with tears, She took a piece of paper from her bosom. "Tanneguy de Treguern," she said, presenting it to the young man, "here is the page that Dowager Le

291

Brec tore out of the register of the parish of Orlan: it's your birth-certificate."

This did not seem to make any impression on the Comte. "There were two cribs at Fanchette Féru's windmill," he said, slowly. "Before being taken to the baptism, they were exchanged, so that the son of Treguern received the name Stéphane, and the *cloarec*'s offspring was called Tanneguy."

Comtesse Torquati was obliged to support Olympe, who was in danger of fainting. The idea, rejected so many times, that Stéphane was her brother returned to fill her soul with dread.

The Commander started speaking in his turn, addressing himself to the Comte: "That which you shall be told is the truth, my nephew Filhol. I was the sole guardian of the destiny of Treguern. Although I divined the substitution, I did not protest at the time of the baptism because I knew that more than one danger would threaten the heir of knights. On the evening following the baptism, however, I slipped into Guillaume's mill, and I exchanged the cribs again with my own hand. That way, I told myself, Treguern will bear his true name, but the false priest and Dowager Le Brec, believing that they see their own accursed blood, will respect his existence."

The Comte lowered his eyes, and remained impassive.

"Do you, then, require more than one further item of proof, my nephew Filhol?" said Malo, placing a hand on his shoulder.

"Yes," the Comte replied, without looking up.

Gabriel had had large mirrors placed on the paneling on every side.

"You said the other day," Commander Malo went on, in a lower and sadder voice, "that Treguern had fallen so low as to have lost the funereal privilege that formerly permitted the divination of the approach of death. You were mistaken, Filhol." Before the Comte had time to reply, Malo seized him by the arms and drew him towards one of the mirrors. "Look!" he said.

The Comte obeyed mechanically—but scarcely had he darted a glance at the mirror than he took several paces backwards, his face livid and his body tremulous. "Is there not in front of that glass," he murmured, in distress, "a black drape sewn with white tears?"

"There is nothing there," the Commander replied.

"Then it's the Veil of Treguern that hides my own image, and I'm condemned to die!"

The Commander nodded his head in affirmation.

"May God's will be done!" Filhol pronounced, drawing himself upright. "I do not deserve to see the renaissance of Treguern."

"A few steps away from us," Malo went on, pointing to the door to the corridor, "there is another man condemned to die. The certainty that you demand is there, close to you. These two young men will look, and you shall doubt no more, my nephew!"

The Comte took Stéphane and Tanneguy by the hand, instructing them to be silent. He led them to the widowed door that gave entry to the hall. Gabriel was still sitting at his desk. The Comte put Tanneguy and Stéphane in front of him and said to them: "What do you see through that window?"

"I see Monsieur de Feuillans, my assassin," Stéphane replied.

"Where?" asked Tanneguy. "I see nothing but a mortuary shroud stretching from floor to ceiling."

Malo whispered in Filhol's ear: "Are you convinced? He is Treguern, *because he can see the Veil...*"

Filhol kissed Tanneguy on the forehead and said to him, while a tear rolled slowly down his cheek: "Treguern, my beloved son, forget your father, a poor fisherman, and remember only the great knights, your ancestors who lived and died for God and the King." Then he knelt on the floor and asked for a priest to administer the last rites.

On the other side of the windowed door, Comte Gabriel was no longer accompanied by the Marquise du Castellat. The negro Congo had replaced her. He held an American pistol in his hand, which could shoot four rounds.

"Will you be able to recognize all three of them?" Gabriel asked.

"Yes, master," Congo replied.

"At the moment when the fireworks begin, three explosions more or less won't be noticed. And in these sorts of festivities, it's rare that one does not have some misfortune to regret. Make perfectly sure that they're dead, this time."

Congo nodded his black head, smiling: "And I'll get 10,000 francs?" he said.

"You'll have your 10,000 francs this very night!"

The Parisian guests were wandering about in the fragrant gardens of the Château de Treguern. Night was falling; it was the high point of the party. Baron Brocard, Champeaux and many others were making fun of the Three Rooks, who had not condescended to show themselves, even though they had been summoned loudly. On each occasion, Champeaux tried in vein to tell the famous story he had got from his aunt.

Despite the absence of the three phantoms, however, the supernatural had its small part to play in the party given by the new Comte de Treguern. In the middle of one group, Noisy-*le-Sec* was speaking, narrating an adventure to which he himself claimed to have been a witness. It had taken place behind the château, on the edge of the forest.

On that very day, Feuillans, taking brief refuge from the crowd, had been walking there all alone. Noisy was going towards him to compliment him on the magnificence of his home, when a woman dressed in white had emerged from the depths of the forest. Dusk was already making things confused, but Noisy claimed to have recognized perfectly the lovely face of Laurence de Treguern, and her soft voice, as it had said to Gabriel: "Think of God! Your minutes are numbered!"

Noisy always had such stories! The first of three rockets giving the signal for the commencement of the fireworks traced a rapid trail of sparks through the air. By the time the rocket was extinguished, Noisy-*le-Sec*'s anecdote was already forgotten.

Everyone moved toward the park. Feuillans, who had not yet come out of the château, would open the ball with his beautiful fiancée, Olympe, immediately after the fireworks. Olympe de Treguern had just been seen passing by on the arm of Commander Malo. The little advocate, Monsieur Privat, was dancing around them, ten times busier than usual.

On the highest story of the château there was a large frieze. Two men were climbing up to the highest window, situated just above the main door. One of these men had no arms. "Mathurin," he said to his companion, "the hour has come; I can hear the false priest coming down the great staircase. Put the cord between my teeth and take care of yourself. What follows is not your business."

"I don't know what you're planning, my brother Etienne," the former Sergeant Mathurin replied, "and I wash my hands of whatever happens." Between Etienne's teeth, he put a cord, with a slip-knot on the end that contained a stone. Etienne got down on to the frieze, balancing himself carefully. At that same moment, Gabriel appeared at the door of the vestibule and gave the signal to fire the third rocket.

Etienne made a movement of the head. Comte Gabriel released a cry and collapsed, struck dead. A stone, fallen from the frieze, had fractured his skull.

The edge of the park resembled a conflagration; in the midst of a thousand fires exploding from all directions, three more powerful detonations resounded. It was the negro Congo, earning his 10,000 francs by shooting three men. Jérôme Clément, Johann-Maria Worms and Filhol de Treguern were no more.

A triumphant voice rose up then to proclaim: "Treguern is dead! It is the third time! Long live Treguern!"

When they removed the planks hiding the Tomb of the great knight Tanneguy, in the choir of Orlan's church, it was observed that the granite tablet was whole, and that the broken corner was no longer missing. Etienne was the only one who could have told what purpose that stone had served before being restored to its place, and how the Prophecy had been fulfilled.

There were three new graves in the cemetery: two simple ones bearing the unfamiliar names of Jérôme Clément and Johann-Maria Worms, the third in beautiful black marble, bearing a knightly coat-of-arms with the name Filhol-Aimé-Tanneguy le Mâdre, Comte de Treguern.

At about this time, the Ursuline nuns at Redon received into their community a young woman who took the veil under the protection of Saint Laurence.

Commander Malo had disappeared, but on the day when young Comte Tanneguy married the pretty Marcelle, a simple peasant girl, joyful lights were seen dancing all night behind the cracks in the Tour-de-Kervoz.

Monsieur Privat was at the wedding. He no longer wondered about the cause of the mysterious protection that had surrounded Gabriel de Feuillans for so long, but you might have taken him for a tormented soul. He was, in effect, a widower; his case had rendered up its last sigh.

It was a true fête, that marriage. Tanneguy was beloved throughout the land. He appointed Etienne, the poor cripple, as one of his witnesses. Then, before going up to the altar, he placed Stéphane's hand in that of Olympe, who was very pale and emotional, saying: "Whatever happens, we shall still be brothers!"

Appendix:

Paul Féval's Preface

This extraordinary story, half-Breton and half-Parisian, was told to me in 1842 by an Englishman, a Londoner, Monsieur J.N. W---y, who was formerly a Protestant but had had the good fortune to finish up in the Catholic communion, in Paris, towards the commencement of the Second Empire. He had not much belief in ghosts, but was convinced that life insurance—especially in the early days of the institution—was the origin of a considerable number of crimes.

Monsieur W---y had occupied a senior position in one of the foremost life insurance companies; he was the head of the claims department and had drawn out some of the details that you will read in the course of an inquiry, pursued in London and Paris in 1820, to relieve his company, Campbell Life, from the obligation of paying out the enormous dividend at issue in our drama.

At the bottom of this story, Monsieur W---y's Englishman's eye saw, above all else, the social menace implicit in the situation of a man "with nothing against him" who might obtain by crime a sum of some ten, 20, or even 100,000 francs, for the payment each year, on a fixed date, a *strictly necessary sum*—independently of his living expenses, since it is his premium—and for whom that premium, paid on a regular basis until the maturity of the policy, represents a future investment of millions.

There is a temptation here: an exorbitant temptation, which must be rarely indulged, although Monsieur J.N. W---y, who knows whereof he speaks, did not think that the curious example that he cited—which forms the basis of this curious history—is unique.

Afterword

The original version of this novel inevitably suffered from the usual difficulties of writing fiction for newspaper serialization. It was made up as the author went along, continually subject to editorial pressure. Modern make-it-up-as-you-go writers retain the opportunity to go back and alter the text already written, in order to "precorroborate" ideas that occur to them belatedly and remove logical difficulties that become apparent in retrospect; Féval did not have that luxury, because his text was appearing in print as he wrote it. He had to be prepared to spin out his stories indefinitely if reader interest warranted extension, and cut them abruptly short if interest declined. He also had to keep recapping material for the benefit of readers who did not begin reading until the story was under way.

Given these conditions of production, it is not surprising that the serial versions of his novels often seem a trifle meandering, and frequently end with loose ends dangling in every direction. This is not necessarily harmful to a work that has far more story than plot, because a reader's enjoyment of a fast-paced story usually depends far more on the intrinsic interest of what is happening at the moment than the appreciation of the entire jigsaw; there is many a best-seller which seems gripping as it is read but can easily be revealed by retrospective analysis to make no sense whatsoever. In a work which is plot-heavy, by contrast—such as a mystery story, in which many events are only important because they add an extra piece to the evolving puzzle—the problems of improvised serial production are bound to become more acute. Most *feuilletonistes*, including Féval, usually paid a great deal of attention to their stories while minimizing their plot-structures, but Féval was never intimidated by a challenge, and he was perfectly prepared to embark upon the occasional *livre des mystères*.

There was, of course, an opportunity for a serial writer to revise his work before book publication, but that was very rarely done, for brutal economic reasons. To produce a thorough revision of a book would require as much labor as writing a new one, and a book would not produce as much income—or, at least, would not produce income as rapidly—as a new serial. Féval, therefore, usually restricted himself to the kinds of trivial revision that could be done at the proof stage, without annoying the printer too much. In this particular case, Féval had a second opportunity to revise his text—and indeed, went out of his way to advertise the version I have translated as "revised and corrected." It is very probable, however, that these revisions, too, were carried out by amending a set of printer's proofs in a conscientiously moderate manner.

In some of the "revised and corrected" texts Féval issued after his "conversion," he made massive deletions, but he does not seem to have made any large-scale additions or done any wholesale rewriting. Most of his additive revisions were very short—rarely more than a couple of lines—and were mostly wrought in the interests of piety, causing his virtuous characters to be more scrupulous in praying to, praising and thanking the Lord. He did not, by and large, make any attempt to repair any of the holes in his plots or clear up any of the puzzles left by his dangling loose ends.

To some extent, the effect of this policy is to leave his novels—especially the more intricately-constructed ones—in a somewhat unsatisfactory condition. On the other hand, the reader is free to regard this as a kind of challenge, whose meeting has its own mildly perverse aesthetic appeal. For that reason, it seems appropriate in this afterword to point out a few of the problematic questions that are partly or wholly unanswered in Féval's text, and to use them as springboards for speculation. For the sake of convenience, I have divided the issues into three categories: (1) questions of fact, (2) questions of motivation and (3) questions of morality.

1. Questions of Fact

(a) What kind of insurance policy did Gabriel buy?

Féval describes it as a "regulated tontine," and must mean it literally. Most literary tontines are informal arrangements in which a number of moderately wealthy men simply put sums of money into a pool that may be claimed by the last surviving member, who thus becomes very rich. The idea was, however, originated in connection with life insurance policies by the man after whom it is named, a 16th-century Neapolitan banker named Lorenzo Tonti. The basic idea of Tonti's version of the tontine is that all the members take out an endowment policy with a life insurance provision, each assuming responsibility for his own annuity payments—but the payments due on death go into an interest-earning pool rather than being paid to the dead person's relatives, and the accumulated sum is shared between the survivors, according to the level of their annuity, when the policy matures. Anyone who misses a premium payment is, of course, thrown out of the scheme.

The informal version of the tontine could easily be construed as an open invitation to murder, and the principal advantage of involving an insurance company was the expectation that the names of the members would be kept secret from one another. Tontines of the kind described may not have been uncommon in the early 18th century—Féval is wrong to imagine that they were a recent invention in 1800—but they must have become much rarer in the latter decades. The British parliament passed a Gambling Act in 1774, which prohibited insuring lives other than one's own. In any case, after 1762—when the Equitable Society first based its premium insurance schemes on actuarial analyses that assessed risk in a statistically responsible manner—the calculations involved in such ventures became much more cautious. On the other hand, 1800 was exactly the right time to get involved in such a scheme, with a 20-year term, because the 20 years in question saw the Napoleonic Wars run their course, costing a great many lives. It is not entirely implausible that Gabriel's payoff could have reached the envisaged level, especially if he was somehow able to include a few of the other participants among his murder victims.

(b) Who was Gabriel's father?

Although many of the characters seem to be unaware of the fact, it seems certain that Gabriel is Françoise Le Brec's son—but the identity of his father is less certain; if it had been her husband and cousin, Jean le Brec, there would presumably have been far less mystery about it. There is no mention in the text of any illicit love-affair but we do know that when Jeanne—the sister who married Filhol's father, the Comte de Treguern—died, Françoise moved into the manor to care for Marianne, only quitting it again when the Comte remarried; it was at that point in time that her hatred of the Treguerns became unbounded.

Is it possible—bearing in mind the quasi-fraternal resemblance between Stéphane and Tanneguy—that Gabriel's father was the Comte de Treguern? Malo claims that Filhol is the first Treguern ever to have told a lie, but that seems inherently unlikely, and the statement is worthless if Malo himself is a liar. The other Treguern candidate is, of course, Malo himself, although that depends on the exact date of his ill-fated engagement to Catherine Le Brec, who may well have been another of Françoise's sisters. Do we really believe that Malo's ostentatious saintliness can be taken at face value, and that the death of his fiancée was sufficient in itself to send him off to join the Knights of Malta? If not, what was the sin he seems to be trying so mightily to expiate?

There is, of course, one other obvious possibility. We do know of one relationship that Dowager Le Brec has that might be assumed to include a sexual component, although Féval could not permit himself to say so in so many words. She has allegedly made a pact with the Devil and is said to be in regular attendance at witches' Sabbaths. Perhaps—and the text hints at this possibility more than once, albeit coyly—Gabriel's father is the Devil.

Whichever of these possibilities is the true one, it does not seem to bode well for Stéphane's prospects as Olympe's husband—although the Bretons do not appear to disapprove of cousin marriage.

(c) Who is the legitimate Comte de Treguern?

In August 1799, the legitimate Comte de Treguern was obviously Filhol, by virtue of lineal descent. After he fakes his death, however, the situation becomes more complicated. Can Filhol still be regarded as the legitimate Comte de Treguern after he has faked his death? If so, then he is still the legitimate Comte until he actually dies—which appears to be at the end of the last chapter, when he is shot by Congo (but see the next question). At that point, Tanneguy becomes the legitimate Comte by reason of descent. It seems unlikely, however, that French law and the French Crown would endorse this view.

If the official registration of Filhol's death is sufficient to deprive him of any continuing claim on his title, then the title cannot possibly pass to Tanneguy, who must be deemed illegitimate from a legalistic point-of-view. This appears to be the official attitude—endorsed, we are specifically assured, by the King himself—since Gabriel is allowed to take over the title of Comte de Treguern on marrying Olympe. But if Gabriel really is the legitimate Comte de Treguern for a brief interval on August 23, 1820, he surely cannot pass on that title. In this case, Tanneguy—even though he may inherit all Gabriel's wealth—cannot become the legitimate Comte de Treguern.

Malo's existence generates a further problem. Why, when Filhol fakes his death, does Malo not automatically become the legally-recognized Comte de Treguern? Even if he formally forsook that privilege when he joined the Knights of Malta, surely he got it back again when Napoleon disbanded the order. Malo, of course, knows that Tanneguy is the hereditary Comte de Treguern, but how can he ever establish that fact in law without revealing that Filhol faked his death? Were he to do that, repaying the money that Filhol gained by means of that deception (with appropriate interest) would only be one of his problems, given the extent to which he subsequently served as Filhol's accomplice.

Whoever French officialdom would have recognized as the "legitimate" Comte de Treguern between September 1799 and the evening of August 23, 1820, it seems likely that the official view would have been that the title was bound to lapse thereafter, with Malo's death if not sooner. There is, however, another way to look at the issue, which appears to be the one that Féval adopts, by which official recognition of Tanneguy's title is neither here nor there, because true legitimacy is a matter of actual heredity. In the view taken by the text, Tanneguy is, and always was, the sole legitimate heir to the title and all that goes with it, by reason of the blood in his veins. The text takes the view that there is a higher law than the law of France, whose endorsement of Tanneguy's legitimacy is worth far more than the officialdom's denial.

(d) How many authentic revenants are featured in the plot?

This depends on the manner in which the textual data is interpreted. The reader is permitted—and perhaps, at least by way of afterthought, encouraged—to take the view that there are none, but it seems far more likely that there is one: Laurence de Treguern. If one takes this point-of-view, the sentence in the last chapter that refers to a novice being admitted to an Ursuline convent must be regarded as a red herring, but that is probably what it is.

Although the narrative voice tells us explicitly that Valérie-*la-Morte* is Olympe, who uses that pseudonym when she is acting as a courier for her father and his associates, it is possible that the original Valérie was Laurence, who took that name after her death was faked—perhaps to save her from the awful fate of marriage to Gabriel—at which point she presumably took up residence with the Three Rooks in the bowels of the manor and the Tour-de-Kervoz. If that were so, however, she would surely make an entrance at the scene in the Louis XV pavilion, or at least warrant some mention by the people there.

When Olympe leaves the enclosed garden, apparently having been summoned by the Three Rooks, she is briefly glimpsed in apparent company with Laurence, but never mentions having been aware of the presence herself. The most likely explanation of Laurence's manifestations in the Marquise's garden—where Monsieur Privat assumes she is alive and the Chevalier de Noisy that she is a ghost—and in Orlan is that she really *is* a phantom.

It may also be worth considering the possibility that although Laurence is the only real ghost in the plot, she is not the only revenant. The "*revenants*" described in Dom Augustine Calmet's treatise, which Féval undoubtedly read, include ghosts, but also include numerous individuals who rise from the dead in the flesh. These are mostly considered under the umbrella term of "*vampires*," although not all of them, by any means, are bloodsuckers. Since we are given no details of what happened to Filhol after Gabriel shot him in the *Trou-de-la-Dette*, the possibility is not excluded that he really did die before returning to life as creature of vengeance incarnate. This might help to explain his remarkable behavior thereafter.

By the same token, it might be worth wondering exactly what happened to Stéphane. Superficially, it appears that he was mistakenly thought to be dead, when he was really still alive. In an era when fears of premature burial were commonplace, this might not have seemed implausible to a contemporary audience—but Stéphane is no narcoleptic, and the description of his wound offered by the Doctor suggests that he might indeed have been dead. If Filhol is some sort of revenant, and Malo cannot see the Veil until he dies irredeemably, then Malo's failure to see the Veil in Stéphane's case might only signify that Stéphane is scheduled for resurrection, presumably by a more benign power than the one that allowed Filhol to complete his vengeance.

2. Questions of Motivation.

(a) Why does Françoise Le Brec switch the babies?

Although the assumed switch plays a significant part in the organization of the plot, it does not seem to have much effect on what actually happens after the switch is assumed to have taken place. Both babies are effectively left in the Dowager's care, and she does not appear to care much about either of them. She is already thinking, at the book's beginning, that Gabriel might one day become the Comte de Treguern—in which case he would be able to pass that title on, quite legitimately, to his own son, and the switch could only confuse the issue. As it turns out, Gabriel is commanded by the supposed phantoms to make Tanneguy his heir rather than Stéphane, but the Dowager could not possibly have anticipated that, so it cannot have played any part in her plan.

Malo says that he switched the babies back again because he thought that the true Treguern might be in danger from the Dowager and Gabriel. This implies that the reason for the switch was to create an opportunity to do away with Filhol's son, thus clearing a potential obstacle out of Gabriel's path—but if that was so, why does the Dowager not follow through with that intention?

Modern readers might well be puzzled as to how the opportunity to switch the babies arose in the first place. Why were both mothers seemingly content to hand over their babies to Fanchette for nursing? This would not have seemed quite so odd in 1852, especially looking back to an earlier era when it was rare for aristocratic women to care for their own children, usually preferring to hand them over to wet-nurses immediately. (The policy resulted in a horrendous infant mortality rate, which greatly assisted the rate at which the direct inheritance of ancient titles failed, causing the titles to lapse and become available for reclamation by distant branches of the family.) We are led to suppose that Geneviève has always lavished the best of care of Olympe, but the extent of that care is never spelled out.

It is possible that the Dowager took the opportunity simply because it was there, and because it was an implicitly mischievous thing to do—she is, after all, the Devil's hand-

306

maiden. On the other hand, it is possible that she did it not because she wanted to take possession of Geneviève's son, but because she wanted and expected Geneviève to take possession of Marianne's. It may well have been the case that she did not expect Geneviève to abandon "her" child and hoped to plant a cuckoo in the Treguern nest. Which leads on to the next question...

(b) Why does Geneviève desert her son?

We are never told exactly why Geneviève leaves Orlan after Filhol's "second death," or where she goes. Although she obviously keeps in touch with Filhol, she cannot have kept close company with him, because Olympe has no idea that "the Comte" is her father. In any case, given that she is such a devoted mother, why did she not take her newborn son with her as well as her daughter?

If Geneviève found out about the switch planned by Dowager Le Brec, that might have influenced her decision not to take the child baptized as her son—but if Malo had told her about the reverse switch, it would surely have allowed her to claim her own son in the full knowledge that he was, in fact, hers. Apparently, Malo did not tell her—indeed, he may well have been instrumental in persuading her to depart and leave her son behind.

The only plausible reason why Geneviève might have left her son behind is that she was instructed to do so by the one person who, in her eyes, had the right to issue such an instruction: Filhol. She had gone along with his plan to defraud the insurance company, albeit with obvious reluctance, and she would presumably have gone along with anything else he required of her. Malo apparently did not tell Filhol about the reverse switch until much later, so Filhol would have been under the impression that, in claiming her son after the baptism, Geneviève would indeed have been taking a cuckoo into the nest. Even so, it is hard to believe that Geneviève would have deserted her son so callously and so completely, even if she were not as certain in 1800 of the maternal instinct on which she relied to make the identification in 1820.

When Tanneguy finally meets his mother, he seems to bear her no grudge whatsoever, and does not even ask her why she left him in the care of a vicious old woman who was unlikely to have lavished any love upon him even if she believed him to be her grandson. What could she have said to him if he had asked? Malo, rightly or wrongly, believed that the whole pattern of events was predestined, and was thus ready to play along with it, even to the extent of doing exactly what he had berated Filhol for—lying—but Geneviève seems remarkably tolerant of his eccentricities as well as her husband's.

(c) Why does Monsieur Privat become obsessed with Etienne's case?

When Privat is giving his own explanation for his lifelong commitment to Marianne, he contends that he simply relishes a challenge. He is, however, also attempting to right a monstrous injustice. By the time Etienne's case comes before the circuit judge at the assize court, and Privat successfully gets him acquitted, Etienne has been in prison for an entire year. How on Earth did this happen?

Privat's defense must have been the easiest ever presented. What, after all, is the prosecution attempting to contend? That a murder was committed, although no *corpus delicti* exists, in order that a valise full of gold, of whose existence there is not the slightest evidence, might be stolen—and that the man who allegedly perpetrated the crime and then hid the gold contrived to complete this task without the use of either of his arms! How were the authorities persuaded to hold Etienne in the first place? Was it not obvious to them that the accusation was nonsensical, and hence malicious? Even if they were prepared to hypothesize that Etienne still had one functional arm when he committed the murder and robbery, how could he possibly have hidden the body and the loot? Who, in that case, fired the shot which deprived him of the use of his other arm? When? Why?

In all probability, Privat's lifelong obsession with the case must have arisen from his perception of this monstrous absurdity—this sudden revelation that the law is not merely an ass but an ass of unparalleled stupidity. It may be worth remembering, at this point, that Paul Féval had trained and qualified as an advocate, but had only ever argued one case in court, giving up the law forever after losing it. According to his version of events (which is hilariously dramatized in *John Devil,* also published by Black Coat Press), it was his client's fault that he lost, and no miscarriage of justice was involved; even so, one cannot help but wonder whether there is a little of Paul Féval in Monsieur Privat—perhaps to the extent that his construction and description of the character is a wry self-portrait. We must remember, too, that the man who really had Etienne thrown into prison for a year to await trial, despite all the evidence proving plainly that he could not possibly be guilty as charged, was Paul Féval.

3. Questions of Morality.

(a) What should Filhol have done?

We can, I think, take it as read that Filhol should not have allowed himself to be tempted by Gabriel in the first place. But what should he have done instead? And, more importantly, what should he have done afterwards?

Filhol is, let us face it, a monumental waste of space. Faced with the prospect of ruination, he simply sits around and waits for it to happen. He does not even consider doing what any sane and responsible person with a wife and family to care for would have done—i.e., find a way of earning a living. He does not attempt to farm the land he still owns (until he sells it to buy his way into the insurance scam), nor does he consider selling the manor and taking his family to Paris, where he might more easily be able to find work. He simply sits around in his crumbling pile, wondering why unkind fate is not serving up a solution on a platter. Is he not as guilty, in his own way, as Gabriel?

If Filhol is still alive after Gabriel shoots him, then he still retains the option of taking his wife, daughter, sister and newborn son to Paris after the catastrophe has unfolded, and searching for an honest job. That, surely, would be the sane, responsible and moral thing for a mortal man to do. What he does instead is to make a plan, in collaboration with the alleg-edly-saintly Malo, not merely to allow Gabriel to continue murdering his way to a fortune, but actually to help him to attain that end. When a couple of Gabriel's murders fail, he does not suggest that the injured parties should reveal that they are still alive, reclaim their fortunes and their families and denounce Gabriel for what he is; instead, he persuades them to play dead along with him, in the hope of obtaining a share in the vast fortune that Gabriel will eventually achieve once he had committed a few more murders. Thus begins their long career as the Three Rooks—who might surely be better named the Three Crooks, or the Three Vultures.

Instead of fighting the evil that has tempted him to be party to the theft of a small fortune, Filhol decides after August 15, 1800 that he will continue to be party, secretly, to further evils of the same kind, in order that he might eventu-ally reclaim his investment, with interest. If he was not quite as bad as Gabriel before, surely he is every bit as bad now. Is it not surprising and remarkable that he seems to retain the full support of Paul Féval (the true author of his plan), not only in the serial version of 1852 but in the "revised and corrected" edition that Féval produced specifically in order to accommo-date it to the convictions of his reinvestment in passionate and pious Christianity?

Filhol does eventually acknowledge that he does not de-serve to inherit Gabriel's fortune, and Féval obligingly has him shot for a second time—but this is surely a poor and very belated substitute for doing the right thing. Had Filhol only done what he should, and owned up to his first crime in August 1800, he could have prevented the lives of his two companions—as well as those of the Marquis du Castellat, Stéphane and anything up to 15 others—from ever having been imperiled. Laurence would never have had to become engaged to the swine, thus being saved the necessity of dying (if she is a phantom thereafter) or faking her death (if she is merely a fake revenant).

Filhol begins the story as a weakling who falls prey to diabolical temptation, but he spends the rest of it actively promoting the Devil's cause. The reader might take the view that this is more understandable, albeit no more excusable, if Filhol really is a revenant returned from the grave in the flesh—and the behavior of his two dread companions might similarly seem a little more understandable if they were in the same condition.

(b) What should Malo have done?

The puzzle of Féval's apparent approval of Filhol's grand plan is redoubled by the fact that he appoints Commander Malo as its active supporter and collaborator. Malo is, after all, supposed to be a paragon of virtue, although the only evidence we have for that is that Féval keeps telling us so, Nothing Malo actually does endorses this view; indeed, he functions throughout the story as Françoise Le Brec's male counterpart—the whole plot is, in essence, a duel between two insanely obsessive sorcerers. Were it not for Féval's repeated assurances that Malo has Providence, Destiny and God on his side, while the Dowager is the Devil's pawn, the reader would surely be at a loss to know which of the two to support.

Filhol may well have been too weak to rally to Etienne's defense on the day after the confrontation in the *Trou-de-la-Dette*, but Malo has no excuse for not coming forward as a witness to prevent Etienne's committal. Malo knows perfectly well, in advance of the event, what the Englishman is delivering, and that Gabriel is planning to steal it—but he does nothing. If Fate is the true author of Filhol's grand plan, then Malo is Fate's chief agent, but does his belief in prophecy and destiny really excuse his decision not to exercise his own moral authority by putting an immediate stop to Gabriel's murderous career? Again, it is truly remarkable that the author, before or after his "conversion," should endorse Malo's decision to let Fate take its course without even lifting a finger in protest.

Malo's belief in prophecy and destiny is not unjustified, of course; although there is a distinct suggestion that Françoise Le Brec really does have the power to lay curses, Malo is the only character in the plot who has manifest magical powers, in that he not only sees the Veil of Treguern several times over but also utters other true prophecies. Even if he does have proof of the workings of destiny, however, can that absolve him of the responsibility to fight against evil when destiny instructs him to do things that are blatantly immoral? Is one really entitled to harm someone—or, by inaction, allow someone to be harmed—if one sincerely believes that it is destined to happen?

Malo's other possible excuse—although it is not one he could or would issue on his own behalf—is that he is barking mad; the modern reader will easily be able to diagnose an obsessive/compulsive disorder. (By the same token the modern reader might take the view that if Filhol did survive the shooting in the *Trou-de-la-Dette*, he must have subsequently have suffered from traumatic stress disorder, and was thus not fully responsible for his own actions.) Féval, on the other hand, appears to think that he is possessed of a greater sanity than his fellows—and it may be worth pointing out that even if Féval can let his character off the hook by citing destiny, he cannot get off it himself. The supposedly-predestinated plan that Malo and Filhol follow is, after all, not God's but Paul Féval's; it is with Féval that the buck stops.

(c) Are the ends of poetic justice served in Féval's plot?

It was the 17th-century Shakespearean critic Thomas Rymer who first pointed out that fiction has an innate moral order. An author always has the power to ensure that, within the worlds of his texts, good is rewarded and evil is punished. Rymer's opinion was that an author has, *ipso facto*, a moral responsibility to see that good characters are rewarded and that evil ones are punished. To do otherwise would be to do wrong.

There are, of course, many authors who disagree with this simplistic thesis, citing the rhetorical value of tragedy and irony—by virtue of which outcomes that violate moral order are not perceived by readers as derelictions of duty but as heart-rending commentaries on the unfortunate lack of moral order in the world of experience. By and large, though, most readers, most of the time, do prefer "happy" (i.e., morally uplifting) endings, and most writers of popular fiction are prepared, most of the time, to pander to that preference. Paul Féval was certainly no exception to the general rule; he was a great believer in morally-uplifting endings, and he did his level best to represent the ending of this particular novel in exactly those terms. The good guys come out ahead, the villains perish ignominiously—except that, as the answers to the previous questions have sought to demonstrate, the means by which this particular conclusion is reached seem very dubious indeed.

Féval's own argument, in response to the charges laid against him in respect of Filhol's and Malo's actions, might not be as brutal as "the end justifies the means," but that is surely the import of his plot. It is, apparently all right for Filhol and Malo to collude in the murders of numerous innocent people, because that is the price of securing the ultimate outcome of the plot: the installation of Tanneguy, the "rightful" heir, as lord of the ancient domain that his ancestral namesake once owned. Had Filhol and Malo behaved morally, and nipped Gabriel's scheme in the bud, they could easily have been provided with conventional "happy endings"—Filhol could have been rewarded with a fulfilling and lucrative job and a happy home, while Malo could have died and gone to Heaven—but there is no way that the actual ending of the text could have been contrived.

One is obliged to ask, however, whether any reward, however vast, can really justify collusion in multiple murder. (It is not clear whether the collusion extends to further murders, although all the talk of removing obstacles from Gabriel's path suggests that it might not have been Gabriel who prevented the Marquis du Castellat from denouncing him.)

On the surface, Féval's plot seems to be proposing that the restoration of an ancient feudal domain really is a goal so admirable that its achievement is worth any moral price, and justifies even the most heinous of means—always provided of course, that it goes to its rightful heir rather than some jumped-up usurper. This is a contention that is perhaps understandable, given Féval's nostalgia for the long-lost Age of Chivalry, no matter how difficult it would be to find a modern reader capable of agreeing with it. There is, however, another way to read the "message" of the text, which is certainly not what Féval intended—consciously, at last—but is nevertheless inherent in the text for the benefit of anyone who cares to look at it from that viewpoint.

It is possible to see the conclusion of *Revenants* not as a conventionally happy one but as a deeply ironic one. It is possible to read it as a commentary on the true nature of the so-called Age of Chivalry, and the manner in which its domains were assembled. Chivalry was itself a literary construct: an invention designed to flatter the feudal barons who were the paymasters and primary audience of the founding fathers of the great literary tradition of Romance. In literary myth, the Age of Chivalry was an age of great knights who fought for righteous causes, whose bloodbaths were not merely forgivable but admirable, because they were endorsed by God and poetic justice alike. In reality, of course, the "Age of Chivalry" was an era of self-seeking, back-stabbing bombast in which the people who had the power to assert their will did so, utterly careless of the cost to others. In reality, the knights of ancient Brittany were petty tyrants, extraordinarily violent if not actively sadistic, who had no cause but their own power, wealth and glory—the last-named item being so important to them that they paid lickspittles to represent them in lore and legend as saintly men beloved by the people they exploited so ruthlessly and consciencelessly.

Is that not what the plot of *Revenants* really tells us, whether or not that was the author's conscious intention? Does it not assure us that the cost of baronial glory is exceedingly high, not merely in financial terms but in terms of morality and sanity? Does it not assert that the builders of chivalric mythology must have been men like Filhol and Malo de Treguern—clinically insane, morally bankrupt and perhaps literally demonic—whose lust for glory laid waste not merely to their own lives but to the lives of everyone around them, including their devoted wives, their beloved daughters, their loyal sons and their amiable sisters as well as their faithful servants?

Perhaps Laurence de Treguern saw that, better than anyone else involved in the plot. Perhaps that is why she was always weeping, inconsolably condemned to misery. Perhaps, if she was a ghost, that is why she could find no peace in Heaven or on Earth—or, if she was only pretending to be a ghost, why she turned her back on her putative share of Tanneguy's fortune and went into a nunnery instead.

If Gabriel really was the Devil's son, the Devil must have been extremely pleased with the work his faithful servant did; unfortunately, Féval never wrote a sequel, so we have no idea what he had in store for Tanneguy.

Notes

Part One

Chapter I

[1] *Pierre-des-Païens* is translatable as "Pagan Stone."

[2] *Trou-de-le-Dette* is translatable as "Hole of the Debt;" "money pit" might be the nearest colloquial English equivalent.

[3] Given the extraordinary number of people who mistakenly thought that the 21st century began on January 1, 2000 rather than January 1, 2001, Féval can surely be forgiven for calling 1800 the first year of the 19th century, when it was in fact the last year of the 18th.

[4] The title of *douairière* (Dowager) implies that the old woman is a propertied widow, although the word is also used colloquially to refer to any old woman of imposing appearance.

[5] The Knights of Malta was the name popularly given to the Order of the Hospitallers of St John of Jerusalem, a company of military monks who played a key role in the Crusades. When Jerusalem was retaken by the Muslims, the Order mounted an unsuccessful defense of Acre before fleeing to Cyprus and then occupying the island of Rhodes. When Rhodes was seized by the Turks in 1522, the Order was forced to decamp again, eventually settling in Malta, whose government they administrated until 1798, when the island was captured by Napoleon. The order was disbanded, its members being "liberated."

[6] I have taken some liberties with the wording of the song in an attempt to preserve the rhyme-scheme. The fact that *digue*—here used purely for auditory effect—translates literally as "dam" means that "dum" is not entirely inappropriate as a substitute.

Chapter II

[7] Members of the Republican Army that fought the Counter-Revolutionary Chouans of the Vendée in the aftermath of the Revolution of 1789 were known as *les bleus* because of the color of their uniforms.

Chapter III

[8] *Grand'Lande* translates roughly as "great heath."

[9] *Kouril* is an alternative term for the mildly malevolent spirits more usually know as *korrigans*, the Breton equivalent of Scottish brownies, Irish leprechauns and Cornish pixies. They are frequently associated with dolmens and menhirs, and have a reputation as wild dancers, although they are sometimes said to live underground, where they often protect treasures.

[10] *Chats courtauds*—loosely translatable as "cats with docked tails"—are giant demonic cats with no tails, which are often encountered in Breton descriptions of witches' Sabbaths.

[11] *Corniquets* are beings related to *korrigans*, sometimes represented as the male offspring of korrigans and humans, often related in a similar fashion to megalithic monuments.

[12] The *laveuses de nuit* ("nocturnal washerwomen"), also known as the *lavandières*, were the specters of bad mothers who were condemned to wash the linen of their victims eternally. George Sand—who was often charged with being a bad mother—wrote an elaborate account of them, represented as a *légende rustique*.

[13] *Belle-de-Nuit*, which translates as "nocturnal beauty," is far more commonly encountered in French than any of the other phrases cited above, being used as the name of a flower and as a euphemistic form of reference to prostitutes, but Féval's reference is obviously to a seductive species of spirit—perhaps the female equivalent of a *corniquet*.

Chapter IV

[14] *Pierres-Plantées* means "standing stones" and *Croix-qui-Marche* means "walking cross". The references are to neo-

lithic monuments of a sort that abound in Brittany and the British Isles, the most famous example being Stonehenge.

Chapter VI

[15] In France, then as now, the sale of tobacco was strictly controlled and subject to a state monopoly—with the result that the manufacture and distribution of such products as snuff was subject to all manner of chicanery.

[16] Féval improvises the word *Janséneux* at this point, presumably to emphasize that he does not intend to signify a literal follower of Cornelius Jansen, bishop of Ypres, whose posthumously-published book *Augustinus* (1640) had been condemned by Pope Innocent X in 1653. The word *Jansenist* was, however, used more generally in French to refer to reformers and agitators within the Catholic faith, so I have substituted the more familiar term here; at a later point in the story, where Féval uses *Janséneux* as a proper name, I have left it untranslated. The actual *Jansenists* engaged in a long ideological struggle with the Jesuits, for whom Féval had a profound admiration, so he would have considered the label suitable for use as a term of abuse.

[17] I have translated Féval's *jureur* literally as "juror," although the English term cannot carry all the implications of the French one. Its reference is to one who has sworn an oath, and is as often used to signify "blasphemer" as "member of a jury." The implication here is that the "false priest" (*faux prêtre*) has sworn an oath of allegiance to the Devil; when the later appellation is repeated, Féval adds *jureur* to the phrase to re-emphasize this point, but there is no easy way to render the compound in English so I have left "false priest" unemphasized.

Chapter VIII

[18] Féval has *lance couchée*. English has no easy way of distinguishing between different types of lance, but the image that will instantly spring to the reader's mind—of the kind of lance

borne by Arthurian knights in tourneys—is correct. According to medieval historian Lynn White, the key invention that made the style of fighting typical of the Age of Chivalry possible was the stirrup; the use of stirrups set a knight so securely in his saddle that he could use a lance equipped with a sort of hilt, which he could brace against his body, rather than one that he had to hold in his hand like a spear.

[19] Charles de Blois (1319-1364) was the nephew of Philip VI of France; in the "war of succession" to which the text refers, he upheld Philip's claim to French sovereignty over the duchy of Brittany against Jean, Comte de Montfort, a descendant of the Anglo-Norman Simon de Montfort, Earl of Leicester. In effect, this means that the Treguerns were fighting for France and the Le Brecs for England in determining the fate of Brittany (or "Less Britain," as the inhabitants of Great Britain were apt to call it). The Treguerns, needless to say, had Féval's wholehearted approval.

[20] The phrase I have translated literally as "slanting groin" (*grouin bridé*) presumably refers to the hogs' genitalia, although it is a slightly odd reference to find in Féval, who tends to be markedly less frank in description than, say, Eugène Sue. *Grouin* is, however, an esoteric term (not to be found in Larousse), which—unlike its English equivalent—is only used with respect to domestic swine, so it is possible that Féval did not expect the majority of his readers to take that implication. (He had used it in previously in Chapter VI of the present text, referring to the pigs sleeping in Marion Lécuyer's farmhouse). A crupper is part of a horse's harness that forms a loop passing beneath its tail. At this point in the text, Féval has a footnote of his own, which says: "*This bas-relief, sculpted on a granite tablet, remarkable in its subject and even more remarkable for the singular boldness of its design and execution, exists at the Château de C*** in Morbihan. Monsieur de C*** has surrounded it with many other artistic treasures in the wall of his armory*." The sarcastic tone of the footnote underlines the outrage expressed in the text at the mockery visited

upon the Age of Chivalry, in the wake of Miguel de Cervantes' *Don Quixote*, by the sophisticates of the Renaissance.
[21] In *The Bride of Lammermoor* (1819).

Chapter IX

[22] Bel was the supreme god of the ancient Babylonians, whose name is usually rendered Baal in English (although the references to him in the Old Testament are more likely to signify Marduk). The term usually has an acute accent in French, although Féval omits it, presumably to emphasize the similarity of the proper name to the less common variant of "beau," meaning beautiful or handsome. The common French phrase *la beauté du diable*, referring to the seductive capacity of *femmes fatales*, has some resonance with this pun.
[23] See Note 16.

Chapter X

[24] There is an untranslatable pun here; the French word *vase*, which crops up twice within the paragraph, means both "mire" and "vase." I have used the intended literal meaning on each occasion.
[25] The feast of the Assumption takes place on August 15; today, the previous night, that of August 14 to August 15, would be referred to as the night of August 14; yet, throughout the novel, Féval constantly refers to it as the night of August 15. I am not sure why Feval follows the usage he does, but I suspect that the discrepancy may arise from a different way of calculating the beginnings and ends of days with respect to feast-days.
[26] The word Féval uses here, *sage-femme*, is a standard appellation for a midwife, but its literal meaning—"wise-woman"—served to emphasize that the role was routinely associated with a certain superstitious awe. Midwives were prominent among those accused of being witches during the days of the great European witch-hunt.

[27] The text's *porté à la commune* could be translated as "taken to the municipal registry" but that would be rather clumsy, and leaving the final word as it is has the advantage of communicating something of the priest's attitude. What the priest is asking is whether the children have been registered with the secular authority established after the Revolution of 1789. The initial purpose of that authority was to replace the religious system, whose abrupt abolition was one of the principal causes of the Chouan Revolt. By 1800, freedom of religion had been reinstituted, but the system of secular registration remained in place: a tacit, if not explicit, rival to the traditional one.

Part Two
Chapter XI

[28] "Madrid" is the Château de Madrid, whose construction by François I first made the Bois de Boulogne a place of festivity. The Jardin de Bagatelle, or Bagatelle Gardens, is at the center of the complex.

[29] *Noisy-le-sec* is a small town five miles east of Paris. The name *Noisy* comes from the latin *nucetum*, meaning walnut tree; the second half of the name refers to the dryness of the area, due to the absence of any nearby rivers; the Chevalier de Noisy obviously objects to being referred to by the same nickname as the town.

[30] I have translated Féval's *Contes de ma Mère l'Oie* literally. Charles Perrault's classic collection of *contes* became widely known under a slight variant of that name in both French and English, although that was not its original title.

[31] In the era when Féval wrote this chapter—let alone the time in which it is set—the term *amazone* had not yet acquired all the connotations it was subsequently to obtain in *fin-de-siècle* Paris, when the opportunity for women to apply to the authorities for official permission to wear male attire was enthusiastically seized by feminists such as Rachilde, Colette and Nathalie Barney; "amazon" then came to signify a member of their select company. The term was, however, already

loaded with the implications that equipped it to fill that role, and therefore carried a particular currency as well as its mythical resonance.

[32] In its original meaning, a *guilloche*—the word is identical in French and English—was an ornament formed by interwoven ribbons or strings, in whose interstices small decorative stones were fitted; by Féval's time, it had broadened out to signify any pattern formed of interlaced strands.

[33] The phrase Féval uses is *chien mouton*, whose literal translation would be "sheep dog," but he does not mean a dog that might be used to herd sheep; he means a dog with a fluffy coat, reminiscent of that of an unshorn sheep.

[34] The word Féval uses here is *courtaud*—as in the *chat courtauds* mentioned in Chapter III—whose metaphorical meaning in this context is difficult to render directly into English. Its literal reference is to a horse or dog whose tail had been docked, but it is also used to refer, in a casually derogatory fashion, to humans of a coarse stripe. "Human cattle" hopefully conveys something of the intended implication.

[35] See the comments on this passage in the Introduction.

[36] Féval has "Brummel." The reference is to George "Beau" Brummell (1778-1840), a close friend of the Prince of Wales (the future George IV), until they quarreled. Brummell became a key model of fashionable dress in London in the early years of the century, until his gambling debts forced him into exile in Calais in 1816, thus extending his dubious celebrity to France. His fame was renewed there by Jules-Amédée Barbey d'Aurevilly's handbook *Du dandyisme et de G. Brummell* (1845). In 1852, Féval had not had the opportunity to witness the extraordinary influence that book was to have in the Parisian literary *monde* in the latter decades of the century, but it is not improbable that he was aware of the figure cut by one of Brummell's earliest Parisian acolytes, Charles Baudelaire. Baudelaire's eulogistic account of the life and works of Edgar Allan Poe appeared in the March and April issues of the *Revue de Paris* while *Le livre des Mystères* (*Revenants*) was being

serialized in *Le Pays*. Baudelaire saw Dumas' version of *Le Vampire* too, and similarly adopted its imagery into his work, although his poem "*Le vampire*" was not published until 1855, and did not acquire that title until it was reprinted, along with "*Les métamorphoses de la vampire*" in *Les fleurs du mal* in 1857.

[37] "Teasing" is as near as one can get to a translation of Féval's *agaçant*, but it cannot convey the full spectrum of the word's implication, which is a near-oxymoronic combination of "enticing" and "tormenting."

Chapter XII

[38] "Dashed" accurately reflects the euphemistic quality of Féval's *diantrement*, but it is worth noting the term was, in 1820, a polite substitute for "devilishly."

[39] The French aristocracy has no definitive guidebook akin to *Burke's Peerage*, and pretentious Frenchmen have always been notorious for appropriating titles—a move that can usually be made, at a superficial level, simply by inserting "de" between a Christian name and a surname. As this passage emphasizes, however, merely appropriating an ennobling "de" was always likely to generate skeptical "discussions." The reader will recall that Dowager Le Brec was enthusiastic to stake a much firmer claim to the prestigious "de Treguern" name for her own family, by wiping out the direct line of descent from the auspicious Tanneguy, so that the title might legitimately pass to a branch associated with it by marriage.

[40] *La Muette* means "hunting-lodge" (from *meute* which is the term for a pack of hunting dogs), that having been the edifice's original purpose—although by 1820 the Bois de Boulogne, while still equipped with "hunting-paths" and a "pheasantry," was no longer the wilderness it had been, and was well on its way to becoming the park that it is today.

[41] The two named towns are very distant from Paris, the former in the far south, the latter in the northwest.

Chapter XIII

[42] The standard formation of a public stagecoach, still repli-
cated in sight-seeing buses, was to have an enclosed compartment topped by a set of seats exposed to the elements. The
cheaper seats were on the upper deck, because it was not unknown for people to freeze to death up there during winter
nights, while summer passengers would have been exposed by
day to the full glare of the Sun.

[43] Jean-Antoine Watteau (1684-1721) was famous as a painter
of rustic scenes featuring shepherds and shepherdesses, whose
imagery was adopted as a fashion in Paris; Marie-Antoinette
occasionally used to dress as a Watteau shepherdess in private
play.

[44] Carbonarism was a Republican movement, formulated as a
secret society, which had originated—according to legend, at
least—among the charcoal-burners of Italy in 1811. It became
a significant underground political organization in Italy, playing an important role in the unification of the nation, but its
extensions in France had a very different context, seeking the
restoration of a very rather different and much more recent
Republican heritage. Féval's suggestion that it was as much a
matter of lifestyle fantasy among "progressive" members of
the *élite* as an authentic revolutionary organization may well
be true.

[45] There is an inevitable temptation to leave the word *noir* in
the final sentence untranslated, as that term now reigns triumphant in English-language descriptions of the direct descen-
dants of Lord Byron, the Vicomte de Chateaubriand and Al-
phonse de Lamartine, but it would be anachronistic. Féval's
own timing may seem a trifle askew in Chateaubriand's
case—the latter's prototypical Romantic hero, René, had been
featured in *Le Génie du Christianisme*, published in 1802—
but that work had gained in perceived stature in the interim,
thanks to the flourishing of the French Romantic Movement.
Lamartine's first collection, *Meditations poétiques*, was hot
off the presses in August 1820, and he was already being

hailed as "the French Byron." Byron had left England for good in 1816, and had written many of his darkest works—including most of "Don Juan," between then and 1820.

[46] The "siren of Lusignan" is Mélusine, a water-spirit originating from the forest of Colobiers, near Poitou, who was said to have been wed by Raymond, Comte de la Forêt; the castle that she built for them was the legendary site of the town of Lusignan. In order to marry her, Robert had to promise never to intrude on her on Saturdays; when he broke the injunction, he found her in her natural state, her nether regions being serpentine. A version of the legend was co-opted as "family history" by Jean d'Arras in the late 14th century, and several other noble families, including those of Luxembourg, Rohan and Sassenaye also claimed descent from Mélusine. The story appears to be descended from Classical accounts of lamias, one of which was co-opted by Philostratus into his highly fanciful "biography" of the neo-Pythagorean philosopher Apollonius of Tyana. Thanks to Philostratus' legend-mongering, Apollonius acquired a posthumous reputation as magician, and the story of his encounter with a lamia, whose serpentine nature he revealed in order to prevent her marriage to a human—which was repopularized by Robert Burton's *Anatomy of Melancholy*—became a popular taproot text of Romantic and Decadent fantasy.

The reference to "Rieux's wanton spirit" is far more esoteric and less easy to decipher. The Rieux to which Féval is referring must be the small town five kilometers south of Redon, whose ill-fated château may well have provided the model for Treguern Manor (which must, on the evidence of Etiennne and Mathurin's journey in Part One, stand at a very similar distance). Jean de Rieux (1342-1417) and his son Pierre (1389-1438) were both Maréchals de France, but Jean IV (1447-1518) only made it to Maréchal de Bretagne; the subsequent history of the family and the edifice was one of long and inexorable decline, although the 16th-century Renée de Rieux, who served as one of Catherine de Medici's maids of honor, achieved celebrity of a lesser sort as "la belle Chateauneuf" (Chateauneuf being a subsequent home of the family). The original castle's "dismantling" began in Jean IV's lifetime, in 1496, and was completed in 1629 when Cardinal Richelieu ordered the remaining defenses to be demolished by means of explosives, presumably leaving little more trace than the ancient castle which once occupied the side of Treguern Manor. There is no mention in Larousse of any family legend involving a supernatural ancestor, and no reference in the omnibus edition of Anatole le Braz' *Magies de la Bretagne* (1994), which is the most comprehensive popular survey of Breton folklore. Jean de Rieux led an expedition in 1405 to assist the Welsh rebellion of Owain Glyndwr, which became the subject of several ballads, but I cannot find one that includes any supernatural content.

[47] This phrase, as rendered at the point in Féval's text—without an accent on the *a* in *Madre*—poses a trivial enigma. Le Mâdre, as the reader will recall from the inscription of the Tomb of Tanneguy, was the surname borne by the first Comte de Treguern before he was ennobled; if the accent has been omitted accidentally, therefore, as I have assumed the reference is to the full name with which the coat-of-arms is associated. However, *madre* is a kind of wood from which armorial shields were once made, so Le Madre de Treguern could simply be an ostentatious equivalent of "the shield of Treguern."

[48] Kadam (now Kadan) is cited in Dom Augustine Calmet's chapters on vampires in *Traité sur les apparitions des esprits et sur les vampires ou les revenans de Hongrie, de Moravie, etc.*, first published in 1746 and reprinted several times thereafter, including an 1850 edition that was the source-text of Féval's information regarding vampire legends and whose titular reference to "revenans" probably played a significant part in the inspiration of the present volume. Calmet mentions Kadam as the nearest town to the village of Blow (which is no longer featured on modern maps). A shepherd was reported in a 14th-century chronicle compiled by Abbot Neplach to have

returned from the dead several times to visit old neighbors in and around Blow, all of whom died within a week, until his body was pinned down by a wooden stake. Although this appears to be the ultimate origin of the stake through the heart that became a central element of literary vampire mythology, the device did not kill the vampire of Blow, who continued to mock his persecutors until he was cremated.

[49] Alectromancy is a form of divination that involves encircling a cock with grains of corn placed on the letters of the alphabet; the order in which the bird eats the grains is supposed to spell out a meaningful sequence of letters.

[50] Toussaint—All Souls' Night—is the feast nowadays celebrated as Hallowe'en, when evil spirits were supposedly allowed free run of the Earth until midnight, when they were banished by the power of God and his Earthly agents. It derives from the pagan festival of Samhain, and came to be associated in post-Medieval Christendom with the witches' Sabbaths.

Chapter XVI

[51] J. F. Campbell appears to be fictitious, and certainly was not the inventor of regulated tontines. Féval renders the phrase *Regulated annuities on survivorship* in English; I have left it as it is, although it is a rather unlikely formulation. A more elaborate explanation and discussion of the kind of insurance scheme to which the text is referring can be found in the afterword.

[52] The French *heureuse* and *malheureuse*, which I have translated in this passage as "happy" and "unhappy," also mean "fortunate" and "unfortunate." The English equivalent retains enough of the double meaning to serve perfectly adequately in almost all circumstances, including Malo's judgment on Olympe, but there is a deeper ambiguity in his (oft-echoed) pronouncement of Laurence's fate, whose possible implications are further discussed in the afterword.

[53] The printed text has *Loetare*, which must be a misprint. The reference in Gabriel's missal must be to the Mass said on the third Sunday of Lent, which is sometimes called *Laetare* Sunday because the first words of the introit to the Mass said on that day are "*Laetare Jerusalem*" ("Rejoice, O Jerusalem"). Gabriel, of course, compares the invitation to rejoice with the opposing injunction of the Requiem Mass. It is presumably not a coincidence, given that he finds *Laetare* on the left-hand page and *Requiem* on the right-hand one that Gabriel then expresses his preference for what English occultists might describe as "the left-hand path" as a choice of "L over R," even though the equivalent French terms (*gauche* and *droite*) have different initial letters.

Chapter XVIII

[54] The reader will recall that Josille was the son of Guillaume and Fanchette Féru, whose recent birth allowed Fanchette to serve as a wet-nurse to the children of Geneviève and Marianne de Treguern. Assuming that this is the same Josille, we may deduce that he is 20 years old, even though the terms in which he is described in this chapter—including the account of his vaguely-formed marriage plans—make him seem younger.

Chapter XIX

[55] Frascati's, near the Opéra, was the most famous gambling house in Paris in the early decades of the 19th century; it features prominently in literary works by Honoré de Balzac and Wilkie Collins, among others.

Chapter XX

[56] A *barbet* is a small poodle; the reference complements the term of address Monsieur Privat applies to the Marquise's dog; bichon is used descriptively of any lap-dog, as well as functioning as a metaphorical term of endearment.

Chapter XXI

[57] The dynasty of Tolbeques, all of whom were composers and conductors, endured throughout the 19th century and into the 20th. Although he would have been rather young in 1820, the one cited here was presumably Jean-Baptiste Tolbecque, born in 1797, who was famous for his dance music in the 1840s.

[58] I have translated Féval's *entamer le chapitre* as nearly literally as I can, although the word *entamer* has other implications in addition to cutting something short; it is also used to mean casting a slur on someone's reputation.

[59] Féval inserts a footnote of his own to explain this item of Breton dialect, which translates as: "An Haute-Bretagne word, which corresponds to the Gaelic *fey*, and which means ensorcelled or, more rigorously, destined to be ensorcelled." (I have used the most immediate English equivalent of Féval's *ensorcellé*, although the more familiar *bewitched* is almost identical in implication.)

Chapter XXIII

[60] This sympathetic reference to Don Quixote contrasts somewhat with the one in Chapter VIII, where Cervantes was charged with being partly responsible for besmirching the memory of the Age of Chivalry.

Chapter XXIV

[61] An octant is an instrument for measuring angles, similar to a sextant; this one must be made of copper to be afflicted with verdigris—a turquoise stain caused by the action of acid on that metal. An alembic is a distillation apparatus, the retort being the long-necked vessel from which the distillate drips.

[62] The first two names in this list, Albertus Magnus and Cornelius Agrippa, were famous scholastic philosophers whose dabbling in alchemy and interests in occult science won them posthumous reputations as magicians. The reference to Gaufridi's *Miroir des Apparitions* would have been interpreted by a contemporary reader as a reference to Louis Gaufridi, a

French priest who became the star turn at one of the most famous French witch-trials, at Aix-en-Provence in 1611. He was charged with procuring the multiple diabolical possession of an Ursuline nun, whose performances during an exorcism had been magnificently theatrical. Like Urbain Grandier in Loudun—as featured Ken Russell's film *The Devils*—Gaufridi's actual crime presumably went no further than debauchery, and his fate provides a graphic illustration of the principle that a scorned woman is more than capable of mobilizing all the furies in Hell to wreak her revenge. He signed the usual confession, under duress, which was every bit as theatrical as his victim's performance, but never wrote a book.

The reference to *L'Hexaméron espagnol* (the Spanish Hexameron) is presumably to a book on various occult disciplines credited to "Antoine de Torquemada," first published in French in 1579; it was allegedly translated from a Spanish version of 1575, but if any such text ever existed, it has not survived.

The final reference in the text is to *Le Voyage infernal de Barthélemy Holzhanser*, but this must be a misprint, presumably caused by the printer's misinterpretation of Féval's handwriting, The intended reference must be to the Jesuit mystic and visionary writer Bartholomaeus Holzhauser (1613-1658), with whose name Féval would have been familiar in 1852 by virtue of a recent French translation of his *Interpretation de l'Apocalypse*. The ten visionary works listed in the Catholic Encyclopedia do not, however, include an "infernal voyage."

Chapter XXV

[63] This moment of recognition contradicts Olympe's conversation with her mother earlier in the day, when she claimed to be searching—so far unsuccessfully—for Etienne. Given that she also claimed to have talked to Monsieur Privat on several occasions, however, it is unlikely that she could have been ignorant of the fact that Etienne was now his servant. One suspects, therefore, that Olympe was not being entirely honest

with her mother, just as Monsieur Privat was not being honest with the Marquise when he suggested that "Valérie-*la-Morte*" might be either Geneviève or Laurence; clearly, the advocate must have found out that evening, if he had not known before, that the person he knew as Valérie was Olympe de Treguern.

Chapter XXVI

[64] Paul Niquet was the proprietor of a notorious cabaret at 26 Rue aux Fers, a side-street of the Rue Saint-Denis very close to the location of this scene.

[65] It had seven stories in Monsieur Privat's account, but he might conceivably have been counting the pigeon-loft, while the narrative voice does not.

Chapter XXIX

[66] An octave, in this sense, is a period of eight days commencing with a feast-day; the reference here is to the eighth day of the octave—i.e., the following Sunday.

[67] The Marquis de Carabas was the name invented by the ingenious feline hero of the fairy tale known in English as "Puss-in-Boots," in order to represent his human master as a man of unparalleled wealth.

[68] The word *factotum* exists, and has the same meaning, in both French and English, although Féval italicizes it in recognition of the fact that it is borrowed from the Latin. It refers to a servant who takes care of many different tasks—and can, by implication, be entrusted with any commission.

[69] Féval adds his own footnote to indicate that this dialect term signifies *le râle de mort*: the death-rattle.